We All Fall Down

© Brian Caldwell

ALPHAR PUBLISHING
alphar@xtra.co.nz
www.alpharpublish.com

alphar

ALPHAR PUBLISHING, Burbank, Ca

www.alpharpublish.com

Copyright © Brian Caldwell, 2006

LIBRARY OF CONGRESS CATALOGING IN PUBLICATION DATA
Caldwell, Brian
WE ALL FALL DOWN
1 Title
ISBN 0-9786024-4-7
ISBN 978-0-9786024-4-4 (at 13 digit)

A Soft Cover edition to be published by ALPHAR on Nov. 15, 2006
ISBN # 97809786024-6-8
PRICE: US $15.95
UK #9.95

Cover Photography: Thomas Moore

Cover Design by Mark Cameron and Thomas Moore

For Kierin and Jenn and Chris,

for their very different sorts of help.

We All Fall Down

© Brian Caldwell

ALPHAR PUBLISHING
alphar@xtra.co.nz
www.alpharpublish.com

Prologue

My wife disappeared out of my life as suddenly and as miraculously as she had first appeared in it. Both times I smiled. The morning Sarah and I first met was a rainy and miserable one, the temperature insisting upon straddling an annoyingly inconclusive middle ground. A few degrees warmer and the rain could have been refreshing; a bit colder and the resulting snow would have covered the town in a beautiful blanket of purity. As it was, the weather refused to commit itself to either extreme, and a thick layer of cold wet slush seeped through my sneakers and froze my ankles.

I was a twenty-four year old graduate student at the University of Massachusetts in Amherst half-heartedly working my way towards a master's degree in English Literature. The previous year had slogged by in useless cycles of failed classes, failed relationships, and failed attempts to forget Jude Gaunt. It had been a bad year, but that particular morning marked a solid month since I'd sat alone in my room, spirit and soul hooked into the Cure's *Kiss Me Kiss Me Kiss Me* CD on an endless candle-lit loop, staring moodily off into the distance, convinced that somehow, Jude could sense my sorrow and felt really *really* bad for me.

It had been a good month in a bad year until I had to go and fuck it up with a dream. The sex was clumsy and awkward; a hodgepodge of fumbling limbs, flailing hair, and brightly colored clothing. Jude writhed through my sleep as a haze of underwear and elbows. Underwear, elbows, and deeply felt joy.

I woke to a brief moment of peace before reality gave me a good, blunt stomp in the gut. I hadn't spoken to Jude in over a year. I didn't even know where she lived anymore.

The ignorant warmth was pelted through by the sounds of thick rain slapping down onto wet snow. My alarm clock had been buzzing for twenty minutes and I was late for class.

With the nasty, early-March weather obligingly reflecting my mood, I trudged towards the bus stop, arriving at the end of my street just in time to see the fucking shuttle pull away. Only one person remained at the stop, a lanky guy dressed in jeans, a white T-shirt, a tuxedo jacket, and a black top hat. He held a thick stack of gold flyers in his hand.

I crossed the street and stepped up onto the curb, hoping that The Top Hat wouldn't intrude upon my funk. Instead, he Chiefed me.

"Heeeeey, take a flyer, Chief."

"No thanks," I mumbled, refusing to raise my eyes from the ground.

The Top Hat shuffled next to me, his hand outstretched with a flyer. "Come on, man, you don't even know what it is. Could be a coupon for a CD you were thinking of buying. Could be a free pass to a movie you wanted to see. Could be anything and everything. Just take one. It's *freeeeeee*."

I attempted a polite smile and turned to face him. His head was bobbing from side to side and he was pushing the flyer towards me and away from me, keeping the motion in synch with the rhythm of his head.

"Thanks anyway," I said.

"What? Come ahhhn! Could be a flyer for a band you've been wanting to see. You take this flyer, go to the show, maybe meet that special someone, huh? Take this flyer and your whole life could change. What've you got to lose? It's *freeeee*."

The sidewalk became crowded as other students arrived, and The Top Hat darted over to each new arrival.

"Could be a coupon for free rubbers. Maybe get you laid if you're not, maybe save your life if you are."

Each person accepted the golden flyer and, as it exchanged hands, The Top Hat would croon a deep throated, *Yeeahhhh*, before dancing over to the next person.

"Could be an invitation to a church that fills that sickening void. Could be your pass into Heaven, Nirvana, the Infinite, and the Holy Nothingness all rolled into one."

Acceptance.

"*Yeeahhhh!*"

The show continued for several minutes until I was the only person who wasn't a member of the flyer club. I sensed The Top Hat's eyes shift onto me. He slid behind me and began dancing back and forth, his head bobbing in and out of sight over my shoulders.

"Come on, man! You're the last one. Take a flyer and change your life. Join the team. Be a Pepper!"

I remained silent and motionless, refusing to look at anything but the dirty slush covering the hard gray pavement. Refusing to raise my eyes even a millimeter.

"Damn, man," The Top Hat yelled, as he hopped off the curb and began moon walking back forth in front of me, sliding through the snow. "This could be your Holy Grail, your Arc of the Covenant, your peace, love, and understanding." He extended his arm in front of him, allowing the golden flyer to float up and down in the cold air. "This could be your free machine-gun, your perfect-pussy, your apple-pie mommy-daddy. Just reach out and take it. If it turns out to be crap, so what? It's not costing you a single, shiny, shitty penny." He halted his dance and jumped back onto the curb, sliding his lips next to my ear and whispering, "It's so *fuh-fuh-fucking free.*"

I spun to face him so quickly that my nose bumped his.

"Look, I don't want the fucking thing, all right? I DON'T WANT IT! Did you hear me that time, you little faggot?"

The Top Hat stared blankly at me

He looked to be about sixteen years old.

The bus pulled up to the curb and I jerked my torso away from The Top Hat and stepped towards it. My legs tangled in the sudden motion and my feet slipped off the curb. As I fell, I tossed my heavy bag over my shoulder in a misguided attempt to save my books and papers rather than myself. The motion occupied my arms and allowed my naked, unguarded face to push through the snow, slapping down onto the hard pavement underneath.

"Jesus fucking Christ," I mumbled, as, one by one, the giggling flyer club stepped over my body and climbed onto the bus.

Avoiding the stares and ignoring the muffled laughter as best I could, I rose up, climbed onto the bus, and sat down in the first available seat. It was one of the three center seats which had its back pressed up against the side of the bus, forcing me to ride sideways. The snow that had settled at the top of my pants slowly melted down into my boxer shorts. I locked my eyes onto the floor, miserably content to be staring at the dirty grime covering the black rubber mat running down the center of the aisle until, out of the corner of my eye, I saw a sudden flash of green.

She had no business wearing a skirt on such a miserable day. I rarely saw her in skirts afterwards and don't remember seeing her wear that particular skirt ever again. It was green and plaid and its hem fell just above her knees, gently pressing up against her legs. *Her legs*. They weren't the skinny, knobby legs of a twelve-year old boy that seemed to be the popular body-fashion back then; they were strong legs, solid legs, and I lingered over them for a moment before following the flesh back up over her skirt, up onto her thick, white Irish sweater. *It was a good combination, the skirt and the sweater*. My eyes rolled in and out of its folds, up to her neck and then onto her face. She had shoulder length blond hair that book-ended startlingly white flesh. I roamed over the white until stumbling onto her pine green eyes, which stood out in sharp contrast to the dark circles underneath.

Pulling my attention back from her parts so as to see the whole of her, I suddenly realized that she was aware of my attention. Her eyes conveyed neither invitation nor rebuff. Our mutual gaze lasted a few moments longer than appropriate and, realizing this, we shared a moment of laughter before breaking off the connection.

I struggled to maintain a calm facade while shredding through my brain in search of some method of introduction. Glancing out the window with a practiced glaze of indifference, I felt a quick surge of panic as I saw that there were only two more stops before mine. Plunging down into the depths of my soul, I desperately flailed about for an introductory phrase, resurfacing with nothing but a handful of limp cliches:

Hey, aren't you in one of my classes?

I know you from somewhere, don't I?

Jeez, this weather really sucks, huh?

Crap, crap, and more crap. The dung piled highest as the bus pulled over to the side of the road and I seriously considered asking what her sign was.

The doors slid open with a hiss of relief and I abandoned any intentions of introducing myself, exiting the bus without even glancing at the woman. My relief was short lived, though, and as I stepped up onto the curb, I turned back towards the bus, hoping to see her looking for me. That, I thought, would be the best case scenario. I was off the bus and could no longer be expected to take any immediate action. But if she were looking at me, if she was displaying any interest at all, then a possibility remained.

I casually looked at the window that should have framed her, but it was empty. Realizing that she must have switched seats, I jerked my head back and forth as the bus pulled away, but failed to find her.

Attempting a dismissive shrug, I joined the departing crowd. As I turned, the woman sauntered past me, so close she almost brushed up against my shoulder.

I crouched down and tugged my shoelaces tight while she made her way towards the Campus Center. I undid both shoes and re-tied them until she was a good twenty feet ahead of me. Secure in my shoe safety, I stood up and followed.

She moved with a tough, confident gait that caused her skirt to swish back and forth against her legs like two puppy dogs panting for attention.

Once inside the Campus Center, I wound effortlessly through the crowd, carefully maintaining a safe distance from her; neither so close as to risk having her notice me and forcing a confrontation, nor so far as to lose sight of her completely. For a moment, I wondered if this was paradise, the ability to have all options available without the pressure to commit or choose.

She disappeared into the entrance to the laundry room underneath the Campus Center Hotel. The hotel was a twelve-story building built directly above the Campus Center, and I realized that if she worked in the hotel, I would have to catch up and introduce myself to her right then, or else run the risk of losing her.

This is it, I thought, feeling the words simultaneously tickling across my throat, *do or die, do or die, do or die.*

Die.

I breezed past the entrance without even breaking stride. I sauntered past the doorway, out of the building, across the campus, into Bartlet Hall, up the stairs, into my classroom, and down into a seat, immune to the obviousness with which my professor glanced at his watch. I never knew what topic the professor was lecturing on that day. *The life affirming poetry of Walt Whitman? The obscene, lucid beauty of Henry Miller's prose? The sobering realism of Sinclair Lewis?* I didn't hear a single word. I was too busy assaulting myself with more fundamental, deeply felt truths: *Loser! Fucking cocksucking, pussy-ass, faggot-wuss, motherfucking loser!* I was in desperate need of the energy, the courage and the determination that rose from within only in the midst of assault. *Weak-ass, man-loving, dick-face, sorry ass-skirt!*

The plan was devised while I tromped back towards the laundry room, maintaining a brisk pace so as to retain possession of my adrenaline rush. I would show one of my soggy books to whoever was working in the laundry room and explain that a woman had dropped it on the bus. I'd describe her and ask where in the hotel she worked so that I could return it to her. Once I knew where she was working, I'd have plenty of time to devise the perfect introductory speech before finding her. My plan, I concluded with satisfaction as I stormed into the laundry room, was foolproof. Armed with it, nothing on Heaven or Earth could stop me.

I stopped dead after looping around the corner, finding myself face to face, not with one of the woman's co-workers, as my perfect plan had dictated, but with the woman herself.

She stopped folding the white sheet she was holding and looked up at me.

My light adrenaline rush became solid and dropped down into my stomach like a sharp brick. It had never occurred to me that she could actually be *working* in the laundry room, rather than simply using it as an entrance, as all the other hotel employees did.

She tossed the sheet over her shoulder and stared at me with penetrating eyes. Then she smiled. Her smile was warm knowing. Her smile, her beautiful smile, was the only thing that stopped me from turning around and running away as fast as I could. She smiled as if she had been expecting me, as if she had been waiting patiently for me to arrive. Her smile was a beautiful silk leash tethering me to her.

I mustered up the slickest line I was capable of on short notice. "Umm, ah, hi?"

"Hi." She laughed a tiny little laugh and nodded.

I returned the nod and tried to look cool and confident for a moment, before releasing a loud groan and dropping my face into my hands. "Shit! Look, I'm sorry, but I have *no fucking idea* how to do this. I don't . . . Christ, I don't even know *what* I'm doing, much less *how* to do it. I . . . Okay, see, I woke up this morning and dove head-first into this shitty, miserable fucking day, you know? I had this dream, and then The Top Hat and, and . . . Well, it was just a bad day. And it was only going to get worse, y'know? I fucking *knew* it was. And then, but then I got on the bus and I saw *you* and it just . . . I don't know, it just felt like everything was good."

Her left eye flinched.

I couldn't decide if it was a good flinch or a bad flinch.

"I know," I continued, "I know that sounds incredibly fucking pathetic and weird but . . . but it's still true. I just, I felt like . . . I feel like everything's okay. I also feel like the biggest fucking asshole in the world." I noticed that her smile had become wider and I took a deep breath and bit my lip. "Look, would you have any interest at all in getting together sometime? We could get coffee or a drink or food or whatever . . ."

She said nothing.

"I know you don't know me from dick," I said quickly. "And I don't know you. But I'd like to. I'd like *us* to. I wish I could come up with a really cool sounding reason to explain why, but I can't."

She tilted her head and narrowed her eyes.

"If you want to tell me to fuck off, I would completely understand. Really. I just . . . Would you like to get together with me sometime? When, where, how, that's all up to you."

She continued to smile and I suddenly noticed that I was smiling too. It felt real and unfamiliar resting on my face.

"Whatever you want to do," I said. "All on your terms."

Her smile opened up and she laughed quietly. "Why not?"

"Really?"

"Sure."

"Um, well, great. I guess . . . I'm Jimmy. Jimmy Lordan."

I extended my hand.

"I'm Sarah."

She took it.

She arrived twenty minutes late.

"Hey," I said with a smile.

"Hey," she said without one.

On my suggestion, we had met at The Spoke, a semi-seedy local's bar.

"You want something to drink?" I asked.

"What are you drinking?"

"Kamikaze on the rocks. It's good."

"I'll have a rum and coke."

When I returned from the bar with two rum and cokes, Sarah stared at both drinks with a look of mild disdain.

"Thought you were drinking kamikazes," she said.

"I was," I said, with an overly enthusiastic shrug. "Rum and coke sounded good."

"Uh-huh." She reached for the drink without looking at me.

We spent the next hour wading into the shallow side of conversation, trading stories about shared teachers, annoying roommates, and the vaguest of future plans. It was a conversation that Sarah was obviously bored with. In the middle of a sentence she'd light a cigarette and allow her eyes to slowly wander the bar, her voice trailing off into silence before completing her question or answer. She rarely met my eyes, and when she did, it was almost as if she were checking to see if I were still there, and was a bit annoyed to find that I was.

After an hour-and-a-half, she tilted her chair back onto its hind legs and began bouncing her leg up and down while drumming her fingers on the table.

"So," she said, her eyes looking over my shoulder at the exit, "you got any good stories you want to tell me?"

The goofy smile dropped from my face as I placed my drink down onto the table and glared at her.

It was the word *stories*. The way she said it, accentuating and drawing out the *st* and then rushing through the rest of the word while harshly raising her right eyebrow. She said *stories*, but it was obvious that the word *lies* would have been a more honest word choice. I felt a rush of anger suffused with the slightly nauseating sensation of failure. I was blowing it, and she had expected, wanted, and knew that I was going to blow it.

"Yeah," I said in a clear voice. "Yeah, I got a good story."

"Well let's hear it, tough guy." She finished her drink and let the glass drop down onto the table with a definitive thud.

"You want another?"

"I'm all set," she said, her eyes still staring over my shoulder.

"Right." I smiled and nodded my head. "Okay, then." I lit a cigarette and inhaled deeply. "So, I dated this girl for about five years. Jude Gaunt. We broke up about a year ago. A few months pass and no matter what I do, I can't stop feeling like shit. It's like I've got this huge fucking hole in my chest and no matter what I do, it won't go away, won't fill up. So, when this girl from one of my classes asks me if I want to have dinner with her, I say *yes*, thinking maybe that'll help. Gretta something or another was her name."

"Is her name."

"What?"

14

"*Is* her name. You said *was*. Unless this woman dies at the end of the story, she still exists."

"Not in my world she doesn't."

Sarah's eyes narrowed and moved away from the exit. She stared at me for a moment before releasing a cold laugh and shaking her head.

"Anyway," I continued, pretending not to notice her anger, "we got dinner. It was painful. She couldn't say something interesting if her life depended on it. I actually groaned when she said she wanted dessert. At that point, I would have rather eaten a gun than chocolate mousse if it meant not having to listen to anymore of her piss-babble.

"Still," I said with a shrug, "after the suck-dinner was over we ended up back at my apartment, messing around. Only, after about an hour of give and take, it becomes pretty clear that she's not real interested in giving, so I figure, *fuck it*, and stop trying to take.

"And I don't even really care. I just roll over and light a cigarette. But after a couple minutes of silence, she gets the brilliant idea of opening her mouth again and says, *So*, and then shuts up so there's this big dramatic pause. *So what?* I ask. *So, I guess I won, huh?* she says. I ask her what exactly she thinks she won, and she says, *Well, you wanted to keep going and I didn't want to keep going and we didn't, so I won.* I'm not even looking at her at this point, but I can feel her smirk. It was like the whole bed suddenly turned into this gigantic fucking smirk.

"So I say something stupid like, *Another hard won victory for the feminist movement, huh?* And my voice is indifferent, but that's total bullshit." I slid one of the ice-cubs out of my drink, rolled it around my mouth and then dropped it back into the glass. "I don't know what it was that pissed me off so much. Even *now* I don't really know. I mean, it was an incredibly stupid thing to say but after spending four or five hours with her, I was used to that. I don't know why it got me so mad."

Without removing her eyes from my face, Sarah crushed out her cigarette. I silently returned the stare and allowed the moment to linger, savoring her attention.

"So what happened?" she finally asked. "What did you do?"

"I talked to her," I said with a shrug while using what remained of my cigarette to light a new one. "I told her stories where I was the butt of the joke and then laughed along with her at my expense. I told her I really enjoyed being with her. I told her she was funny and interesting. I told her I could peg most people right away but there was something elusive about her. I told her she was beautiful."

"All bullshit."

"Yeah. She was okay looking, but nothing special, and she was about as elusive as a five-lane highway. I could sum up who and what she was in less than five sentences. You want me to?"

"No."

"Fine. Anyway, we start screwing around again. Real slow at first. I'd laugh and let my hand fall on her stomach, or tickle her leg and leave my hand there afterwards. Eventually, I kissed her. Real gently, almost as if I was afraid of her. When I started touching her, I was tentative, soft. After an hour or so, things started becoming more intense, but I made sure that the focus stayed on her. I wouldn't let her do anything to me, it was all about her.

"Pretty soon, I knew. I can still remember the exact second when she let herself go. I pushed her legs apart only, it wasn't really a push, or if it *was* it was like pushing air. She pulled me on top of her and I slid inside. Just a little. She let out this throaty little gasp of consent and arched her back. I pushed myself all the way in and she inhaled like she was stuttering. I moved delicately. Lovingly, even. After a few minutes I pulled almost all the way out and looked down at her. She had her eyes closed and her chin turned up. The back of her head was pushed into the pillow and her lips were parted, opened up almost like she was trying to say something beautiful but couldn't quite come up with the right words. Corners of her mouth were curled into this faint smile. Right then, at that moment, she really *did* look beautiful. Innocent.

"Then I banged away at her like a drunk high-school quarterback.

"My eyes were closed and all I could hear were the sounds of my hips slapping up against hers." I blew smoke out of my nose while staring at Sarah's blank expression. "It was this pink noise that kept pushing into the darkness. It just . . . I remember that I felt this, this rush of anger. Hate. It was so strong, it was . . . it was so *fucking* big.

"After maybe a minute, I pulled out and shimmied up onto her chest. She turned away, but I kept staring at her, and the only thing going through my mind is, *Now who won, bitch? Now who fucking won?*"

The cold look on Sarah's face shifted into one of confused rage. She slipped a cigarette between her tight lips and reached across the table for my lighter. She flicked it open but quickly snapped it shut without lighting her cigarette.

"Why the hell did you tell me that story?" she asked, while throwing down the lighter and yanking the cigarette out of her mouth. "Was I supposed to think it was funny? Should I be impressed that you *won*? Guess you showed that bitch, huh?"

I dropped my eyes away from her and stared down into the dirty ashtray.

"After the whole thing," I continued in a quieter voice, "I dropped next to her. Neither one of us said anything. It was this huge silence where the smallest movement sounded like a scream. I just wanted her to go. No. No, I wanted her to *already* be gone, to have never come. I was turned away from her, so I couldn't see her or feel her, but I *knew* that she was there and knowing that, it was like, it felt like, like God or something. She felt like a judgment. She . . ."

"Gretta," Sarah said with clenched cheekbones.

"What?"

"Stop calling her *she*. Use her name."

I nodded my head and looked away.

"Gretta." My voice felt small. "Eventually, sh . . . Gretta left. Didn't say anything, just got up and left. After she was gone, I was . . . I mean, I didn't cry or anything but, Jesus, I . . . I just . . . I needed something good. Something as good as Jude or at least good enough to let me forget her for one night. Just one fucking night. That's all I wanted. Jude was gone so I had to try and make my own paradise. All I ended up capable of was shooting my hell onto that poor girl's face. Gretta. Gretta's face." I crushed out my cigarette. "So, there's your story."

I kept my eyes locked onto the ashtray for several minutes.

"Why did you tell me that story?" Sarah finally said, breaking the silence. Her voice wasn't angry so much as uncertain.

"I don't know," I said in a dismissive voice. "You said you wanted a story and that was the first one that popped into my . . ."

"No," she interrupted. "No, don't do that. Why?"

I took a deep breath and forced myself to look at her. Her face looked sad and confused.

"Does it really matter?" I asked.

"Yes."

"Why?"

She ran her fingers over her lips and looked as though she was trying to figure something out. After a moment, she shook her head and dismissed the question.

"Just tell me why," she said.

I chewed on my tongue for a moment before looking into her eyes and sighing. "Look, that's who I am, okay? Or at least that's a part of who I am. I . . . Jesus, I don't know, Sarah. I thought I was telling you because I was blowing it and you wanted me to and I was pissed, so fuck it, right? Why not just blow it big. But then . . ." I turned away from her again.

"I don't want to be like that," I said quietly. "I can hide it, but it's still there. I don't want to lie to you. I don't want to pretend that I'm something better than I am. And I know that that's stupid, because I don't even know you. It shouldn't matter, right? But for whatever reason, it feels like it matters a lot."

I looked back towards her and saw that she was slightly, almost imperceptibly, nodding her head.

"Sarah, why do you even care? Let's be honest, you wanted to leave before I even started that story. Shit, you wanted to leave before you even got here. If you didn't have a good enough reason then, you sure as hell do now. Why are you still here? Why do you care?" I shook my head. "I don't get you, Sarah. When I asked you out the other day, you smiled. Jesus, you looked like a fucking angel. You . . . you looked happy. Then you come here and you act like you want to kill me just for saying hello. I don't understand."

She leaned back into her chair and stared past me. "I don't know," she said in a far-away voice. "I don't . . ." Her voice trailed off and she shook her head, regaining her focus before leaning across the table. "Okay," she said in a strong voice, "I hate men."

I smiled gently.

"No, Jimmy. I don't mean that like I hate math class or I hate a bad movie. I mean I *hate* men. I hate them the way a Jew hates a Nazi. The way a mother hates a baby molester. And I don't hate them because I'm gay, because I'm not, or because I was raped by my father, because I wasn't, or because my old boyfriend hit me, because he didn't. *Your* story is *exactly* why I hate men." She leaned even closer. "Jimmy, I've never met a man who *doesn't* want to come in a woman's face."

"Yeah, well . . . Yeah." I leaned back and tried to distance myself from her words. "But that still doesn't answer my question. If anything, it just makes me wonder all the more why you're still here."

Her hard features softened a bit.

"Jimmy, your story repulses me. It repulses me but it doesn't surprise me. What surprises me is that rather than hide it, you pushed it at me. This is our first date. You're supposed to be trying to impress me, to charm me. Instead, you tell me that horrible story. It's almost like, I don't know, almost like you're confessing." She shook her head. "You stumbled into the laundry room last week and you were so goofy and scared. You were incompetent and . . ."

"Yeah, thanks. I get it."

For the first time since arriving, Sarah smiled. "It was sweet. It was. But between then and now, it struck me that it was probably just another act. That you'd be sweet until you didn't have to be anymore."

"I still don't . . ."

"Look, I don't either, okay? Not really. Maybe it's just that after hearing so many lies over the years it was nice to hear a guy tell the truth. Or maybe it was just that you sounded guilty. I don't think I ever met a guy who felt guilty about that stuff before. Or maybe it's something else. I don't know. I just know that I *am* still here."

I reached across the table and grabbed Sarah's glass, slipping an ice cube out from it and dropping it into my palm. It quickly began melting and the cool water felt good.

"So . . . so, what now?"

"I don't know," she said intently. She stared silently at my hand and then suddenly grinned and looked up. "I'll tell you what, though, if this is how you want to play it, *I'll* tell *you* something." She lit a cigarette, grabbed what remained of my original kamikaze and, in a combination of words and motions that I would have assumed were impossible to occur together, shot back the last of my drink, took a long drag off her cigarette, and said, "I'm a Christian."

I faked a shrug of indifference. "Yeah, me too. I'm Catholic."

Her grin grew wider. "No, it's not the same. Not the way you mean it. I'm an Evangelical Christian. Born Again. I've handed my life over to Christ. I trust in Him to take me where I should be, to help me become who I should be. It's not a hobby or a Sunday morning once a week thing, it's my life."

I bought a moment by taking a drag off my cigarette.

Sarah's silent grin remained fixed, as did her stare.

"Bullshit," I finally managed to say. "You've got a cigarette in one hand, booze in the other, and you swear as much as I do."

She inhaled through her smile, her words mixing with exhaled smoke. "I never read anything in the Bible that said smoking is a sin. I drink in moderation and I never take God's name in vain. Beyond that, *motherfucker* is just a word, or maybe two, and short of blasphemy, I doubt very much that God cares about our word choice. It's the intent that matters and the intent behind *fudge* and *fuck* is the same. The only difference is one sounds a whole lot stupider than the other. Besides, from the sounds of it, Jimmy, no one swears as much as you do."

I managed a weak smile. "*Stupider* isn't a word."

"You're stalling."

"No, I . . ." I took another drag off the cigarette, but it felt forced. "Why would I need to stall?"

"You tell me."

"I don't. . . Look, I. . . I know all about the Bible and, you know, Christianity and everything."

"Is that right?"

"Oh, you don't believe me? Okay, the, um, you know, the. . . Revelations! Yeah, just as an example. Revelations. It's the final book of the Bible. It says God's going to place a final judgment on mankind. The first thing is the, um, the Rapture, where God pulls all of the Christians up into Heaven. After that, there's all the different judgments. Over seven years, there's the Seven Seals, Seven Trumpets, and Seven Dishes . . ."

"*Bowls.*"

"Right. Right, Seven Bowls. There's the Antichrist that'll lead the world and fuck everything up, and when the seven years are over, Jesus comes back and judges everyone. There's more. I mean, I could go on about the whole Mark Of The Beast stuff and how Israel would be the only safe place left on Earth, but, you know, that's the gist of it."

Sarah considered me for a moment, her expression shifting between surprise and distrust. "And," she said slowly and carefully, "you believe that?"

"What? You mean do I believe it's true?"

"Yes. That it's *literally* true."

I tried to decide what the right answer would be but, after a moment, allowed what had become an uncomfortable smile to drop from my face and simply told her the truth. "No."

"I didn't think so. Why do you know so much about it then?"

"I just think shit like that's fascinating. You know, Terrence McKenna, Nostradamus, Revelations, it's interesting. But no, I don't think it'll happen. It'd be nice if it did, though."

"*Nice?*" she asked in an incredulous tone. Her eyes opened wide with disbelief. *Her eyes were so beautiful.* "The end of the world is going to be seven years filled with death, torture, starvation, war, lies, plagues, and every other form of suffering and evil known to man, and you think it'd be *nice?*"

"Sure. I mean, yeah, it'd suck for seven years, but think about it. If one morning you woke up and half the population disappeared and they were all Christians and then the rest of Revelations started happening, then you'd finally know. All the questions would be answered. Is there a God? Yes. Is the Bible true? Yes. Is there a Heaven, a Hell? Yes and yes. No more doubting or searching or wondering. Everything would become clear."

"I don't know that it would work like that, Jimmy."

"Of course it would. If you knew that there was a God, I mean knew it as an *undeniable fact*, what possible reason could there be for not being happy and doing the right thing?"

"I *already* know that there's a God. It *is* an undeniable fact."

"Yeah, well that's great for you, but a hell of a lot of the rest of us don't know that."

"Jimmy, God's always been in front of you. If you haven't seen Him, it's only because there's something inside of you that doesn't want to look. I don't know that that would change even if the world were ending, because *you'd* still be the same."

"Yeah. Well, anyway." The serious tone in her voice pulled me away from my theoretical enthusiasm and I lit another cigarette. "Look, why did you tell me this like it was a bad thing? Like it's the same kind of thing that I told you?"

"Because in most people's minds it's not as *bad* as what you told me, it's *worse*." She laughed. "I'm not stupid, I know what people think about hard-core Christians. They think we're judgmental, uptight morons who don't have the courage to face up to life in a godless universe and instead, make up fairy tales so we can sleep better. Try this out, Jimmy, you go and tell your friends the Gretta story and then tell them that you're dating a Born Again Christian. Fifty bucks says they all get a good laugh over Gretta and that the Christian thing is met with uncomfortable silence at best."

"You're a Christian but you hate men? You know, that's half the population that you hate."

"Just because I believe in God doesn't mean I'm perfect. If anything, it makes it all the more obvious when I'm less than I should be. I know it's wrong and I struggle with it. I suppose that's part of why I showed up here today." She sighed. "Look Jimmy, the way I see it, you told me the one thing about yourself that would probably make me want to have nothing to do with you. I did the same thing. You told me who *you* are, well, this is who *I* am."

I nodded my head and we stared silently at each other for several minutes. Sarah's eyes seemed to be gazing through me, evaluating my very being.

She got up and walked away.

21

The hole in my stomach returned and I suddenly realized that I hadn't noticed it since that day in the laundry room. Staring at Sarah's empty seat re-opened it, only now it was larger, its emptiness more vacant.

She came back carrying two kamikazes.

"So," she said, "you got any more stories you want to tell me?"

The hole was gone.

One year later we were married.

Twelve years after that, she was gone. I never saw her again.

I

Good Intentions

One

The sun pushed down relentlessly as I brought my slow march to a halt two hundred yards outside of the Israeli camp. The sudden halt caused my knees to buckle and I fell onto them, down into the sand. I slid my backpack off and the straps ripped painfully over my sunburned shoulders. I gasped for air that burned in my throat. Grains of sand burrowed into the tender red flesh covering my knuckles. I strained my eyes staring through the glare of the desert, desperately looking at the camp, searching for something new, something that would encourage me to rise up off my knees and return to it with enthusiasm. After several minutes, I stopped looking and struggled back up onto my feet, resuming my march without the enthusiasm.

Physically, the Israeli camp was a scene out of the *Grapes Of Wrath*. Every aspect of its physical construction reminded me of photographs I had shown to my American History class of Depression-era shanty towns. The dwellings were ineptly constructed out of whatever randomly available materials were on hand. Tin cans, slabs of cardboard, sticks, scrap metal, anything and everything was fair game for building material. There was no discernible logic to be found in the location of the shacks, neither in relation to each other nor to the topology on which they were constructed. One end of a 'home' was often two or three feet higher than the other, due to the incline on which it had been haphazardly built. With the single exception of size, the Israeli camp being hundreds of times larger than any shanty town ever was, the camp was a Hooverville.

The difference between the two lay in its inhabitants. The men in those grainy black and white photographs possessed hard, gaunt faces, touched with elusive shame. The women were dirty and obstinate, their expressions set with a haggard determination that refused to surrender, or even admit to, the fatigue that permeated their entire being. The children were forty-five year old men trapped in the bodies of pre-pubescents. They stared at the camera with a sneer that dared the photograph to document any vestiges of innocence. The children in those pictures looked as though they would have been more comfortable with a pack of cigarettes, a bottle of whisky, and a revolver than with a dolly or a rubber ball.

24

In the Israeli camp, every mouth wore a smile, every eye owned a twinkle, and every step displayed a happy bounce. The men moved with a gleeful sense of purpose, the women with a slow, gentle serenity. The children were tanned and ruddy-faced, looking as though they were gearing up to be painted by Norman Rockwell. The whole big bunch of them seemed to be constantly on the verge of bursting into song.

I entered the camp and felt a familiar knot of queasiness return to my stomach. The people swarmed like worker bees; interchangeable drones possessing a single-minded determination to accomplish a task whose significance was beyond their care or comprehension. They built huts, taught, tended crops, talked, and of course, prayed. Lots of praying. The chants, songs, hymns, and confessionals, all accomplished in Hebrew, English, Spanish, Arabic, French, and every other language conceivable, combined to form an ever-present, incomprehensible, maddening buzz.

I wandered aimlessly for a few hours, vainly struggling to close my ears to that buzz. Each step reminded me that I had returned to the camp for good, and each *Amen* that managed to rise above the collective din, reminded me how much I hated that fact.

"Jimmy!" a voice yelled. I recognized it as Bezalel Roth's, and began walking faster.

"Jimmy," he repeated, scuffling across the sand as he bridged the gap between us. "You are back."

"Fuck off," I muttered, and began walking more quickly.

"We were not certain if you were to return," Bezalel said, keeping pace with me. "You did not tell anyone that you were leaving, and we feared that a patrol might have perhaps arrested you. I myself had thought that. . ."

"I don't give a shit what you thought, Roth. Just get the fuck away from me."

"Jimmy, we must speak."

"Fuck off."

"We must speak."

"No we *mustn't*."

"This is important." He ran a few steps ahead of me and then turned and stopped in my path. "Jimmy, we must speak."

I stopped in front of Bezalel but the surrounding flow of foot traffic continued. An elbow jammed into my back and I stumbled forward.

Bezalel caught me.

I shoved him away.

"Sorry," a voice said.

"Shit-head!" I spun around but the person had already disappeared into the crowd. Reluctantly, I turned back to Bezalel.

He was still wearing the same beat-up brown pants that he had been wearing two-and-a-half years ago, when I had first met him, and the same black sweater, torn in six places now instead of just one. He was thirty-six years old, three years younger than I was, but he could have passed for twenty-five, with his dark brown hair and wrinkle-free face. I looked closer to fifty, almost sixty, with the red in my hair already giving way to a bleached, unhealthy white.

"Jimmy . . ."

"Save it, Roth. I came back because I *had* to come back, not because I wanted to. And frankly, you're one of the main reasons I don't want to be here, so turn around and get the fuck out of my face."

"Jimmy," Bezalel said, his voice dripping with sympathy, "if this is about what happened two weeks ago . . ."

"I got nothing to apologize for," I said too quickly.

"I am not here with the desire to make you apologize."

"No?" I felt a momentary flash of shame.

"No," he said earnestly.

I laughed, allowing the shame to transform into anger.

"Yeah, well, maybe that's part of the problem. Maybe you *should* be expecting me to apologize." I stared at Bezalel's guileless expression and scoffed. "What do you want, Bezalel? Shouldn't you be off observing the Sabbath? It's Saturday." Bezalel winced for a moment and I pushed forward. "Oh! Oh, I'm sorry, I forgot. You're a Christian now, so *Sunday's* your special day. Must be tough keeping track of things with all your holy days out of whack."

"I do fine," he said stiffly.

"Little Bezalel Roth," I said in a singsong voice, "a loyal soldier in Christ's army, working hard for his savior even on a Saturday. How proud your father would have been. He was a rabbi, right? I'd say that he must be smiling down from Heaven except, of course, being a Jew, Jesus didn't let him in there, did He? Well, maybe he's smiling up from Hell. What do you think?"

The words were useless as, per usual, a barely discernible stiffness in Bezalel's voice was as far as I could push his anger. He took a deep breath and, when he spoke again, even that stiffness had disappeared.

"I know that you hate it here, Jimmy."

"Why would you say that? I love being in Sunday School twenty-four hours a day, seven days a week. It's been my dream ever since I was an altar boy."

"As I said. Still, I believe I have discovered a solution."

"Oh yeah? You leaving and taking all the rest of the Christ-freaks with you?"

"Actually," he smiled, "it would be versa-vicea. Jimmy, how would you like to return to America?"

"Are you . . . Are you threatening me, Bezalel?" I couldn't decide if what I was feeling was anger or admiration. "Are you actually threatening me? *You?*"

"What? Oh!" He began waving his hands back and forth and shaking his head. "Oh, no. No, no, no. Of course I am not . . ."

"Because that sounded like a threat to me, you fuck." I grabbed onto his wrist. "What's the matter?" I asked, yanking his arm down and jerking him close. "You take me into your little paradise figuring you'll save my soul and add another Christ-freak to your resume? Another conversion and maybe your throne in Heaven'll get moved closer to God's? That don't happen so I get my walking papers? Is that it, you self-righteous piece of shit?"

"Jimmy . . ." I could feel his arm tense underneath my grip.

"Was the last straw two weeks ago? Huh? Who the fuck are you to tell me that I have to go? A yid who sucks up to Christ is going to judge *me?* Who are you to tell me anything?" I squeezed harder and the bones in his wrist bent and shifted.

He winced and then looked into my eyes. For a moment, I saw a jolt of rage, and it appeared as though Bezalel was ready to meet my anger with anger, my hate with hate. It felt good, seeing a piece of myself coming from him.

The moment passed quickly, though, and Bezalel's wrist relaxed underneath my grip while the anger disappeared from his face. In its place, a look of bemused understanding appeared, and he began chuckling.

"Always the angry man, yes? Now you let go of my wrist before I kick hell out of you, Jimmy." His threat contained a smile, and I knew that if I forced him to follow through on it, even his violence would possess an understanding grin, robbing me of any satisfaction.

I opened my hand and suddenly felt empty. Turning away from Bezalel, I collided with a passing drone. His shoulder dug into my neck and I stumbled back, hacking up phlegm laced with desert sand.

The man grabbed my shoulders and steadied me. *"Pardon,"* he said in a concerned tone.

I knocked his hands off my shoulders and shoved him away.

He shrugged an apology, smiled, and turned to rejoin the swarm, yelling, *"Je regret,"* over his shoulder before disappearing.

"Fucking faggot frog," I muttered, while rubbing my throat. "So what's this about America?" I asked Bezalel.

"Yes. Correct," Bezalel said, taking a deep breath. "Yes. Now, you have been away for the last two weeks, so would not have heard the news. Four days ago, we ushered in the Third Trumpet. Russia deployed its salvageable chemical weapons into Europe. They targeted Morrison's primary fresh water sources, so a very large percentage of Europe's drinking water is now poisoned, utterly contaminated."

"Uh-huh," I said, the interest in my voice minimal, "and that was the Third Trumpet?"

"And the third angel sounded," Bezalel quoted effortlessly, *"and there fell a great star from heaven, burning as if it were a lamp, and it fell upon the third part of the rivers, and upon the fountains of waters; And the name of the star is called Wormwood: and the third part of the waters became wormwood; and many men died of the waters, because they were made bitter."* Bezalel stared at me with a beatific look of self-satisfaction.

"Anyone ever tell you you talk like an asshole, Roth?"

"I . . . I simply wanted you to understand what . . ."

"Yeah, I understand just fine. Let me guess, most of Russia's chemical weapons came from Chernobyl, which translates into Wormwood, right?"

"That is right," Bezalel said, sounding impressed.

"Fuck you. Don't talk to me like I'm an idiot. So Russia jammed up Morrison's drinking water. Good for them. What's it got to do with me?"

"Good for them? Jimmy, do you comprehend how many people are now to die because of what Russia did?"

"Yeah, less than died when Morrison nuked Russia."

"I do not condone what Morrison did to Russia, but how can more death be a good thing? Especially when there is no point?"

"No point?" I asked.

"Of course not. Russia has been in ruins for more than three years now. Obviously some leaders managed to survive in bunkers, but what they did accomplishes nothing. It did not return to them their country or their dead. Yes. Of course there was no point."

"Hate, Bezalel. Hate is the point."

"Yes, it makes no sense," he said, continuing as if I had agreed with him. "Now Morrison shall simply bomb Russia more, and perhaps even send in troops to ensure that all are dead. What few people survived will now be massacred. There was no point. Yes."

"You know, you say *yes* like you understand what I'm saying, but you don't. You're not even listening. It's the hate. Their country's destroyed, their people are dead; hate's all they got left."

Bezalel stared at me as if I was speaking in a foreign tongue.

"Who the hell are you to judge them, anyway?"

"I am judging no one," he said with surprise.

"Yeah. Yeah you are, and you know what? When God fucks the rest of the world up the ass and gives *you* the reach around, you forfeit the right to bitch about the other guy being a bad sport, okay?"

"Jimmy . . ."

"No! No, the rest of the world's suffering and dying but not here, right? God protects *His* people here. No invading armies, no killer earthquakes, no death, no destruction, plenty of water, plenty of food, and plenty of free time to sit around wondering how the rest of the world could be so filled with ingrates too stupid to suck up to God while He pisses down their throats and tells 'em it's holy water."

"You make me sick, Roth. You're Noah, bobbing up and down in your arc, praising God for sparing your life while conveniently ignoring the millions of bloated corpses floating in the water. Corpses *your* God drowned. You ought to be ashamed of yourself, you . . ."

"Damn it, Jimmy! This is not what I wanted to speak with you about."

"Oh yeah," I said sweetly, my grimace transforming into a honeyed grin, "you wanted to know if I wanted to go back to America. I'll keep my answer short and to the point. No, and go fuck yourself."

"You are not happy here, Jimmy," Bezalel said with a sigh.

"No. No, I'm not. But I am safe here. And as much as I might hate it, I don't have any reason to trade in that safety."

"Is Judith Gaunt a good enough reason?"

The blood drained from my face.

"Jude?" I asked, the name feeling strange in my mouth.

"Yes."

"Wha . . .? What about Jude?"

"She is alive. In America." He began speaking in a short, clipped tone. "We can get you to her. Once we do, you convince her to return with you to Israel. Jimmy, I am offering you the opportunity to help save Jude Gaunt."

An elbow slammed into my slack body and I stumbled onto the ground. My sunburned face scraped against the hot sand and my teeth dug into my cheek, chomping through a chunk of flesh. I flipped over onto my back and a swarm of hands reached out to me, anonymously pleading for the opportunity to assist. I kicked and slapped the limbs away.

"Leave me alone, you fucking freaks! Get away from me!"

I pushed myself back up onto my feet and turned around in circles. The crowd that had offered their help had already moved on and disappeared. The new drones passing by ignored me, their faces blurry and indistinct to my eyes, their noises indecipherable to my ears.

"WHAT'S THE MATTER WITH YOU PEOPLE? WHAT THE FUCK IS WRONG WITH YOU?"

It had been more than a decade since I had heard anything from or about Jude. Our last contact had been waiting at my father's house after Sarah and I had returned from our honeymoon in Europe. It was a brief note, which simply read:

Jimmy,

Congratulations. I hope you're happy.

Love,

Jude.

I never could figure out whether the note was intended to be sarcastic or sincere. Knowing Jude, it was probably a little bit of both.

I pushed my way back through the crowd, towards Bezalel.

"Are you all right?" he asked.

"How come no one ever bumps into you?" I asked, jabbing my finger into his face.

"They do," he laughed. "Everyone bumps into everyone here. It is too crowded to be any different. I simply have learned to roll with the bumps. You, my friend, are too stiff."

"How do you know about Jude? I never told you a goddamn thing about her."

"Yes." He inhaled deeply. "You have been here for over two years. You arrived a bit more than a year after the Rapture. Yes?"

"So?"

"So, in that time, you have made it abundantly clear that you wish nothing to do with our community. This is your choice, but it has stopped you from understanding much of what we accomplish here."

"What? Like the praying? Oh, no, I've always been real impressed with the quality and quantity of your praying."

"Yes, Jimmy, We pray. But we pray not simply to worship and give thanks. We pray for direction. We pray for the wisdom to carry out God's will. The Lord has provided us with sanctuary, and despite your desire to believe the worst, we are not simply biding our time while the rest of the world is dragged down to Hell. It would be the greatest of insults to the Lord if we were to accept His gift of sanctuary and ignore the needs of the rest of humanity."

A shoulder slid across my back and pushed me forward. I tried to roll with it, clenching my teeth and remaining silent. My hands began shaking and I could feel the faint stirrings of a migraine.

"What does any of this have to do with me or Jude?"

"This camp is the focal point of a global network. One of our operations is an Underground Railroad of sorts. We have accessed the OWC's database and we use that information to bring people here."

"What's the point? We've got what, three, three-and-a-half years left? What difference does it make if they die now or then?"

"Yes. Well, certainly you worked very hard to get here, yes? When I found you in the desert, you were near dead. Regardless, though, the Railroad is not about maintaining the flesh, it is about salvation for the spirit. Many people have already made their decision. They have chosen the flesh and allowed themselves to lose salvation by being tagged, or they have chosen the spirit through Christ, and have been executed by Morrison and the OWC for their refusal of the tag. But what of those who have not yet chosen? How likely is it that they will choose Christ when they are surrounded by evil, and all who could speak the truth to them are dead or in hiding? How likely is it that those people will choose eternal life through Christ when all they know of Him is that to do so means almost certain physical death?"

He paused and stared at me expectantly.

"Bezalel, don't ask me rhetorical questions and then expect me to answer them. Just get to the fucking point."

He sighed. "We attempt to bring those people here. To bring them to a place where they are given the freedom and the information to choose wisely. Ms. Gaunt is one of those people."

"And she's still alive, huh?"

"You sound surprised."

"I don't know," I said with a shrug. "I guess I just assumed she had died in the nukes or the earthquakes or all the other shit. Hell, knowing Jude, I'm kind of surprised she even made it to the Rapture in one piece."

"Yes. Well, she is alive. More important, she has not been tagged. We can tell her the truth, help bring her to God."

"Yeah, good luck with that."

"God does not need luck."

"Shut up. You still haven't answered my question. How do you know about me and Jude?"

Bezalel nodded his head. "More than a year ago, we gained access to the OWC files. *Hacked*, I believe is the word. Their information possessed is astounding. Ms. Gaunt's time in jail, her drugs, where she has lived, those she has dated, where she has worked, her medical records, all of it is possessed in the OWC files. What is ironic is that it was not even the OWC which collected most of the information. The U.S. government did so before Morrison took over. All the OWC did was to make use of those files and keep them updated.

"After the hot-wires were laid and the System became centralized, the U.S. government introduced a tracking and filing program. With TV, the telephone, and the computer all combined into a single system, the government was able to possess very deep files on nearly everyone. Phone talks, money, personal writings; anything accomplished using the Centralvision was sorted and filed. When the OWC took over what remained of your country, they inherited that information. That was how Morrison was able to track and categorize so many of you so quickly.

"And that is how we learned of Ms. Gaunt. After gaining access to that information, we introduced a program into the System. We put in a name and learn if it is mentioned in any other files. If other criteria are met, a match is returned. We entered your name and the System returned Ms. Gaunt's."

"What's the *other criteria*?" I asked.

"If the person is still alive, if they have been tagged, if their location is known, if they are affiliated with any specific religions . . ."

"Yeah," I laughed, "and I bet the Christ-freaks get bumped to the head of the line, right?"

"No."

"No?"

"No. Christians have already made their choice. They need no further assistance from us."

"Even though they'll probably end up tortured and killed."

"As I said, Jimmy, we are concerned with the fate of the spirit, not the flesh."

"You're a cold bastard, Roth, you know that?"

"Jimmy," he laughed, "why do I suspect that if we did prioritize Christians, you would accuse me of favoritism. Yes?"

A person squeezing past nudged me forward, his chest sliding against my back. I said nothing and the migraine began to throb.

"Jimmy, I am not attempting to force you into doing something which you do not wish to do. I am simply presenting an opportunity. If you wish to help Ms. Gaunt, you can. I read her files, I know that the two of you were very nearly married. My hope was that, knowing how you feel about this place, about God, that you would want to do this. In truth, after what happened with Maria, I felt that this might be something that, indeed, you *needed* to do."

"I . . . Look, Bezalel, I'm a teacher, or at least I used to be. I'm not some kind of ex-commando that you can bring out of retirement for *one last mission.*"

"No one is handing you a gun, Jimmy. You are not going to kill anyone. We shall bring you to Ms. Gaunt and then return you here. You simply need to convince her to return with you."

"Well Jesus, if you can get me in and out, why do you need me at all? Why don't you just go and get her yourselves?"

"Because you know her, Jimmy. Because she knows you. We have attempted sending strangers to these people and it simply does not work. Most people are not even aware that there is a section of Israel under God's protection. Morrison has been very successful in squelching any rumors of this camp's existence. These people are not going to trust a stranger telling them some fairy story about a paradise in the desert. You know Ms. Gaunt, you tell me; if I went to America in your place, do you truly believe that she would return with me? Would she even listen to what I had to say?"

"No," I said, and laughed at the thought. "Not the Jude I knew, anyway."

"Yes. Good. Correct. That is why it must be accomplished in this fashion. If you want Ms. Gaunt to be saved, *you* must go."

I nodded and turned away, trying unsuccessfully to focus my thoughts. People swarmed around me in droves and the omnipresent chatter crushed any attempts at clarity. A long, drawn out buzz rattled its way through my ears, scratching away at my brain.

"How would I get there?" I asked, turning back to Bezalel in desperation.

"On a human transport."

"A prison ship! Fuck you. Everyone knows what happens on those ships. Without a tag I'd be pegged as a Christ-freak in a second. I'd end up raped or dead or both."

Bezalel scratched the back of his neck and averted his eyes. "Yes. Correct. Yes. Well, that would be a part of it, Jimmy. Even aside from the transport, once you arrived in Boston, you would need to be tagged so that you could move freely about the city in order to find Ms. Gaunt. Yes. Yes, you would need a tag."

"Didn't I just say that? I'm not tagged, it won't work."

"Yes. Yes." He nodded his head and stared at the sand. "If you choose to go," he said in a quiet voice, "we would tag you."

"What?"

"We possess the instrument needed for tagging. We have a tagger. You would need to be tagged to do this. We can do that."

"It's a fake? You can counterfeit a tag? Would that work?"

"No," Bezalel said, and then remained silent.

"*No*, what? Quit dicking around, Roth, what are you saying?"

"No! I am saying no to both questions. No, a false tag would not work and no, it would not be a false tag. The tag would be real. It took several months and many lives to secure it, but we possess a real tagger."

"So . . . you'd put a real tag on me? As real as the OWC's?"

"Yes," Bezalel said, still refusing to look at me.

"If . . ." I looked down onto the sand, at the same spot upon which Bezalel's vision had become transfixed. "If you tag me with a real tag, then I go to Hell, right?"

"Not necessarily," he quickly said. "The tagger we possess? All of the taggers, I would presume, they are also capable of removing a tag. We would tag you, you would go to America, get Ms. Gaunt, and if you returned, we would then remove the tag."

"*If* I get back." My stomach became a tight knot and my brain shrank down into a compact pellet of solid pain. "And what *if* I don't get back? Huh? What then? What *if* some fuck on the prison ship decides, tag or no tag, that I look like an easy mark and beats me to death? What *if* the OWC ends up shooting me in the back of the head before I even get on the boat? Jesus Christ, Roth, what *if* I trip over a banana and break my fucking neck before I even leave the camp? What *if* I don't make it back? Then I go to Hell, right?"

Bezalel took a deep breath and met my eyes.

"Yes. If you die before we are able to remove the tag, then you will go to Hell."

The pellet in my brain continued to shrink, becoming more and more dense. The knot in my stomach twisted so tight that I felt certain it would burst.

"You arrogant fuck. Where the hell do you get the balls to ask me to risk my soul? My fucking *soul*?"

"Oh please, Jimmy. Your *soul*?" Bezalel asked, with astonished laughter. "Your *soul*? If you tripped and broke your brain open on a rock right here, right now, where is it that you suppose you would end up? You believe, what, that because you are not tagged you are not damned? Jimmy, if you desire to hide from the world, that is your choice, but do not lie to yourself. What is it that you believe? That God is going to take you to Heaven so that He may spend an eternity listening to you rail against Him and spew your contempt in His face? If you died right now, right at this moment, we both know where it is that you would wind up. Yes?"

An arm gently brushed against my back.

"MOTHERFUCKER!"

The nugget in my brain exploded. The knot in my stomach tore. I spun around and, through a wall of red, saw an eternity of indistinct, identical faces. I had no idea who had brushed into me, but it didn't make any difference; they were all the same.

I swung my fist towards the first man I saw, my knuckles digging into the back of his neck. He stumbled into the crowd and I pounced onto his back, screaming like an animal. We tumbled onto the ground and I began pounding away at the back of his skull.

"Stop it, Jimmy!" It was Bezalel's voice, but it was far away.

Strong arms grasped me.

The crowd stopped its eternal noise and motion as hundreds of drones stared at me silently, their faces draped in pity.

"DIE!" I screamed, flailing my legs and kicking at them. "FUCKING DIE! ALL OF YOU SHOULD BURN IN HELL YOU FUCKING PIECES OF SHIT! DIE!"

I struggled until I was exhausted, and then went limp in Bezalel's grip. Barely able to hold my head upright, I watched as the man I had attacked was helped up off the ground. He looked to be about sixty years old and he stared at me with fear and confusion. He reminded me of my father, and the heavy exhaustion tugging down at my body transformed into even heavier feelings of guilt.

Bezalel lowered me back down onto the ground and released me. I pushed back at him with rubbery arms and stumbled forward, elbowing my way through the gawking, sympathetic crowd.

"Fuck off," I mumbled, pushing to the outskirts of the camp.

Once again, I found myself in the desert. After wandering several hundred yards away from the camp, I stopped. Staring out into the empty desert and then back towards the camp, I felt like a magnet helplessly hovering between two opposing poles. My hands began aching and I looked down at my knuckles and saw that the skin had been scraped off them. Grains of sand were wedged into the open sores and I realized that I had punched the sand as much, if not more, than I had that old man's head.

The knowledge didn't change anything, and I surrendered to the guilt and exhaustion, collapsing down onto the desert floor.

Bezalel was preaching to a large group near the camp's makeshift hospital. I waited until he had completed his sermon, hovering far enough away to ensure that I couldn't hear his words, and then slowly approached him after the people had dispersed.

"Hey," I said, my voice horse.

Bezalel stared at me blankly.

"So, um . . . Russia screwed Morrison's water supply, huh? It's funny; everything's so fucked-up now that that doesn't even seem like that big of a deal."

"It will be for the OWC."

"I guess. Hey, you know what really disappoints me?"

"No."

"Well, for thousands of years, people have been waiting for the Apocalypse. People thought, even hoped, that Nero was the Antichrist, that Napoleon was, Hitler, Saddam Hussein, all of them. And then, when the real Antichrist finally shows up, he's this sissy little Englishman in a three-piece suit. He brings his empire of evil with him and then gives it a pussy name. *One World Community*. *Nazi* sounds scary, *OWC* just sounds pathetic. Couldn't he have come up with something like, *The Legion Of Doom*?"

"I believe that was the name of the villains the Super-Friends fought on that cartoon show, yes?" Bezalel asked, without the slightest trace of humor.

"I don't know, but you know what I'm saying, right? Even *666* ended up watered down. Instead of being these huge ominous numbers branded on people's forehead or hand, it ends up being a fucking microchip attached to a tiny hand bone."

"It still contains three sixes. There are always three sixes contained in the identification number of all the chips."

"I know, and that's my point. Instead of a big 666, it's just three numbers randomly tossed in the middle of a few hundred other numbers on a microchip. Even the name sounds faggy. *Tag, taggers, Oh no, I've been tagged!* It sounds like a fucking game."

"Technically it is called an *identification implantation*."

"Yeah, well, that's my point, what the fuck happened to *666: The Mark Of The Beast*?"

"Yes. I doubt that Morrison could convince many people to accept the tag if he named it *The Mark Of The Beast*."

"Yeah, but you know what I'm saying, right?"

He said nothing.

"You have no idea what I'm talking about, do you, Bezalel?" I smiled weakly.

"What? No. Yes. Yes. Of course. It is just . . ."

"Doesn't matter. Forget it." We stood in uncomfortable silence for several minutes. "So," I finally said, "do they still have cigarettes in America?"

"I believe so."

"Well, that's something, I guess." I shifted my weight back and forth and stared at the ground. "I'll do it."

Bezalel nodded.

"Yeah, well, I don't want any misunderstandings about why I'm doing it, Roth. I'm not doing it for you and I'm not doing it for me. And I sure as shit am not doing it for God. This is about Jude, plain and simple. You got that?"

Bezalel stared at me and said nothing.

I tried to return his solid gaze, but couldn't.

Two

I allowed Bezalel to blind me. Once the rag was tied securely around my eyes, he boosted me up onto the horse and then climbed on in front of me. We rode in silence for several hours and I began to suspect that we were mostly just riding around in circles, I doubted that Bezalel would really allow his precious tagger to be maintained as far away from the camp as he was trying to make it appear. Still, the silence was pleasant and I was disappointed when Bezalel yanked back on the horse's reigns and soothed our transportation into an unsteady halt. After being helped down off the horse, I heard tiny snippets of sound fraying the edges of the silence, and assumed that Bezalel was exchanging glances or signals with someone else. I heard what sounded like a tent being unfastened as Bezalel grabbed my arm and gently led me forward. The sun's glare, perceivable even underneath the blindfold, disappeared, and I knew we had moved inside.

"Stand still for a moment, Jimmy," Bezalel said, his words loud and inappropriate, a clumsy smashing of the blessed silence we had been respecting. I heard motion and what sounded like machinery being disassembled and removed. Bezalel's fingers fiddled with the back of my blindfold for a moment and the cloth dropped from my eyes. We were standing inside a small tent, which was empty except for Bezalel, myself, and a heavy looking table with a small black box resting on its center.

"That's it?" I winced, my voice sounding loud and embarrassing, a belch in the middle of confession.

"Yes."

The tagger was completely black, and appeared to be made out of plastic. Its surface possessed no dials, no buttons, no switches, and no brand names. There was no goat's head or pentagram or inverted cross plastered across its surface. It presented an alluring simplicity, its only distinguishable feature being a small rectangular opening in its center. The opening appeared to be just the right size to accommodate the entrance of a human hand.

"I don't see any controls. How do you operate it?" I crouched down and peered into the box's opening but could see nothing but more black.

"There is a laptop connected on this side," Bezalel said, as he walked around to the back of the table. "It has already been prepared so, whenever you are ready, simply place your right hand into the opening with your palm faced downward."

My knees became light and airy. I was unable to inhale anything but the shallowest breaths which, gentle and quiet as they were, sounded deafening. The air in the tent became thick and dank. I stared at the black box and felt a rush of panic sweep through me. I knew what I was staring at.

Early in our marriage, Sarah and I had taken an extended trip through Europe. While in Poland, we had visited the former death camp, Auschwitz. It was fall and the cool air had been motionless while we toured the peaceful grounds. It wasn't what either of us had expected; mostly empty fields and a few brick buildings, buildings that could have easily been mistaken for a school house or a fire station. There were no obvious indications of the evil that had once festered there, no glaring Swastikas or screaming Nazis with leather boots and whips. There was no rancid smoke funneling out from the long dormant chimneys or emaciated corpses littering the plush, green grounds. Even the railroad tracks had become obscured, robbed of their dark immediacy by the soft weeds tangling themselves around the rusted steel.

It was an affective simplicity. Absent the garish distraction of obvious evil, my mechanisms of perception shifted. The physical serenity of the camp, its silence and its stillness, the lack of visual and intellectual distractions; it all allowed me, forced upon me, a deeper knowledge of where we were. I could smell it in the odorless air and touch it with the bottom of my stomach. It prodded my soul with a voice of silent obviousness. It was the opposite of Sarah. It was black black evil in its most honest simplicity.

Standing in front of the tagger, my soul remembered.

"Jesus Christ," I whispered, turning away from the black box. "I don't know if I can do this."

"Yes. The choice is yours, Jimmy. You would not be the first to withdraw."

"What if . . . what if it doesn't come off? What if you put it on me and you can't take it off?"

40

"This is not the first time we have done this. It will come off, Jimmy. I promise."

"But what if it doesn't? What if it won't let you?" I stood transfixed, unable to speak or move, unable to think.

"You feel it, yes?" Bezalel asked.

"I . . . Feel what?"

"The evil." Bezalel stared at me as though we finally understood one another, as if I had suddenly realized something that he had known all along. There was a conspiracy of Those-In-The-Know conveyed in his voice, a conspiracy of common understanding into which, his tone told me, I had just been initiated. He spoke to me as if we were suddenly brothers, as if we were suddenly the same.

"You want to know what I feel?"

"I believe I already know," he said, while nodding solemnly.

"Yeah, huh? Tell me something, Roth, you ever try heroin?"

"Have I . . .?"

"My little brother OD'd on it. Did you know that? Oh, wait! Of course you knew that. You know everything, don't you? You knew that when he was fifteen someone sold him a hot bag, some uncut junk. You knew that my mother found him in our bathroom, dead on the toilet. You've got the OWC files, so even though *I* never saw fit to tell you, you already knew all that, right?"

He looked away.

"Yeah. Well, here's something you probably don't know. A couple of years after we put Scotty in a box, Jude convinced me to shoot up with her. I didn't want to. She knew about what happened to Scotty and what happened to my mother after she found him. She knew how I felt, but she . . . she . . . Well, anyway, I told her I'd do it. So, I roll up my sleeve and Jude pushes the needle into my vein. I didn't even feel it go in. I was too busy thinking about Ma, and how fucked up she got after finding Scotty. I'm thinking about Dad telling me it was my fault. I'm remembering how Scotty looked in that box. He had . . . You know they put make up on you when you're dead?"

Bezalel said nothing.

"Yeah. Well, anyway, I'm thinking about all this while Jude's pushing the needle into my arm and I just, I felt evil, like I was spitting on Scotty's grave and pissing in my parents' eyes."

Bezalel stopped looking away and nodded sagely; obviously approving of my use of the word *evil* and relieved at the path my story was taking.

"Yeah. Well, you know what happened then?" I asked. My tongue felt thick and wet in my mouth. I pushed it out and ran it across my lips. "The smack hit my heart and my dick got harder than it's ever been in my entire life. It was almost a shame, that hard-on, because the rush itself was so incredible, so sexual, that physical sex, actually *fucking*, it never entered my mind. It felt *so* good. And it wasn't just the heroin, it wasn't just the drug. It was like I had stepped through a mirror and once I was on the other side, everything that made me *not* want to do it, everything that made me feel guilty, *that* was what made my dick hard once I *had* done it."

Bezalel shifted back and forth uncomfortably. "Yes, well . . . Yes. Well, have no illusions about this, Jimmy; there is nothing sexy about getting marked for Satan."

His stiff words knocked me away from the memory, and I laughed. "You're a fucking moron, Roth. I'm going to tell you something. You won't understand it, but I'm going to tell you anyway. Pissing your soul away for a lark; shooting the same shit into your arm that killed your little brother and broke your family; squeezing the trigger on a machine gun aimed at a line of innocent people; fucking some skank up the ass who smells like a toilet and isn't half as attractive as your loyal wife; guzzling so much booze that you piss and shit yourself; all of it; it's all sexy when *you're* the one doing it. It just depends which side of the mirror you're on."

A look of disgust grasped Bezalel's face.

"Yeah. Don't ever think that I'm like you, Roth." I rolled up my sleeve. "Let's just do this."

Highh on adrenaline and stupidity, I stepped up to the black box. I looked to Bezalel and he nodded his head without meeting my eyes.

"When you are ready," he said.

"I'm ready right fucking now." I pushed my hand into the black box's open mouth and was surrounded by a cold, cave-like emptiness. It was as though there were no machinery inside the box, its outward simplicity duplicated by the dark emptiness of its interior.

Bezalel pressed a button. One clean, quiet tap.

For a long pregnant moment, I waited silently.

My hand remained untouched.

Noticing that I was holding my breath, I forced my lungs to descend, releasing the pent-up air.

The pregnant moment succumbed to a bloody birth as unseen leather straps inside the black box hurled themselves around my hand and wrist.

A tiny noise, which I had a difficult time recognizing as my own, escaped from my throat.

I pulled back instinctively, trying to reclaim my hand.

In response, the straps contracted, solidifying their grip.

I tried to squirm my hand loose but was unable to move it in the slightest. Up, down, backwards, forwards; every avenue of escape was blocked. The straps were cold and clammy and they responded perfectly, countering my every motion. It was as if the leather was alive, and I suddenly realized that I had placed my hand, not in a simple mechanism, but into the mouth of a black demon. Its tongue, colored I felt certain, an unnatural mesh of red/white, had slipped itself around my hand, claiming me as its own.

I quickly abandoned all thoughts of Jude and Sarah and Scotty and Bezalel and Dad and Ma and God and every other damn thing on the planet. All I wanted was my fucking hand back and I couldn't get my fucking hand out of its fucking mouth.

"Jesus Christ, let me go!" I screamed, more scared than angry, more pleading than demanding.

In response, the Demon bit down into my flesh, a quick, piercing jab followed by a dull, hard pressure that pushed itself onto, and then into, my bone. The attack opened up an entire universe within me, one that existed in the tiniest millimeter in the smallest bone in my right hand. The Demon displayed that universe to me, brought its vastness of existence to my attention, and then raped it while I remained a helpless spectator.

I slammed my eyes shut as the pain ripped up through my arm and then tore into my brain before dropping down into my stomach like ten tons of wet shit. I fought to stop myself from puking.

I fought. Yes. Fight. Fight this cocksucker.

I forced my eyes open. My body began convulsing but my head remained completely still as I located the Demon's eyes. They were black eyes, visually indistinguishable from the rest of it, *but I could still fucking see them.* I gathered up everything within me that was strong and pushed it all into those eyes. All the hate, all the anger, everything that was left to me was stuffed into those pitch dark eyes so that I could beat the Demon, beat the black box, beat the Auschwitz that was trying to claim me.

The Demon responded by squeezing me tighter with its tongue and digging its teeth deeper into my bone.

It's nothing. I can beat it. I know I can.

This faggot tagger, this cocksucker Demon, this pussy Auschwitz.

I can beat it.

I can stick my hand into its slot, stuff my hand down into its mouth, push my soul into its gates of death, and win.

Alone, I can meet it, fight it, beat it, and walk away clean.

You can't touch me, you fuck.

Nobody can.

I'm better than all of you.

I can win.

I can't not win, you fucking faggot.

And then it was over.

The pressure disappeared and the leather straps dissolved into the vast recesses of the machinery. I stumbled back, drunk off sudden victory, gasping for breath and curling my lips into a smile that felt as though it were stretching all the way up to my eyeballs.

"Fuck you," I gasped. "Fuck you. I won. Me. Teach you. Teach you who you're fucking with. Goddamn right."

I spit at the black box and turned away, dropping my vision down onto my injured hand. Next to my thumb, about an inch bellow my index finger's knuckle, was a thin black line. The line was one-eighth of an inch in thickness and one full inch long. I felt an unnatural itch underneath the skin. My *bone* itched.

The smile slid off my face.

I was tagged.

I raised my head and stared at the black box.

Through the still, motionless air, I heard the Demon's silent, victorious laughter.

It had poisoned my blood and gassed my soul.

I bolted out of the tent and dropped down onto the ground, vomiting until my throat bled.

The plan itself was simple. Bezalel would accompany me to Jerusalem where I would be arrested and then sent to Boston on a prison ship. Once in America, he had arranged to have one of his contacts get me out of custody and bring me to Jude. After convincing her to return to Israel with me, the contact would arrange for transportation back, and that would be that.

Unfortunately, Bezalel was still finalizing the details of the plan, and while he did so, I was stuck in the camp, where the situation had become unbearable. Nothing was ever said, but from the moment I returned with the little black line on my right hand, a vast chasm suddenly existed between myself and the rest of the camp. It was, to be fair, a chasm that I had desired for some time. But I quickly realized that there was an enormous difference between fighting tooth and nail for your own space and having said space thrust upon you.

I'd pass people, good Christians all, and notice their quick, twitchy glances towards my hand. The looks commenced and ceased in less than a second; more than enough time for me to notice, but not enough to justify a confrontation. But it was more than just the looks. The Israeli camp packed people together tighter than a Japanese subway, yet suddenly, I seemed to have developed a force-field two feet wide in diameter. In a camp that was both severely congested and severely happy, avoiding physical contact had previously been an impossible task. People slid past one another, shook hands, slapped backs, hugged, and kissed; anything and everything short of actual sexual relations were a constant. Not me. Not after I was tagged. What was amazing was how natural everyone made it appear. No one ran or pushed or shoved; the foot traffic simply flowed around me as naturally as a raging stream flows around a rock.

And while a small part of me enjoyed the newly granted space, a much larger part began hating the people for imposing that space upon me. After all, who were *they* to reject *me*? After several days of quiet ostracism, I began intentionally bumping into people, grabbing them in an unnecessary attempt at steadying them, maintaining my grip on their shoulders far longer than appropriate, and reveling as they squirmed uncomfortably in my arms. Familiar faces that tried subtly ignoring me were greeted with enthusiastic smiles and the offer of my tainted hand of friendship. After severe hesitation, their faces would drop as they surrendered to the demands of both common courtesy and Christian charity by limply accepting my contaminated hand into their own.

It was a bitter, short-lived satisfaction, though, and when Bezalel finally informed me that everything was ready for my trip to Jerusalem, I felt a surge of relief. We were to leave the following morning at sunrise.

Unfortunately, the next day, the sun never rose.

The Forth Trumpet of Judgment wasn't quite the spectacular event that it had promised to be. The sun didn't bleed out of the sky, the moon didn't engulf its inferno, and nuclear explosions didn't hurl tons of soil into the atmosphere, obscuring its fiery presence. We all went to sleep and, the next morning; there was simply no sun to see.

I woke up every half-hour, each time expecting to see the dawn's tepid light poking itself through the cracks of my tent. Each time, I assumed that I was simply being overly eager, and would force myself back to sleep. After eight false wake-ups, I finally stopped trying to sleep, noticing that the buzz of prayer was particularly loud for so early in the morning.

When I walked outside, the sight of hundreds of bonfires tearing into the darkness greeted me. The people were praying, but they were doing so at a shockingly fevered pitch. Prayers were screamed rather than chanted, songs of grace were accomplished through lacerated throats, and instead of kneeling upright, petitioners splayed their torsos across the sand, pressing themselves into the dirt as deeply as they were able.

An older woman bumped into me and I asked her what was happening.

"The Forth Trumpet," she told me, her eyes bulging. "The Angles of the Lord have blighted the sun from the sky."

"*Blighted?*"

She dug her fingers into my forearm and tried yanking me down onto my knees alongside her.

"Let us pray! We must beg for forgiveness! Humble yourself with me before Christ!"

"Piss off." I jerked my arm out of her grasp and walked away.

After pushing my way to the outskirts of the camp, I paused and turned around for one final look. The bonfires raged into the perpetual night, spewing forth a violent orange glow that danced across the people's faces, the twisting light and frantic shadows imparting the appearance of passion and complexity. It was more than they deserved. More than they had earned. The fires created an illusion of depth that had never existed within the people, and I felt resentful that my final view of them would be framed in such an intense light. It would have been more appropriate to leave when the sun was centered in the sky, casting a bland, uniformed illumination across the people. I closed my eyes and created that picture in my mind.

Keeping my eyes shut, I turned my back on the camp, trying hard to engrave the duller of the two images into my memory while casting out the false evidence of my own eyes.

I left without looking back, relying on the camp's residual light to lead me through the darkness.

Bezalel had already arrived at our meeting place. He wasn't alone. Towering over and beside him was an immense black man. The huge man was holding a violently flaming torch in his right hand and, if his skin had been green instead of black, I might have mistaken him for the Statue Of Liberty. His other hand grasped the bridles attached to three horses; all apparently sane enough to remain completely still while under his control.

Bezalel's warm smile was ridiculously overshadowed by his companion's hateful scowl, a scowl that was directed towards me. It wasn't a grimace of frustration or annoyance, it was pure hatred, so intense that it looked as though the excess was feeding up through his arm and funneling into his torch, fueling its bursting red flame.

Bezalel was either ignorant or indifferent to the hatred looming over him. He smiled with innocent enthusiasm as I approached.

"Jimmy, you found us! This is something, yes? Do you understand that it is nearly noon? Morrison's scientists and press are going to have a very difficult time trying to explain *this* away."

"Yeah." I looked back at the huge man and kept my eyes locked on him while I spoke in as non-threatening a voice as I could manage. "Bezalel, who's your friend?"

He glanced over his shoulder as if he had forgotten the looming rage.

"Oh! Yes. Good. Jimmy, this is Amhad."

At the mention of his name, Amhad glared at me, his hatred sharpening into rage.

"Amhad. Super. Who is he?"

"He is your guide. He will lead you to Jerusalem."

"I thought you were doing that."

"No. Not in this darkness. I could bring you a small way, but very rapidly we would become lost. I will follow for a bit, but Amhad will take you all the way. He is Egyptian, but he grew up in this area and knows the land like the front of his hand."

"Great. Why isn't he saying anything?" As far as I could tell, Amhad had yet to blink even once.

"He speaks no English."

"Okay. Fair enough. And, you know, just out of curiosity, why does he look like he's about to disembowel me?"

"I do not know that word."

"Kill me, Bezalel, why does he look like he wants to kill me?"

"He hates Americans," Bezalel said with a shrug.

"He what?"

"Yes. Correct."

"Uh-huh. Well, that's something. Should have told him I was Scottish."

"Yes. Well, he hates them also."

"What? Who the hell hates Scottish people?"

"Yes. Perhaps it would be more true to say that he hates white people."

"Not very Christian of him." Amhad had yet to move and I began wondering if he wasn't a statue.

"He is putting effort into change. Be happy that he does *not* speak English or you would have to pass the whole journey listening to him complain about white men. He would tell you how Jesus and the Apostles were black and how it is no coincidence that the Antichrist is *not* black."

"But he's not American either, he's English."

"Yes. But he is still white, you understand? Yes?"

"Right right. He's still white." I nodded pleasantly towards Amhad and turned back to Bezalel, who was sporting a big, dopey looking smile. "Could I speak with you alone for just a minute, Bez?"

"Why? We really should be leaving."

"Yeah. Just a quick minute, okay?"

I gently grabbed Bezalel's shoulder and we walked far enough away from Amhad for me to feel certain that he couldn't hear.

"Jesus fucking Christ, Roth! What is this bullshit?"

"What?" He stared at me with a look of genuine confusion.

"*What?* Are you kidding me? Is this a fucking joke? You're going to send me into the desert with a racist with a pituitary problem? You figure I didn't have enough bullshit to deal with? Now I've got to watch my back in case Malcolm X on steroids decides to avenge his people's suffering on my white devil's ass."

"Jimmy, do not be such a baby."

"*Don't . . . ?* Fuck you, Roth! What's he got to be pissed about anyway? I didn't even think they had white people in Egypt."

"Relax. Yes? He is trying to overcome his prejudices. Helping you is simply a part of the process."

"He doesn't seem to have a problem with you. Why not? You're as white as I am."

"Yes. Correct. But I am Jewish. Amhad does not consider the Jewish people to be a part of the white race."

"Lucky you. Fucking unbelievable." I looked over at Amhad and smiled. Despite our distance, I felt certain that I could hear his teeth grinding. "Jesus Christ. Fine. Whatever. Just get me out of here, Roth. Get me away from you fucking people."

The three of us mounted our horses and Amhad extinguished his torch. Without the light, I experienced the total darkness of God's judgment. There was no moon or stars or even a slight glow upon the horizon. The darkness was absolute, nothing but thick black in every direction.

In order to keep track of one another, we loosely wrapped a connecting rope around our left hands. At first, it was difficult for the three of us to fall into a smooth riding pace. I was in the middle, with Amhad riding in front and Bezalel riding behind and, for the first few hours, I bore the brunt of our lack of cohesion. Amhad would ride too fast, yanking me forward and tearing the rope across my hand or Bezalel would slowly fall behind, gradually increasing the rope's tension and causing it to burrow into my flesh.

After several hours, though, we fell into a comfortable rhythm, riding without incident, until I felt Bezalel tug the rope to signal for a stop. I continued the signal up towards Amhad, who brought his horse to a steady halt while simultaneously giving the rope a quick, violent yank, which, as far as I could remember, hadn't been an agreed upon signal for anything. *One tug stop, two tugs speed up, three tugs slow down.* Apparently Amhad wasn't comfortable with the breadth of our created language and, in an attempt to express himself more fully, introduced into our common rope-language the violent tug that tears into my hand and almost yanks me off my fucking horse.

Bezalel jumped off his horse and lit a torch. I clumsily slid off my horse and walked towards Bezalel. Amhad remained mounted as he coiled the rope.

"This is my end," Bezalel said. "Amhad shall take you the rest of the way."

"You're not going any further?"

"Yes. No." Bezalel's torch flickered in the dark wind, sprinkling light and shadow across his face in an ever-changing pattern. "This is as far as I am able to go in this darkness and still be able to return alone."

"Oh." I felt oddly disappointed that he wouldn't be continuing on with us, although perhaps that was simply my fear of being alone with Amhad. "Why don't you just go all the way then, and come back with Amhad?"

"No. No, you still have two days of riding and there is much to accomplish at the camp. Time is short, yes?"

Behind us, Amhad's horse was impatiently tromping its hoof into the sand.

"Okay. But you never really told me anything about my tag."

"How do you mean?"

"Well, what's my name? What am I classified as? A thief? A deserter? What's my identity?"

"I . . . Yes. Or, no." Bezalel rubbed his ear. "No, it does not work that way, Jimmy. We have access to the files, but if we begin changing them, then the OWC will become aware of that and change all their access codes. All that we did was place the tag on you, which already contained your information."

"I don't . . . What does that mean?"

"You are going as James Lordan."

"Oh." I was nowhere near as fond of the idea of re-entering the world as *James Lordan* as I had been of doing so as someone else. "Okay, well, what's my status then? Am I just a deserter?"

"No. No, we cannot change your status either, Jimmy."

"Yeah, yeah I get that part. But what am I?"

"Jimmy, I do not think that that is necessarily . . ."

"Is it possible for you to answer a direct fucking question, Roth? What am I?"

"You are a murderer, Jimmy."

"What?" I stepped back. "But why? I mean, I . . . I'm . . . "

"Louise Toth."

"Lou . . . She was . . . Look, that was when the earthquakes had . . . I mean, it's not like I . . ."

Bezalel continued to stare at me but said nothing.

"Yeah." I turned away from his glare. "Anyway. Look, about Maria . . ."

"Yes. Good. Do not worry. I believe that she understands."

"Yeah. Well, it's just that, you know, I never saw her after I came back. I just never ended up bumping into her, you know? I mean, you know how big the camp is. Anyway, I was just thinking that maybe if you see her you could tell her that I'm . . . Well, maybe you could just talk to her for me when you get back."

"You speak to her yourself when you return, Jimmy. There will be plenty of time then."

"Right." I smiled and nodded at the easy lie.

Amhad prodded his horse into a painful sounding whinny. I wasn't at all interested in knowing where he had stuck his foot in order to produce such an unnatural sound from his horse.

"Guess I better get going before I give Superfly-Shaft here any more excuses to hate me." I climbed onto my horse.

"You have a chance here, Jimmy," Bezalel said as he approached me. "Do not throw it away because of the past."

"Yeah."

Bezalel's torch fizzled out and there was an uncomfortable moment of silence, a discomfort illuminated, rather than concealed, by the darkness. I awkwardly began reaching my hand out into the darkness but, before I could complete the motion, heard, "Remember, Jimmy, *The Lord our God Sayth that he who. . .*"

I dropped my hand. "Jesus Christ, Roth! What the fuck did I tell you about quoting scripture to me? Stupid dick."

Amhad hurled the rope, slapping me in the face with it. I wrapped it around my hand and gave two light tugs. He answered my signal with a yank that lifted me two inches off my saddle. Behind me, I heard Bezalel climb onto his horse and ride away. Amhad and I began galloping in the opposite direction and, as the gulf between Bezalel and myself grew larger, I felt the Israeli camp melt away like the false oasis I had always known it to be.

I bathed in the cold, dark day. The wind pushed through me, making my blood course like an electric current. I was free, headed back to where I belonged and, for the first time in more than two years, I felt alive.

We rode for what felt like decades into the forever night until the warm glow of rediscovered freedom disintegrated into a terrifying, timeless mind-fuck. The darkness was simultaneously invisible and omnipresent. It crushed me with its engulfing presence while tearing at my brain with its intangible distance. Without the sun, time became meaningless, dissolving into an eternal black moment. My horse navigated the desert terrain, requiring neither direction nor control from me, and as I pushed nowhere, I dissolved into an abandoned ghost, listlessly hurtling through a vast, crushingly compacted void. I was neither protected nor persecuted, neither observed nor ignored, neither hated nor loved. I was a spark of useless consciousness rapidly traveling nowhere through nothing.

Amhad, riding solidly ahead of me, became, in the surrounding sea of zero, my anchor to reality; our connecting rope my lifeline to sanity. His brutal signals periodically shocked me away from delirium, ripping into my hand, tearing away at the flesh, and allowing me to momentarily reconnect with a linear sense of time. The wound began as a tender spot and then, as time moved forward, progressed to an increasingly painful open sore with strands of rope embedded in the mangled flesh and blood. The pain dragged me back towards actuality and allowed me to maintain a tenuous grip on reality.

We stopped twice to sleep, but it was an unceremonious affair. Amhad would violently signal for our stop, slide off his horse down onto the ground, and fall asleep without saying a word. When he had slept enough, he would throw a stone at my back and angrily gesture for me to get back onto my horse. We didn't eat at all.

Amhad's final tug, a particularly brutal one, felt as if it stopped just short of burrowing the rope into the bone itself. We halted the horses and Amhad lit a torch and jammed it down into the dirt, allowing it to stand alone. He pointed past the torch, indicating the direction I should continue to walk and then marched towards my horse, his movements harsh and precise.

I gazed towards his reassuring reality with something that felt like love. He stood by my horse and glared at me with his usual hatred. That hate was so tangible, so physical, so solid and real, that I felt grateful, and smiled warmly.

A growl escaped the back of Amhad's throat and he shoved me off my horse.

"Mother*fucker*!" I scurried up onto my feet, shaking the cold grains of sand out of my clothes. The jolt from the fall knocked my head clear and transformed my love into anger. I ran around the horse, stopping just short of bumping into Amhad. Standing in front of his huge frame, I quickly realized that there was no way in hell I was going to even try and vent that anger on him.

Ignoring me, he tied the bloody rope that had connected us onto my horse's bridle and then turned towards me and pointed past the torch, indicating the direction I should continue traveling. I had no idea how far away from Jerusalem I was, but I implicitly trusted Amhad's sense of direction. I had no idea how he had managed to navigate his way through the darkness without hesitating or faltering even for a moment, but I respected the incredible, almost supernatural skill he had displayed in doing so.

Perhaps it was that feeling of admiration that prompted me into offering my hand. Perhaps it was simply that I was still angry with nothing to release it on, and decided instead to try and make myself believe that Amhad didn't deserve my anger. Perhaps. It's difficult, sometimes, to trace backwards to the origin of stupidity.

Staring at my outreached hand with amazed contempt, Amhad smacked it away and spit in my face.

The spit felt thick, slapping against my nose and lips.

I stepped back as Amhad pushed his face towards me.

"Nigger," he hissed.

I took another step back and forced myself to relax.

Amhad noticed my calm and became indignant.

I began laughing. Loudly and deeply.

He began shaking and spat at me again, this time towards my feet. He missed, and the spittle landed harmlessly on the sand.

I looked down at the ground and my laughter splintered into fractured giggles.

Shaking with rage, Amhad stormed past me and climbed onto his horse. He began riding and jerked the rope, his pull so violent that for a moment, I thought my departing horse was going to tumble over onto its side.

I continued my loud laughter until I was certain that Amhad was no longer close enough to hear. The moment I was sure of that, I stopped the laughter dead and wiped the spit off my enraged face.

It took more than a little effort to free the torch that Amhad had stuffed into the ground. Once I had, I looked in the direction Amhad had signaled for me to walk, toying with the idea of going in the opposite direction, just to spite him. The foolish, self-destructive temptation was stronger than it should have been, but I managed to ignore it, and began walking in the right direction.

After about an hour, I stumbled upon a road and followed it until, just as my torch was burning out, a vehicle approached. It was a jeep with a huge spotlight mounted on its rear and it screeched to an immediate halt in front of me. The spotlight blinded me and I discarded the dead torch and raised my hands over my eyes to block out some of the light. I saw shadowy blurs of movement and heard voices screaming at me in a foreign tongue. Someone grabbed me and I was tossed onto the hood of the jeep.

After carefully frisking my body, I was spun around and pinned against the jeep. With the spotlight behind me, I could finally see the men clearly. Their uniforms were Israeli and they were younger than I would have expected. Two baby-faced kids wearing fake tough-guy expressions and playing at war. They pointed their guns at me and shouted loud, incomprehensible questions.

"I don't understand a single fucking word you guys are saying."

"OWC?" one of the boys asked.

"American," I responded, a touch of indignation in my voice.

One of the soldier-babies whispered something to his partner-playmate, who walked past me, towards the rear of the jeep.

"Your hand!" the remaining kid demanded.

"No need to yell, junior," I said, and raised my left hand.

"Other hand," he said with an exaggerated scowl.

I shrugged and raised my right hand, which he grasped and, noting my tag, quickly dropped.

"Shouldn't you kids be back in the city trying to get laid instead of playing Cowboys and Indians out here in the desert?"

"Who are you? How are you here?"

"Well, I was with this big huge seven foot Christian/Egyptian guide who had this uncanny knack for direction, but wanted to kill me because I'm white. So I . . ."

"Quiet!" His voice cracked when he yelled and he looked embarrassed. "What are you here?"

"You mean *why*? Boy, that's a big one. Okay. About three and a half years ago, Jesus took my wife up to Heaven in the Rapture. I stayed behind because I had this stupid idea that I could save my family, but when I finally got back to Boston, and this would have been after the spacemen came and the nukes had flown, mind you, my mother had . . ."

"Quiet!"

I shrugged. "You asked."

The other kid returned with a scanner, which he passed across my tag.

"I'm a political refugee," I said. "I demand asylum. Take me to your leader. Bring me your women."

One of the boys looked up from the scanner and whispered something to the boy who spoke English.

"Political refugee?" he asked.

"Yup."

"Murderer!" he snarled, in an unconvincing tone he must have picked up from television.

"Yeah, well, you know, six one way, half dozen the other."

He swung his gun around and stabbed my cheek with its barrel, slicing off the piece of flesh I had chomped through when Bezalel first told me about Jude. It lay by my tongue and, for a moment, I had the strange urge to chew at it. Instead, I stumbled backwards and covered my face with my hands, leaning over and spitting out a mouthful of blood.

The two boys stared at me, uncertain at what to do next.

"What?" I yelled. "Did you think you were going to hit me once and knock me out? What is this, your first day on the fucking job? This isn't a movie, idiots, you have to hit me more than once." Using my teeth, I tore at the remaining flap of skin in my mouth and spit it out. Jolts of pain flared through my jaw and I continued talking in an attempt to ignore it. "First, you don't ever hit anyone with the barrel of your gun. It'll bend. Besides, it's too fucking narrow to knock anyone out. You use the butt of your gun, okay? Second, and this is the important part, kids, you don't just hit the person once and then wait for them to fall. You keep hitting 'em until they stay down."

They looked at each other and then back to me.

"Goddamnit, if you're going to do a job, do it right! Take some pride in your work, you stupid little shits!"

I walked towards the two boys and the one who spoke English swung his gun into my face, using the butt.

I fell down.

This time, they did it right.

"Jesus Christ," I mumbled, waking up with a painful throb in my head and a mouthful of torn flesh.

"Little late to ask Him for help, don't you think, buddy?"

The familiar words and tone cut through my fog.

"Stan?" I asked, fighting against a stiff neck and turning to my right. Sitting next to me was a pudgy, scruffy looking man who was silently chuckling. The flab around his cheeks jiggled with the motion. It wasn't Stan.

"Hey brother, good to see you up. I thought I might have to make this trip without any conversation. Kikes do that to you?"

"What? Do what?"

"Yer face. Whole side's all black and blue and swollen. Hell, the way yer lip's all puffed up, if it wasn't for the blue, I mightta mistaken you for a darkie. Get it? *Black* and blue? Swollen lips? Darkie? Heh heh. Anyway, who did it?"

"Students of mine," I mumbled painfully. "I'm very proud. Where are we?"

He peered out the small window next to him. "Ah, I don't know. I can't see a goddamn thing in this darkness. Somewhere over Europe, I guess."

"*Over?*" I glanced around and realized that I was in a small plane and that my hands were cuffed to my seat. All the seats were occupied with similarly chained prisoners and there were ten other men standing in the aisle, chained to a metal bar running down the ceiling of the plane. Two armed Israeli soldiers stood at either end of the plane, looking bored and tired. "Where are we going?"

"Can't say for sure, but I hear they're gonna be shipping us outta Spain."

"*Shipping us out from Spain*," I repeated, my head beginning to clear. "To where?"

"America." He grinned into his double chin. "Land of the free. We've had our fun and now Big Daddy Morrison's sending us to our room without any supper." He made a flapping sound with his lips. "Like I care. I wasn't cut out to be no soldier anyways, and since I ain't no Christ-freak, I'll just end up doing a few months in a camp before getting work in the States. That's where all the real goodies are."

"*Goodies?*"

"Oh yeah! Most of these chumps here are Christ-freaks and Morrison ain't got no use for their kind. You and me, though, brother, we got the tag. We'll get good work over there and, the way I hear it, there's plenty of fringe benefits for guys like you and me. 'Sides, anything's gonna be better than getting shot at by the Camel Jockeys or the Chinks when Morrison finally decides to wipe 'em out, right?"

"Uh . . ."

"Goddamn right it's right. What'd they pick you up for?"

"I don't, um, murder, I guess."

"You *guess?* Damn, brother, if you can't remember it than it wasn't worth it, right? Yeah. They got me on a rape beef."

"Rape?"

"Yeah. No big deal. We'll do okay in America."

"Did you do it?"

"Huh?"

"Did you rape someone?"

He stared at me with a confused expression, which eventually transformed into a grin. "Couple of kike slabs," he whispered. "Can't say it wasn't my own fault though, right? Morrison don't wanna be stepping on their toes right now and I knew that. Still, the way I figured it was, if they're gonna ship us over there to help build their stupid temple, the least they can do in return is cut us a little rhythm when we bend a rule or two. But no, they gotta make a big stink over two lousy slabs and *I'm* the one who gets screwed. Shouldda stuck with the Palestinians; no one gave a fuck about what we did to them. Oh well, live and learn, right?"

My face crumpled into a look of disgust.

"What? What's the matter?"

"You raped two women?"

"Hey, I'm just making conversation."

"You're a rapist?" I asked, my voice rising with disgust. "You . . . Get the fuck away from me." I shifted as far away as I could, as far as my constraints would allow me, which wasn't very far.

"What the hell is this? You too good to talk to me?"

"Fuck you."

"You something special?"

"I'm no rapist!" I said, angrily spinning back towards him.

"Yeah, well I ain't no murderer."

"I'm not a murderer, I just, I just . . ."

"Yeah, and I ain't no rapist, *I just I just . . .*"

"Fuck you, you sick bastard. I'm nothing like you."

"Yeah, you got that right, pal. You don't see me making up no pansy-ass excuses like some little kid. At least I own up to what I am, you freakin' hypocrite."

"Good, I'm a hypocrite. Just shut up."

"Fine, we'll fly in silence. That'll be fun."

"Good."

"Fine.

"Good."

For several minutes there was silence.

"Stuck up little prick," he mumbled.

The plane landed and we were quickly transferred out of Israeli custody and into OWC custody. Didn't seem to make much difference; Israeli soldiers wore brown uniforms and carried guns while the OWC soldiers wore dark blue uniforms and carried guns. I was scanned and then led to a room where my hair and beard, both of which had grown long in Israel, were shaved. After being stripped and subjected to a body search, I was given one minute in a bathroom.

The whole process took less than an hour and I experienced an odd feeling of security while being led from one task to another. After the disorienting freedom of the desert, the intense, if impersonal, attention I received while being processed through the de-assembly line was strangely reassuring.

With my hands cuffed behind my back, I was led into a brightly-lit courtyard where hundreds of naked men were already standing in tight, efficient rows. I was placed at the end of one of the rows and told, "Stand. Don't sit, don't talk."

The prisoners continued arriving and I stared up at the spotlights, which were throwing light at us from all directions. The illumination was too intense to stare at directly and produced a bright, pulsing glow, which made it impossible to see beyond the surrounding chain-linked fence. At the head of the yard, in front of the prisoners, stood a tall wooden platform with a lone microphone perched on its center. Soldiers with guns hiked over their shoulder and cattle prods dangling casually from their wrists roamed the ranks. Being careful to avoid the guards' eyes, I focused my vision on the glow, straining unsuccessfully to see past it, to see what, if anything, was behind it.

The temperature continued to plummet and the pain began in my toes. After my digits had become mercifully numb, the frigid ache slowly spread out, eventually becoming focused at the tip of my penis. It was a stabbing pain that flared with every pump of my heart. I attempted to focus on something else; anything that would allow me to ignore the pain, but the silence and stillness of the courtyard made that impossible. I stared at the lights, trying to escape in their warmth, but their harsh luminance only increased the pain.

Long after I became convinced that the cold had ensured that my penis would never properly function again, a man in an OWC uniform climbed up onto the stage and stared down at us from the microphone. He wore a thick, well-groomed, white mustache and had a heavy head of hair. He stood completely erect; his shoulders arched so far back that it looked as though they had been severely dislocated.

He turned his head back and forth, inspecting us silently for several minutes before grimacing in utter disdain.

"Remain perfectly still and perfectly silent while you listen to me," he said into the microphone. His voice was that of a British aristocrat and each impeccably pronounced syllable bounded out of the speakers with an existence and a meaning of its own. Each clipped syllable dug into my penis, causing it to throb in agony.

"Proper protocol demands that I introduce myself before commencing my address. I shall *not*. I am a proud, productive member of the One World

Community. An energetic contributor to the future of humanity. You. All of you, are non-persons. You are nothing!" He paused and allowed the word to echo through the courtyard. "You are traitors and malingerers. You are selfish animals!" His head jerked back and forth as he spoke, but his immaculate posture remained motionless. "Each of you, regardless of past indiscretions, was offered a room in our loving home, a wing in our mansion. You are here now because you have, in one fashion or another, rejected that offer. You have not only rejected it, but have tried to destroy our house, and in doing so, have declared yourselves to be enemies of our family.

"Your father, Charles Grant Morrison, the man whom, even as we speak, is in the midst of selflessly leading humanity towards a greater destiny, is, like all fathers, merciful. He is in the possession of no greater desire than to open his arms to his prodigal sons. You are, therefore, not to be shot in the head as you should be, you rotten little ingrates. No. Instead, you are being sent to the North American Quadrant for re-education, in the hope that you shall return to the flock.

"Do not, however, mistake mercy for weakness; do not believe that your punishment will be easy. Harbor no illusions on that count, you parasites. You *will* be punished!

"However, after your richly deserved chastisement, you will be offered a place in our home. If you refuse, we will kill you.

"I am not, by disposition, a merciful man. Were the decision mine, I'd save Mr. Morrison a lot of bother and put a bullet in your brains right now. RIGHT HERE AND RIGHT NOW! I'D DO IT! I'D DO IT MYSELF! DOES ANYONE DOUBT THAT? DO ANY OF YOU MISERABLE BASTARDS DOUBT THAT?" He darted his bright red face back and forth. No one seemed to doubt him and, satisfied with the silence, he nodded his head, wiped the spittle from his chin, and tugged down on his uniform.

"Right. Well then, my personal feelings notwithstanding, I bow to the superior wisdom and judgment of Mr. Morrison, and try to share with him a hope for your future. Although looking at you now, it is difficult to do so. This is your last chance, you pack of pig-wankers.

"Now get on the damn boat, staring at you for this long has actually managed to make me physically ill."

My penis hurt worse than ever.

Three

One by one, we were led out of the courtyard and onto a huge freighter. Once we boarded the ship, our handcuffs were removed and we were brought to a small hatch. The hot, rancid smell drifting up from the hole made my stomach clench. "Down," the soldier told me. Lowering myself to my waist, I swung my feet back and forth, searching for a ladder. Before I could locate one, the soldier stomped on my shoulder and sent me hurtling down into the dark heat.

I crashed down onto an accumulation of bodies, people who either hadn't possessed the foresight to move out of the way quickly enough, or had been injured in the fall, and weren't able to move. The bodies cushioned my impact and I wound up bruised rather than broken. I quickly rolled out from under the hole and, the moment after doing so, heard the thud of another dropping body. I continued to role, struggling to relax as elbows, knees, hands, and various other appendages jammed into my back and stomach and wrapped themselves around my limbs.

When I finally rolled free of the heap, I splashed into a liquid, which was more than a foot deep. The slime was heavy and chunky, and consisted of various colors, including red, green, brown, and white, all refusing to bleed into one another. If the colors alone hadn't identified the ingredients, the putrid smell would have. The stench clung to the back of my throat and, while crawling away from the pile of bodies, I added to the mixture with my own vomit.

I continued to crawl forward until the top of my head bumped into a wall, and then flipped over and leaned against it. Initially, my body rejoiced at the opportunity for rest and warmth, but quickly enough, the pleasure became pain as the muscles in my back clenched and the quiet numb coursing through my body transformed into a hot, painful throb. The pain subsided as I allowed my feet to push through the watery top of the slime, into the thick denseness underneath. As my toes were gently warmed, I slumped down and began spreading the heavy liquid across my legs and groin. The smell and knowledge caused me to retch several times, but in truth, the gags felt more obligatory than necessary; with the pain in my body subsiding, I was already beginning to feel comfortable with my surroundings, which were dimly lit by several low-wattage light bulbs perched at the top of the hull. Spaced about twenty feet apart from each other, and apparently covered in heavy dust, they emitted a mild, brown-tinted illumination.

Feeling securely situated, I turned back towards the hatch and watched as bodies dropped down into our Hole, one after another.

Whump.

Whump.

Whump.

Whump.

Whump.

Usually after the fall, there would be some shadowed, frantic movement as the person struggled to free himself from the tangled mass of limbs. Occasionally, though, someone would become tangled in the various limbs and claustrophobic screams of terror would last until the dropping bodies bludgeoned the sound into unconsciousness. At other times, the simple noise of a fleshy fall was accompanied by the sound of a breaking bone, followed by a distinct lack of motion and quiet groans, which were quickly silenced.

Whump.

Whump.

Whump-Snap!

Whump.

Whump.

When the hatch finally closed, I was relieved to discover that we weren't packed in as tightly as I had feared we might be. Every person, or *non-person* I suppose, owned a surrounding foot of personal space. I was in possession of a coveted space against the wall, a location that allowed me to sit upright and relax my back muscles without having to sink my entire body down into the slime. As a consequence, I was jammed shoulder to shoulder between two men.

As the journey began, the Hole remained in possession of a peaceful quiet. The steam rising out of the slime mingled with little more than quiet murmurs and restrained whimpers. A few tepid shoving matches began, but quickly dissipated before amounting to anything. No one had enough energy to begin anything serious.

I stretched my arms up over my head and arched my back until I felt a satisfying crack. When I dropped my arms back down to my side, I felt a single fingertip gently tapping my shoulder.

Turning to my right, I saw a young, sweet looking kid smiling at me. He looked like he was somewhere between his first wet dream and his first shave.

"I'm Robert," he said, and offered me his hand.

I turned away from him.

He nudged me again.

"What?" I asked in an annoyed voice.

"Has anyone ever told you of the glory that is Jesus Christ?"

I groaned.

"Everything that's happening is the fulfillment of six thousand years of Biblical prophecy. It's not too late to turn away from evil and embrace your savior, Jesus Christ."

"He's not *my* savior, kid."

"Of course He is. Jesus saves all who accept His grace."

"Mm-hmm. Let me guess, you got picked up trying to sneak into Israel."

"Only in the wilderness of Israel are God's people spared from His wrath and protected by His grace."

"Right. Listen kid . . ."

"Robert."

"Whatever. Now is not the time to be talking that Jesus shit. Especially not to me, you understand?"

"So, you *have* accepted Jesus as your savior?"

"What? No, that's not what I'm saying, I . . . Did you not hear what I just told you?"

"I heard. But *you* have to understand that it's every Christian's duty to spread his love and knowledge. *Especially* now."

"Do you have any idea where you are?" Lowering my voice, I leaned over and spoke quietly into Robert's ear. "Look around. God's not going to help you here, kid. Pull your head out of your ass and smarten-up. You need a savior? Fine, *I'll* be your savior. First commandment; shut the fuck up about Christ. You tagged?"

"Identification implantations are abominations. They're the Mark Of The Beast and an outward symbol of the internal rot of . . ."

"Yeah, I'll take that as a *no*. Okay, listen to me; people are going to fuck with you. When they do, don't let them see that you're not tagged. Cover your hand in slime. If someone tries and check you out to see if you're tagged, get in their face and act like you're insane. Hopefully, they'll buy it and leave you alone, if not, go for the eyes or the balls. And for Christ's sake, wipe that stupid fucking grin off of your face!"

"I'm sorry, but I can't do any of that. Well, I suppose I could stop smiling."

"I . . . Do you understand where you are? What's going to happen to you? It's quiet now, but pretty soon, people are going to get bored. They're going to start looking for trouble. When they do, the first thing they're going to look for is who's tagged and who isn't. Odds are they'll stay away from you if they think you're tagged, because anyone with a tag being sent back to America has pulled some serious shit. Violent shit. No one's going to bother taking that risk with so many of you Christ-freaks available. On this ship, you're marked because you *don't* have a tag."

"Look, I appreciate your concern, I really do. But I can't turn my back on God for any reason."

"I'm not telling you to turn your back on God, just shut up about Him for the next few weeks."

"I won't deny Him the way Peter did. No matter what the circumstances, it's my duty to help lead others to salvation."

"Not *here* it's not."

"Here *especially*."

"Fine. You don't want to listen to me? You get what you deserve. Don't fucking talk to me again."

I turned away and slumped down into the warm slime, spreading its warmth over my body before falling into a deep, comfortable sleep.

Time completed its descent into obsolescence. It had begun to lose its meaning in the desert and, in our unchanging Hole, it had become a complete anachronism. I suppose that I could have paid attention to how much thicker the slime was becoming and, through that, gauged the passage of time. Some things however are simply not worth that level of commitment.

Food was sporadically thrown down to us in the form of moldy bread. Water was served up by a high-pressure hose that shot in all directions after being lowered down through the hatch. We'd open our mouths and hope to get smacked in the face, swallowing down a bit of liquid before being knocked over by the pressure or, in my case, having the back of my head slammed up against the steel wall.

The warmth of the hull, along with the food, water and rest, returned some of our energy to us. That was when the rapes began.

No one worked alone. There were always at least two or three men in a group. Their black silhouettes could be seen slowly moving across the ship, grabbing people's hands and inspecting for tags. They casually slipped through the mist, sliding anonymously through the shadows as they chose their victims.

I didn't see the first few rapes, but I heard them. The sounds of quick scuffles, muffled protests, and the sickening grunts of pleasure lingered like the hot, static steam. The noises were always the same and they blended in seamlessly with the brown, stifling atmosphere.

Like the slime, the rapes were sickening at first, but it didn't take long to become accustomed to them.

I was dozing in and out of sleep when my turn for inspection came. A thick, meaty paw grabbed my wrist and sloppily wiped the sludge off my right hand. I felt an empty swish of fear for a moment, a sensation that pleasantly converted into relief as my hand was gently released and I was left unmolested. I pretended I was still asleep, but slightly opened my eyes and saw three men covered in slime.

Moving past me, they surrounded Robert and I hoped that, despite his protests to the contrary, he had listened to me. I hoped that he still had some space left in his brain for someone other than God.

"Hello." Robert smiled the smile that I had told him to hide.

"Hi there," one of the men said.

"Have you heard the message of Christ?"

"What?"

"Jesus Christ. It's not too late to turn to Him for salvation."

"Why would you do this to yourself, boy?" the man asked.

"Just do him," one of the others said.

"Shut up."

"Why would I do what?" Robert asked.

"You know what we are, boy. You know what we're going to do. Why would you say that? Why would you talk about Jesus?"

"I . . . I don't have any choice. I'm a vessel for God."

The man considered his words for a moment. "Okay. Go on and turn over."

"But . . ."

"It's okay. Turn over." The man bent down and gently lifted Robert's body, turning him over onto his stomach.

"But," Robert asked as tears flowed down his cheeks, "but why would you do this?"

The man froze and stared down at Robert's vulnerable body, thinking about the question for several minutes.

"Because you're a vessel for God," he finally answered. Then he raped him.

Through his screams and tears, Robert prayed. *"Yea, though I walk through the shadow in the valley of death, I shall fear no evil, for the Lord is with me."*

He sounded desperate to believe the words.

The man bent his face next to Robert's and gently whispered into his ear as he delicately pushed his face down into the slime.

I rolled Robert onto his back. His eyes were glazed; his mouth filled with the slime that had choked him to death and silenced his prayers.

One of the three men who had raped Robert returned and tossed his corpse onto the pile that had accumulated under the hatch.

"I knew you weren't asleep," he said as he slid down the wall next to me, claiming Robert's space as his own. "Just thought you should know that."

I was awoken by an odd noise.

Still groggy, I stared down the length of the ship.

Through the dark brown, a lone figure slowly walking towards me. His body slumped to the right. Drooping arm shattered. Face covered in blood. Singing in a quiet, dreamy voice.

"Ring around the rosy."

Feet never rising out from the muck. Floating.

"Pocket full of posies."

Elbow bent backwards. Jagged bone clinging onto torn flesh.

"Ashes."

Floating towards me, occasionally stumbling, never falling. White eyes gleaming through a red, wet face

Unnaturally white. Staring into me. Into my soul.

Floating towards me, eyes locked onto mine.

An angel. An angel in mangled flesh.

I smiled.

Holy. Clean.

"Ashes."

I struggled to my feet as he moved towards me.

Here to save me.

"We all fall down."

A black shadow broke free from the surrounding darkness and punched the Angel in the face.

"SHUT UP!" the Shadow screamed.

I jolted back.

Angel falling down into the slime.

Shadow kicking its head.

"SHUT UP!"

I slid onto the floor. Covered my face with my hands.

Angel's head slamming down onto the hull.

Vibrations tickling through me.

Spurts of laughter echoing through the dirty air.

"SHUT UP!"

I slid my face between my knees and cried, praying no one would notice. Praying *someone* would notice.

Four

Time, always such an essential aspect of American life, returned to our world when the sun, as simply and as inauspiciously as it had disappeared, reappeared. At dawn, thin slivers of flawless gold sunlight pushed down through the corners of the closed hatch and a slice of my heart uncoiled with relief. The final leg of our cruise seemed to pass quickly once the sun had returned from wherever it had gone and, a few hours after the third dawn had arrived, the ship slowed itself into a steady halt. After several hours, the hatch above us opened and a thick beam of sunlight ripped down into our darkness. The concentrated white was too much for my eyes to bear and I jerked my face away from it.

"When your name is called, climb out," a voice from the white yelled.

After several minutes, I forced my eyes open and quickly slid them across the light. When I closed them again, an image had implanted itself upon the inside of my eyelids. A rope ladder had been tossed down into our hole; its excess gently draping over the bodies that had accumulated underneath the hatch.

In the darkness, the corpses had been indistinct; a large black shadow with frayed edges. The sunlight stole that illusion, transforming the simplicity of darkness into a well lit, techincolored obscenity. On the inside of my eyelids, I saw blood so red it was almost black, crusted and thick as it clung to ears and mouths and noses. I saw pale broken bones ripped free of the confines of flesh and stabbing into the air like morbid erections. I saw skin, pink and black, intertwine as limbs tangled in a frozen, passionless orgy.

I saw Robert's face, his empty eyes staring at me with unbliking accusation.

One by one, our names were shouted out, occasionally leaving momentary silence in their wake; the only eulogy the dead would receive. More often, though, a groan of relief would be heard, and a man would rise out of the muck and ascend the ladder into the light. The procedure took several hours and, by the time my name was called, it was already dark, the boat nearly emptied of life.

I stumbled towards the pile. The dead stared at me with silent, unwavering eyes as I stepped up onto their bodies. After taking several hesitant steps, my foot snagged underneath an elbow and I fell forward. My hands slapped onto a stiff back. I felt two nubs of vertebrae underneath my right palm and a shoulder blade under my left. When I tried to push myself up, the slime covering my hands caused me to slip. My chin dug into a dead shoulder while an unbending finger pushed into my eye.

I struggled to push myself up, but continued to slip and fall. Slowly, the left side of my body began sliding down, wedging between two of the dead. I panicked and lurched forward with a frantic body spasm.

Was that a knee pressed into my stomach? A chin?

I writhed and began flailing my arms.

What was scraping against my toe? A tooth? A broken bone?

My fingers brushed against the rope ladder and I clutched onto it as a frightened squeal of panic burst free from my throat. Straining my arms and shoulders, I pulled myself out from the dead and scaled the ladder as quickly as I could, rising towards the soft cool glow of the beautiful moon.

Soldiers surrounded me, their machine-guns casually dangling from their shoulders. I stood in front of them, nervously awaiting direction, half-expecting to receive another beating. Looking down at myself, covered in filth and blood, my body hunched and emaciated, I couldn't help feeling that I deserved a beating, that I had become less than human.

When the beating failed to arrive, I looked up at the surrounding soldiers and saw them more clearly. In Spain, the OWC soldiers had looked like real soldiers. They had short hair, were in good physical shape, and carried themselves with a sense of purpose and authority. The only similarity between those soldiers and the ones surrounding me on the boat were the uniforms and the guns. The American soldiers ignored me while they smoked their cigarettes and chatted casually with one another. They slumped lazily against the rails and two of them appeared to be sleeping. Most of them had long, unkempt hair hanging listlessly across their shoulders. Their pot bellies strained against their stained and wrinkled uniforms, threatening to tear through the filthy fabric. More than half of them looked to be well into their sixties while the others were younger, even than the two Israeli soldiers who had captured me.

Eventually, a few of them glanced over at me. There was a spark of hatred in their eyes, but it was a lazy hatred, one that seemed to stem from annoyance more than anything else. In Spain, the revulsion had been different, a disdain blossoming out of a genuine sense of morality. Both viewed me as a cockroach, but in Spain, I was a cockroach that had scurried into a five-star restaurant and required a quick and efficient disposal; my existence amongst the grandeur necessitating a proper display of moral outrage. In America, I was a cockroach in a run-down tenement building in the projects; I had to be dealt with, but my presence was routine and, if annoying, certainly not surprising.

One of the soldiers, a young kid with terrible acne and a squiggly dirt mustache crawling across his upper lip, hobbled over to me and scanned my tag. He accompanied me off the ship and jammed me into a huge shower-room packed tight with prisoners. For a brief moment, I wondered about gassing, but quickly dismissed the notion, realizing that Morrison would never exterminate us cockroaches in a fashion which would so easily associate himself and the OWC with such a universally condemned period of history.

The water was frigid, but I forced myself to stay underneath its stream. The cool night had transformed the slime covering my body from warm and protective to hard and constricting. It tore at my skin, and I would have happily scrubbed myself with solid ice in order to free myself from its filthy grip.

Wet and naked, we were led outside, into a huge parking lot surrounded by a chain-link fence. We were placed in loose forming rows and scanned once again before being split up into two separate groups, one comprised of Christians, the other, violent criminals. My crew was the most heavily guarded, despite the fact that the Christ-freaks more than quadrupled us in number.

Hunched over and exhausted, most of the Christians looked as though the journey had defeated them, but a few stood upright, seemingly undaunted by their plight. A few even appeared to possess the threat of a smile dancing underneath their lips.

The prisoners surrounding me stood tall, looking hard and bored. Some of them glared towards the Christ-freaks with disdain, and I wondered who had done the raping and killing on the ship. I found it impossible to guess who might have been guilty, as none of the surrounding faces betrayed even the slightest hint of shame.

"James Lordan! James Henry Lordan!"

71

I pushed myself to the front of the crowd, where an old man with long white hair and a thick beard stared at me without emotion. It was Kris Kringle in an OWC uniform.

"James Lordan?" Santa asked.

"Yeah."

He grabbed my arm and began leading me out of the parking lot, back towards the main buildings.

"Where are we going?" I asked, wondering if this was the man Bezalel had contacted to get me out of the camp.

"Shut up," Santa said, his voice bored and dismissive. He carried his gun over his shoulder absent-mindedly, as if it were a sack of toys.

We had walked about a hundred feet away from the other prisoners when someone else called out my name. This time, the voice sounded uncertain and hesitant.

"Mr. Lordan?"

Releasing an annoyed groan, Santa stopped walking.

"Mr. Lordan, is that really you?" A small soldier in his early twenties walked towards me with a pronounced limp. "Mr. Lordan, right?"

"Yeah."

"You don't remember me?" he asked, stopping in front of me and grinning.

I stared at him and wondered if he, rather than Santa, was the person who was supposed to help me.

"Yeah," I muttered. "Yeah, you look familiar. I just . . . I'm not . . . I can't seem to place you."

"Mark Perry?" the soldier asked. "Michigan? I had you for tenth-grade History. Remember?"

And suddenly I did, his name unlocking my memory. "Oh my God! Mark Perry! Of course I remember you. You always sat in the back. Never turned in your homework. Jesus, I can't believe it's really you!" I was suddenly filled with joy. Intellectually, I knew that I had once done something as normal as teaching, but on a deeper level, I had forgotten it long ago. That job had become the possession of another man, the work of another lifetime. Seeing Mark Perry, I suddenly remembered that life, remembered it, not in my head, but in my heart. I remembered sneaking smokes behind the field house with Joe Lukas. I remembered fighting with the school board over the curriculum, back when something like that still seemed important. I remembered hanging around my house over summer break, drinking coffee and making fettuccini alfredo for Sarah.

Sarah.

I remembered being Sarah's husband.

"Boy, you look like shit, Mr. Lordan. That happen on the boat?" Mark asked, pointing at my face.

"Huh? I don't . . . Oh, this. No. No, it's nothing. Israel."

"It doesn't hurt?"

"No. No, not anymore."

He snickered the same annoying laugh that used to emanate from the back of my classroom, stepped forward, and dug his knee up between my legs.

I dropped down onto the pavement and curled into myself, desperately grasping for the air that rushed out of my stomach.

"How about that Mr. Lordan? Did that hurt?"

He began kicking me, digging his boot into my back.

Santa casually lit up a cigarette.

Mark grabbed onto my face and jerked my head off of the ground. "You don't even remember me, you fucking asshole?" he asked, pushing his mouth next to my ear, his words and breath giving me shivers. "Every fucking day it was something. No homework. Showing up late. Talking in class. You always found some way to fuck me with, some way to make me look like an asshole." Without releasing my head, he gave me another quick kick. "Did it make you feel good, Mr. Lordan? Humiliating a fifteen year-old kid? *You* try doing your homework while your father's kicking the shit out of your mother in the next room. See if *you* can focus on the emancipation intoxication." He kicked me again. "If I went to class, you'd humiliate me, if I skipped class, my Dad'd kick the shit out of me. I couldn't win with you fucking people. I couldn't win!"

He dropped my head back down onto the concrete and resumed the kicking. They were hard, solid kicks, and my back felt as though it were about to burst. In the midst of the pain, I experienced a sudden epiphany of the obvious; Mark Perry was going to kill me. A runt who couldn't even tell me what century the Civil War occurred in was going to take my life away from me.

"Fucking cocksucking faggot! Think you're something special, huh? I'll give you something to suck on, you fucking piece of shit faggot cocksucker! We'll see who's better, you faggot . . ."

His words began sounding further and further away. Not that it really mattered, as he was apparently incapable of coming up with any fresh, imaginative insults and instead, simply repeated the same basic refrain over and over again with only the slightest variations.

I managed a tiny smile at the irony, realizing that such criticisms were identical to the ones I had subjected him to in class.

The smile disappeared when I suddenly remembered the tag. Mark Perry was not simply going to murder me; he was going to send me to Hell. Mark Perry, a moronic piece of white trash, who thought FDR resigned over Watergate, was going to be responsible for my spending an eternity in Hell. *Mark Perry*!

"Hey!" a voice yelled. "Knock that shit off right now!"

"What?" The kicking stopped.

"Just stop it."

"Fuck you."

"No. Fuck *you*, Perry."

"Mind your own goddamn business, Glass."

"Is that man James Lordan?"

"Maybe."

"*Maybe*? Okay, then *maybe* it is my business. This hump's my responsibility. Givens here was bringing him to me when you decided to have your fun. I'm in charge of transporting him to New York and they expect him to be in one piece when he gets there, so *maybe* step the fuck back unless you wanna go in his place."

I uncovered my face and looked up at the two men.

"What's so special about him?" Mark asked.

"How the hell would I know? Since when do the bosses tell us anything? Someone dropped dime on his ass and they want him for questioning. Something about Israel. Beyond that, I don't see, I don't know, and I don't fucking care."

"Yeah." Mark's tone relaxed. "Fucking bosses."

"Smells like teen spirit, am I right?"

"Ain't wrong. Questioning in New York, huh? Good. That place is an even bigger shit-hole than here." Crouching down next to me, Mark grabbed my face, digging his fingers into my flesh. "You think about me when they're scooping your eyeballs out with a spoon, Mr. Lordan. You remember what you did to me."

He dropped my face and the other soldier helped me up onto my feet. My back felt bloated and I couldn't stand upright.

The soldier cuffed my hands behind my back.

I yanked myself free and leaned towards Mark. "If . . . if . . . I ever . . . see . . ."

The soldier I pulled free from slapped me across the face and grabbed onto my arm. "Shut your mouth, slab. You pull free from me one more time and I'll beat you to death myself, understand?"

Mark snickered.

Santa Clause continued to look bored and took one last drag off his cigarette before dropping it down onto the ground and grinding it into the pavement with his boot.

"**Y**ou always make friends this fast, Lordan?" the soldier asked, while I slipped into the black jeans and sweater he had given me.

"Fuck you."

"That'd be a *yes*, huh? Y'know, I didn't expect head, but I did figure you'd be a little nicer to the guy who's helping you get your little honey out of this toilet."

"*You're* the guy Bezalel set me up with?"

"So to speak. Consider me your tour guide."

I looked him up and down while the beat-up Honda Accord warmed up. He appeared to be a little older than Mark, but not by more than a few years. His dark brown hair looked as if it had once been stylishly cut, but had since grown past it. Loose tufts of hair hung over his ears and brushed across the tops of his eyes. His beard was thick and untrimmed, his body stocky but not muscular, just puffy and flabby.

"*Guide*, huh?" I asked. "Do you hate white people, too?"

"What?"

"Forget it."

"Listen, I'm sorry about slapping you back there, but I kinda had to do it. Would've looked hinkey if I didn't, what with you mouthing off and everything."

"You ever touch me again, I'll fucking kill you." I was hunched over in the passenger seat, unable to sit upright after the beating.

"Uh-huh. Anyways, I'm George. George Glass."

"You couldn't come up with a better fake name?" I scoffed.

"It's not fake," he said with a smile.

"Seriously?"

"Seriously."

"Jesus Christ," I said, while shaking my head. "Well, *George*, you still dating Jan?"

"You're wasting your breath, Jim. I've heard 'em all. 'Sides, I always thought Peter was the cutest one out of the *Bunch*." He slipped the car into gear we pulled out of the lot.

"You gay?" I asked.

"What, you mean happy? Sometimes."

"I mean are you a fag."

"A British cigarette?"

"A fucking queer."

"Odd?"

"Homo!"

"Same as what?"

"Huh?"

"*Homo* means *same*. Too bad, we had a good riff going. But yeah, I'm a big fat boy-kisser."

He grinned and, despite myself, I grinned along with him, turning away so he couldn't see.

When I looked out the car window, what I saw made that grin disappear.

I grew up in South Boston, *The Best Place In The World*, as everyone who lived there called it. Southie was an Irish enclave, hateful to outsiders, but mythic and wonderful to the people who grew up there. It was a community that prided itself on loyalty, toughness, and a strong sense of kinship. We called it *Southie*, instead of *South Boston*, because it felt like its own world, as alienated from the rest of Boston as Boston was to Siberia. It was a closed off neighborhood and some of the older men and women used to boast that they hadn't set foot outside of its confines in more than thirty years. It was an extended family, where everyone knew everyone else's business, but with outsiders, silence was the golden rule. When I was ten years old, Seamus Collins stabbed Michael O'Connell to death outside of the Aces High Tavern with a *nigger-knife*, a broken bottle. He had stabbed him in front of more than thirty witnesses. Before the night was over, everyone in the neighborhood knew that Seamus was the killer, but when the police investigated, they couldn't find a single witness who would talk. Michael was a well-liked kid while Seamus was roundly considered to be a no-good shitbird, but that didn't matter, because Seamus was still a Southie-boy, and as such, was owed the loyalty of silence. There existed no morality outside of familial neighborhood obligation; stealing was fine, but only if it was done outside of the neighborhood, stealing in Southie being considered *niggerish*.

My family lived on Patterson Way, next to Old Colony Project, and we were, in many ways, the envy of the neighborhood. We owned our own home and, unlike most of the families in Southie, our home contained a father. What's more, that father actually worked. We hovered just above the surrounding poverty and as a result, I grew up experiencing the best of both worlds, slipping out from the mundane safety of a working-class home while still insulated from the true dangers of poverty.

During the day, I hung out with my friends from the Projects. We'd fight with the *white nigger* gangs from the D-Street and Old Harbor Projects across town. We'd sneak into McDonough's Gym and watch the boxers, occasionally catching glimpses of some local gangsters who were setting up fixed fights, and who'd occasionally slip us a few bucks for candy. None of my friends had fathers who lived with them, and the mothers never seemed to care what kind of hell we raised in their rent-controlled apartments. During the days, I experienced the freedom and adventure granted by poverty.

At night, I was able to slip away from the consequences. While my friends returned to their alcoholic mothers and cockroach-infested apartments, I returned to the security of a working-class home. Whereas most of the other mothers had to keep their apartments in a constant state of disaster in case Social Services made an unexpected visit and decided that the living quarters were too decent to require continued welfare, my mother possessed the freedom to maintain an immaculate, quiet home, a home without abusive boyfriends or centralized heating that couldn't be turned off, even in the middle of a scorching summer. At night, we'd turn off our lights, in the Projects, they burned continually, keeping the cockroaches from scurrying out of their hiding places in the dark.

Southie was my playground. I knew every corner and ally as well as I knew my own father's face. I knew that the owner of Jolly Donuts could always be counted on for some free crullers, whereas the prick who ran Mug and Muffin across the street would throw out all of his old donuts at closing time, preferring to let the rats devour them than give any away for free. I knew that the best place to see a street brawl was outside of the Rabbit Inn, where the Mullen Gang drank. I knew which bums leaning against the Long Wall next to Southie Savings should be avoided, and which ones would offer up a sip of their whisky for a quarter.

Southie was as much a part of me as my arm or my leg.

"Glass, where are we? What city is this?"

"It's Boston," he said. "South Boston. I thought you grew up here."

"I did."

The buildings had either been destroyed in the earthquakes or were fire-scorched and beaten down in the riots. The streets and sidewalks, littered with broken glass and rubble, teemed with rats and possums. In the fifteen minutes we had been driving, we had yet to pass another motorist and, apart from the occasional pack of soldiers, the only humans I saw were a group of five children who quickly darted into a ruined shell of a building when they noticed our approaching headlights.

It was their playground now.

"How long you been out of country, Jim?"

"Not that long. Couple of years."

"That's a lifetime nowadays," he said, swerving around the rubble and abandoned cars with confidence. "Okay. I'm gonna give you a crash course in America or, more properly, the new and improved North American Quadrant of the One World Community." He squeezed the car between a fallen telephone pole and the burnt-out husk of a truck, with barely an inch of space on either side.

I pressed my foot down on a phantom break, causing jolts of pain to shoot through my back. The speedometer read thirty-five. It didn't feel like thirty-five.

George glanced at me while he spoke, maintaining a casual eye on the road. "In a nutshell, we're Morrison's toilet. He disposes of his waste here."

"Land of the free."

"Yeah. Well, to be fair, I think he honestly intended on salvaging what was left of the country after the nukes totaled the West Coast and the South. But after the earthquakes ripped down whatever he had rebuilt, he just cut his losses. All the decent folks, the women and the children who had accepted the tag, they all got shipped over to Europe, where I guess he's still trying to build his little paradise. Most of the men got shipped over there too and inducted into his army.

"In return, we get the garbage. The *non-persons*. Christians, deserters, men with injuries that keep 'em out of active military service, psychos that even the army can't keep under control, we get 'em all. Christ-freaks get whacked right away. Anyone who's got the tag is given a choice: help run the camps or get whacked along with the Christ-freaks."

His foot slammed down on the breaks and the car screeched to a halt. I fell forward and smashed my face up against the dashboard.

"What the fuck?"

George motioned for me to look out the window.

Standing in front of the car was a little girl who couldn't be older than seven or eight. She stared numbly into our headlights, seemingly unable to move. She wore a filthy MIT sweatshirt and was naked from the waist down. Dangling from her hand was a clump of three dead rats, which she clutched by the tails. The only motion came from the animals as they twirled around in a circle, their thick, pink tails twisting around each other.

I tried sitting upright, but pain coursed through my back.

George rolled down his window and leaned his head out of the car. "Better get off the roads, kiddo. Take what you got and go on home. Don't push your luck."

She was gone in an instant, spinning on her bare feet and bolting out of sight.

George slipped the car back into gear.

She thought we were going to kill her and yet her face had expressed no emotion. No fear. No regret.

"You know," George said while glancing at me from the corner of his eye, "you don't have to duck down. We're safe. You can sit up."

She was only seven or eight. Maybe younger.

"I'm just saying, as long as you're in my custody, you don't have to worry about the OWC."

She didn't even have any underwear.

"You can sit up."

"No I can't fucking sit up," I growled. "If you had gotten me out of that fucking camp before Perry dug his fucking foot into my fucking back a hundred fucking times, then I might be able to sit up. But that didn't fucking happen, did it?"

"What are you pissing and moaning about?"

"You saw what he did to me!"

"Ah, just be grateful he didn't kneecap you."

"What?"

"Isn't that what you Irish do, shoot each other in the knees?"

"What, the IRA?"

"Yeah."

"What the fuck makes you think I'm a mick?"

"*Lordan.* That's Irish, isn't it?"

"It's Scottish, you fuck-head."

"Ah Ireland, Scotland, what's the difference? You're all too wussy to have kicked England out."

"Fuck you."

"That sounds Irish, to me. See, no difference."

"You know what the difference is? The Irish might kneecap you, but the Scottish'll hack off your head, piss down your throat, and then turn you into a fucking belt."

"Poetic people, you Scots." A possum ran in front of the car and I slammed into the door as George swerved the car to avoid it.

"Who the fuck let you drive, Glass?"

"You sure do swear a lot, Jim."

"Fuck you."

"If I was ten years old, I'd probably be pretty impressed. Hey, where do you know Perry from, anyway?"

"I was his teacher in high school," I mumbled as I pushed myself off of the door and made another unsuccessful attempt at straightening myself out.

"Really? Huh! Guess you didn't quite *reach* him, huh?"

"Fuck's that supposed to mean? You saying it's *my* fault he kicked the shit out of me?"

"Nah, I'm not saying anything. I'm just talking here. Just seems pretty clear you pissed him off when you knew him and it ended up biting you in the ass. Instant karma and whatnot, huh?"

"Fuck you, Glass."

"You really like that word, don't you?"

"I wouldn't have to use it so much if I wasn't constantly surrounded by fuck-heads." I tried to sit up again but it felt as though I were pulling against a thick, taut rope. "Fuck this," I growled, and placed my hands onto the dashboard. It hurt and it hurt and it hurt some more, but I finally managed to push myself upright. Once my back was straightened, I swung my hands around the back of the seat and held on tightly.

"You okay?" George asked.

"Fuck you."

George nodded his head and we drove in silence.

"Anyone ever tell you that you're kind of an asshole, Jim?"

I turned towards him angrily.

"Just wondering, is all," he said with a shrug.

Despite myself, my scowl disintegrated into laughter. My grip on the seat slipped and my back clenched up again, forcing my face back down towards my knees. The laughter made the pain worse, but I couldn't seem to stop.

After several minutes, I wiped away my tears and tried to regain my breath.

"Oh, shit," I mumbled. "No George, no one's told me that for a long time."

"Yeah, huh? I gotta tell you, Jim, I find that hard to believe."

"Yeah. Yeah, so did I. And listen, call me Jimmy, okay?"

The car rocked with a thud I felt in my stomach.

"What the hell was that?" I asked.

"A small dog or a big possum."

"Good. I hate possums."

"Yeah, well I'll tell ya, they're better than the dogs we got running around here. Wild packs. They're like wolves. Seriously though, Jimmy, are you okay? You look like hell."

"It's just my back. I'll be fine."

"Yeah, you look like you'd be used to it, anyway."

"Used to what?"

"A beating. Your face, your back, that gash on your hand; you're a mess. And that's not even mentioning that nasty looking scar on your chest. I saw it when you were changing."

I lifted up my sweater and touched a perfectly square scar. It had never healed properly and the flesh was thick and discolored.

"Souvenir from the OWC," I mumbled. "A lesson on race relations."

"What happened?"

"Nothing. Anyway, why does Morrison bother shipping people over here? Why not just kill them in Europe? It'd save him a lot of trouble."

"Well, this is just a guess, but I'd say he's trying to hide his dirty laundry."

"From who?"

"I dunno. Himself? Kind of hard to build a paradise when you've got a death camp sitting across the street from your kindergarten." The casual amiability in George's voice left and he began speaking in an artificially level tone while keeping his eyes locked onto the road and slowly increasing his speed. "There's about thirty death camps here. Most of the people you got shipped over with'll get bussed out to Western Mass and whacked. You went to school out in Amherst, right?"

"Yeah. UMass. I met my wife there. We . . ."

"It's a death camp now. Biggest in the state. New York handles more people than we do. Massachusetts has eleven camps, New York the rest."

"And you help with this?"

"No." He clipped off his words one by one. "The harbor is *not* a death camp. It is a point of arrival and departure. I sort out and guard the prisoners. That's all."

I stared at him for a moment, but decided not to intrude on his denial. "Where are we going?"

"My apartment," he said, his voice relaxing a little.

"What about Jude? Do you know where she is?"

"Yeah. She's hiding in the North End right now, but we can't get to her just yet because they're conducting sweeping raids there for the next few weeks. The whole section of town's closed off. No one in or out."

82

"Jesus Christ, George! What makes you think she'll still be there when the raids are over? The only reason that *you* know where she is is because *they* know where she is."

"Jimmy, what you've got to understand," he said, easing up on the gas and turning towards me with an understanding smile, "is that, at its core, the OWC, for all the evil shit it does, is nothing more than a bureaucracy. It's like the IRS; ultimately efficient, but slow and encumbered. *Yes*, they know where Jude is, *yes* she's on a roundup list, and *yes*, they will eventually get her. But she's not a Christ-freak or a violent criminal, and they're the priority right now. As long as she doesn't do something retarded like wander in front of a sweeping party, she'll be fine. Luckily for her, there's still too damn many of those dangerous Christians running loose."

George's head was moving ever so slightly back and forth, as though he were listening to a song that only he could hear.

I smiled and looked out my window.

"You're pretty happy for a guy who works in a death camp."

George hit the breaks and I went crashing into the dashboard.

"It's not a death camp," he yelled, turning towards me and pushing his finger into my face. "It's a point of arrival and departure. It is *not* a death camp!"

"Hey, George . . ."

"No! No, we're going to be together for the next few months, and I'd like it if we could be friends. But don't you ever judge me, Lordan. You gonna sit there and tell me that your hands are clean?"

"Hey asshole, I wasn't judging, I was joking. And yeah, I never worked in no fucking death camp."

"Yeah, I'm sure you're a real saint."

"Get your faggot finger out of my face before I snap it off."

"That right? Maybe that oughtta be second on your list of priorities, right after you manage to sit up straight without turning beet red and sweating like a pig. I do what I gotta to get by, and I'm not gonna listen to . . ." Suddenly, he dropped both his finger and his jaw. "You were joking?"

"Yeah, you fucking asshole, I was joking."

"Oh. Shit. I'm sorry, Jimmy. I thought . . . I thought . . ."

"Fuck you."

He began driving again and we remained silent.

"Sorry," he repeated.

"Suck a dick."

"Can I make it up to you with a present?" He leaned over and opened the glove compartment with one hand while steering with the other. "You'll like this. Roth told me about you." Keeping his eyes on the road, he blindly fished through the compartment. "C'mon," he muttered, "I know it's in here somewhere."

I licked my lips as George flipped the small, red and white box into my lap.

I picked it up, my hands shaking a little as I turned it over and over in my fingers. I dropped it into the palm of my hand and it rested there snugly. *Such a perfect size. Such a perfect weight.*

Tossing the box into my other hand, I turned it upside-down, gently placing my middle and index fingers across its bottom while my ring finger and thumb grasped it solidly by either side. I packed the cigarettes tightly, my smile growing wider and wider with each slap. The thin strip of gold cellophane peeled easily around the box, and I yanked up before completing the circle, ripping off the top third of the package's clear cellophane. There was the slight sound of cardboard separating from cardboard. I tugged out the silver foil.

If there exists in this world, a more beautiful sight than twenty identical cigarettes tightly pressed together in three perfect rows, you'll have a hard time convincing a desperate smoker of that fact. Twenty tan filters with white, rounded ends are beautiful perfection housed within the world's most efficient container. No wasted space. No false pretense.

I licked my thumb and slid a cigarette out, tossing it between my dry lips.

George handed me a pack of matches and grinned. "They didn't have any cigarettes in Israel, huh?"

"Not where I was. I don't think God approved."

"You sure you want to start up again?"

"I never stopped. Quitting's only quitting if it's your choice. I didn't decide to quit, I had it forced on me, ergo, I never quit."

"Well, you could quit now."

"The world's ending in what, three years? You want to tell me what kind of a fucking moron quits smoking three years before the world ends? Now shut up. You're killing the moment."

I dragged the match up against the flint and watched it explode into a flame. The faint smell of sulfur lifted into my nose. I raised the match up to the tip of the cigarette, inhaling the fire and hearing the delicate crackling of burnt tobacco. It smelled like freshly cut wood. The smoke drifted into my mouth, but I stopped short of inhaling, allowing it to linger, savoring its warmth as it wafted around my tongue and gently slid across my cheeks. When I released the smoke from my mouth, I admired its purity of color.

Sliding the cigarette back between my lips, I drew hard against the filter, this time gulping a mouthful of smoke down into my lungs. My head felt light and my stomach full. I pushed the smoke out through my nose and leaned back into my seat effortlessly.

"Jesus, I feel like a Peeping Tom," George said with a smile.

"Fuck you," I said and returned his smile, this time without trying to hide it.

Five

"Umm . . . well, I guess all of `em are mine," George said in an uncomfortable voice.

"*All* of the apartments? The whole building?" I asked, staring up at the six-story apartment complex.

"I only use one of the apartments myself," he said quickly.

"Jesus Christ, I couldn't even manage to get my own fucking *tent* in Israel."

"C'mon, man, cut it out. I already feel like enough of a Republican. It's not like I asked for a whole building. They just gave it to me. Besides, what with the Rapture, the migration to Europe, the nukes, the `quakes, and the rest of the crap that's happened over the last few years, well, there isn't really much of a housing shortage. I mean, in the last three years, the county's population's dropped from something like three hundred million people to ten or twenty. It's not like I . . . ah, screw it. Look, I'm on the top floor, in 6B. Just pick any apartment you want and let me know which one you're staying in so I don't have to pound on seventeen doors to find you, okay?"

"Yeah. Okay."

"Okay."

"Do any of them have a bed?"

George scratched the back of his head and winced. "They all have beds, Jimmy. Beds, books, TV's, soap, shampoo, jewelry, photo albums, booze, drugs, magazines, clothes, furniture; pretty much any damn thing you want is probably in at least one of the apartments. Two hundred fifty million people are gone and they all left their shit behind."

"Jesus, George," I said, following him up the stairs and into the building, "if there's so much shit lying around, why the hell is an eight year-old girl eating dead rats?"

"I . . ." George's shoulders slumped forward. "Look, I don't like it anymore than you do, but there isn't a damn thing I can do about it. It's not going to do that kid any good if *I* stop eating. So yeah, I've got enough food for five years and enough fresh water to drown a whale. Hell, I've even got a refrigerator full of cigarettes because Roth mentioned that you might want 'em. But the only reason I've got all of that crap is because I'm tagged. You were here for the earthquakes?"

"Only the first wave. After that I got out. Got to Israel."

"Yeah, well, like I said, right after the 'quakes ripped most of the city down, Morrison did a complete turnaround with his plans for America. First thing he did was burn down the suburbs. He herded everyone he could find into the cities and then closed 'em up tighter than a dolphin's ass. South Boston, Somerville, and a few other places that weren't completely destroyed in the earthquakes had their water and electricity repaired and were reserved for OWC personal. The rest of the city, Kenmore Square, the North End, Jamaica Plain, all of it, it's all rubble, a garbage dump. That's where the Christ-freaks hide. No food, no water, no electricity, and no heat. If you've got the tag you can go to a Distribution Office and get anything you want. Gas, food, cigarettes, water, anything perishable gets shipped in from Europe. There's other things too. Buildings that cater to special interests. There's still some bars run by the OWC. There's also drug houses and buildings with . . . women."

"Women?"

"Yeah."

"You mean . . .?"

"Yeah."

"Jesus."

"Yeah."

"I don't . . . look, if you've got so much food, why don't you give some of it to those people out there? Why don't you help them?"

"I'm not Robin Hood!" he said angrily. "I'm just trying to survive. Most of the guys I work with on the docks are sadistic bastards. And they might pass the day stoned or drunk, but they still notice things. A flash of compassion, a moment's hesitation when you push a little boy onto a bus that's bringing him to a death camp. They notice that shit and they're not above reporting it. I get caught handing out food to Christ-freaks and I'm dead, you understand?"

"Yeah I understand. I understand that Jude's out there living like a fucking animal."

"Jimmy, I . . . we can't get her now. I'm sorry, but there's no way. One month. I can't do any better than that. Look, why don't you just pick a room and get some sleep. We'll talk later."

I choose an apartment on the third floor and stayed there for three weeks. George occasionally visited, laughing at the red hair that began sprouting out of my bald head and telling me I looked like I was gaining some weight. Mostly though, I spent the days alone, staring out the window and smoking cigarettes that tasted slightly moldy. George told me that if I wanted to, it would be safe to leave the apartment and visit the surrounding area. I declined.

Strolling the area Southie had decomposed into would have been like gazing down into Scotty's coffin, staring at the back of my father's head after it had been torn open by a bullet, or talking to Stan while he was down on his knees, his head crushed by God. I'd already spent what felt like half a lifetime seeing the hollowed-out shells of the people I loved, and the last thing I wanted to do was tromp around the festering corpse of the neighborhood that had helped raise me.

Unfortunately, the surrounding decay wouldn't be ignored that easily. During the night, the sounds of rat and possum claws scratching their way through the rubble scurried into my ears, never quite drowned out by the louder howls of wild dogs chasing after God-knows-who. The closed windows kept out neither the sounds nor the smell of death, the putrid aroma of human waste and decomposition passing through them as easily as a ghost, refusing to be overpowered or ignored no matter how many cigarettes I smoked.

I began feeling claustrophobic, as if I had closed myself up in an inverted coffin where I was alive and everything outside was dead. That death pushed softly against my box, always increasing its morbid pressure, constantly threatening to shatter the fragile separation between my world and its own.

After three weeks of it, I left the apartment and went to see George. He was slouching down in a leather recliner, absent-mindedly bouncing a tennis ball off the wall.

"Hey," he said when I entered his apartment, looking both surprised and happy to see me, "what are you doing here?"

"I want to . . . You said that I could walk around the city and I'd be safe, right?"

"Yeah."

"Does that mean that I could go anywhere?"

"Well, you can't get into secured areas, but other than that, sure."

"Explain it." I lit a cigarette. "Why wouldn't I get arrested?"

"Because you're not red-tagged. Okay, let's say that you leave the apartment and, while you're walking around, you get stopped by a patrol. If you didn't have a tag, they'd automatically arrest you. You do have a tag, so they'd scan it. There's two kinds of scanners. One is attached to a computer console, and when they scan you with that, they can bring up your entire file and see your status. But those expensive and coveted. Every muckity-muck in the OWC cooks up a story about why its imperative that they own and operate one, so the underage losers who patrol Southie and do the rest of the shit work don't have access to 'em. Random patrols and most other places just use the Stoplight Scanner. If the red light flashes, they arrest you, a green light and you're all set. The red light'll flash if the System's red-tagged your file."

"But my file lists me as a criminal, so wouldn't I be red-tagged?"

"No," he said, dropping the ball on the floor and sitting up. "While you were on the ship, Roth called in an anonymous report to the OWC, saying that you had special information about the Israeli camp. OWC intelligence is stationed in New York, so he knew they'd want to transport you there for interrogation. I volunteered to bring you. That's how we got you out of custody so easily. When you were scanned out with me, your status was updated. As far as the System's concerned, you're still in custody, headed to New York for interrogation, we're still *en route*."

"Yeah, but that was three weeks ago," I said, while looking around the apartment for an ashtray. I couldn't find one and, when the ash fell onto the floor, George didn't seem to mind. "New York's only a few hours drive."

"Right. We've just slipped through the bureaucracy's cracks. The System's been clogged for months because Morrison's sending so many people to America. The System assumes that if you'd escaped, I'd have reported it, so until then, it's patiently awaiting our arrival. Red-tagged just means you're not accounted for in the System. We are. Sooner or later, someone'll notice that we never showed up and then both our files'll be red-tagged. But that'll take a couple of months, and by then, you, me, and Gaunt'll be in Israel, and it won't matter. Understand?"

"I guess."

"Why are you asking? You want to go outside?"

"No, I . . . You said the OWC still runs some bars, right?"

"Sure. Best way to maintain a death machine is to keep the executioners drugged or drunk. Why, you want to go to one?"

"Could I get in?"

"Sure."

"Would you . . . would you take me? I need to get drunk."

"I can take you, but you know, there's plenty of booze right here in the building if that's all you want."

"Yeah, I know. But I . . . I need to be around people. People who are alive. And I have to be drunk to do that." Another heap of ash fell down onto the floor.

"The Rat."

"What?"

"The Rat," I repeated, staring at the boarded up building. "The Rathskeler. When I was a kid, me and my friends used to sneak in here. I saw REM here before they got big. Someone threw a bottle at Michael Stipe's head and called him a *pissy little faggot*."

"Cute."

"It was a big moment in my life."

The building was guarded by a legless soldier who scanned our tags and allowed us inside when the green light flashed. As I pushed open the door, I was enveloped in a thick cloud of smoke. The walls were dark red, absorbing and reflecting the light from the purple lamps, making it appear as if a simmering fire was burning behind the walls, threatening to push through. The glow reflected onto the men, dressing their faces in a scarlet hue. John Lee Hooker blasted out of the speakers, drowning out most of the conversation, although every once in a while, a sharp burst of laughter would rise above the music. Some of the men were engaged in conversation, but most sat silently, staring off at nothing with a faraway look, absently swaying their bodies in synch with the music.

George pushed his way to the bar while I grabbed a table. Returning with drinks, he sat down across from me and we quietly drank. The conversation was minimal; each of us lost in his own thoughts. We took turns going to the bar for drinks, but it felt like a hollow custom; the drinks were free and the tradition of buying rounds required currency to retain its significance.

Slowly, after an hour or so, the booze began to take effect and our tongues loosened.

"I don't suppose there's any alcohol in Israel," George asked, staring at the gin in his glass.

"Nope," I said, lighting a cigarette and leaning back. "No devil rum allowed in paradise."

"Hardly seems like it can be paradise then, does it?"

"That was pretty much my experience."

"Yeah, I figured as much." He swung his glass in a circle, silently staring down at the swirling ice. "Still, it's worth it to get this damn tag off."

"Why'd you take the fucking thing in the first place?" I asked, sipping on a kamikaze and trying to bury a recollection of Sarah.

George stared down into the black line on his hand, as if the answer to my question lay within it.

I blew smoke into his face and he coughed, shook his head, and finished his drink.

"I'm gay," he said with a shrug. "Even in kindergarten I liked the boys. Didn't know what it meant, but I knew I liked 'em. It felt good. Pure, y'know? That didn't last long. By the second or third grade, kids were already calling each other *faggots*, and I knew that what I felt was wrong, that I had to hide it. You got any idea what that's like, Jimmy? Spending your entire life hiding who you are?"

"Yeah. I got an idea of what that's like."

"I doubt it. I grew up in Brooklyn. Everyone was always talking about getting laid, always talking about pussy. I tried to imitate 'em, tried to sound as exited as they were, as real as they were. I got pretty good at it, but never had any real friends. I mean, I hung out with people and stuff, but I could never let myself get too close. I was always afraid that if I did, I'd be tempted to do something stupid."

"What, like kiss them?"

"Like tell 'em the truth about me."

"Ah, it couldn't have been that bad," I said, placing the tip of my cigarette onto the ashtray and turning it around, peeling off the excess soot. "I mean, I'm not going to say that I knew what it was like for you, but things were getting better with shit like that. Especially in places like New York. That was a real liberal city."

"*Liberal?*" He dropped his empty glass down onto the table. "Yeah, it was real liberal. If you had money. Poor and gay? You were still a piece of shit faggot. Rich homos whose parents could afford to send 'em to Yale would get themselves a big round of applause when they climbed up onto a lunchroom table and screamed about how *fabulously* gay they were. Then they could move to

Manhattan and get work as the token fag at a company that wanted to pat itself on the back for being so progressive."

He glanced over his shoulder to see if anyone had been listening. When he spoke again, it was in a quieter voice. "That's great for them, but I lived over the bridge, and that ain't the same as living over the rainbow. My parents were blue collar. My Dad drove a dump truck, my mother ran a register in a supermarket. You try climbing on top of a table in *my* neighborhood and screaming about how fabulously queer you are. See how much applause *you* get. Or better yet, get caught in the high school bathroom with your hands down another kid's pants. I didn't get any applause; I got a lead pipe upside the head."

He eyed his empty drink and I went to the bar and got us two more, even though mine was still half full.

"So what happened?" I asked as I sat down.

"Ah," George said while making a dismissive gesture with his hand, "I spent a few weeks in the hospital. Fractured skull and two broken ribs. Messed up my knee pretty bad, too. It never really healed, which is why I'm still here instead of in Europe waiting to get whacked by the Arabs and Chinese and whoever else Morrison's gonna try and wipe out next. Anyway, when I got out of the hospital, I just disappeared. Never went back to school, never went home. Dad never visited me in the hospital, so I knew he must have heard why I got the beating. Knew that if I tried going home, he'd have given me a worse one. So I'm fifteen years old and I'm on the street with nothing. All 'cause I like boys instead of girls. That's how fuckin' *liberal* New York was, okay?" He nodded his head angrily and lifted his glass in the air. "Cheers."

"Top o' the morning."

"Thought you said you weren't Irish."

"Don't know any Scottish salutations. So that all kind of sucked, huh?"

"Ah, we all got shit to deal with. I ended up working down at the piers, unloading the ships. It was like high school all over again. Everything was *pussy, pussy, pussy*. During the day I'd talk the same shit as everyone else, then at night I'd head out to the bars and end up getting laid by some stranger in a bathroom. Never had a . . . I don't know, a boyfriend or anything." He stared down at the table with a pained expression. "I hated them so much," he mumbled.

"Who?"

"The faggots. The faggots I slept with. I fuckin' hated 'em. Hated myself, too. Every time I walked out of one of those bars, I expected to get a pipe upside the head. Worst part was, I *wanted* to get a pipe upside the head, felt like I deserved it. I don't know."

"I don't . . . George, what does this have to do with getting tagged?"

"I was made to feel like a freak, like I was less than human. And I believed it. I *agreed* with 'em. I had never been in love. Never knew what that felt like. Figured I never would. And then all those people disappear, and the Celestine Prophets or space-men, or whatever the hell they were say that they took 'em. The nukes, the riots, I mean, hell, you remember what it was like, Jimmy. The whole world went insane.

"And then Morrison takes over and stops it all. You remember watching him on TV that first night?"

"Not really. I had other stuff going on at the time."

"Yeah, well I remember. He told us we had to stop hating each other. Said we had to stop treating each other like second-class citizens because of the color of our skin or our different religions or who we liked to sleep with. He asked for our help. And he named us. None of that *lifestyle choice* crap. He says the word, says he wants *homosexuals* to be an active, prominent member of his community. You remember Clinton? Son of a bitch wanted our votes but still treated us like we were garbage. Can't adopt, can't vote, can't serve in the military unless we hide what we are. Morrison spoke to us with respect."

He finished off his drink and took a sip from mine. "Those first few months were weird. It was like everything before had been a game. Morrison yells, *ollie ollie oxen free*, and the game's over, everybody comes outta their closet and stops hating. Not just the queers, but the blacks, the Jews, everyone; it was like all the hatred had been a game and we just stopped playing. It felt real. For the first time in twenty years, I remembered what it felt like to not be ashamed of what I was. To not be sickened by myself. I remembered what it felt like in kindergarten.

"So I joined up. Got myself tagged and became a proud citizen of the One World Community."

"I've got to take a piss." I drained what was left of my drink and stood up.

When I returned, George was staring down at his empty glass. I raised my drink and guzzled what was left.

"So if you love Morrison so much, why aren't you over in Europe sucking him off? Why help me? Why get rid of the tag?"

"They thought I was stupid," George laughed. "I was a high school dropout who worked on a loading dock, so they just naturally assumed that I was an idiot. They put me to work burning books. I was one of the guys who went around to libraries and bookstores with a list of titles to confiscate. Mostly Bibles and books on Christianity. They assumed I wouldn't read 'em, too stupid, right? Yeah, well I read 'em. Didn't understand a lot of it at first, but bit by bit, I saw. Books by Texe Marrs, Hal Lindsey, Grant Jeffery, all that stuff talking about the Apocalypse."

"I read some of those guys in college. Most if it was shit."

"Yeah, it was kind of tough to stomach a lot of it. But once I got through the self-righteous crap, it was a revelation. They were talking about exactly what had been happening, but they'd been written ten, twenty years ago. All of a sudden, I knew what was really going on. Can you imagine what that was like? Realizing that you've sold your soul? That you've damned yourself to Hell?"

"Yeah," I said while raising my right hand, "I can imagine."

"No you can't. Why don't you stop telling me you know shit that you don't?"

"Well why don't you stop asking me rhetorical questions?"

"Look, you knew what you were getting yourself into, Jimmy. I was *conned* out of my soul. I got fucked!"

"Everybody gets fucked, George," I said while lighting another cigarette. "Get used to it."

"Don't hand me that crap. I had no idea what I was getting into. You did. If you got fucked, you fucked yourself."

"Is that right?" I nodded angrily. "Fine. Tell me this, though, you read the Bible, right?"

"Cover to cover."

"You notice the part where it says a man fucking another man is an abomination? Where it says gays should be put to death? Just getting the tag off isn't enough to get you through the Pearly Gates, Glass. You're going to have to put yourself under God. You telling me that you can do that, knowing what He thinks of your kind?"

"*My kind?* And what kind is that? A sinner? I didn't just read part of the Bible, Jimmy, I read the whole thing. I might be a sinner, but so are you. So is everybody. Fucking another man's a sin, but no more so than anything else. You read the part where it says if a kid doesn't respect his parents he's gotta be put to death? Were you the perfect son?"

"Fuck you." I ground my cigarette into the mound that was overflowing out of the ashtray. "You just got through telling me that being gay is who you are, not something you do. There's a difference. You're really telling me that you're okay with a God who tells you that who you are is evil?"

"First off, it's not *a* God, it's *God*. It's not like there's a few hundred of 'em and we get to choose which suits us best. If that was the case, sure, I'd take the one who let me do whatever I wanted to. Unfortunately, that's not an option. Second, my understanding is that we're *all* evil. Original sin doesn't just apply to fags. Besides, I never said that being gay is who I am. It feels that way sometimes because that's how the rest of the world sees me, but it's not the way I see myself. A straight guy isn't defined by the fact that he has sex with women; his personality, his job, his beliefs, all of it defines him. Sex is just a piece of it. Same with me."

"Yeah, but God gave you that part, you said you've felt it since kindergarten."

"So?"

"So, how can you accept a God who creates you in a certain way and then judges you for it?"

"It's just another temptation, no different than anybody else's. Didn't you ever wanna sleep with a woman without marrying her? Weren't you ever tempted to steal? To lie? Did you ever get angry or jealous? We're all born with different temptations."

"So you think being gay is evil? You're okay with that?"

"Look, I can understand why sleeping with another man's wife is wrong, but I can't understand why *thinking* about doing that is wrong. I remember that feeling when I was in kindergarten, that *thing* I felt towards a boy, I don't understand how that can be evil. But that's me, that's my limitation. If God says it's wrong, there must be a reason, I'm just too small too understand it."

"Sounds to me like you pussed out." I gulped down the last of my drink. My head no longer felt connected to my neck, more like it was floating on top of it. "You became a skirt who can't think your own thoughts. A fucking yes-man."

"I still have my own opinions. I just try and accept that they're not as valid as God's. I mean, isn't that what handing yourself over to God's all about? What faith's about?"

"I wouldn't know, Glass, I never handed myself over to someone. I never fagged-out."

"Bullshit," George said with a scoff. "Everyone hands their lives over to someone. A wife, a husband, a parent, a president: we all hand it over to someone."

"Wanting someone to run a country and surrendering your life to someone is completely different."

"The impulse is the same. Deep down, we know we can't make things right, not by ourselves, so we keep looking for someone to *make* it right for us."

"Whatever. I need another drink." When I stood up my legs buckled underneath me, but I persevered.

"See, the thing is," George continued when I returned with the drinks, "we keep screwing up. We need someone to make things right for us. The problem is we keep handing control over to human beings, who are inevitably gonna screw things up as badly as we would."

"If that's true, then how come most of humanity seems to be running away from God rather than towards Him? If we're all so needy and desperate to surrender ourselves to someone, why aren't we bowing down to God rather than spitting on Him?"

"Pride and delusion. We wanna be saved, but at the same time, we wanna be able to fool ourselves into thinking that we're still in control, that we never *really* needed the saving. That's what makes a successful politician. You ever notice how politicians were always spouting off about smaller government and keeping the state outta our faces and then, two seconds later, would be telling us that the government needs to restore family values and make all the rest of our problems disappear? How can you do both? How can they stay out of our lives and still fix them?"

George stared at me silently.

I took a swig of my drink.

"I ever tell you how much I hate rhetorical questions?"

"You mean like the one you just asked me?"

"What," I asked with a slur, "is your point?"

"Politicians were successful when they quietly let us know that they were gonna take complete control and make everything all right while, at the same time, allowing us to believe that that's not what we were asking them to do. That's exactly what Morrison did. He let us know he was gonna save us, but told us that we were gonna do it ourselves."

"So?"

"So, God doesn't do that. He tells us that we *do* need His help, that we *can't* do it on our own. People don't like hearing that, so they reject Him. He's a lousy politician because He won't lie to us and tell us what we want to hear."

"Yeah, well, that's great, assuming God doesn't suck."

"Well, that's faith, right?"

"*Faith?* Just another fucking word for stupidity."

"What, you think you don't have faith?"

"I don't need it."

"Jimmy, every day, every one of us gets by on faith. The signal says *walk* and, like a bunch of sheep, we all walk into the path of traffic. We don't know that the cab'll stop, that he'll obey the traffic laws. We have faith that he will. You'll have faith in someone you don't even know, someone driving a ten ton hunk of steel towards you at forty miles-an-hour, someone who could be drunk or crazy, and you'll put your life on the line 'cause you have faith in him. *A cabbie!* You'll put your faith in a pilot, the guys who builds your house, a doctor, almost anybody, and you think that makes more sense than putting your faith in God?"

I finished my drink in one gulp, drooling a bit of it out of the side of my mouth. "If you're so smart, how come you got conned out of your soul?" I asked, and reached across the table, grabbing George's untouched drink.

"Ain't that a black line on your hand too, Jimmy? Who conned you?" His words expanded and contracted, slipping into and out of one another.

"*I* did."

"Rather be conned by someone else than be stupid enough to con myself."

"Fuck you! That's not what I meant and you know it! I meant . . . I meant that I, that no one conned me. I know exactly what I'm doing and why, and . . . and . . . Hey Glass!" A lisp that I thought I had conquered in grade school reappeared. "When the fuck are we getting Jude?" The words sounded round, lacking clarity or edge. My tongue felt bloated. I lit a cigarette and it slipped out from between my lips, falling into a small puddle of booze on the table. The fiery tip extinguished with a weak sizzle.

"Just one more week, Jimmy. When the sweeps are over." He stared down into his palm for a moment. When he spoke again, his voice was quiet, tentative. "You haven't seen this woman in more than ten years, man. Why are you doing this?"

I felt a sudden collapse into depression, uncertain if it was caused by the thought of Jude, the morose look on George's face, or just the booze.

"I don't know, George. I . . . You know, my father was, he was a lot of things. Not all of them good. No. But they, he . . . I always knew that he'd be there for me if I was fucked. He wasn't the kind of guy who'd give me a hug or anything, but if I said I killed some guy, he'd do everything he could to keep me out of jail, he'd stand up for me. He'd have died for me. I mean, I know he would have. And I . . . how do you turn your back on that? How do you say it's all okay just because it's God? How can you turn your back on that and still claim to be a good person? If you don't stand by the man who raised you, if you don't stand by your family, what kind of man are you? How can . . .? I . . . I need to find Jude. I need to . . ." I slumped over the table. The Paul Butterfield

Blues Band was playing on the stereo. I slowly nodded my head in synch with the music, allowing it to bear some of the weight that was pushing down on me.

"Yeah," George said, and nodded his head.

"Goddamn right, *yeah.*" I stared into the ashtray for a while and then suddenly raised my head off the table and pushed my finger towards George. "Hey, Glass, if you want that tag off so bad, let's go back home and get a knife. *I'll* cut the fucking thing outta you."

"Thanks," George laughed, "but I'm not looking to die."

"A little cut won't kill you, you homo."

"It will when . . ." George stopped what he was saying and stared at me thoughtfully for a moment. "They didn't tell you."

"Tell me what?"

"Jesus Christ, they didn't tell you."

"Tell me *what?*"

"Jimmy, all of the tags, they all contain a small capsule of poison in them. It's not a lot but if any non-organic object, like say a knife or a scalpel, comes into contact with the microchip, the poison is expelled into the bloodstream, killing you the instant it reaches the heart. You can't remove it without a tagger. Roth didn't tell you?"

"Fucking cocksucker!"

"Well, I guess now we know who conned you, huh? Was that your backup plan in case things ended up going sour? Just dig it out before you die?"

"Fucking kike! Where the fuck does he get off not telling me something like that? Not right to play games with someone's life. Fucking kike." I stared down at the table, my neck feeling like a rubber band. When I finally bounced my head back up, I saw George staring at me, studying my face. "What the fuck are you looking at?"

"Nothing. Just guessing that you might not be in a position to judge someone for using other people."

"Fuck's that supposed to mean?" I asked, bouncing my head up and down, finding it hard to stop the motion once I had started. *Up and down, up and down . . . It was kind of fun.*

"Y'know, I can't figure out if you're a happy drunk or an angry one."

"I'm happy with my anger, how's that?"

"Sounds about right."

"Hey George," I said in a whisper, halting the nodding and leaning across the table. "When do we get Jude? What's the plan?"

"There's not much of a plan, Jimmy. Don't worry about it. It's gonna be a milk run."

"Sure you're not being overconfidence?"

"I know exactly what I'm doing here, Jimmy," he said, laughing good-naturedly at my mispronunciation. "Don't worry, in one month, we'll be back in paradise with souls as clean as . . . as . . . hell, I don't know, as clean as something real clean, okay? I'm in complete control."

I smiled and thought about Israel, wondering if it would be different if Jude was there with me, if George was there with me. I wondered if it would be different if I had a friend.

"One more drink."

"Let's just head home, Jimmy."

"One more, then home." I rose up too quickly and a feeling of hot emptiness rushed into my head. I grabbed the back of my chair and stared straight ahead, locking my eyes onto the bar in an attempt to steady myself. My vision was blurry and it was difficult to see clearly through the red lights and the smoke, but there was something familiar about a figure at the bar. The way he slumped down into his barstool and fiddled uncomfortably with his drink reminded me of someone. When I suddenly recognized who it was, I turned towards George with an enormous grin.

"You okay?" he asked.

"Look at my face, George. You will never see a happier man. Not in this life and not in the next one. I'll be right back."

I waltzed across the bar, gracefully pushed forward by what felt like the breath of God. I picked up a bottle from one of the passing tables and then pressed my chest into the back of the man sitting at the bar. Licking my lips, I leaned my head next to his ear and quietly whispered into his ear. "Where's your homework, Mark?"

Mark Perry turned around in his barstool and stared at me.

In a perfectly smooth arc, I lifted the bottle from my side and swung it into his face. He jolted backwards and I dropped the bottle's remains onto the floor before grabbing his shoulders and jamming his runt body against the bar. I climbed up onto his lap, straddling his body and pinning his arms underneath my legs while grabbing onto his throat. I squeezed tightly for a moment and then loosened the pressure as I began punching him in the face.

His nose had just collapsed underneath my knuckles when George grabbed the back of my shirt and yanked me off of Mark, who stumbled off the bar stool, bent over, and spit out blood and teeth.

I swung my foot and kicked Mark in the face, sending him crashing into the bar and down onto the floor.

The crowd remained silent and still for a few moments before turning away and returning to their drinks.

Mark rolled over and sat up, leaning his back against the bottom of the bar. His nose was spread across the left side of his face while a thin stream of blood spurted out towards the right. His cheek and forehead were torn open from the bottle and he stared up at me through puffy, wet eyes.

"Mr. Lordan?" he asked meekly.

Before I could answer, George spun me around.

"What the hell are you doing, Jimmy?"

"God provides," I said with a smile. "Almost got me willing to give faith a shot."

Mark wiped the blood and tears from his eyes and stared up at George.

"Glass," Mark whined in a frightened voice. "Glass help me, he . . . what are you doing with . . .? I don't . . ."

George turned away from Mark and back towards me.

"Mark Perry?" he asked in an astonished voice.

I nodded my head, proud of the fact that I had beaten Mark so badly that George had to confirm that the bloody mess in front of him was indeed Mark.

George clenched his jaw and darted his eyes back and forth, between Mark and myself. He began breathing heavily and jerking his head in all directions, as though he was looking for something.

"You stupid son of a bitch, Lordan," he said, tightening his grip on my shoulders and staring at me with rage.

I stepped backwards and glanced around, suddenly feeling ashamed, although of what I wasn't sure. The bar felt unbearably hot. The red light began hurting my eyes, but even when I closed them, the scarlet glare was still visible. Smoke seeped between my eyelids and burned my pupils.

"Goddamn you, Jimmy," George said in a quiet voice. "Goddamn you."

I opened my eyes.

George pulled a gun out from underneath his jacket.

I tried to step forward but froze, afraid to move.

George raised the gun towards Mark, whose eyes opened wide with fear and confusion.

It was so easy to see the white in Mark's eyes with the dark red surrounding them.

"Why?" Mark asked softly.

My body jolted at the sound of the gunshot.

The front of Mark's face imploded as the back exploded.

The bar became a splattered painting of red and gray. Small, triangular flecks of white skull speckled the painting, their hard angular presence offsetting the swirls of blood and brain matter.

George grabbed my limp body and pushed me out of the bar and through the indecisive crowd.

When I gulped down a mouthful of fresh air, my head cleared and I slapped George's hands off of me. He stepped forward and grabbed my shirt, violently yanking me towards him.

"You stupid son of bitch! You fucking asshole! Do you know what you've done?"

"Get the fuck off me, Glass!" I tried to break away but he held me too tightly.

His face became red with fury, his jaw quivering with rage. Making a noise filled with disgust, he pushed me away from him.

"I don't believe you, I don't fucking believe you," he muttered.

"Hey," I yelled, "I'm not the asshole who went nuts in there! You are! Why did you shoot him? I was just getting even for what he did to me, I wasn't going to kill him. Why the fuck did you shoot him?"

"He saw me, you idiot!" He continued pacing back and forth for several moments, eventually stopping and taking a deep breath. When he began speaking again, his voice was a thin cover of calm failing to hide the anger and fear underneath it. "He saw me with you, Jimmy. He would have reported it. He knew that we were supposed to be in New York. He saw you in a bar with me. He would've gotten both of us red-tagged by tomorrow. If we're red-tagged, we can't get Gaunt. If we're red-tagged, we can't get out of the country." He slapped his hands against his face and abandoned his thin calm. "Goddamnit, you're gonna be red-tagged no matter what! They'll go through the records of everyone who was scanned into the bar tonight and see that you're supposed to be in New York." He began pacing back and forth again, slapping the butt of his gun up against his forehead. "This is bad, this is so fucking bad. I . . . Oh Jesus, I just shot a man. I just . . . I killed . . . FUCK!"

He kicked a bottle laying in front of him and sent it skidding across the pavement, shattering into pieces.

The sliding, tumbling glass sounded beautiful.

"Fuck it," he said. "Let's go, we're getting Gaunt now. Right now. It won't take 'em more than a couple of days to put my name with yours and I'll be red-tagged too. We gotta get Gaunt before this whole thing turns to total shit." He stopped pacing and stared at me. "I hope it was worth it, Jimmy," he said in a cold voice.

I followed limply as George stomped towards the car, waiting patiently while he fumbled with his keys.

"Fuck!" I shouted, as something sharp jabbed into my ankle.

"What now?" George asked with supreme annoyance.

"I don't know." My leg felt numb and, when I shook it, a huge bug that looked a like a giant black grasshopper scurried out of my pants leg. "Nothing. Let's just go. It's just a bug. A grasshopper or something. It bit me. Forget it, let's go."

"A grasshopper?" George's keys dropped down onto the ground, making a pretty sounding jingle. "Tell me you're kidding."

"I'm fine." My head began spinning and my stomach felt like it was about to burst open. "It's just the booze."

"Oh my god. A locust? A FUCKING LOCUST? HOLY CHRIST, NOT NOW! NOT NOW! I DON'T FUCKING BELIEVE THIS! NOT NOW!" He began pounding his fists on the roof of the car. "NO! NO! WE'RE DEAD! WE'RE ALL DEAD! Holy Christ, I'm going to Hell. This can't be happening."

My stomach surged and contracted. It felt as though a horde of maggots was swarming through my intestines, taking millions of tiny bites every second. My leg swelled-up and pushed against the confines of my pants and shoe.

"I'm fine, George. Really. This'll still be a milk run." With that reassurance uttered, I felt free to allow my legs to die underneath me. I fell forward and smashed my face onto the hood of the car. Rolling off the steel, I fell onto the ground, cracking the back of my head up against the pavement and causing a cool stream of blood to flow into my eyes. I heard George crying and, behind that noise, approaching sirens. Through the blood, I watched a black mass of enormous bugs skittering towards my body.

Why was this happening to me?

My mouth and face became engulfed in a swarm of insects.

What had I done to deserve this?

II

Original Sins

Six

On New Year's Day, the world woke up with a hangover. Or at least I did. Our bed was cold and I began moving my arm towards Sarah, slowly reaching out for her warmth. I pushed forward gradually, each millimeter of extension accompanied by the expectation of discovering Sarah's warm, reassuring presence.

Nothing.

Nothing.

Nothing.

Still half asleep, I smiled. *Where the hell was she? Had she scurried all the way over to the edge of the bed? Was she watching me creep towards her, playfully staying out of reach?* Over the years, we had fallen into the habit of sleeping in each other's arms, or at most, a few inches apart. January in Michigan was not the time of year to begin altering that tradition. I emerged from sleep a bit more and my smile grew at the thought of locating Sarah, wrapping my arms around her stomach, and yanking her towards me. She'd make a grumpy noise and I'd say, *Your husband demands warmth, perform your wifely duties and warm me with your butt.* Her back would press tightly up against my chest, my chin resting perfectly on top of her head, like the Mad Hatter at the tea party.

My arm continued pushing forward, playfully.

Nothing.

Nothing.

Nothing.

We had forgotten to turn up the heat before we went to bed. Too drunk to remember. Too drunk to have sex, too. It was the first time since we had gotten married that we didn't have sex on New Year's Eve. We were thirty-five years old and I suddenly wondered if drunken sex was for the young. I had never thought of myself as old before, but the New Year seemed to have erected a gap, a fence separating me from youth.

My hand continued its forward creep, now lecherously.

Nothing.

Nothing.

Nothing.

Jesus Christ, how far away was she?

I felt oddly pleased at her distance, realizing that, had I woken with Sarah already in my arms, I'd have taken her warmth for granted. Having experienced that chill, the warmth would feel all the better.

My hand reached the end of the bed.

Sarah was gone.

Gone, I assumed, simply from bed.

I frowned and looked at the alarm clock, which read 12:36 PM. The bathroom door was open and the light was off.

"Fuck it," I mumbled, and flipped over onto my stomach. I closed my eyes, but was unable to fall back asleep. It was too cold.

"Hussy," I yelled, kicking off the sheets and stumbling out of bed. "You abandoned me to the cold! Vixen!"

There was no response and I left the bedroom and saw that the kitchen was also empty.

"Sarah!"

I rolled my eyes at my own stupidity. Our apartment consisted of a bedroom, bathroom, and living-room/kitchen combo. Assuming that she wasn't hiding in the shower or the closet, it was obvious that she wasn't in the apartment. I scanned the room for a note, but couldn't find one.

"Sarah!"

If one of her clients from social services had called, I felt certain that the phone would have woken me, and even if it hadn't, Sarah would have left me a note. I decided that she must have run to the store and, having settled the mystery, started a pot of coffee and took a shower while it brewed.

After drying off from the shower, I pulled a box of Marlboros from the freezer. Before I could open them, though, I looked down at the kitchen counter, down at the dirty ashtray overflowing with black soot and crushed cigarettes. Some were Sarah's, but most were mine.

I dropped the cigarettes onto the table.

Sarah's cigarette butts were smeared with red lipstick, and the bright color seemed out of place amidst the filthy gray. She had talked about quitting for years, but never followed through, knowing that she wouldn't be able to kick the habit unless I joined her in the effort. Sarah was strong enough to quit without my help, but not without my temptation, not when she had to watch me smoke two packs a day. We were bound together in love and addiction and for the first time, I felt guilty about the latter part of that union. I didn't want our marriage to drag Sarah down into lung cancer, to drag her down into death, and decided that it might be better if I allowed her to drag me up instead.

Four cups of coffee later, I lit a cigarette and threw Sarah's cold, untouched coffee into the sink.

I dropped down onto the couch, trying not to worry, and reached for the remote control. We had had the Centralvision for almost a year, and I still couldn't figure out how to work it. Trying to turn on the television, I accidentally booted up the computer, and when I finally figured out how to shut that down, I mistakenly dialed my parents' house in Boston on the videophone. Luckily, the line was busy, and after several more screw-ups, I finally managed to turn on the television.

The black guy with glasses was anchoring CNN and I settled back into the couch, glancing towards the door for a quick moment, expecting to see Sarah walking through it. When she didn't, I tried to distract myself by focusing on what the anchorman was saying.

" . . .fiber-optic lines have partially collapsed, as literally millions of missing person reports have continued to flood police, fire, and federal agencies. As of yet, no discernable pattern has been detected connecting the disappearances. Both men and women have been reported missing, as have people from all races and ages. Initial figures seem to suggest the possibility that more women than men have disappeared and a proportionally larger number of African Americans and Hispanics, but those numbers are far from confirmed.

"There has still been no comment from the President, and there are unconfirmed reports that high governmental offices, including those of the President and Vice-President, are now vacant, their holders amongst the missing. Local officials are requesting that citizens remain in their homes and refrain from reporting missing relatives until communication lines are repaired."

He paused and drank deeply from a glass of water. For a moment, the anchorman's eyes wandered past the camera and the muscles around his nose quivered. He shook his head, took a deep breath, and, carefully placing his hands on the desk in front of him, returned his eyes to the camera, once again composed and detached.

"For those of you just joining us, an unknown phenomena has apparently resulted in the disappearance of millions of people across the globe. Estimates range from several hundred million, to perhaps as high as one billion people. The disappearances occurred simultaneously at 3:23 AM Eastern Standard Time. As of yet, there are no indications as to what caused these disappearances. Witnesses describe the people as simply vanishing into thin air. Some of these disappearances were caught on camera, and we'll . . ."

The remote control dropped out of my limp hand, falling onto the couch with a muffled thump. I suddenly realized just how much effort I had always expended in keeping the muscles in my jaw and face tensed when, in an instant, those muscles released, allowing my jaw to sag and my eyelids to droop.

"Oh my God," I whispered.

The TV continued to drone, the anchorman's voice flowing through my ears in a continuous stream of words, only the smallest clumps of which registered in my consciousness.

". . .newly ordained Pope has made a plea for unity, specifically directing that plea towards his native country of Nigeria, where violent rioting has . . ."

It happened. It really happened. It . . . Jesus Christ.

" . . .were operating machinery. A TWA 747 crashed in . . ."

My wife was gone.

No, not my wife. Not a title, a position that could be filled. Sarah. Sarah's gone.

My face remained as motionless as oak. I stared at the TV, but couldn't see it. I was looking past it, through it, through the wall, through the earth, and through the universe; pushing so far that the line of vision beginning at the front of my cornea, ended at the back of my head. I stared straight ahead and saw the inside of my brain, which was dark and empty.

Sarah. Sarah's gone. I'm still here.

" . . .claiming governmental cover-up, militiamen in Ohio and Colorado have . . ."

Sarah left me.

" . . . Sir Richard Grant Morrison, newly elected chairman of the United European Community, professed confidence that . . ."

No. No, she didn't leave me. She was taken. God took her.

Something began slithering within my body, a sensation keeping to the shadows of my chest and the corners of my skull, staying just out of reach, just out of sight.

God did.

" . . . have denied responsibility, as have the IRA, the National Front, German Separatists, the Texas Militia, America First, the PLO, British Separatists, . . ."

Sarah, I'm . . .

The elusive Thing wrapped around my ribs, squeezing tightly before disappearing back into the darkness. My body shivered at the cold it left in its wake and my hands began trembling.

She's gone. Jesus Christ, I . . .

" . . . coup in Russia by former communist hard-liners . . ."

How did I live without you? I don't remember how to. How could you do this? How could you . . . ?

My eyes became wet.

"Sarah."

" . . .no answers, no traces, and no . . ."

The Thing sprang out of my shadows and coiled itself around my heart. It was dark and it was cold and it squeezed.

I lurched over in pain and then sprang up from the couch, my knees knocking over the coffee table. I leapt over the table and kicked the TV screen with my bare foot, cracking it. I grabbed the ashtray off the counter and hurled it at the cracked glass. A cloud of black ash floated behind the ashtray as it dug into the screen, causing it to shatter in an explosion of sparks and fire.

"CUNT!"

The sparks fizzled and the screen went blank.

I dropped down onto the floor. Lying next to me was an empty bottle of wine from the previous night. The floor was covered in dead cigarettes and black ash.

The air fled my lungs easily, but it was a chore to pull it back in. I curled into a ball and began rocking back and forth.

The apartment was cold.

"Jimmy," a voice said.

I jerked my head up, but saw no one.

"Close your eyes, Jimmy," the voice said. The voice was so clear that it sounded as if someone were whispering in my ear.

"Sarah?" I gushed, and jumped up onto my feet.

It hadn't sounded like Sarah's voice, but it was so familiar.

The living room was empty, so I ran into the bedroom.

She was going to be pissed off about the TV.

"Sarah?"

I looked under the bed and in the closet.

"Sarah?"

I pushed open the bathroom door.

"Sarah?"

I tore down the shower curtain.

"Sarah . . ."

I fell back onto the toilet and began crying.

"Jimmy," the voice said, "you want to close your fucking eyes so that you can see me?"

I suddenly realized that the voice was coming from inside of me. I wondered if I wasn't going insane. A part of me hoped I was.

I closed my eyes.

In the darkness of my mind, stood an alien. It looked exactly like I would have expected an alien standing in my brain to have looked like. It had yellowish gray skin and its body was small and frail. Its enormous, hairless, earless, noseless head was perched on top of a wiry body. It stared at me with huge black eyes, looking exactly like the alien that had been described thousands of times by supposed abductees. Its presence was solid and real, and when I opened my eyes, it disappeared, its image replaced by the torn brown shower curtain covering my knees.

I closed my eyes again and the alien was still there, its soulless gaze blacker and deeper than the surrounding blackness of my mind.

It grinned.

"Relax Jimmy," it said in the same voice I had heard in the living room, a voice so familiar that I had mistaken it for Sarah's.

"You're not going crazy." Its grinning mouth barely moved. "I'm not here to fuck with you. I'm not going to hurt you. I'm speaking to you," it casually pointed its long thin finger towards me, "and everyone else in the world," it raised its hand and twirled its finger in a circle, "at the same time. This is how my race communicates. I'm sending the same fundamental message to your entire species, sending it to your neocortex. You're receiving the message and then processing and filtering it through your individual speech patterns."

The voice was familiar because it was my own.

The alien's grin widened.

"Okay," it continued, "I know that this is a lot to take in, but try and follow me here. I've come to deliver a warning and to give you some advice.

"We've been watching you for a long time. We've watched your species grow and evolve. You've got a lot to be proud of. Democracy, art, science, philosophy, humor, irony, spirituality, love, history, and on and on. Your level of growth is almost unique.

"But there's a problem, isn't there?" It paused for a moment and then grinned. "Sorry, I hate rhetorical questions, too. The thing is, for every baby-step forward in growth, you insist upon taking a corresponding leap in hatred. For every Einstein, you've got a Hitler, Stalin, and Mussolini; for every Gandhi, a Nero, Napoleon, and Nixon; for every Jesus, a Bundy, Reagan, and Pol Pot. You are a hateful motherfucking race.

"You slaughter each other over the flimsiest of excuses. You draw imaginary lines in the sand, calling them countries, and then murder because of them. You concoct fairy tales about angels and devils and then burn each other for believing in a different fairy tale. You kill people because you don't think they should be sleeping with who they're sleeping with. You hate each other, and this is the one we can't get over, because of the *color of your skin*. Think about that, someone else's hue is a little lighter or little darker than your own, and you *murder* them. You are a violent, petty species." It shook its huge head pityingly.

"Okay," the alien said, leaning back into the darkness and slouching up against an invisible wall, "having said that, let me say something else: you remind us of ourselves." It winked. "You're what we were billions of years ago. That's why we've been watching you, why we borrowed a few of you over the years to study. You possess the same limitless potential that we once did, and you're the first species we've ever discovered to share that potential.

"Do you have any comprehension of what you're capable of? You are not a three-dimensional creature, that's just how you view yourself. You are actually a five-dimensional creature growing in the soil of space-time. If you develop, you'll learn that space and time and matter are not constraints, but tools that you're able to manipulate. Time doesn't move in a linear, forward motion, it's a crystal, where all moments occur simultaneously. You know that, but you haven't allowed yourself to see, so you only view one aspect of that crystal.

"I know that none of this makes any sense to you, but if you embrace your potential, it will."

Staring at it, I realized that it wasn't just my voice that the alien had appropriated. The grin, the cynically crinkled brow, the slouch, the hand gestures; they all belonged to me. It was like staring into an extremely fucked-up funhouse mirror.

"Anyway, here's the warning: right now, you're at the most important crossroad you'll ever have. Intellectually, you've raised yourself to amazing heights. Your quantum physicians are already beginning to understand some of what I've explained to you, but to truly understand, to *live* in that reality, you've got to evolve spiritually. And spiritually, you're a fucking retard. You've allowed yourself to grow up intellectually, but have been indulging in a spiritual adolescence for way too long. You're tearing yourself in half."

I remained silent and stupefied.

"The next few years are going to be hard ones, the hardest you'll ever face. You're either going to make the next evolutionary jump or you're going to continue wallowing in your own hatred and end up choking to death on your own shit. You've got a chance to become something unique, to fulfill your potential and discover the truth about yourself. If you don't, you're going to die.

"It's your decision," it said with a shrug. "We can't force you to make the right one. What we *can* do is nudge you in the right direction and give you a little head start. That's what we did last night, when we removed nearly one-and-a-half billion people from your planet. They were the most closed-mined amongst you, the fucks-heads who were totally unwilling to think in different ways and who were the most intolerant of those who did. They were weights pulling you under, drowning you, and if we hadn't taken them, you wouldn't have had a chance in hell. They're alive and they're happy, but you will never ever see any of them again."

Sarah.

"Still, don't start thinking you've got a free ride. We left plenty of fuck-heads behind. We're not saving you; we're just evening up the odds a bit."

There was something missing. The alien possessed my voice, my gestures, my posture, even my profanity, but there was still something missing.

Before I could figure out what it was, its absence was rectified as a half-smoked cigarette appeared in the alien's hand.

"Okay," it said, and inhaled on the cigarette as if it had been smoking two packs a day for all its millennia, "so that was the warning. Here's the advice." It took a long drag off the cigarette, using the pause to heighten the dramatic tension. "Smarten-up." It ashed into the blackness, licking its lips and tilting its head.

I began chuckling.

"Pretty soon," it continued, "you're going to realize that most of the people we took were Christians. There's a reason for that. Nothing against Jesus, he was one of the best people you ever produced. But *Jesus* wasn't enough for you, was it? You just had to go and add *Christ* to the end of his name. Rather than seeing him as an example of human potential, you turned him into a god, conveniently creating a situation where you no longer had any possibility of meeting his standards or even the responsibility to try. After all, who can be as good as god, right?"

It shook its head and inhaled more smoke.

My chuckle tumbled into full-blown laughter.

"And then," it continued, "you formed a religion around a man who preached nothing but love, and used it as an excuse to judge, torture, ostracize, and murder one another. He says, *don't judge*, and you judge in his name. He says, *love* and you hate in his name. Fucking unbelievable!" It scoffed and ran its hands over its bald head. "Grow up! Stop lying to yourself! You spend all your time staring into the sky, looking for someone to come and make it all okay, and it stops you from remembering that you have to do it yourself. You create gods that make you feel small, create something so big that it justifies how small you behave. Stop it. Look inward for a savior. Remember that *you* are God. All you have to do is remember."

"Well, I guess that's it." It took a final, shallow puff off the remaining cigarette and then dropped it down onto an invisible ground, crushing it out with its tiny, toeless foot. "Oh, and hey, don't even *think* of turning us into gods and praying to us for any more help. You won't get it. You're on your own from now on. Do what's right and we'll meet again as equals, don't and you die.

"Good luck, Jimmy, god knows you're going to need it."

It smiled one last time and then disappeared.

I opened my eyes and continued to laugh, my body shaking uncontrollably. Every time I began calming down, the image of the alien grinding out the cigarette underneath its yellow/gray stub of a foot reappeared in my mind, throwing me headlong into hysterics.

When, grasping for breath, I finally regained control of myself, my guts ached and my face was covered with tears.

I closed my eyes and stared at the space where the alien had stood.

"Nice try, cocksucker. Next time why don't you just try offering me the fucking apple?"

I began laughing again.

Seven

I allowed myself a full week to pack, carefully sifting through years of accumulated memories and possessions, trying to decide what was important enough to lug to Boston and what could be abandoned. After stuffing the final bag into my car, I looked around the apartment one last time. It somehow seemed a shame to simply walk away, and an adolescent part of me wanted to set the building on fire, to leave a burning husk in my wake.

A knock on the door tore me away from thoughts of fiery infernos and, when I opened the door I saw Joe Lukas, the principal of my high school, standing in the snow, frantically rubbing his hands together.

"Jimmy! Oh man! I knew that *you'd* still be here."

"Yeah. Hey, Joe," I said with a polite smile. "Listen, you kind of caught me at a bad time. I'm out the door to Boston."

"Boston?" He shook his head as if I had just uttered an unacceptable statement. "No. No way. We've got to talk."

"Look, I'm . . ." My voice trailed off and I stared at Joe, who didn't appear to be listening. He was bobbing his scrawny frame left and right, shifting his weight from one foot to the other, looking like a child who needed to use the bathroom.

"Yeah, sure. Come on in, Joe. It's good to see you."

He nodded his head and shuffled past me, his movements even more harried and frantic than they usually were. I closed the door and followed him into the kitchen, where he was already pacing back and forth across the linoleum.

"Have you been watching the news?" he asked.

"Not for about a week," I said, and lit a cigarette. "I kicked in the TV."

"Yeah, it's just amazing, isn't it? Something new happens every ten minutes. Right before I left the house I heard that Texas was trying to declare itself an independent state."

"That's nothing new," I said as I began brewing a pot of coffee. "Bunch of fucking rednecks." I doled out my words at a leisurely pace, hoping that Joe would catch the hint and slow his rapid stream of babble. He was speaking so quickly and moving so frantically that I began to wonder if he was on something.

"The UEC looked like it was all done, but Morrison saved it."

"Richard Grant Morrison?" I asked. "The English guy?"

"Yeah. He's amazing. He's talking about pulling the world together the same way Europe did, abolishing countries, doing away with war, focusing on cooperation instead of competition. If he can do it, we'll finally be able to concentrate on the *real* problems."

"Morrison, huh? Hmm. He's the Antichrist."

"Yeah," Joe mumbled without listening, "it's great. It's finally falling apart. Capitalism's done and now we'll finally be able to do it right."

"Joe . . ."

"I've been talking about this for years, and everyone always laughed at me."

"Joe . . ."

"But I told them we had to do it differently, and now our kids are finally going to have a chance."

"Joe . . . "

"This has been a long time coming."

"JOE!"

"What?" He stopped his pacing with a jerk.

"Fucking simmer down, huh? Smoke a cigarette."

"I quit."

"When?"

"A week ago."

"Good thinking. Listen, what do you need? I mean, I want to help, but I've really got to get going. Boston's a long drive."

"What?" He stared at me with horror and confusion. "Jimmy, I told you, you can't go."

"I can't, huh?"

"Oh no. No, no, no, no, no, no. We need you here. The last few days, I've been tracking down all the teachers that are left. We need you, Jimmy. We've got to start teaching our kids."

Neither Joe nor I were parents, *Our kids* was Joe's way of referring to the students at the high school.

I crushed out the cigarette and drank a cup of black coffee. Without the cream, which I had run out of three days before, it tasted bitter.

"School's closed, Joe. Just about everything's closed."

"Exactly!" He nodded his entire body. "We've got to open it up, start teaching our kids the truth and help them evolve. Jimmy, didn't the Celestine Prophets talk to you?"

"*The Celestine Prophets?*"

"That's what they've been calling them. Haven't you been watching the news?"

"I told you, I kicked my TV in. But yeah. Yeah, my *Celestine Prophet* spoke to me." I began chuckling. "We smoked a butt while he explained the universe."

"What? I . . . look, this is important, Jimmy. Even *you* must know that."

"*Even* me?"

"We've got to prepare our kids. For Christ's sake, Jimmy, we've got to tell them what's happening!"

"Do you think you *know* what's happening?"

"That's just it!" He jumped back and spilled some of the coffee I had handed to him. "That's why you can't leave. We've got to decide on a new curriculum."

"*A curriculum?* Jesus Christ, Joe, I . . ." I gently grabbed his frail arm and led him over to the couch. "Look, if you want to teach them the truth, Joe, just take the kids and . . . Wait, *are* there any kids left?"

"Of course! Our kids are our most precious resource! They're our future! They . . ."

"Shut up. Have you seen them? Have you actually *seen* any children since last week?"

"Of course."

I threw what was left of my bitter coffee into the sink and frowned. It didn't seem right to me that children had been left behind.

"Well, anyway," I said, trying to ignore the thought, "just take whoever's left, spend a few days teaching them Revelations, and then send them home to their families."

"The *Bible?*"

"It's the truth," I said with a shrug.

"It's illegal!" He stared at me as if I had just proposed that we sell *our kids* into prostitution.

"What is?"

"You can't teach the Bible in public school, it's against the law! Our entire society's based on the fundamental separation of church and state . . ." He continued ranting and became so animated and excited that I feared he might hyperventilate.

A familiar feeling of annoyance crept up on me, but that emotion quickly gave way to something else. Looking at Joe's flushed, frantic face, I felt sorry for him. For all his grating enthusiasm and self-righteousness, he was a good man. He didn't deserve to go to Hell.

"Joe," I said, raising my hand and shutting him up, "I want you to do something for me. Will you do something for me?"

"Yeah, sure, but listen, the first thing we have to do, is . . ."

"No." I shook my head. "No, *will you do something for me,* yes or no?"

"Yeah. Yeah, sure." He nodded his head and calmed down.

"Okay, I want you to sit still and listen to what I have to say."

"I *am* listening," he said in a slight whine.

"Joe, you haven't listened to a goddamn word I've said. You never do." He tried protesting but I cut him off. "No. Look, I don't care about that. It's who you are, I understand that. But right now, I need you to sit down on the couch and listen very carefully to what I'm going to tell you. I need you to promise not to interrupt, okay?"

"Okay."

"Not a word? You promise?"

"I'm listening."

"Okay, Joe." I took a deep breath. "This is what's going on. This is the truth."

In the beginning, six thousand years ago, God created man and placed him in Paradise. He did this because He was a loving God, and as such, wished both to love and to be loved. Man lived together with God, possessing no knowledge of evil. He did, however, possess free will, for without free will, man could not freely choose to love God. In exercising that freedom, man choose to know of evil, and thus expelled himself from Paradise, separating himself from God.

For two thousand years, God allowed man to live without rules, allowed him to live as he chose; he chose to become hateful, selfish, and petty. Man brought murder into the world and worshipped false gods. He ran further and further away from Paradise and, in response, God created the Law, a covenant between man and God which would help him understand how to bridge their separation. God gave the Law to the tribe of Israel, so that they might follow it, serving as an example to the rest of mankind.

Once again, man failed, proving himself either unwilling or unable to follow the Law. Even those most favored in God's eyes failed: Noah was a drunkard; David, the greatest of Israel's kings, arranged to have a loyal soldier murdered so that he might possess the soldier's wife; Solomon, Israel's wisest leader, became possessed with jealousy and spite, and attempted to have loyal David murdered. Two thousand years of Law passed and man continued to spurn Paradise, to reject God.

Seeing this, God brought forth the New Covenant. For in his time spent under the Law, man proved unable to save himself. To remedy the rift between man and God, God created a Son, gave Him human form, and allowed Him to become the redeeming sacrifice for man's sin.

For the following two thousand years, all that was required of man if he was to be reunited with God, was that man accept the sacrifice made by Christ on his behalf. When man consented to the need for forgiveness and salvation by placing his life under Jesus Christ, he would be cleansed of sin and allowed back into Paradise. This was the New Covenant.

Some accepted this gift, while others spurned His mercy.

Six thousand years has passed since the beginning. There will be no new covenant. The time of final judgment has arrived.

God raptured the true believers, raising those who had accepted Christ's sacrifice to Heaven, so that they need not suffer alongside the sinners, who had spurned salvation. For seven years, those who remain on Earth will be punished. Twenty-one separate judgments will be placed upon man for his evil. Seven Seals, Seven Trumpets, and Seven Bowls. During this time, an Antichrist will arise and serve Satan, deceiving man and turning him away from God, leading man into damnation while proclaiming himself to be his savior.

When the time of tribulation has ended, both the living and the dead will be judged by Christ, judged and accepted into Paradise or condemned to spend an eternity separated from God, cast down into Hell, where they will suffer that separation.

The final judgment has arrived.

Of course, Joe attempted to interrupt me several times. His mouth would begin to open or he'd edge forward on the couch with a flustered face. Each time, I silently reminded him of his promise to shut up and listen by pointing my finger at him, or simply raising an eyebrow. When I had finished speaking, I sat down and lit a cigarette.

"I . . ." He stared towards me with disappointment, confusion, and what looked like horror. "Jimmy, *please* tell me that you don't really believe all that."

"Jesus Joe, how *can't* I believe it now?"

"How *can't* you? How *can* you? I . . . I . . ." He took a deep breath and tried to calm down. "Okay, if all of that's really true, then what about the Celestine Prophets?"

"Jesus Christ, Joe, would you stop calling them that? It's the dumbest fucking thing I ever . . ."

"Just answer me. What about them?"

"It was Satan." The word felt odd coming from my mouth.

"*Satan!*" He jumped off the couch and dropped back down.

"Think about it, Joe. The Devil can understand the Bible as well as we can. He knew that the Rapture was going to happen sooner or later, and he knew that if he didn't come up with a damn good explanation for it, a lot of people would understand what was going on and turn to God. He's been setting up this cover story for decades. Think about all the alien abduction stories in the last thirty years, how they've been increasing in number every year. I mean, were you even *slightly* surprised that the alien looked like it did? We've had that image burned into our consciousness so that this whole thing wouldn't seem so ridiculous."

"Satan setting up a cover story? Are you listening to yourself?"

"Look, I know how fucked-up it sounds, but why is it so much easier for you to believe in a little yellow alien telepathically contacting you than is to believe in the possibility of God and Satan?"

"Jimmy . . ."

"Have you ever read the Bible?"

"Why would I?"

"I don't know, if nothing else so that you'd know what you were talking about when you dismissed it as an *opiate for the masses?* I mean, I read the Bible figuring that I'd punch a million holes in it and at the same time, shut Sarah up. But it ended up making sense. Look at it numerically. *Six* is the number of man and *seven* is the number of God. There were two thousand years after the fall from Eden, then two thousand years of Jewish law, then two thousand years after Christ, which was the time of the Gentile. That's six thousand years, six being the number of man. After the Tribulation, Jesus is supposed to rule the earth for a thousand years. That's the seventh millennium, seven being the number of God. Seven years of tribulation, seven thousand years on earth, three sets of seven judgments."

"Jimmy, what the hell are you talking about?"

"I'm just saying that it all makes sense."

"Yeah," he scoffed, "it makes sense if you ignore evolution and the fact that mankind's been on earth for millions of years, not six thousand."

"Genesis says God made every living creature, then on the next day, made man."

"Big difference between millions of years and a day."

"Yeah, but what I'm saying is that maybe what happened was that millions of years ago, God set the wheels of evolution in motion, but only gave mankind a soul six thousand years ago. Hasn't it ever struck you as being ridiculously out of proportion that for hundreds of thousands of years, humanity's only real achievement was walking upright, making a few scribbles on a wall, and lighting a fire or two? But then, in just a few thousand years, we suddenly transformed from nomadic, hunter-gatherers with primitive language and thought capacity into a species capable of building cities and planes and artificial hearts? Capable of engaging in complex philosophical and abstract thought? In *hundreds* of thousands of years, we went from a cave to a cave, then in a *few* thousand, we went from a cave to New York City."

"That's evolution, Jimmy."

"But it doesn't make sense. It's the complete opposite of how it works in the real world. We experience the *most* development in the *first* years of life. It's not like we spend eighty years learning to walk, talk, and shit in a toilet, and then the last day or so developing empathy, philosophical thought, and social skills. We experience most of our growth and development in the first decade or two of life. After that, it takes an enormous amount of energy to grow or change even a *little* bit. Why would that be true for us as individuals but the exact opposite as a species? It seems to me that something happened a few thousand years ago that changed us dramatically."

"I . . ." He shook his head and ran his hands through his greasy hair. "Jimmy, it's a book written by men. Scared, ignorant men who couldn't understand the universe and made up fairy tales to explain it. Men wrote it, Jimmy. Not God."

"God wrote it *through* men."

"Jimmy . . ." He gently placed his hand on my shoulder.

"Don't you fucking condescend to me, Lukas." I knocked his hand off. "I . . . I'm sorry, I just . . . Okay, take Israel. Everything in Revelations revolves around the state of Israel being in existence. The Bible says that the Jews were going to turn their backs on Jesus and because of that, they'd be dispersed around the globe and persecuted. That would happen until the end was near, at which point, they'd return to their homeland and reform their nation. That's exactly what happened! In 70 AD, their temple was destroyed by Nero and they've spent the last two thousand years getting the shit kicked out of them by just about every country in the world. Despite all that, they still held on to their identity and returned to reform their homeland."

"So?"

"*So?* You're not stupid, Joe. How many people retain their national identity after being expelled from their country and dispersed across the world? Where are the Mesopotamians? Where are the Sumerians? The Bible said Israel was going to reform exactly where it did. Exactly! No one in history's ever done what the Jews have done. Two thousand years ago, the Bible predicted they would. Doesn't that tell you something?"

"Coincidence."

"*Coincidence!* The Jews were supposed to be dispersed, persecuted, rebuild their country, and then become surrounded by enemies. All of that happened! What are the odds of that? The Christians disappeared just like the Bible said they would, is that coincidence too? The Antichrist is supposed to be a leader coming out of a collection of ten nations. Morrison comes from The United European Community, which is comprised of ten nations. Coincidence? Jesus, Joe, you might as well say that if you turn on the light switch a million times and every time you do, the light goes on, that's a coincidence too, because the odds are about the same! It's over! The world's done, finished!"

"How can you say that?"

"How can you act surprised? Fuck man, even if you weren't looking at it from a religious angle, the signs were still all around you. The population explosion, the environment, race hatred, technology, violence, information, all of it, it was all blowing out of control. Everything was getting faster and faster, time was doubling up on itself, one invention led to the next twice as fast, one problem spawned another in half the time. How many times did you think the population could double itself in half as much time before it had to stop? How fast, how dense did you think it could all get before we hit the wall? Wasn't it obvious that there had to be an end? Couldn't you see it coming?"

"It's not the end! It can't be!"

We stood silently for several minutes. I lit a cigarette and tried to calm down. Joe turned his back to me and his shoulders began bobbing up and down, as if he were crying.

"Joe," I said quietly, "the people who disappeared were Christians. Pretty soon a third of the world is going to be wiped out. I don't know how, but it's going to happen. That's the First Seal of Judgment. I know how hard it is, but read the Bible. Turn to Christ to save yourself." I cringed hearing those words come from my mouth.

"If you believe all of this," Joe said, jerking around and staring at me through angry tears, "then why are *you* still here? Why aren't *you* in Heaven?"

"I . . ." I stepped back from him. "I don't know. I suppose that there's a difference in belief and faith. Living with Sarah all of these years, I guess I began believing that maybe it *was* all true. But I think I believed it the way you believe you're going to die. You might know it in your head, but in your heart, you really think you're going to live forever. Besides," I smiled, "how could I go to Heaven if it meant leaving my family behind to burn in Hell? If I really put my faith in Christ and got raptured, who'd be left to save them? Who'd tell them the truth about God? They'd never have listened to me before, but now, with all of this happening, with everything so clear, how *couldn't* they believe me? I'm going to save my family."

Joe wiped away his tears and looked at me with disgust.

"You're happy," he said in an astonished voice. "You honestly believe what you're saying and you're happy. You think there's a Hell, where people burn for eternity and you're happy. You think the world's going to end in seven years and you're actually smiling. What the hell's the matter with you, Jimmy?"

I shook my head, trying unsuccessfully to rid myself of the rush of energy fueling my smile. "I don't know, I just, I . . . You ever been in a car crash?"

"What?"

"A car crash. A big one."

"I . . ."

"Maybe ten years ago, me and this girl Jude where driving home from New York City. Jude was sleeping next to me. We were driving down 95 and a car driving a hundred yards ahead of us just crumbled apart. It just fucking disintegrated. But it was going like eighty miles-an-hour, so when it disintegrated, it basically just exploded. A BMW driving behind it swerved into another lane to avoid it, right in front of an eighteen-wheeler. The truck plowed through the BMW and then jack-knifed." I took a quick, sharp drag of smoke.

"So, I'm staring at this fucking inferno in front of me, roaring towards it at seventy miles-an-hour. And I should feel fucked, right? I mean, there's metal and glass and huge pieces of shit flying all over the place and an eighteen-wheeler skidding out of control, shooting sparks and fire with a BMW welded onto its front. But I don't *feel* fucked. Instead, I get this tunnel vision and everything becomes clear.

"I take half a second to look at Jude. She's still sleeping. The only time she ever looked innocent was when she was sleeping. Her life's in my hands and she doesn't even know it.

"Everyone else slams on their breaks, swerving and smashing into one another. But me, I press down on the gas and everything becomes perfect. The car stops being a car, and becomes a part of me. I swerve around an engine and cut in front of the truck, the BMW still wrapped around its fender. Debris is flying all around us, metal, plastic, glass, but none if it touches us. I look in the rearview mirror and the whole highway's shooting up sparks and fire. It's like hell itself's trying to climb up my ass.

"I outran the whole fucking mess. All of it. Past the wreckage, the highway was abandoned. I owned it. I had outrun death. It was fucking beautiful."

I took a final drag from my cigarette and then dropped it onto the rug and crushed it with my foot.

"That's how I feel now, Joe. Everything's clear. I know what's going on and I know what to do. *I'm* in control, and just like then, I can push through this fucking mess and do the right thing."

Joe threw his coffee cup past my head. It shattered against the wall, splattering coffee all over. His tears began flowing.

"The world *can't* be ending! Think about our kids!"

"Goddamnit, Joe! Would you shut the fuck up about *our kids*?"

"No! No, we have to decide what to teach them. We have to! You and me! That's all that's left."

"Joe, I . . ." I rubbed my hands over my face and sighed. The energy that had been powering my enthusiasm abandoned me and I suddenly felt drained and empty. "Why don't you head home, okay? Just think about what I told you. Go on home to Sandy, you should be with her now."

He dropped back onto the couch, his coiled body suddenly losing its electricity. His shoulders slumped and he dropped his head into his hands. When he lifted his face back up, his eyes had retreated backwards, withdrawing into their sockets.

"She's gone," he whispered.

"Oh. Oh. I'm sorry, Joe."

"Yeah." He began slapping his palms against his forehead. "That bitch. That fucking bitch." His body tightened up again and he sprang off the couch, pacing back and forth like a fighter waiting for the bell. "All this time. All this time I thought she was like me. I thought she was trying to make things better."

"She was a good woman, Joe. Look, be happy, she's in . . ."

"LIAR!" He jumped towards me and pointed his finger into my face. "She was a liar! Behind my back, Jimmy. She was a whore. A slut! She was a Christian and she never told me. I had my suspicions. Don't think I didn't notice that all of a sudden there was a Bible sitting on the bookshelf. I noticed. But I . . . I never . . ."

"Joe . . ."

"I never knew. She was part of the problem, Jimmy. She wasn't trying to make a better world for our kids; she was part of the problem." He stared down at the carpet, muttering more to himself than to me. "All that time it was lies. Filthy whore."

"Joe . . ."

"Where's Sarah?" he suddenly asked, raising his head.

"She's gone."

"Yeah? Yeah. Yeah, you see? How could we have known? Couple of bitches. Lying little bitches."

"You got to go, man." I grabbed Joe's elbow and gently led him to the door. "Come on, you got to get home."

He continued to mutter as I led him out into the cold.

"Jimmy?" he asked before I could close the door.

"Yeah?"

"She was pro-choice." He looked desperate.

"What?"

"Sandy. She believed women had the right to choose, she told me so all the time. How could I have known?"

"I don't know, Joe. I guess maybe you couldn't."

He nodded his head and his features once again became hard. "Yeah. Two-faced little Janus cunt. We'll teach our kids, though. Our kids'll know better."

In theory, the drive from Michigan to Boston can be accomplished in a little under thirteen hours. In reality, it took me twice as long just to edge my car onto the highway. Apparently the entire country wanted to be exactly where they were not, and had decided to drive there. Traffic would move forward at a steady clip for a few minutes or so before coming to a dead halt for hours, sometimes days at a time. Pulling off the road for gas was a five-day affair. It took me seven days just to get out of Michigan. Thirty-six days later, I finally reached the Massachusetts Turnpike. That was when I first heard the news.

We all abandoned our cars when we heard, understanding that if traffic had been an endless purgatory up to then, it was certain to become hell after a nuclear war.

Eight

A hushed wind of murmurs blew across the highway, quietly telling of nuclear holocaust. The traffic had been at a standstill since the previous day, and I climbed out of my smoke-filled car feeling stiff and frigid. The other motorists also exited their vehicles and, one by one, we lifted our faces to the sky. It was a beautiful February day. The air felt cold and strong and clean. The sky was virginal, unmarred by even a single cloud. I stared up into the blue sky and smiled at its innocence while waiting for the bombs to drop down on my head.

We waited in complete silence. There were no screaming voices begging for mercy or anguished cries of despair. We stared into the heavens with a stoic hush, a collective nod of acceptance. Extinction through lack of spiritual evolution had felt like a ridiculous and obtuse way to die, especially when the herald of destruction had been a skinny, dorky looking alien; destroyed in a nuclear fireball of our own creation, that made sense. We stared into the cloudless sky and waited for the fire and light that, somewhere within us, we had always expected to witness. We stood patiently, a resigned groom waiting at the altar for his shotgun bride to arrive.

She never showed.

The hours crept by and, eventually, the sun sank peacefully down into the earth. The day had passed and we were still alive.

One by one, we stopped staring into the sky, abandoned our cars, and began marching east. We walked during the day, thousands of us trudging next to the motionless highway, slowly moving through the white snow at a languid pace. At night, we would disperse, scattering off the highway and swarming into the surrounding towns to locate an abandoned house where food and shelter could be found. The sun would rise and we'd trek back onto the highway to continue our pilgrimage.

Two and a half weeks after abandoning my car, I finally reached the outskirts of Boston. It was late afternoon, and while the sun set behind me, an orange glow continued to permeate the city. From a distance, I guessed that the sun's fading light caused the glow, but as I approached, I realized that the glow originated from the city itself. Clumps of buildings burned out of control while dirty black smoke pushed up into the sky, covering Boston like a decrepit umbrella.

As I entered the city, I felt a rush of fear mixed with wonder. People ran through the streets in an orgasmic free for all, hurling bricks and rocks through windows, setting cars aflame, and fucking each other while the burning buildings kept their naked bodies warm. A group of kids were taking turns running towards a burning car, diving into the flames and then rolling over the car's roof, expunging their burning backs in a spurting fire hydrant waiting on the other side. The city echoed with primitive screams of freedom and release.

I smiled at the surrounding madness. Despite the chaos, there was a conspicuous lack of physical violence. Property was destroyed, stores were looted, and any flammable object seemed to be fair game for destruction, yet it all felt innocent, joyous even. Young children remained unmolested as they warmed themselves around burning cars and buildings. It was like a Loony Toons cartoon: frantic action, but with no real malice or consequence.

That changed as the sun disappeared completely and I wandered deeper into the city. None of the streetlights were operational, not even the ones that hadn't been destroyed, and any moonlight was blocked by the heavy smoke covering the city. The resulting darkness was immense, offset only by the fires that turned the city into a chessboard of light and dark; the flames illuminating one block but casting a heavy black shadow upon the next. The burning buildings warmed the night, but it was an unnatural heat, making the air thin and difficult to breathe.

The congested streets quickly became sparse as the joyful squeals of late afternoon were replaced by wails of terror. I saw the first bodies in Chinatown. Two men and a young boy were sprawled amongst the garbage and the glass, their faces hidden by blood. I turned away and kept moving.

Packs of men began roaming the streets with baseball bats, knives, guns, and pipes; anything that looked frightening and could inflict damage upon another human being. I stared straight ahead and tried to conjure up a fierce looking countenance with which to intimidate the locals. It didn't work.

I looked over my shoulder to see four men following behind me, moving faster than I was. I darted down a brick ally and began running. They were quicker than I was and two of them dashed past me, blocking off the other end of the ally. I quickly spun around to see the other two approaching me from behind. I looked back and forth towards each of the parings and could hear my own breathing. It sounded loud and afraid. I was certain that they could hear it too, so I leaned back against the brick wall and lit a cigarette, trying to look unintimidated.

They sauntered up to me and I inhaled deeply on the cigarette before looking into their faces. They were four white kids who couldn't have been much older than sixteen. They weren't *men*, they were *boys*. Their ages humiliated me. They were twenty years younger than I was, but I knew that if they wanted to, they could kick my ass up and down that ally. Their condescending smiles told me that they knew it, too.

Three of the kids stopped a few feet away from me, but the forth, a beefy, pale-skinned Italian kid with greased back hair and a dirt mustache moved to within inches of my face, staring at me with a silent smirk. I tried to look bored and unaffected, but was certain that each loud swallow I took betrayed that attempt.

"You got a problem?" I asked, failing to keep my voice from quivering.

The world suddenly seemed very unfair. I had lived for more than twice as long as these children, had seen and experienced things that they had only imagined, and yet *I* was the one who was afraid.

"A problem?" the boy asked, his smirk becoming a wide grin. "Nah, we ain't got a problem. How about you? *You* got a problem?"

His friends laughed and my shame became anger. I thought about my father, knowing that if this had happened to him, he would never have run. As soon as he realized that he was being followed, he would have stopped, turned around, and walked right up to the four of them. When he saw how old they were, he wouldn't even have bothered talking. He would have taken out whichever kid was closest to him with one punch and then given the remaining three about two seconds to get running before they got some of the same.

I pushed myself off the wall and closed the distance between the kid and myself. "Why don't *you* tell me if I've got a problem," I said, trying to sound like my father.

"Oh yeah." He pulled a straight razor out of his pocket. "Yeah, you got a big fucking problem, man." He opened the razor and held it up to my face. The building across the street was burning and the blaze reflected in the razor's metal. I stared at the silver blade and felt my false anger collapse into real fear.

The other three began moving towards me, but stopped with a jolt as the sound of a shotgun blast tore through the ally, echoing across the brick walls.

A middle-aged black man in a suit was standing at the far end of the ally, holding a smoking shotgun. Behind him stood a number of other men, whose faces were obscured by the shadows.

"Jesus Christ," I mumbled, dropping my face into my hands, "the Niggers and the Wops are gonna to fight it out to see who gets to kill me."

"WHO YOU CALLING A WOP, MOTHERFUCKER?" the kid screamed.

"Leave that man alone, son." It was the black man's voice, deep and authoritative. It possessed sternness mixed with compassion and understanding, the perfect voice for a teacher. It was the kind of voice that in all my years of teaching, I had never quite been able to cultivate.

"Fuck you, nigger," the kid said. Despite his words, he stepped away from me, obeying the voice without even realizing that he was. "Go find your own bitch. This one's ours."

I hoped that I had managed to hide the quiver in my voice better than the Italian kid had.

"This man belongs to Christ. As do you. Go on home before you get hurt."

The three kids looked to their leader with uncertainty. He wavered for a moment, the razor in his hand slightly shaking. When he noticed the doubt on his friends' faces, he wiped the identical doubt off his own and pointed his razor at the man.

"Who the fuck're you kidding, Christ-freak? You ain't got the balls. Go find someone else to save before I slice your black ass." He stepped towards the black man, but halted when he heard a fresh round pumped into the shotgun's chamber.

"Son, in my heart, I possess nothing but love for you. But don't think, not even for a moment, that I'll hesitate to blow your nuts off." He paused. "Go home, boy. All of you, go on home."

The kid darted his eyes back and forth, frantically searching for an option. Seeing none, he slipped the razor back into his pocket and, turning to leave, bumped shoulders with me.

"Yeah," the kid muttered, "we gonna meet again real soon, nigger." He didn't say the words loud enough for anyone but me and his friends to have heard.

Once the four boys were out of sight, I collapsed backwards, slumping against the brick wall. I reached for a new cigarette and realized that the one I had lit minutes before was still in my hand, unsmoked but burnt down to the nub. I dropped it and pulled a fresh one out of my pocket. I lit it with shaking hands and inhaled deeply.

"Jesus fucking Christ." I exhaled and, after a few moments, turned towards the men, all of whom were standing utterly still. "Thank you," I said. "Really, thank you, guys. That was," I laughed, feeling a sudden rush of relief, "that was seriously fucked up. Thank you. Jesus Christ, I think a fucking nuke's about to fall on my head and I don't bat an eye, but a guinea with a razor almost make me piss my pants. Fucked up. Seriously, thank you."

"What's your name?" he asked, lowering his gun and walking towards me.

"Jimmy. Jimmy Lordan." I tossed the cigarette between my lips and leaned over; suddenly afraid I was going to vomit.

"The end is here, Jimmy," he said in a deadly serious tone.

"Yeah," I said, before spitting out the cigarette and gagging.

"The judgment of our savior Jesus Christ is upon us."

"Uh-huh." I wiped my mouth and glanced down at the other side of the ally, half expecting the kids to return with their mobbed-up uncles dressed in pinstriped suits and brandishing tommy-guns.

"You must choose. Christ or Satan. Heaven or Hell. The flesh or the spirit. There is no middle ground."

"Yeah." I stared past the man and looked at his companions. They remained hidden by the shadows, the fire behind them casting its light over and around them, allowing me to see nothing more than their dark, motionless silhouettes.

"Jimmy, the Word of God . . ."

"Hey," I said, shaking myself out the haze and standing upright, "I know, okay? Seriously. I know what's going on. Revelations, the Bible, all of that crap. I know."

The man gazed at me with doubt-filled eyes.

"Seriously," I repeated, not wanting him to doubt me, although uncertain as to why I cared. "Okay, look, the um, the First Seal was the White Horseman, right? The false peace. That idiotic alien telling us all we've got to do is love one another. All this, the riots, the nukes, this is all the Second Seal, the Red Horseman, the Sword. I understand what's going on. That's why I'm here."

His eyes narrowed. His face looked weatherworn, but resilient, his flesh a brown leather shoe that had proven its durability, having become wrinkled and worn-in rather than ripped and worn-out. His hair possessed just enough gray to bestow distinction without implying weakness of age.

"Christ has brought you to us, Jimmy," he said, his leathery face suddenly bursting into a smile.

"Yeah, okay. Anyway, thanks again." I reached out to shake his hand, turning to include the others in my gratitude. They remained obscured, silent, and motionless.

He grasped my hand and shook it with the perfect balance of warmth and strength, firm without that solidity feeling forced, and gentle without being soft.

"You don't owe *us* anything. Give your thanks to Christ."

"Yeah." He was only two or three inches taller than I was, but his presence seemed to tower above me. His gray suit was expensive and it looked as though his body were exploding underneath, his energy and power pushing against the material.

"I'm Marv," he said.

"*Marv?*"

"You sound surprised."

"I . . . Yeah, I guess so." I laughed. "I don't know, I was expecting something like Ezekiel or Samson. Not Marv."

Marv laughed a laugh that encompassed his entire body. "Well, I'm sorry to disappoint." He stopped laughing but maintained a strong smile. "Come with us, Jimmy. You say that you understand what's happening, and if that's true, your place is with us, accomplishing God's work. Christ has brought you to us, follow His will and serve Him alongside us."

"Yeah." I scratched the back of my neck. "Yeah, that's nice of you, Marv, but I can't. I mean, I came here for a reason."

"Christ's work?"

"Umm . . ." I considered the question. I had always thought of it as *my* work. "Yeah. Yeah, I guess so."

Marv retained his smile but, almost imperceptibly, his expression changed. He locked his eyes onto mine and it felt as though he was rummaging through my brain for a more insightful answer than the one I had provided.

"Where exactly are you headed, Jimmy?" He sounded like a teacher speaking to a gifted student who refused to do his homework.

"Across town. I . . . Southie. Patterson Way. I . . . Southie." Jesus Christ, I thought, now he's got me *sounding* like a guilty student. "I'm going to South Boston," I said more firmly.

"All right." He slowly nodded his head. "But not tonight."

"Not tonight?" I said, as though asking permission.

"No."

"And ah, and why is that?"

"We need to rest."

"*We?*"

"You wouldn't make it there by yourself, Jimmy. Anyone moving alone through this mess is going to get pulled down. You'll spend the night with us and, if tomorrow morning you still want go to South Boston, we'll make sure you get there safely."

I tried to consider Marv's offer, but couldn't. My thoughts were constantly returning to his presence, to how perfectly *right* he seemed. His words, his posture, his face, his handshake, his suit, the way he casually but carefully held his gun, his laughter, all of it; it all fit together seamlessly.

I knew that he was right about the dangers of the city, and that the sensible thing to do would be to accept his offer of protection. But his flawlessness, the utter perfection permeating everything he did and said, made me yearn to refuse that offer.

"I don't know, Marv. I mean, I appreciate it and all, but I've been traveling for almost two months, and I'm so close . . ." I trailed off and Marv continued to stare at me as though I hadn't said a word.

Turning away from his penetrating gaze, I quickly realized that my attention had been so fully focused on Marv, that I had closed out the rest of the world. No longer transfixed, I became aware once again of the sounds emanating from every corner of the city. I heard roaring fire and shattering glass. I heard gunshots and explosions. I heard a scream that, to my ears, sounded exactly like a man having his face slit open by a razor.

Marv's companions stood silently. The fire behind them continued to erupt, its orange glow welding their silhouettes together, creating a single, solid object. Behind them, people ran in and out of view like sputtering bottle rockets, their bodies appearing as little more than flailing cloth puppets in comparison to the solid mass of flesh formed by Marv's companions. They were an impenetrable wall separating me from the violence.

Four kids and my heart still hadn't returned to its normal rhythm.

"Yeah," I said, turning back to Marv, "that sounds good."

He nodded his head without betraying the slightest trace of surprise, as if my answer had been the only possible one. He clasped his hand against my back and pushed me forward, into the center of the group.

When we left the ally, I was able to see the other men more clearly. There were nine of them, three black, the rest white. They were all in their mid-forties and dressed, like Marv, in suits.

I wanted to ask who the other men were, but the group maintained a strong silence as we moved through the anarchy and, not wanting to break the noiseless spell insulating us from the violence, I said nothing. Marv kept his eyes locked straight ahead. Each step he took was solid and confident. I could hear his breathing, deep and full, above the sounds of the surrounding melee.

We moved forward unhesitatingly, stopping only when we had arrived at our destination, a seven story brick building on Beacon Street. The glass door was shattered and, one by one, we slowly stepped through. We climbed three flights of pitch-black stairs and felt our way down a hallway. The hallway became illuminated when Marv opened a door and a splash of light spilled out. Before following him into the room, I read the brass plate on the door:

Marvin J. Davis: Attorney At Law

Personal Injury Claims

A huge fire burned in the middle of the office, contained and tended by three men who smiled at us as we entered the room. Everyone gathered around the fire and knelt in a circle. I tried to exclude myself, but Marv motioned for me to crouch next to him. I reluctantly stepped forward and lowered myself to my knees. Everyone dropped their heads and closed their eyes.

"Pray silently," Marv whispered.

I stared into the flames while the others prayed. Feeding the fire was a pile of blackened, shattered office furniture. Beneath my knee was a singed piece of paper with the words, *Writ Of Appeal* printed boldly at the top. The paper connected to others, and I followed the trail underneath the bricks, which surrounded the blaze. The flames swished and swirled, colors majestically flaring up before instantly folding into themselves and disappearing from existence. I marveled at the fire's power and wondered how the meager bricks kept it contained, stopped it from exploding and engulfing the entire room and everyone in it.

"Amen," Marv said, and was echoed by the others before rising off their knees and casually scattering across the room. Some began quiet conversations while others disappeared into a back room, emerging with food and water.

Remaining on my knees, I pulled a cigarette out from my pocket and carefully placed it between my lips. Closing my eyes, I began slowly edging my face towards the fire. The inferno became louder and my face started to sweat. I sucked dryly on the filter and blindly closed in on the heat. I had grown a beard while traveling, and could smell its singed hair. Continuing to move forward, I tasted a sudden swish of smoke. I pulled away, opening my eyes and grinning before blowing my smoke back into the fire.

I climbed off my knees and wandered into a dark corner, sliding down the wall and smoking anonymously. None of the others approached me, and I was glad for that. The fire's light made the men's faces fluid and indistinct. Nameless and faceless, they floated across my vision like flickering shades, luminous spirits occupying this reality and another simultaneously.

Only Marv seemed real. With a loaf of bread and a jar of peanut butter, he crossed the room, his presence exuding a denseness, a hyper-reality that contrasted with the surrounding phantoms. I narrowed my eyes and vainly attempted to locate the simple lawyer he had once been. He moved with such presence that if one of the other men were in his path, I wouldn't have been the least bit surprised to have seen Marv pass through him as easily as a car moves through fog.

"Take some food, Jimmy," he said, offering me his bread and peanut butter. "We have plenty. The Lord provides for His servants. Besides, bread doesn't last long, even in ice, so eat it before it gets moldy."

"Umm . . . yeah, thanks." I stuffed the bread into the jar, scooping out a thick glob of peanut butter and then jamming it all into my mouth. Marv handed me a gallon of water and I gulped a mouthful, enjoying the feeling of the food slowly oozing down my throat and into my empty stomach.

"So," Marv asked as he sat beside me, "what's in South Boston?"

"Muh fumluh." I took another drink of water and washed the remaining food down into my throat. I wished it were milk, and realized that I probably wouldn't taste milk or anything else that was highly disposable, ever again. "My family."

"And you're sure you belong there instead of here?"

"Yeah," I said, shrugging and scratching my nose. "Hey, let me ask you something, If I counted right, there's twelve of you guys. Is that intentional?"

"How do you mean?"

"You know, twelve of you, twelve apostles. Did you do that on purpose?" I thought of a theoretical thirteenth man who had begged for the security Marv's group offered and had been turned away.

"Oh, I see." Every task, no matter how mundane, was reflected, not simply in Marv's face, but in his entire being. He centered himself completely on whatever thought, action, or emotion occupied him, even if that focus was necessary only for a few seconds.

"No," he said. He smiled and his body stopped thinking and began smiling. "No, it's not intentional. It is interesting, though."

"What?"

"Well, we didn't set out to create a group of twelve men; it just turned out that way. But there's a pleasant correctness in the fact that there are twelve of us. That seems to be the way things work though, isn't it? Life forms symbols and patterns on its own accord. People who claimed that existence was a random mess were too cynical, or perhaps just too lazy, to look past the surface chaos and see the vast depths of order that lay underneath."

"Chaos theory," I said offhandedly.

"I'm sorry?"

"It's a mathematical theory. You never heard of it?"

Marv shook his head, unashamed to admit his ignorance.

"Well," I continued, "its basic premise was that there was a verifiable order to the universe. Things like air turbulence, weather patterns, even stuff like politics and the stock market follow a precise pattern. It's based on fuzzy logic and fractal mathematics. It said that stuff like traffic always follows a mathematically ordered pattern, clustering up in certain areas, freeing up in others, and that that pattern's orderly, not a random mess. You can't predict the future, because there's an almost infinite number of variables, but you can trace the past and see that events follow a precise, if complex, pattern of order."

Marv rubbed his chin.

"No big deal," I said with a shrug, "I just mentioned it because it was pretty much the same thing you were talking about. You know, unintended order and patterns and stuff."

Marv continued staring at me, but his attention wavered for a moment as a look of pain and sadness crossed his features.

"What?" I asked. "You don't like it?"

"No, it's very interesting. I was just thinking about how it was probably received. My guess would be that people used it as another excuse to disavow the existence of God."

"Why do you say that?"

"I'm sure you've seen it, Jimmy," he said while smiling sadly. "Every time science explains some aspect of our universe, that explanation is used to deny God. People have a tendency to assume that since we have the natural explanation for events, there's no longer a place for God in the universe. People don't seem willing to take the next logical step and ask who or what set such an intricate process in motion in the first place. I would guess that tendency was repeated with this. *There is order in the universe, and it is natural, thus we no longer need to create a higher power to explain that order.* You see?"

"I guess." I put down the water and lit a cigarette.

"Don't misunderstand me, Jimmy. I'm not suggesting that Christians should condemn science or bury our heads away from the natural world. If what you're saying is right, then I'd say that when order was first recognized underneath the chaos, we were seeing an aspect of God. What saddens me is that science is not objective. How we view these discoveries reflects who and what we are, and it makes me sad to think of all the people who might have used this as an excuse to push themselves farther away from God when the opportunity existed in this discovery to bring them closer."

He paused and, for a moment, his entire body became sad. In the next instant, though, it transformed, becoming eager and inquisitive. "It is an interesting idea, though. With something like traffic, it says that the patterns would always be the same?"

"Well, no. The patterns are different, but there's always an orderly pattern of some sort."

"What are the consequences for free will?"

"Well, people still have it. They can step on the gas or the break whenever they want. Free will exists, it just operates and contributes to a larger order."

"I like that." Marv smiled widely and I felt like a student who had just given his favorite teacher the perfect answer. "I like that very much. It helps us to understand the paradox of how humanity can possess free will and still exist in a world ruled by God. Take the nuclear disaster that just happened . . ."

"It *really* happened? I mean, I heard rumors, but when nothing else . . . when we didn't . . ."

"I don't know, Jimmy. I haven't heard anything official, just rumors. Still, I've heard enough of them to make me believe that it did indeed happen. The West Coast and the South were destroyed."

"I . . . Why not the rest of the country? Who did it?"

"Jimmy, if I knew, I'd tell you, but I don't have any more information than you do." We remained silent for a moment and Marv's whole body mourned the dead for several moments before he returned to our previous topic. "What I was going to say was that the destruction fulfills the Lord's Second Seal of Judgment. Whoever made the decision to attack us had free will in that choice. God didn't order them to do it, but in the course of exercising their own agendas, they were also working within the confines of God's plan."

He smiled and his face and body seemed to glow with contemplative, humble satisfaction.

"Marv, what the fuck are you still doing here?"

"What do you mean?"

"Why weren't you raptured, yanked away with the rest? The Rapture was only two months ago, and I can't believe you've given as much thought to this as you obviously have in such a short amount of time. Obviously you knew about all this before, so why are you still here?"

"Knowing and believing are two very different things," he said while gently touching his lips. "Belief and faith are even more different. Yeah, I knew about God before the Rapture. I was raised Catholic. In CCD, they used to tell us that God allowed men of faith to perform miracles." He smiled. "When I was a kid, I once prayed and then tried talking Spanish to the Puerto Ricans in my neighborhood, tried speaking in *tongues*, like the Bible said. It was just a bunch of gibberish. They thought I was making fun of them and beat me for it. As a child I was very religious, but people get older, and childhood faith falls away. Girls, school, work, family, money, simply living a life; it all distracts from God, pulls you further away from Him. I never lost my belief, but I forgot my faith.

"My wife was religious," Marv continued, "I went to church because it was important to her, but I never really listened to the priest's words. Money, upcoming cases, scheduling problems, even what was on TV, they all laid claim to my thoughts, blocking out the Lord. The priest would place the Eucharist on my tongue, my mother always told me it was a sacrilege to take it in your hand, so he'd put it on my tongue and say, *Body of Christ*, and I'd say, *Amen*, but it had become a hollow ritual. When I was child, that word was powerful. It felt like a magic, holy word, and I felt strong when I said it. Somewhere along the way, though, it had became just another word."

His eyes were full of shame, but he never turned away. In fact, he made a point of staring directly into my eyes so I could view his disgrace. "I treated Christ the way a nigger treats a whore, turning to Him when I was in need, but ignoring Him when I wasn't. He was my savior. He was tortured and murdered for me and I still treated Him like a whore. He should have been my wife, I should have opened my heart to Him, but I was blinded by *my* needs, by *my* wants. I'm still here because I *deserve* to be here."

"And your wife?"

"Susan," Marv said, his face trading its shame for bliss, "was miraculously raised to Heaven two months ago. She lives with Christ."

"And that doesn't bother you?" I asked, his bliss somehow annoying me. "To have your wife stolen while you're left behind?"

"I loved my wife," he said, his face suddenly becoming confused. "Why would I be unhappy that she was spared suffering? Better she ascend to Heaven alone than we remain in Hell together."

"Just like that, huh? No anger or resentment?"

"Towards who? Towards Susan? Towards God? Should I be angry with Susan for being good? Angry with God for creating a situation which showed me the truth about my life? Had this happened a hundred years from now, had God not ripped my wife away from me, I might never have seen the error of my ways. I might have died believing myself a decent, religious man, and awoke to find myself spending an eternity in Hell, suddenly realizing that I had spent a lifetime lying to myself. That's the purpose behind Revelations, not to punish, but to help. In the quiet of a mundane life, we've been able to lie to ourselves about who and what we really are. God's creating a situation so extreme, that that's no longer an option. Before this is over, every one of us will be faced with the truth of who we really are. And from that truth comes a choice. No, Jimmy, no anger. I serve Christ with an open heart and praise His mercy and wisdom every second of every day."

"Jesus, man, why do you got to talk like that?"

"Excuse me?"

"When you talk about this stuff, you sound as if you grew up with Moses. That's obviously not you. I mean, when you told that little fuck with the razor that you were going to blow his dick off, you had a totally different, I don't know, speech pattern or tone or something. Why can't you just talk about God normally? Why does it have to sound like you're auditioning for the Ten Commandments?"

"Does that bother you?"

"I . . . Yeah. It'd be one thing if that's the way you normally spoke, but it isn't. No one talks like that. Why can't you talk about God and still be yourself? It's like you're surrendering a piece of yourself every time you want to talk about God."

"That's *exactly* it, Jimmy. Only, I'm not just surrendering a *piece* of myself, I'm surrendering everything. Jesus, Heaven, God; these are holy subjects which demand a language of their own, a language which needs to be respected. Have you ever heard a priest trying to talk with kids about God using their own language? *Christ is the most radical dude you'll ever know. You'll never live in a crib as rightous as Heaven.* Which sounds more ridiculous?"

"Yeah, but you're making it sound stupid on purpose. There's an in-between."

"No there isn't. Not with God. God only wants the hot or the cold; he spits out the warm. That was my mistake, that was all of our mistakes. We all knew God, but we shuffled Him off into the corner of our lives. God has to be center stage. Complete acceptance of His will is the only path to salvation. There is no in-between; therein lies the path to Hell."

"*Therein*, huh?" I stubbed out my cigarette and lit another one while staring into the fire.

"Jimmy, why are you going to South Boston?"

"Already told you, I'm going to see my family."

"Why?" The tone of his question implied that he already knew the answer.

"Because they don't understand what's going on. I need to tell them what's happening so they can make the right choice. They need to be saved."

"For whose glorification? God's or your own?"

"Fuck's that supposed to mean?"

"Christ told us to abandon our families and serve only Him."

"So I should just fuck my family? Let them burn?"

"You can't save them, Jimmy." He leaned towards me. "Only Christ saves."

"Bullshit. *You* saved me tonight."

"God saved you."

"I didn't see God holding a gun."

"Then you might as well say that the gun saved you, because it was as much an instrument in my hands as I was an instrument in the Lord's. Abandon your schemes Jimmy, because if they're undertaken with a selfish heart, they'll come to naught."

"*Naught?*"

"They'll blow up in your fucking face, Jimmy. How's that?"

I laughed. "Look Marv, I'm just trying to do what I think's right."

"Yes, what *you* think is right. That's the problem, Jimmy. You're a human being, and as such, you're selfish and evil and foolish. What humans think is right, seldom is. If you really want to do what's right, accept that you have no real concept of morality. Accept that *Christ* does and hand yourself over to Him."

"Which would mean joining you guys, right?"

"Christ brought you to us. Follow His will."

"I don't own an expensive enough suit."

"We dressed respectfully when we conducted our own business, should we be ashamed for doing the same now that we are conducting the Lord's?"

"I'd throw off the whole number scheme you've got going."

He stared at me without speaking.

"What exactly is it that you do, anyway?" I asked. "Walk around with guns?"

"We go where God leads us. We pray for guidance and He provides it."

"And how exactly does that work? God's never spoken to me. He hasn't told me a damn thing. How do you know you're doing what God wants? Did you hear a voice that led you to me? Did an angel tell you to save me? How exactly does God provide you with guidance?"

"Are you asking or mocking?"

"I . . . Look, all I'm saying is, a lot of people with a lot of bad ideas have claimed to have heard the voice of God telling them what to do. Those things usually end up sounding more like, *Burn that woman over there, she's a witch*, then *Give that bum a dollar so he won't starve to death*. I'm just wondering how you're so certain that God's talking to you. How do you know that there's not a part of you guys that just always wanted to walk around the city with guns and fuck with people, and that you're not just using God as an excuse to do it?"

"Okay, firstly, you're referring to what, witch-hunts, the Crusades, the Inquisition, things of that nature?"

"Yeah, that and things like assholes who hold up signs that say stuff like, *God Hates Fags Dead*."

"All right. For one thing, don't confuse God with religion. Religion is man made, and as such, flawed. God is neither. As to how God speaks, it's . . . Well, it's subtle. I believe that it's a question of honesty. People who hate and kill in the name of Christ are, in my opinion, simply justifying the evil in their own hearts by hiding behind God. It's a shame, but those actions don't sully God, only man."

"You looked like you were willing to kill that kid tonight. Isn't that the same thing?"

"No. I was *not* prepared to shoot that boy. I was prepared to *allow* the Lord to work through me however He saw fit. I've stopped asking God to take me where *I* want to be. I allow Him to take me where *He* wants me to be.

"As to how that process works, I wish I could tell you. Can the scientist who came up with chaos theory explain why the traffic is so orderly? They can witness the order, but can they explain the forces behind it? If we can't understand how traffic works, how can we understand how the Lord works? I trust in my actions because I have opened myself up to God. We do what He desires."

"What you should do," I said, "is get your asses into hiding. World's going to become a pretty fucked-up place for Christians."

"Yeah. I heard rumors that Richard Morrison is sending troops to occupy what's left of America. He's the Antichrist, you know."

"Yeah, I know, and if those rumors are true, you guys are going to find yourselves knee-deep in shit. Why don't you get to Israel while you can? If the Bible's right, it's going to be the only safe place left for people like you."

"People like *us*? Aren't *you* one of us, Jimmy?"

I stared at Marv for several moments. His eyes were unbending. They were full of love and warmth, but it was a firm warmth, one that demanded change and acceptance to bask in their glow.

"No," I said. "No, I'm not one of you. I appreciate what you did for me and I have a lot of respect for you, but I'm not going to abandon my family."

"You can't save them, Jimmy. Place your faith in Christ and trust in Him to do what's right. If you're going to play any part in redeeming your family, it'll only happen through the Lord. Become His instrument and, if it's His will, your family will be saved."

"And what if it's *not* His will?"

"If that's the case, you have to accept it. There's nothing you can do to change it. If you try fighting it, it'll still come to pass, and you won't accomplish anything but your own damnation."

"Y'know, Marv, the only reason *we* met is because I came here to save my family. If I hadn't come here to do that, I'd still be in Michigan. If coming here to save my family is against God's will, then how can it *also* be God's will that we met?"

"You're not a lawyer, are you?" Marv asked, laughing loudly and slapping his hand down onto my shoulder.

"Uh-uh. High school teacher."

"Really?" He sounded surprised. "Well, I think you missed your calling. If I had ever argued a case against you in court, I think you'd have won. You've mastered the alchemy of law; mix enough truths together and you magically create their opposite. I don't think I could've answered your question if you hadn't already provided me with the answer yourself."

"*I* did?"

"Chaos theory. You can step on the gas, step on the break, hell you can even pull off the highway, and none of it'll affect the larger order. Like you explained, you have free will, but in the end, you cannot help but contribute to a larger order. Whatever choices you make, whatever actions you take, you are still following and contributing to God's plan. You cannot escape that fact, Jimmy. And as for God having never spoken to you to let you know what your part in that plan is, He did tonight. He's speaking to you through me. Do the right thing, Jimmy. Follow God's will."

Marv's blue eyes earnestly and imploringly pushed into mine. His all-knowing stare made me feel uncomfortable, and I turned away from it, crushing out my cigarette and staring into the fire. The other men had fallen asleep, their bodies surrounding the flame. As had happened in the alley, they once again became black silhouettes, their bodies merging with one another, becoming a thick black snake wrapping itself around the burning flame, keeping it in check. Each individual motion became a small twitch in the larger whole.

They weren't real, they weren't even human anymore.

Together, they created a powerful force, a wall separating me from the violence, a snake containing an inferno. I could acknowledge the strength created in such a union, and feel secure in its presence, protected. But it also sickened me. By surrendering themselves, they had created something powerful, but not even Marv was truly in charge of that power. They had surrendered control. They had offered it up to God, and in doing so, had become nothing but hollow puppets.

Behind them, the flame continued burning, its triangular peak growing and shrinking, splitting and wavering.

I pulled out another cigarette.

"Coffin nails," I muttered.

Jude had started me out on the habit, but it was a habit I always knew I'd allow myself to fall into. Sometimes, when I picked up Sarah from church, I'd sit on the edge of the car, waiting for her to find me with a cigarette dangling between my lips, smiling as the church-goers stared at me with unease. Sarah smoked, but never in front of people it might offend.

I tilted my head back and blew smoke up at the ceiling.

Marv was still staring at me, his hand still resting on my shoulder.

"I appreciate the offer," I told him, "but I've got to do what *I* think is right. I'm going to my family."

"All right, Jimmy." He nodded his head solemnly and removed his hand from my shoulder. "It's your decision. Get some sleep and we'll make sure you get there safely."

"I appreciate that."

He smiled grimly as he rose to his feet. "You accept and appreciate everything I offer except the one thing that really matters." He turned away and joined the others. As he crouched down, his legs and waist having already disappeared into the black snake, he quietly called my name.

"What?" I asked.

"It's warmer by the fire. Why don't you sleep over here?"

"I'm fine where I am."

"Mmm. Remember that chaos highway we were speaking of?"

"Yeah."

"If you jerk the wheel and smash into the car next to you, if you cause an accident and kill someone, it doesn't matter whether the accident conforms to a preordained pattern or not. The blood's still on your hands."

"You're not too good at hearing *no*, are you, Marv?"

"I felt it was important to point that out."

"Yeah. Thanks a lot."

He sank down into the others.

I inhaled some more smoke and flicked my cigarette over the snake and into the flames.

The corner I remained in was cold, but I slept well.

Nine

Bleached morning sunlight pushed through the windows and I awoke feeling dirty and foolish. The Twelve Apostles, already risen, were busy bustling around the room, preparing for the day's holy activities. With the uniformed sunlight replacing the extinguished fire, I saw the Apostles clearly for the first time. Their suits were dirty and wrinkled. They were wearing sneakers instead of shoes. Some were eating, using their hands to scoop cold cereal out of a box before sloppily shoving it into their mouths. One was hunched over a pile of shotguns, cleaning and loading them. Each time he pushed a shell into one of the chambers, he slid his tongue across his lips. Four were lined up outside of the bathroom, shuffling from foot to foot, impatiently waiting to empty their holy bladders.

I remained in my corner until they approached me. They asked if I was ready to go and I stared at them with a smirk.

"Are you ready to go, Jimmy?" asked Marv, who stared at me from across the room. His presence was unchanged from the night before, which stunned me. It was as if a dream had carried over into reality. The harsh sunlight was unable to strip Marv of his power and dignity as it had the others.

"Yeah," I said, feeling ashamed. "I'm ready."

The rumors were true. Earlier than anyone had expected, Richard Grant Morrison had taken over the country. Soldiers dressed in dark blue jumpsuits with an earth insignia on the right shoulder and an OWC insignia on the left, filled the streets. Most carried guns. Big guns.

Marv acted as though their presence was inconsequential, and we began moving towards South Boston.

"They got the power back on," I said, after seeing a flickering TV in a window.

"No doubt Mr. Morrison will quickly get the trains running on time, also," Marv said.

"It was just an observation."

"As was mine, Jimmy."

"Yeah. Anyway, it looks pretty safe out here, now," I said, staring at him disdainfully. "I'll be okay on my own."

"We made a promise." His voice left no room for argument.

"Fine." I suddenly wanted to be anywhere *but* with Marv and the Apostles.

OWC soldiers used bulldozers to remove the rubble from the streets, clearing paths for fire trucks and ambulances, which were racing back and forth across the city. They had already extinguished most of the fires, and those that were still burning were being fought by soldiers and civilians working together.

"You know, seriously, Marv, I appreciate what you guys have done for me, but I can make it home by myself. I'm sure you guys have got lots of important God-stuff you could be doing instead."

He ignored me and continued moving forward.

"Fucking prick," I mumbled.

The whole affair was beginning to feel like a bad one-night stand. I had been intoxicated by fear the previous night, and in that adrenaline-drunk state, had mistaken Marv and the Apostles for a beautiful beast of power. In the sober morning's light, the beautiful beast had revealed itself as a transvestite with a hairy back and bad breath.

The steely determination in Marv's walk told me that I'd never be able to persuade him to let me go home alone.

"Cocksucker."

The soldiers all spoke English when conversing with the civilians, but reverted back to their native tongues when speaking amongst themselves. A flow of thick accents and foreign languages floated through the air. As we moved, I heard snippets of French, Spanish, and Italian conversations, and smiled when I heard two soldiers arguing with each other in Scottish brogues.

The kaleidoscope of foreign languages sounded exotic and civilized, and I looked around me at the Twelve Apostles, feeling a guilty sense of embarrassment. I knew that they had saved my life the night before and, conversely, that the OWC soldiers were working for Richard Morrison who was,

146

after all, the Antichrist. Still, in the cultured atmosphere conjured by the intersection of so many foreign tongues, I couldn't deny the embarrassment I felt at being surrounded by a gang of Dirty-Harry-gun-tottin'-NRA-Republican-Shyster- Christ-freaks. While the OWC put out fires, cleaned the streets of rubble, and helped the injured, Marv and his gang walked around in their sneaker/suit combos with shotguns tossed over their shoulders.

I was beginning to seriously consider making a run for it when an OWC soldier, backed by fifteen others, halted our posse.

"Excuse me sir," a middle-aged soldier said to Marv in a British accent. "I'm afraid I cannot allow you to walk the streets with those weapons."

"My name's Marv Davis." He took a confidant step forward and offered his hand to the soldier.

"A pleasure to make your acquaintance, sir," the soldier said, accepting Marv's hand and shaking it vigorously. "My name's Richard *Davis*, if that isn't just the damnedest of coincidences. You wouldn't happen to be of British ancestry, would you?"

Marv smiled and shook his head.

"Yes, well, it's important not to make assumptions in our new Community." The soldier broke off the handshake and took a formal step back. "Well, Mr. Davis, as you have no doubt already ascertained, these lads and myself are members of the One World Community. We're here to help you get back on track. We're here to save you."

"You're here to *save* us?" Marv asked in an incredulous tone.

"Well someone has to, now don't they? Riots, murder, looting, arson; you've made a right bloody mess out of things."

The soldier and Marv focused all of their attention on each other, ignoring me.

"Back to reclaim the Colonies, wot?" I said in a horrible imitation of a British accent.

"Yes. Right." A look of distaste crept across the soldier's face. "At any rate," he said, returning his attention to Marv, "one of our first priorities is the confiscation of all illegal firearms, so at this point, I'm going to have to ask that you and your companions surrender your weapons."

"Jeez, the NRA was right all along, give up your weapons and the king of England comes back and starts pushing you around again."

"Quiet, Jimmy," Marv said before stepping up to the soldier. "Mr. Davis, I happen to be a practicing attorney-at-law, and I can assure you that our possession of shotguns violates no existing legal statutes."

"Humph," the soldier grunted. "No doubt it's not illegal in America to walk the streets brandishing shotguns. You Yanks and your obsession with firearms. Last year, there were less than one hundred shooting fatalities in all of England. America surpassed that number in a week. Right lot of good your *right to bear* arms did you."

"You got to understand, your lordship," I said, stepping up to the soldier, my arm pressing against Marv's, "after we kicked your faggot king out of here, we got kind of attached to our weapons."

"Shut up, Jimmy," Marv said.

The soldier still refused to acknowledge me.

"Hey Guv'ner!"

"Jimmy, shut up."

"Fuck you, Marv. Hey limey, I'm talking to you!"

The soldier slowly turned and faced me.

"The reason no one dies of gunshot wounds in England is because you're a bunch of fucking faggots. Too chicken-shit to pull a trigger and too fucking incompetent to hit the side of a barn when you do, ya tea-drinking fairy."

"Regardless," the soldier said in a drawn-out, phlegmy voice, "the laws you cite, *Mr. Davis*, are void. Your country has become a member of the OWC, and as such, is subject to its laws and regulations. So once again, please relinquish your weapons."

"Fine." Marv smiled gently. "Hand them over, guys."

The Apostles hesitated.

"Well, we're hardly going to shoot it out with them, are we?"

"Fucking faggots," I mumbled, and then suddenly realizing that I could use the confusion to slip away from Marv and the rest of the Apostles, I made a quiet exit.

I crossed the city without incident and, within three hours, was standing on Patterson Way, staring at the house I grew up in. It looked old and fragile, its dark green color having deteriorated into a softer shade of lime. Scraps of faded paint pulled away from the walls, revealing the naked wood underneath. I stepped onto the stairs and wrapped my hand around the wooden banister. It was waterlogged and weak and I knew that if I tightened my grip, the plywood would tear. Easing my hand off the fragile timber, I saw that the sharp corners of the banister had become rounded where my fingers had grasped.

Behind me, a van with speakers attached to its top slowly rolled down the street, blaring a message: "It is now 6:47 PM, curfew will commence in thirteen minutes. Only authorized citizens of the One World Community will be allowed outdoors between 7:00 PM and 7:00 AM. If you have access to a television, please turn it on at 7:30 PM for information and an important announcement."

As the van continued its slow drive, repeating the same announcement on an endless loop, I imagined a young woman sitting inside the van, reading the same message over and over again, each time managing to sound just a little less human, each time managing to eliminate a bit more personality from her voice.

The thought depressed me and I turned back towards the front door. Rather than decrepit, the house suddenly appeared warm and inviting, and I eagerly rang the doorbell. When no one responded, I pulled out my keys and hoped they hadn't changed the locks. The key turned easily and I pushed open the door and stepped inside, inhaling deeply and then smiling. The smell was something I could never attach to any particular origin, but it was the fragrance of home, and that was enough. I glanced around and saw that the same tacky, yellow-striped wallpaper that had always cursed our entrance hall still stood. To my left was the wooden desk which, in thirty some-odd years, had never been used for anything except piling junk on top of. Under my feet lay the violet welcome mat, whose *E* and *O* had been erased twenty years earlier.

A wave of happiness washed across me, and I wondered why I had never appreciated the fact that I had such a solid memory to which I could return, why I had allowed three years to pass without indulging myself in the warmth and nostalgia of home.

I stepped into the living room and heard the loud clack of a shotgun. Two cold, perfectly round barrels pressed roughly and snugly into my neck.

"Keep your hands where I can see `em, punk," a haggard voice growled. "Now turn your ass around and get the hell out of here before I redecorate the wallpaper with your so-called brains."

"Hi Dad."

My father was a retired police officer who had become a cop in the late fifties, joining the force along with the last wave of pre-Miranda police to naturally assume that a criminal's rights both could and *should* be ignored. Beating a

149

confession out of a suspect, tossing a rapist off a roof, making sure that the Niggers kept to their side of town; that was the police force that my father had joined and that was the man that he had become. He was tough and he was fair and he was brutal. He was old school.

Now he was just *old*.

In three years he had aged twenty. His once broad shoulders hunched into a heavy slump, a slump so low that it appeared as if his very bone structure had been altered. He had always stood a good two inches taller than I had, but his newly acquired posture shrank him, forcing his head to hover three inches lower than mine. His clothing, always a perfect synthesis of flesh and cloth, was now a tent in which his frail body hid. His hair, gray and red when I had last seen him, had turned completely white. Not a stately, vibrant white, but a color that existed only because all other colors had abandoned him.

His face was even worse. It appeared as if his skull had shrunk, allowing the excess skin to accumulate underneath his eyes, where it drooped listlessly. His lips, the first feature on his face to reflect his moods, either in a sly grin or a ferocious snarl, had grown rubbery and lifeless. His blue eyes, once shallow and certain, had faded into a gray depth, leaving his appearance vacant and drained.

"What the hell are you doing here?" he asked, as he dropped the gun and wandered across the room.

I turned away from the unrecognizable old man standing in front of me, my awkward motions making it obvious that I was looking at nothing except away from him.

Noticing my unease, Dad looked away and leaned his gun against the wall before slowly and carefully lowering himself into his recliner. "Well," he muttered, "sit down. Since you're here, you can watch this Republican bastard give his speech. Prick probably got the power running again just so he'd have an audience."

"Yeah." I wandered next to his chair. "Um, where's Ma?"

He stared at the blank TV and ignored my question.

"Dad?"

"What?"

"Where's Ma?"

"Gone."

"What do mean, *gone*? Gone where?"

His face quivered and began twisting into itself. His movements seemed delayed and uncertain.

As a child, I instantly knew if my father was happy or angry, his tight features immediately reflecting his disposition. Now, it took several seconds for his doughy face to rearrange itself. He frowned deeply and slowly, his excess flesh curling into his wrinkles. Once his features had finally set themselves, he turned towards me.

"I don't know, and I don't care," he said. "The Moon, Mars, Outer Mongolia. The *Celestine* faggots, or whatever the hell they were, took her. How the hell am *I* supposed to know where she is?"

"She's *gone*?"

"Well, I'll tell you where she's not." He leaned over the arm of his chair, pushing his body towards me with obvious difficulty. "She's not *here*. She's not with me, that's for goddamn sure." He dropped back into his seat and slouched down, nodding his head up and down, emphatically agreeing with what he had just said.

"Jesus." I took a deep breath and ran my hands over my face.

"Yeah, *He* ain't here either."

It had never occurred to me that mother could have been among the raptured. My father had always been the nexus of the family, the undisputed dictator. I knew that he would never be raptured and from there, just naturally assumed that my mother would follow his lead, remaining earthbound and in need of salvation. Over the years, Sarah had become close with my mother, speaking with her more frequently than I ever did, and I wondered if she had anything to do with my mother's unexpected conversion.

A part of me admired Ma for pushing out on her own and accepting salvation without Dad's okay, but another part was annoyed, angry that Sarah had interfered in a family dynamic that had remained constant for more than thirty years. She should have told me that what I had assumed to be nothing more than friendly, casual chit-chat had actually been a mission of conversion. What's more, if my mother had accepted the Bible as truth, she should have included my father in the equation, rather than ignoring him and leaving us behind while she and Sarah skipped off to Heaven.

"Fuckers," I mumbled, and instantly felt guilty.

I loved Sarah and Ma, and they were both in Heaven.

Once again, I tried to smile.

"What the hell are you grinning at, you jackass? I tell you that your mother disappears and you think that's funny?"

"She's in Heaven, Dad."

"Yeah, *she's in Heaven.*" He sneered and sputtered his lips. "She don't have to put up with me anymore, right? That'll make anyplace look like Heaven. *I'm* the son of a bitch, right?"

"No, I mean the real Heaven. Jesus and angels. I mean . . ."

"Yeah, yeah, I know what you mean, smart guy," he said, while waving his hands at me to be quiet. "I might not've had anyone give me fifty-thousand dollars so I could go to college and learn how much better I am than everyone, but I'm still not as stupid as you and your mother seem to think I am."

"I don't think you're . . ."

"Just sit down and shut up, huh?" He shifted his body away from me and turned on the TV. "I want to watch this speech, if that's okay with you."

"Dad, we have to talk."

"I'm watching this," he said, motioning towards the static filled screen."

"This is important."

"Mister, you haven't set foot in this house for God knows how many years," he said, turning towards me. The excess flesh on his face relocated to his forehead, looming over his eyes in thick waves of angry wrinkles. "Don't think that you're just gonna waltz in here like the queen while we all hold our breath waiting to hear how important you are. If you're thinking you're gonna be waited on hand and foot, you've come to the wrong house, pal. Your mother ain't here anymore."

"That's not what I'm saying, Dad. What the fuck?"

"Hey! You keep it on the streets, pal!"

"I don't . . . Why can't we just . . .?" I shook my head. "Fine, let's watch TV."

"Thanks for your permission."

"Yeah." I pulled a chair out from the corner and placed it next to my father's recliner. He knew I was looking at him and his features assumed an exaggerated appearance of indifference.

We sat silently for several minutes until the screen changed from white to black. I assumed that the darkness was going to give way to an office or a podium, and was surprised when an unassuming man calmly walked into the center of the black. There were no props or background, the darkness ensuring that all attention would remain focused squarely on one single figure.

He was a man in his early forties with dark black hair, slightly graying at the temples. He appeared fit and trim, though not muscular. His face was open and inviting, his voice serious, but possessing a slight undertow of self-effacement. He was British, but I could detect only the faintest accent in his voice. Everything about his presence was reassuring and pleasant. His name was Sir Richard Grant Morrison. He was the Antichrist.

"Good evening. Some of you folks watching this broadcast probably recognize me. Most, I'm sure, do not. My own father wouldn't know who I was if not for the fact that I happen to be his only son. He wouldn't have learned about me through the papers or the television, because he stopped reading the papers and watching the news years ago. Found it too damn depressing, and frankly, I don't blame him.

"So, for those of you who don't follow the news and don't happen to be my father, allow me to introduce myself. My name is Richard Grant Morrison. I was formerly the elected chairman of the United European Community. I was the first individual to hold that office and I will be the *final* person to do so, for, in response to the monumental events of the past two months, I have dissolved the UEA and, in its place, formed the One World Community.

"The One World Community is not an alliance of nations, but rather, its opposite. It is, I hope, the first step towards doing away with the outdated and inherently destructive notion of the nation-state. It is an organization that will dissolve the artificial boundaries we have created, both as nations and as human beings. It is an attempt to unite our planet under one banner, so that we might solve our problems as a community, rather than working in opposition. I'm speaking to you now, because it is my intense hope that each and every one of you will join me in building this new community.

"But, before I delve into the nuts and bolts of the future, I'm sure that most of you are more concerned with the present and the immediate past. We have just experienced the most traumatic period in our planet's history. Rumor and innuendo have been your only sources of information, so allow me to explain what's really been happening. Following this, a much more detailed explanation will be broadcast, but for now, allow me to answer at least some of your questions.

"In the early morning of January first, approximately one-and-a-half billion humans disappeared from the planet. Beings we have come to refer to as the Celestine Prophets communicated with each and every one of us telepathically, claiming to have been responsible for the abductions. They brought us an important message, warning us of the perils of what would happen to our species if we continued clinging to our hatred and our pettiness. Unfortunately, some people did not heed that message.

"Immediately following the abduction, former hard-line communists formed an alliance with the Russian army and staged a coup; overthrowing Russia's democratically elected government. In your own country, with the President, Vice-President, and many other members of the government among the abducted, civil war and chaos erupted. Texas attempted to break away from the Union while California and several southern states exploded in racial violence. Your elected officials squabbled amongst themselves trying to decide who would lead, and while they argued, your country fell to pieces. In South America, governments were formed and overthrown on a weekly basis. Tribal genocide has plagued the continent of Africa. The Arab League maintained an internal order by imposing swift and brutal martial law. Only the United European Community, with myself as its elected head, maintained a humane democratic order.

"In forming the United European Community, a coalition of ten European nations, we managed to pull together in this time of crisis. We chose love instead of hate, and because of that, we survived. It was, however, a bitter success, for while we flourished, people outside of our community suffered and died.

"By including only ten nations in our community, we had succeeded only in forming another, larger nation, one that would doubtlessly be at odds with other nations sooner or later. The success of our community, I concluded, would only be complete when humanity in its entirety was included within it. What was needed, was a nation that included *all* nations.

"Accordingly, I disbanded the UEC and founded the One World Community. Israel, which was on the brink of total annihilation as the Arab League threatened invasion, was the first to join. Canada soon followed, as did India. China, which closed its boarders to the outside world immediately following the disappearances, has not responded to our offer.

"Russia rejected our invitation and, instead, allied themselves with the Arab League, which also rejected our call for unity and declared an Islamic Jihad against the West. Nine days after the Russo/Arabic alliance was formed, Russia swooped down from the North in an attempt to destroy Israel. The reasons for the attack are unclear, although it's possible that such an attack was a prerequisite for joining the Arab League. While invading Israel, Russia simultaneously commenced a nuclear attack against the United States of America. The reasons for this attack are even more baffling than its aggression towards Israel, although the possibility exists that Russia feared eventual retaliation for its attack against Israel, a nation strongly supported by America, and felt it best to destroy the United States while your country was vulnerable due to its internal chaos.

"With a heavy heart, I commenced a full-scale nuclear assault against Russia. Their nation has been completely destroyed. Fortunately, when Russia attacked your country, they used only third-generation nuclear weapons, or *mini-nukes*. These weapons are much more contained than second-generation thermonuclear weapons and that, combined with our swift action, spared your country from total destruction. Still, the West Coast and southern US has been completely destroyed, and much of the Midwest is contaminated due to radiation. Only the Northeast appears to be unaffected by the devastation.

"In addition to the nuclear assault, I dispatched soldiers to Israel to aid in their defense against the invading Russian army. OWC soldiers fought side by side with Israeli soldiers and prevailed despite incredible odds. Mother Nature lent a helping hand when earthquakes ripped across much of the country, cutting off Russian supply lines and decimating much of their army. It was a truly miraculous event; one, which I suspect, was instigated by the Celestine Prophets.

"In the wake of nuclear destruction, your country and others disintegrated into a violent state of anarchy. In response, I have dispatched OWC troops to Africa, Latin America, and the United States, in an attempt to halt the appalling violence and begin distributing much needed food and medical supplies.

"I am standing in front of you today to tell you that it is essential in this time of crisis that we work together as a community. I've dispatched soldiers to control the violence, medical personnel to tend to your wounded, and engineers to help rebuild your infrastructure, but they cannot do it alone. If you wish to be saved, you must save yourselves. You, all of you, must make a choice. Will you set aside your prejudice and indifference and help me build something better? Are you willing to embrace a vibrant new world or will you cling to the old one, perishing along with it? The consequences of these choices are clear: we shall change or we shall die.

"I've made my decision and I hope that you will follow me. And when I say *you*, let me be very clear about who I mean. I want *everyone*. I want white people, brown people, red people, yellow people, black people, and, hell, if there's any green people out there, I want you, too. If you're heterosexual I want you, if you're homosexual I want you, if you're bisexual I want you, and if you're asexual I want you. If you're Christian I want you, if you're Jewish I want you, if you're Hindu I want you, if you're Buddhist I want you, and if you're Muslim I want you. I want the atheists and the agnostics. I want the men and the women. I want the children and the babies. If I've left anyone out, I apologize, because I want you, too. *I want you all.*

"If you do choose to become a citizen in our Community, you'll notice a great many changes in your life. First amongst them, is a tiny mark just as you see here on my right hand. This is an identification implantation. It's a microchip implanted under the skin. It identifies me as Richard Grant Morrison and as a citizen in the OWC. You'll receive one yourself when you join our

Community. They're painless to receive and, if you look real hard, you'll notice them on the soldiers helping to rebuild your country.

"Now, I understand that America has a long, proud history of freedom, and that such a history might make some of you wary about accepting the implantation, so allow me to explain its purpose. In the past two months, more than a billion people have disappeared from the planet. The nuclear conflict, starvation, war, anarchy, and natural disasters have claimed the lives of hundreds of millions more. Before we can move into the future, we must mourn the past. This system will help us determine who is alive and who is not. We can reunite relatives and inform others of the death of loved ones, allowing them the opportunity to mourn their loss.

"Another function of the implantation is to aid in the proper rationing of food and supplies. Money, like nationality, is a concept whose time has passed. No longer will three percent of the population live like royalty while the other ninety-seven percent struggle just to survive. We shall see to it that every person receives food, medical care, and shelter. The implantation works like a bar code, and can be read by a scanner gun, which you've doubtlessly seen a hundred times in your local grocery store. This system will ensure that everyone receives the proper amount of food and supplies. No longer will a select few be permitted to gorge themselves at the expense of the starving multitude.

"I was the first to receive an identification implantation and, already, nearly three quarters of the citizens living in the former UEC have received them. As we speak, registration centers are being set up in your local community. The sooner you register, the sooner we can begin distributing food and providing you with information on missing loved ones.

"These are our goals for the immediate future, restoring order and providing all of you with the basic necessities. Once we have accomplished these modest goals, we will begin expanding our efforts into higher education and spiritual growth, so that we might fulfill our potential, a potential the Celestine Prophets assured us is within our grasp.

"That, however, is the future, and as the past two months have shown us, the future is by no means guaranteed. To achieve it, we will have to work together. We need to set aside our differences and join together as one world, as one Community. We have pushed our species to the brink of oblivion, now we must pull back.

"The Celestine Prophets told us that the key to salvation exists within each and every one of us. Working together, we can locate that key and unlock our perfection. We are standing at a crossroad. One path leads to extinction, the other to salvatrion. Choose wisely. Follow me, and together, we shall create for ourselves a paradise.

"Thank you."

"**S**tupid limey son of a bitch," my father mumbled as he turned off the TV. "How stupid does he think we are?"

"What do you mean?" I asked, indifferent to the answer.

"All of it," he said, turning towards me. His face seemed to have regained some of the energy and life it had been missing. "There's no way that all of that crap about Russia and Israel is true."

"What are you talking about?"

"Let me tell you something, pal, I learned more in my first year on the streets than you could learn in thirty years of college. I know when some fucking skell's lying to me."

His use of the word *fuck* make me wince. I had never heard him swear like that. I was fairly certain that he swore a blue streak when he was working, but he had never done so in the house, not in my mother's home. Our family had always possessed very strict rules when it came to the use of profanity. My mother never swore, my brother and I were permitted the occasional *hell* or *damn*, and my father was allowed *hell* and *damn* for general use and *bastard* and *son of a bitch* when talking about Republicans. *Shit, fuck*, and the rest of the baddies were outright banned.

We're working class, he used to say, *not white trash.*

Hearing him say *fuck* made me realize just how far he had fallen since I had last seen him.

"You see, Jim," he continued, "his story doesn't add up."

"Makes sense to me."

"That's because you weren't listening." He smiled and, for the first time since returning home, I saw a bit of warmth in his eyes. "Okay, why would Russia invade Israel?"

"I don't know, Dad. Who cares?"

"Well think about it, for Christ's sake! We spent fifty thousand dollars so you could think, didn't we?"

"I . . . Okay, fine. I don't know, what did Morrison say? Russia invaded Israel as some kind of pre-condition for joining the Arab League, right?"

"Right. Now it makes sense that Russia wouldn't want to join Morrison's One World thing, because Russia's always been wary of the West.

They hated it when NATO included some of its former satellite states in its alliance, and they'd see the OWC as just another attempt by the West to dominate the world. But they'd also realize that something like that would be a huge world power, and that they'd need to form an equally powerful alliance of their own. So, they ask to join the Arabs, and the towel-heads use it as leverage to force the Commies into attacking Israel and wiping out the Jews."

"Dad," I said impatiently, "this is exactly what Morrison said."

"Okay, okay, but why would Russia nuke America? If they were really worried, why not attack Europe? They're the real threat. And if they were going to attack us, why nuke the West Coast? Why the South? Washington, New York, and Boston would have been the first places to hit, where all the political and financial power's located. And that crap about mini-nukes? Russia never developed third-generation nuclear weapons. They've spent the past fifteen years disarming, not developing. America and Europe were the only countries who had that technology. It doesn't add up."

"Fine, it didn't happen exactly like Morrison said. It still happened, so who cares about the details?"

"You don't care who destroyed your own country? Why don't you try using your brains for once instead of your mouth? I'll bet you five dollars that Morrison told the Russians that he wouldn't interfere with whatever they did to Israel just so long as they didn't interfere with what he did to America. So Russia invades Israel and Morrison nukes America. Strategically, destroying the West Coast and South instead of the East Coast doesn't make any sense, but what it did do was get rid of the country's most troublesome areas. California and the South with the race riots, and Texas with those redneck assholes trying to start their own country. It softened us up and made the country manageable, eager for us to let Morrison in."

"If that's true, why would he turn around and destroy Russia when he had a deal with them?"

"I think this idiot really believes this One World crap he's spouting. I think he wants to take over the world. He knows Russia won't go along with it, so he lets them distract themselves with Israel and then, when they're not looking, jabs the knife in their back. With them out of the picture and America prepped to think of Morrison as their savior, all that's left to worry about is China and the Arabs."

He stared at me with a satisfied, expectant smile.

"Whatever," I said, and shrugged indifferently.

His smile disappeared and he leaned back down into his chair and began staring at the blank TV once again.

"Where's your wife?" he asked, after several minutes.

"Gone. Outer Mongolia."

"Oh. I'm sorry to hear that. She was a good woman."

"Yeah? I never heard you say anything like that when she was here."

"When the hell *was* she ever here? When were either of you here? You went to college and that was it, buddy, you were gone. How many years has it been since you've graced this house with your presence? Four? Five?"

"Three years, Dad. Three."

"Oh, *three* years! My mistake, you're the perfect son, a super guy. Only *three* years, well, I apologize."

"Jesus Christ, Dad, I had a wife and a job. I lived a thousand miles away, I couldn't just pop in for the weekend."

"Yeah, yeah, you had a job and a wife. You also had a mother who needed you. No one forced you to move a thousand miles away, pal, that was your call. You could have lived your life and still shown some respect for your family. I didn't care for me, but what about your mother? She needed you and you could have cared less. You had to go and be a big shot, the big college man."

"Hey, did you send me to Harvard and I'm forgetting about it? I am so fucking sick of this blue-collar bullshit. I was a high school teacher, not a corporate lawyer. And I don't remember you *ever* coming to visit us in Michigan. And as to why I didn't come home more, well, I can't imaging why I wouldn't want to spend more time in this house, what with the way you spread your fucking sunshine around."

"Watch your mouth! You keep it on the fucking streets!"

"Yeah, I'm a big college snob. *You're* the one who insisted I go to college. *You're* the one who said you'd kick my ass if I ever brought home anything less than a *B*. And you know what, Dad, I worked for the state the same as you, and probably got paid less for it."

"I'm not talking about money!" He struggled out of his chair and hobbled towards me, his face red with anger. "I'm talking about respect, you son of a bitch! I'm talking about obligation and family. I'm talking about loyalty! After Scotty died, you were all your mother had left, and you turned your back on her!"

"I didn't turn my back on her. I lived my life. I never heard Ma complain, she said I should do what made me happy."

"You could have slit her throat and she'd have told you how proud she was of you for handling the knife so well, that don't make it right! I raised you to have a sense of loyalty. You pissed on that, pissed on your family." He turned away and wandered back to his chair. "Should've kept a better eye on your little brother, too."

"*I* should have?"

"You were his brother!"

"You were his father! Where the hell were you?"

"I was right here!" He slammed his arms down on the chair. "For forty-two years, I was right here! I took care of my family! Where were you?"

"Oh fuck this. I don't have to listen to this bullshit."

"You're goddamn right you don't, you know where the door is, so why don't you get the hell out of here? It's already been a whole hour, so I'm sure you're burning to get back to your big important life. Go on and get out of here, you little shit. I didn't ask you to come."

"No, but I came anyway. You want to know why?"

"Yeah, sure. That and a turd oughtta fill a toilet."

"I came here to save you."

"To save me? *You're* going to save me?" His voice oozed contempt. "From what?"

"From Hell, Dad, from Hell."

"From . . .? Get out, Jim, get the hell out of my house."

"You want me gone? Fine, FUCK YOU!"

"Yeah, yeah, don't let the door slam you in the ass. Grace me with your presence in another three years if you're not too busy."

I stormed out of the living room and out onto the porch, hesitating as I stepped down onto the first stair. I lit a cigarette and smoked it. After smoking three more, I went back inside.

Dad hadn't moved, he was still sitting in his chair, angrily staring at nothing. I took a deep breath and walked towards him. Crouching down next to his chair, I looked into his red, haggard face. His breathing was loud and raspy. I reached my hand towards him, but at the last moment, redirected it, placing it on the back of his chair.

"No, Dad," I said quietly, "not this time. This is too important. I don't know why it always has to be like this, but it can't be, not this time. Look I'm sorry if . . . Well, I don't know what I'm sorry for, but . . ." I shook my head and ran my hands over my face while taking a deep breath. "Okay, I don't how to say this, so I'm just going to say it: I know how you feel about God and religion, I know you don't believe in any of that anymore, but . . ."

"Just go, Jim." His voice was quieter than his breathing.

"You went to parochial school, Dad, I know you read the Bible. That's what's happening. It's Revelations. The Rapture, all the deaths, the false hope for peace, it's all in the Bible. This is God. Morrison's the Antichrist. There's less than seven years left."

"Enough, Jim."

"That implantation Morrison talked about, that's the 666 of the Bible. You can't buy or sell without it, and if you get it, you go to Hell. Forever."

"Jim . . ."

"He'll start going after Christians soon. We have to get to Israel while we can, it's going to be the only safe place left. We have to accept Christ. Mom and Sarah, . . ."

"Enough."

" . . . they're in Heaven. Scotty, too. We can be with them forever. We can all be happy."

"ENOUGH! SHUT UP!"

"WHY GODDAMNIT? WHY DOES IT ALWAYS HAVE TO BE LIKE THIS? WHY CAN'T WE JUST TALK? I'M YOUR SON, FOR CHRIST'S SAKE, I'M YOUR SON!"

"Yeah." He jutted out his chin. "Yeah, you're my son. That and a nickel'll get you a cup of coffee. Go let the dog in."

"What?"

"Molly. She's out back barking. Go let her in."

"Dad, we have to talk."

"I'm done talking. The world's over, your mother's in Heaven, some limey Republican's the Antichrist, and you're my son. See how good I listened? Now go let the fucking dog in."

My father playfully pushed his face into the chocolate retriever's, warmly rubbing his hands behind her floppy ears.

"That's a good dog, isn't it?" he cooed. "Yes she is, she is a good dog. Molly's a good girl."

The dog whipped her tail back and forth while the old man slapped his hand up against her ribs. Molly squirmed with delight. Dad reached into his pocket and pulled out a treat, placing it on top of Molly's nose.

"Leave it. Leave it," he said with mock severity.

Molly remained completely still.

"Get it," Dad yelled, at which point Molly jerked her nose into the air and snapped the treat into her mouth.

"Good dog! Good girl!"

I remained in the kitchen doorway and watched silently for twenty minutes while my father played with the dog.

"You want to know why you're wasting your time?" he asked without turning away from the dog. "You want to know why you don't have to worry about saving me from Morrison?" His voice was less harsh than it had been.

"Okay." My voice was weak and exhausted.

"You remember Tim O'Reilly?"

"Kind of. He was your partner, right? The guy who stayed with us that summer when his wife threw him out?"

"Yeah." Molly flipped over onto her back and squirmed as my father scratched her belly. "Anyway, you remember back in, oh Jesus, I guess it would have been in the late sixties, early seventies? Back when I was doing night tours?"

"No, I don't remember that, Dad. Probably because I either wasn't born or was too busy shitting in my diapers."

"Don't be a smart-ass, Jim, just say you don't remember. Anyway, me and Tim were doing night tours down in the North End. Heroin was making its first big push."

"Jesus Christ, Dad, does this have anything to do with what I was talking about?"

"If you'd shut your mouth and listen, you might find out."

"I'm listening, I just don't see . . ."

"Yeah, you don't see because you don't listen. You don't listen to anybody but yourself, pal, and you never have. Now, do you want to hear this or don't you?"

"Yeah."

"Because if you just want to be a smart-ass, you can take it out onto the street, understand?"

"I want to hear it, Dad, okay? Jesus Christ."

He frowned at me and then turned his attention back to Molly. He slipped his hand between her teeth and she gently clamped down, allowing him to shake her head back and forth. She growled playfully and a smile replaced my father's frown.

"Like I was saying, heroin was starting to make its first big push, but it was regulated, because back then, the Italians controlled everything. The Wops ran it all, and if someone wanted to deal, they had to get permission. Even the Irish had to get permission to operate, and back then the Micks were crazy bastards. Nowadays, you see Irish kids walking around talking a big game and dressing the part, but they're all show. Back then, the Irish were like the Niggers are today, dirt poor and don't give a shit about anything or anybody. And even the Irish weren't crazy enough to go up against the Italians. They operated out of Southie, and they still had to get permission. That's how strong the Italians were back then; they made the Irish ask permission to operate in their own fucking neighborhood.

"I'll tell you, Jim," he said, laughing and shaking his head, "it was a different time back then. People followed the rules. I grew up in Roxbury, and my mother walked five blocks every night to buy groceries. She was never touched. Nowadays, some nigger'd slash her throat before she made it halfway down the stairs."

He sighed and sent Molly into the corner. The dog obeyed and my father sat up in his chair, his slump less severe.

"Anyway, the Guineas're finally letting the drugs into the neighborhoods. They kept them out for a long time, but there was too much money to be made in it. But it was orderly. Respectful.

"Then, from out of nowhere, this colored kid starts moving major amounts of heroin. Lionel Dershowitz. We called him the Colored Kike. We didn't even have a sheet on this kid because he'd come outta Harlem, and back then, cops didn't trade information. We didn't even know what the little spade looked like, and all of a sudden he's a major player.

"We couldn't figure it out at first, because the Italians never did business with the Niggers. It took us a little while to realize that the Colored Kike never *got* permission. That's how he became so big so quick. He brought his crew up from New York and just started dealing without ever getting permission. What's more, he's dealing in other people's territory, dealing to kids, he's even dealing in the North End, right in the Italians' own neighborhood.

"This kind of shit was unheard of back then. Like I said, even the Micks had to get permission to operate in Southie, and then this fucking nigger comes along and starts dealing in the Guineas' own fucking neighborhood." He laughed and ran his fingers over his smile. "Kid had balls, I'll say that for him.

"Obviously the Italians are pissed, but they don't know any more about this kid than we do. They can't whack him, because they can't find him. So they put out the word that they want a sit-down with him, probably planning to offer him some pathetic slice, knowing he'll refuse, but at least then they'll know what he looks like and can whack him. Lionel agrees to the meeting, but ends up turning the whole thing into a fucking bloodbath. Seven guineas and two niggers wind up dead. After he killed 'em, Lionel cut off their heads and balls. He waited until after the funeral, so they couldn't have open caskets. Then he started sending the heads and nuts back to the families. One head at a time, one ball at a time. Kid was an animal, a real fucking savage.

"Of course, this starts a war, and bodies, mostly Italian, are turning up left and right. In the middle of all this, me and Tim are walking a beat. Me, I could give a shit how many of the fucking humps get whacked. I'm half hoping they end up wiping each other out. We just keep doing our job; we see a piece of shit on the street, we roust 'em. Mostly, we're picking up colored guys, because back then, if you saw a nigger in the North End, you knew he was up to something he shouldn't be. The other thing was, the Italians aren't out on the streets anymore. They're holed up, half trying to figure out how to handle this crazy motherfucker, and half just plain hiding.

"See, they were still playing by the old rules. They don't want to whack someone in public and they don't want any innocent bystanders getting hurt. They're not choir boys, they just know what'll bring down the heat, and what's bad for business. But Lionel and his boys, they don't give a shit. If one of 'em saw a mobbed-up guinea on a school bus, they'd have blown up the whole fucking bus just to get to him. It's all standard stuff nowadays, but back then, nobody would have dreamed of shooting into a crowd of civilians. Lionel and his boys were something new, and they scared the shit out of the Italians.

"So, what with the Italians in hiding and the Niggers being so obvious, that's mostly who me and Tim rousted. After a while, Lionel assumes we're on the pad, and starts putting feelers out to me and Tim, trying to get us to switch-up. Every time we arrest a nigger, the first thing out of his mouth is an offer from Lionel: *Lionel'll make your lives easier; Lionel'll double what the Wops are giving you; Lionel'll spring for a hotel room to sleep your shifts off and even toss in a couple of broads with the room.*" My father shook his head disapprovingly. "No class, that Lionel. Balls as big as the Twin Towers, but no fucking class.

"Me and Tim, we'd nod our head politely while they're making their offers and then give 'em a good fucking beating once we got 'em back to the station. Goes on that way for a couple of months. Lionel sends his boys in with offers; we send 'em home with a few less teeth. This starts pissing Lionel off, and, maybe three months after Lionel whacked those first seven Italians, I go down to the Diamond Cafe, for breakfast, like I did every Sunday. The place is empty except for a skinny little nigger sitting in a booth. He's a tiny little shit, and he's smiling at me like he's sitting on top of a pile of fried chicken and watermelons . . ."

"Jesus Christ, Dad," I groaned. "Would it be possible for you to tell the story without sounding like the biggest racist in the world?"

"Who's racist? After Tim retired, I partnered with Chris Tenson for four years. He's a colored guy and was a hell of a partner. We never had no problem between us."

"Yeah, but you . . ."

"They're just words, Jim. Now shut up, will you? I'm trying to tell a story here. Okay, so I'm standing there looking at this fucking nigger . . ."

"Dad!"

"Quit being such a skirt, Jim. So, I'm staring at this nigger and he's staring back, giving me a big, shit-eating grin. I figure he's one of Lionel's mules come to make me another offer and lose a few more teeth. I slide into the booth and he's still grinning from ear to ear. He's grinning so wide, that I can see his gums. After a minute, though, I look past his grin, look into his eyes, and I realize that this ain't one of Lionel's mules. It's the Colored Kike himself. His eyes are happy and crazy and totally fucked-up. I stare into his eyes and I think, *Yeah, that's what you'd have to have in your eyes to be able to scare the Italians.*

"He knows I know who he is, so he gets right to the point. He tells me that if I leave his people alone, he'll give me twenty-five thousand in cash. I say no. He nods calmly, but he's still got that look in his eyes, and he leans over the table and in a real soft voice, tells me that if I ever arrest one of his people again, he'll show up at my house while I'm working and hack my family's heads off. And he names you too, just to let me know he's not blowing smoke up my ass. *Little baby James*, he says, *and your beautiful pregnant wife, Sharon.*

"I nod my head and step out of the booth. Lionel stays seated and keeps grinning. I tell him we understand each other and offer him my hand. When he takes it, I break his arm in four different places."

He took a deep breath and appeared lost in the memories. After a minute, he called Molly back over and began patting her.

"So, what happened?" I asked. "You broke his arm and he just left us alone?"

"Nah. I broke his arm because he pissed me off. His body turned up in the river about a week later. The Guineas had finally caught up to him. You could tell they brought in the experts. His balls were crushed so badly that they were almost liquid, his dick was cut off and stuffed up his ass, and his teeth were all knocked out. He had burns and bruises all over his body and his left arm was almost completely hacked off. They even scalped him. They must've spent days working him over, and I'll tell you this, when they found his sorry fucking corpse, he wasn't grinning any more.

"He had given the Italians a good scare, but it was only a matter of time before they caught up to him."

"And you knew that? You knew they'd get to Lionel before he got to us?"

"No. No, I didn't know that."

"So you . . . you thought breaking his arm was enough to keep him away?"

"Hell no," he laughed. "If he was crazy enough to take on the Guineas, a broken arm wasn't going to scare him off of *me*. No, I looked into his nigger/kike eyes when he threatened all of you, and I knew he was stupid enough and crazy enough to kill a cop's family."

He ran his hands softly over Molly's fur.

"I don't . . . So, he could have killed us?"

"Yeah."

"Well why the hell didn't you do something about it?"

"Do what, Jim? If I'd arrested him, he just would've gotten his mules to do the job. Should I have taken his money?"

"Jesus, Dad, I don't know, but it'd be nice to think that our lives meant something to you. Some crazy fucking nigger tells you he's going to chop our heads off and you do nothing?"

"You know, my father's name was James. I named you after my father. Your mother was pregnant with Scotty and you . . . well, you were my son. There was nothing more important to me."

"Well, I don't . . ."

"Jim, listen to me," he said, rising up out of his chair and facing me. Once again, he was taller than I was; his slump vanished. "This is a rotten, miserable fucking world. People do the right things for the wrong reason and vice-versa. People let you down and disappoint you. They're evil and cruel and selfish, though most of the time, they're just weak and stupid. It sucks, but that's the world we live in and you can't change it. All you can do is try not to be one of the bastards.

166

"I would've died for any of you. I'd have taken the torture that the Guineas handed to Lionel if it would've meant saving any of your lives. The one thing I couldn't do, though, was compromise who I was by taking that nigger's money. If I had done that, I'd be just as bad as the rest of 'em, just another bastard doing the wrong thing and making excuses. I wouldn't and I won't bend over for anyone, because that's the only thing in this whole rotten fucking universe that any of us have any control over."

He nodded his head and stared at me.

"I . . . Okay. But what does any of this have to do with what I was talking to you about?"

"Fifty thousand dollars right down the fucking toilet. You still aren't listening, Jim. You come here and tell me that you want to save me, that Morrison's Satan and . . ."

"The Antichrist. He's human, he just works for Satan."

"Uh-huh. Fine, he *works* for Satan. Then you tell me that if I accept the identification thing, I'll be condemned to Hell. Okay. I think you're full of shit, but either way, it doesn't matter, because I know that there is no way in hell that anyone will ever scare me as much as that crazy fucking nigger did when he told me he was going to murder my family. And if I didn't bend over for Lionel when your lives were on the line, then you can be damn well sure that I won't bend over for some faggot Republican, Antichrist or not."

I stood uneasily in front of my father, his regained height making me feel small and awkward. The house seemed huge to me and I chewed my lip and shifted uncomfortably from one foot to the other.

"Well then," I said in a tiny voice, "will you come to Israel with me?"

"No one's going to run me out of my own house."

"But . . ."

"You came here for a reason, Jim. Now, I just told you why you don't have to worry about that anymore. You want to go to Israel, go. Your conscience is clean."

"But it's more than just that. You have to . . . you have to accept Christ."

"Is that right? You want me to get down on my knees and beg Christ for forgiveness? For acceptance?"

"Yeah, I . . . I mean, you don't have to beg but . . . Dad, this is about forever. I mean, I know how fucked up it all sounds, but look at the world now. Everything's changed."

"Nothing ever changes."

"How can you say that? Look at everything that's happened."

"*People*, Jim. People never change."

"Dad, don't do this. This is about forever. Mom and Scotty, they're already in Heaven. We can all be there together. Please Dad, come to Israel with me. Accept Jesus. Please."

He had flinched when I said that we could all be together, but he quickly covered-up the hesitation with a tight face, and began nodding his head slowly and solidly. When he spoke again, it was the voice I remembered from when I was a child, bereft of age or weakness.

"Jimmy," he said clearly, his eyes cutting a quick flash of blue through the gray, "if I didn't bend over for the Colored Kike, and I won't bend over for that limey fuck, then what the hell makes you think that I'd ever let Jesus push me down onto my knees?"

Ten

I quietly slipped into my brother's room and closed the door behind me. The air was fresh and new, the blue wallpaper looking as if it had been hung the day before. The purple, plush carpet stood unruffled. Feeling as though I had just crossed a police barricade, I silently crossed the room, stopping in front of Scotty's bureau. I opened the drawer and saw his socks; all rolled up in perfect little balls, and his underwear, neatly folded in halves and carefully piled in two separate rows. I placed my hand on the soft, white, virginal underwear. Closing the drawer, I looked across the room at his bed. The *Peanuts* bedspread was pulled tight and Charlie Brown, Snoopy, and Linus stared back at me without a single wrinkle marring their faces. Scotty had stopped using that bedspread years before he died, but the first day after his funeral, my mother had unpacked it from the basement and spread it perfectly across his bed. I quietly left the room.

Across the hall, I opened the door to my old room, which had long since become a storage space for accumulated junk. Squeezing past the boxes and exercise machines, I flopped down onto the unmade bed and stared up at the ceiling. The room was smaller than I remembered, and I was amazed I had been able to live in its confines for eighteen years.

I tried falling asleep, but the bed was small, and I kept waking up, afraid that if I turned over, I'd fall.

The next morning, I woke up with a heavy knot in my stomach and walked downstairs, determined to talk with my father, ensuring that I would never have to sleep in that room again. He was already awake, standing in the kitchen wearing blue slacks and a tan, button down short-sleeved shirt. His tie was wide and garish, the color so red it hurt my eyes to look at it so early in the morning. He was cooking over the stove and I could smell the bacon.

"Still here, huh?" he asked without taking his eyes off the sizzling pork.

"Yeah."

"Two days in a row, that's a record."

I sat down at the kitchen table.

He cooked in silence and then lifted the pan off the fire and drained the grease into an empty coffee can. He flipped the bacon onto a paper towel and then folded the towel over, absorbing some of the grease. He brought the food over to the kitchen table and then poured himself a glass of water. Sitting across from me, he stuffed a piece of bacon into his mouth and began chewing loudly, looking everywhere except at me.

"We don't have any bread for toast," he said after he had eaten three pieces of bacon, "but I think there's some cream of wheat in the cabinet."

"Can I have some bacon?"

"Thought you were a vegetarian." He wiped his mouth.

"Where'd you get that idea?"

He gobbled two more pieces of bacon and then looked at me. "Well eat some, then."

I pulled a slice out of the tangled mound of meat and chewed it slowly. The grease didn't mix well with the knot in my stomach.

"You on a diet or something?"

"Yeah, I'm on a diet."

"Quit sulking like a little girl and eat your food."

I dropped my half-eaten piece of bacon onto the table. "Dad, can we talk?" I asked quietly.

"MOLLY!

I jolted at the noise and the pork in my stomach seemed to expand, making me feel nauseous.

The dog ran into the kitchen, its claws scraping across the linoleum, sounding like an incompetent, but enthusiastic tap dancer. She slid to a halt in front of my father and he turned his chair away from me in order to face her. He dangled some bacon in front of her and the tongue rolled out from between her teeth. My father smiled.

"You love bacon, don't you girl? Yeah, you do."

The dog panted and its thick brown torso shimmied.

"Okay, sit, Molly. Sit!"

The dog remained motionless; its eyes locked onto the meat.

"Sit!"

Molly lurched forward and snapped at the treat.

"Bad dog. No!" He whapped Molly on the snout and shook his finger at her. "Sit!"

The dog's rump dropped to the ground with a quiet thump.

"Good girl!" He smiled warmly, and dropped the bacon.

Molly snapped it up before it touched the ground.

My father clasped his hands around Molly's thick neck and began rubbing her fur. "Did you see that, Jim?"

"Yeah, I saw." I lit a cigarette.

He frowned at me and grabbed another piece of bacon.

After forty-five minutes, the pile of bacon had disappeared and he reached across the table without looking at me, grabbing my half-eaten piece and enticing the dog to play dead for the sixth time.

"That's it," he said, after she had gulped it down, "no more." He led her to the back door and shooed her outside.

I lit another cigarette and waited while he watched the dog out the window.

Five cigarettes later, he finally turned away from the window and shot me a momentary look of disdain before walking over to the sink. "When'd you pick up that filthy habit?" he asked while washing the frying pan.

"College."

"Well, that was money well spent."

"Yeah, somehow I managed to find the time to smoke in-between making fun of my ignorant, blue-collar parents who I thought I was so much better than."

"When are you leaving?" The words were sharp and curt.

"I . . ."

"You what?"

"That's what I wanted to talk to you about," I said quietly.

"What? Speak up, you sound like a little girl."

"I said that that's what I wanted to talk about!"

"Your mother was a slob," he said as he dried the frying pan and put it back into the cabinet. "You make a mess, you clean a mess." He returned to the window and stared at the dog.

"Dad, if you'd just listen to me for an hour. Give me an hour without interrupting. Just one hour where you really listen to me."

He stared at the dog.

"Dad!"

"What?" he asked without turning to face me.

I got up out of my chair and walked over to him, but he still refused to look at me.

"Look at her," he said. "You'd swear she's still a puppy."

"Dad, if you'd just listen to what I'm saying."

"Well what the hell does it look like I'm doing?" He turned away and walked into the living room.

"Dad," I said, trailing behind him, "I can prove that what I'm saying is true. Okay, the um, the disappearances were the Rapture. Then Morrison taking over America is the Third Seal. And then, um, everyone that died in the nukes and the riots and stuff, that was the Second, or maybe the First Seal. But then, next, Morrison'll start persecuting Christians, and then they'll be an earthquake. And then the sun'll disappear, or maybe it was locusts. But see, when this stuff happens, you'll know that the Bible's right. And then you'll . . ."

I continued speaking to my father's back as he paced the living room. My words were garbled and unconvincing. My brain was a tangled knot, and the harder I tried tugging the words free, the tighter the knot became. I thought about Marv, about his presence and eloquence, how words like *Satan, Jesus, Judgment,* and *Salvation,* wouldn't have sounded foolish coming out of his mouth. I wondered why he was able to speak about God so articulately while I could spew forth nothing but embarrassing blather.

When my father located the leash he had been searching for, he turned to me and frowned.

"Okay," I said, looking away. "And Israel . . ."

"Shut up, Jim."

"But . . ."

"Shut up and listen to me. You're family, so you're welcome to stay here. But this is still my house, and if you're going to stay, you're going to keep your language out on the street, your smoking out on the street, and your God out on the street. Understand?"

"But . . ."

He walked back into the kitchen, and when he returned with the dog, paused at the front door. "I'm taking Molly for a nice long walk," he said without turning to face me. "If you can't follow those rules, you won't be here when we get back." He tugged at the leash. "Come on, Molly."

That night, I slept in my old bed again. It didn't feel too small anymore.

When he wasn't playing with the dog, he was watching TV. They didn't show sitcoms or dramas or movies; only news and documentaries. The documentaries, all newly produced, covered a variety of topics, delving into the history of homosexuality, religious groups, homeopathic medicine, warfare, and a host of other topics. Some were horribly violent, showing graphic footage of animals being experimented on by cosmetic companies, public executions in Arab countries, and any other image that clearly displayed our recent barbaric heritage. The news programs focused exclusively on the OWC and Richard Grant Morrison. Morrison was shown in a variety of different settings; in Israel, reviewing architectural plans for the new temple he was helping the Israeli's build; in Rwanda, becoming dewy-eyed while touring an OWC medical tent filled with babies dying of AIDS; in New York City, being cheered on by thousands of men, women, and children as he unveiled the reconstructed Statue of Liberty, now holding a globe rather than a torch. The news showed OWC soldiers guarding the Israeli boarder and European children meditating in an OWC yoga center; it showed OWC soldiers reuniting families with relatives mistakenly thought to have perished and environmental specialists destroying the equipment once used to bulldoze the Amazon rain forest.

Through it all, my father maintained a running commentary. When a news segment showed the Pope and Morrison giving a hug to the first black, female, lesbian priest, I thought my father was going to shoot the TV with his shotgun. None of his comments were directly addressed to me, but I didn't mind. I knew his opinions were vocalized for my benefit. It was a form of communication, and I grudgingly accepted it as such.

That same grudging acceptance, however, did not carry over to the dog. The two of them played for hours. He patted her eternally, and I felt certain that sooner or later, either my father's flesh or the dog's fur would rub off. He took her for long walks and occasionally even crouched down on the floor, wincing in pain while wrestling with her. He fed the dog three times a day, doling out scraps from his own plate.

I cooked for myself and ate alone, eventually developing the habit of leaving the house while my father played with the dog. I'd wander around the neighborhood smoking cigarettes, or walk down to the grocery store and pick up the supplies that were distributed four times a week. At first, identification implantations and membership in the OWC had been portrayed as voluntary, but one month after giving his first speech, Morrison explained that there would be a six month deadline for receiving identification implantations, or *tags* as they had quickly been dubbed. In the corner of the TV screen, twenty-four hours a day, a countdown was displayed, informing viewers as to how much time remained until the end of the deadline. No one said what would happen in the event of a failure to comply, and the unspoken threat scared me more than a spoken one would have.

Until then though, supplies were handed out to everyone. As the months passed, I noticed more and more people wearing thin black lines on their hands, and found myself eyed with suspicion, both by the OWC soldiers handing out the supplies and by the civilians reaching for their food and proudly displaying their tags.

Outside, I felt like a fugitive, inside a ghost. I was unable to form a coherent thought or plan a reasonable course of action. I had never counted on convincing my father to worship Christ and come to Israel with me; I had counted on convincing my mother. I knew that she'd listen to me and that, faced with going to Israel with my mother or staying in Boston alone, my father would grudgingly go to Israel in order to keep the family together. Once in Israel, I was counting on seven years of subtle pressure from my mother, myself, and other Christians to push my father into salvation. It was a good plan, but it depended on the presence of my mother. With her gone, I was lost.

Twice, I broke the house rules and tried speaking to my father about Israel and God, but the speech, so streamlined and beautiful in my mind, became thick and ugly by the time it traveled down to my tongue. The first time I attempted talking to him, he told me to shut up. The second time, he didn't need to, as I shut myself up, realizing how ridiculous and empty my words sounded. I remembered Marv, and how when he was a little boy, he had tried talking to the Puerto Ricans in Tongues. He got the shit kicked out of him, too.

Ignoring my father's complete refusal to leave Boston and travel to Israel, I called Logan Airport one day to find out if it was least *physically* possible to get there. I was told that the airport was open, but OWC permission was required to fly anywhere, and that the passenger must be tagged. Jews were exempt due to Morrison's special treaty with Israel and Judaic law, which forbids tattoos of any kind. Judaism had been declared a race, not a religion by the OWC, making it impossible to convert in order to fly without a tag, since strict bloodlines determined who was and was not Jewish.

174

Two months before the deadline for registration, I took the long walk to Logan Airport. I saw that it would be next to impossible to sneak in, as there were three rows of tight checkpoints that had to be passed before anyone could even enter the airport.

I walked home slowly, feeling as if my entire life had been sucked into quicksand. Back at the house, my father was wrestling with the dog on the living room carpet. I stared at the two of them for an hour. My father never looked up at me.

I lit a cigarette.

"Take it outside, pal," my father immediately said.

I smiled and walked into the bathroom, throwing the cigarette into the toilet. The sizzle of its dying flame ended just as our doorbell rang. It was a sound that I hadn't heard since I had arrived home five months earlier.

I stepped out into the hall and my father pushed past me, gripping his shotgun in his hand. He peered out the window and then swung the door open, keeping the shotgun hidden behind the door. I looked over his shoulder and saw a young man in his mid-twenties standing on our porch. He was carrying a small, hand-held computer and was wearing an OWC uniform. He smiled warmly at my father.

"What the fuck do you want?"

"Good afternoon, sir," the soldier said, ignoring my father's hostility. "My name's Thomas McBride and I'm a citizen of the One World Community."

"I don't give a rat's fat ass who you are. Get off my property, you little shit."

"Sir, I'm here to inform you that the backlog of people waiting to register for citizenship has been alleviated and that we're now able to process your induction in a single day. We understand that a lot of you became discouraged when you were told that there was a month-long waiting list for registration, and I'm here to tell you that that's no longer the case."

"Hit the bricks, junior."

"If you'd like, I'd be happy to accompany you and help facilitate a quick registration. Grab your coat and we'll have you back home before nightfall."

"Stick your tag where the sun don't shine, punk."

"Sir . . ."

"While you're at it, cram it up Morrison's faggot ass, too."

"There's no need for profanity, sir." The soldier stiffened, his words and smile gaining a slight edge.

"Fuck you and fuck your mother. You don't come onto *my* property and tell *me* how to talk."

"When America became a member of the OWC," the soldier said, his smile becoming arrogant, "all personal property became communal. You don't own this house."

My father's knuckles became white as he squeezed his gun.

"Sir," the soldier said, returning the warmth to his smile and dropping the arrogance from his voice, "after you become a citizen, you can request to be assigned to this property as your official living space. I'm sure that your request would be honored."

"*Request?* You think I'm going to *ask* to live in my own home, you smart-mouthed little punk? I worked for forty years to pay for this house. You just try and tell me I've got to leave. Go ahead, pal, try it and see what happens."

"Hey, listen . . ."

"Get the hell outta here before I break your goddamn neck."

"Is that right?" The soldier stepped forward and his voice suddenly lost its generic quality, lapsing into a thick Boston accent. "And who's gonna do that, old man? You gonna break my neck?"

I saw my father's cheeks open into a wide smile. He lowered his arm and dropped his gun into the corner before stepping towards the man.

The soldier suddenly noticed me.

"Who's that?" he asked in a surprised voice.

"None of your fucking business," my father said, the smile dropping from his face. He quickly stepped back, blocking me from view. "What did you say your name was? McBride?"

"That's right, Thomas McBride." The soldier jutted his chin.

"McBride," my father mumbled. "*Tommy* McBride?"

"Thomas," the soldier said hesitantly.

"*Thomas* my ass. I knew I recognized you, you little perv."

"I don't know . . ."

"Shut up! Fifteen years ago I rousted your ass outside of Bea Cleamont's house. You remember that?"

"I don't have any idea . . ."

"Don't you lie to me, Tommy! You remember."

"I . . ." Tommy dropped his eyes away. "That was a long time ago, Mr. Lordan."

"That's *Officer* Lordan to you, buddy, and it wasn't as long ago as you'd like to think. Jesus, McBride, she had to be eighty-five if she was a day, you weenie-wagging little pervert. I'll tell you, I busted a lot of people for a lot of things in my day, but smacking your pecker while watching an eighty-five year old woman get undressed, that really took the cake."

"Look Mr. Lordan, I . . ."

"*Officer* Lordan!"

"I . . . Officer Lordan. I never . . . "

"Shut up!"

Tommy stepped back and looked as though he might cry.

"Go fiddle with yourself somewhere else before I grab you by the scruff of your neck and drag your ass over to your father's house like I did ten years ago."

"Look," Tommy said sheepishly as he backed off the stairs, "I just came to tell you that its only two more months until the registration deadline. And besides, that was a long time ago. I don't do that kind of stuff anymore."

"Save it for the priest, junior. And just remember, if I catch you in any more bushes, I'll whup your ass good, you hear me?"

Tommy sulked off and my father slowly closed the door. As soon as the door was shut, he looked at me with a mixture of anger and alarm.

"I don't want you going outside again," he said. "And don't you ever come to the door if one of them comes around again."

"That's stupid, Dad, I've got to get the food."

"I'll get it from now on."

"Dad, there's no reason to . . ."

"Goddamnit, Jim, don't argue with me!" He looked sad and afraid and quickly turned away. "Just, stay in, Jim. Just stay inside."

"We can't hide in the house forever, Dad."

He sighed and leaned on the desk for support.

"We have to talk about what we're going to do," I said.

He turned around and looked at me without anger or disgust. He even nodded his head slightly, and seemed to be waiting for me to continue, seemed to be open to what I needed to say.

The moment passed quickly, though, and before I could say another word, he jerked his face away from me and looked over my shoulder, towards the backyard.

"Where's Molly?"

"Who cares where . . ." I trailed off without bothering to complete the sentence. There was no one left to hear it, as my father was already gone, busy looking for the dog.

Her white/pink stomach bobbed up and down as she slept, her long tongue drooling out of the side of her mouth. Her claws scrapped the floor as she kicked her feet, unable to remain still even in her dreams. I crouched down next to her and gently ran my hand over her warm stomach. I whispered her name and she awoke with a start, scrambling up onto her feet. She darted her head back and forth and began trotting around the kitchen. I attached the leash onto her collar and quietly led her out of the house, into the night.

We crossed Broadway and walked over to the playground behind St. Augustine's Grammar School. My father had pulled me and Scotty out of O'Reilly Public School when the busing riots were occurring and enrolled us in St. Augustine's. Had we stayed in public school, we would have been bused over to Roxbury, to a predominantly black school. *This isn't about black or white*, he told us, *it's about money. It's no coincidence that they're pulling this crap in the poorest white neighborhood and the poorest black neighborhood. You can bet that you won't see kids in Topsfield or North Andover getting shipped to Roxbury. It's rich people thinking they can tell working class folks what to do, and I'm not going to have it. I've got nothing against the Coloreds. It's not about that.*

All the same, when the riots broke out and the black kids from Roxbury were being attacked by angry mobs as they were driven into Southie, my father called in sick to work, refusing to put on his badge and arrest his neighbors.

"Go on dog, go," I shouted after releasing her from the leash. She bolted away and began running around the perimeter of the field. While she ran, I walked across the street, over to a construction site. Finding what I needed, I walked back to the playground and sat down on a swing, tightly holding onto the supporting chains.

Swaying back and forth on the swing, my feet scuffling through the dirt, I watched as the dog flung herself around the playground. Occasionally, I'd lose sight of her in the shadows, but I could always hear her heavy paws rapidly thumping onto the cold soil. After an hour of constant running, she moved into the center of the playground and began tearing up the grass, ripping it with her teeth and then spitting it back onto the ground. A squirrel crept onto the field and the dog spun around to face it. The two creatures stared at each other for a moment before the dog bolted after it. The squirrel scurried up into a tree and the dog, trying to stop, slid across the wet leaves and dewy grass, slamming into the trunk. She shook her head back and forth and, unfazed, returned to her laps.

Realizing that her reservoir of energy and enthusiasm was endless, I called her name and she slid to a halt, jerking her ears back and forth. I called her name again and she charged over to me, flinging tufts of grass and soil behind her. She ran between my legs and pushed me back into the swing. I slid out of the seat and crouched down onto the ground. She pushed her face into mine and began licking my cheeks and nose. I pulled away from her slobber and placed my hands on her strong shoulders.

"Sit!" I tried pushing her down onto the ground, but she refused to budge, staring at me with exited, ignorant eyes. "Sit!"

She sat down and panted excitedly.

I slipped my fingers underneath her collar, grabbing her tightly while my other hand searched for the brick. I shivered slightly as my fingers passed across its hard, sharp corners.

I took a deep breath, closed my eyes, and swung.

My arm vibrated at the impact.

The dog stumbled sideways as a yelp of surprised anguish escaped her throat.

It was the same noise my mother made when she found Scotty dead in the bathroom. The exact same.

I slipped my fingers out from underneath her collar as she staggered back and forth, refusing to fall.

The brick had caught her on the side of her head, ripping off a strip of fur and flesh directly above her right eye. Her fur absorbed the blood, and a slowly darkening hue spread outward from the gash.

"Good girl," I said grimly. "Good dog."

I steadied my arm and swung again.

The brick smashed her in the jaw, knocking out several teeth and pushing her swaying body over. Once on the ground, she began shaking and whining. She stared at me through the blood with a confused eye. No hate, no anger, just confusion. I cupped my hand over my mouth and began shaking.

"I'm really fucking sorry, dog. I don't want . . . I don't . . . I'm so fucking sorry." I began crying. "Dad has to . . . I'm sorry."

Her legs kicked at the grass, running nowhere like they did when she slept.

My father always pointed that out to me.

Look at that, Jim, he'd say, his voice draped in love, *She's chasing after something in her dreams.*

I raised the brick and finished the job.

There was weakness in my father's voice.

"Wake up," he repeated, while pushing down on my shoulder, bouncing me up and down on the bed. "Molly's gone. My dog's gone, Jim."

I wanted to stay hidden under the covers. The previous night in the playground felt like a dream, and I was shocked to wake up and discover that the consequences of that dream had carried over into morning. I stared down at my clothes; afraid that they might be soaked in blood, feeling relived when I saw that they were clean. I allowed myself to believe that it really had been a dream, that the dog's disappearance was simply a coincidence. I savored the lie for as long as I could, but reality reared its ugly head as I remembered that I had thrown my bloody clothes in the ditch along with the dead dog.

"What do you mean?" I asked.

"She's missing. I don't know where she is."

"She's probably in the backyard."

"No, no I checked, she's gone."

"Well, she's probably just running around the neighborhood, like before." I was referring to my three previous attempts to abandon her, only to hear scratching on the front door three hours later. She had possessed an uncanny knack for returning home, a factor which didn't seem to make her any more desirable to the people I had tried to give her to. Although there was no shortage of food, there was a general fear that there could be, and no one wanted another mouth to feed. After a month of trying to lose her or give her away, it had become obvious to me, that there was only one way for me to separate the two of them for good.

"No," he said, "it's not like those other times. I can tell. She's gone, Jim, she's gone." His face was frightened and confused and he was inhaling short, loud breaths. His lower lip hung slack and he kept turning his head back and forth, as though the dog might be hiding somewhere in my room.

"Dad."

He snapped his attention towards me, his eyes begging for an answer.

"Dad, I don't know where she is, but we'll find her," I said, retreating into cowardice. "I'm going to get dressed and we'll go looking, okay? We'll find her."

He nodded his head and his face looked like a child's, a child who knows he's being lied to, but is grateful for that lie all the same. He walked out of my room, continuing to slowly nod his head.

The morning after we had decided to give up the search for the dog, I came downstairs and found my father sitting in his recliner, dressed in pajamas. In my entire life, I had never once seen my father in anything but pants and a shirt. Once or twice, I had seen him in a T-shirt, but never in underwear or pajamas. From that moment on, I never saw him in anything *but* his pajamas.

I'd cook his meals and try engaging him in conversation. He'd accept the food, halfheartedly nibbling on it while ignoring my words. Most of the time, he stayed in his chair, staring at the TV. After a few weeks, he stopped turning the television on, and would simply stare at the blank screen for hours at a time. Every once in a while, he'd tilt his head so his ear pointed towards the front door, and I knew he was listening for the sound of the dog's claws up against the wood, scratching to be let back into the house. We spent entire evenings silently listening for those scratches.

"I wish," he said one night, shocking me with his voice, "I wish you had met my father. He died two years before you were born." Each word was a chore. He paused and took deep breaths between the sentences. "He grew up in Scotland. When he was thirteen, he took a job on a steam ship and, when the boat was a few miles off the coast of Ellis Island, jumped overboard and swam to shore."

He lifted up the glass of water I had brought him, but paused before drinking it, and set it back down. His chest heaved as he chased after each breath, exhausted by the effort of lifting the glass.

"He made his way to Boston and met my mother there. They were sixteen years old when they got married. We named you after him, did you know that?"

"No," I lied. "No, I didn't."

"Yeah. They were Catholic and after nine years of marriage, they had seven kids. I was the last. I was the baby. He worked odd jobs to support us, usually two or three of `em at the same time. And they weren't easy jobs, either, they were hard labor. He was an *Illegal*, so he had to work with the Chinks and the Micks, doing the dirtiest work around for pennies.

"But I never heard him complain. I never once heard him say that he was tired or that the work was too much. He just did what he had to do. As simple as that. He made it seem easy. And maybe by today's standards, their marriage wasn't the best, but they stayed in it. He took care of his children and his wife. She took care of him. He never left."

"I wish I had met him," I said.

He looked over at me, surprised to discover that I was still there, that he was speaking to someone other than himself.

"He died two years before you were born. Probably just as well. He never got his citizenship. It used to kill him that he couldn't vote. You think I'm a Democrat, you should have heard Pop. Some Sundays, he'd take me down to the Common after church. Back then, all the different groups would be there, the Communists and the Socialists and the Democrats and the Nazis and the Unions and the Republicans, and they'd all be giving speeches. We'd listen to the Democrats for a while, but Pop always ended up drifting over to the Republicans. He'd start screaming at `em, calling `em dirty son's of bitches. Of course, back then, everyone was shouting at everyone else. Sometimes, a fight'd break out and Pop'd be right in the middle of it, thanking God for the opportunity to take a poke at a Republican.

"But he could never vote. He wanted to so badly, and he never could. Never complained about it, but you could see it on his face election day, you could see how much it hurt him to not be able to vote. Still, I never heard him complain about it. He carried it.

"Anyway," he placed his trembling fingers on his lap and stared at them. "He had a . . . He had a breakdown three years before he died. He got more and more scared that he was going to get deported and eventually, he just, just snapped.

"I went to see him in the hospital. He had always been a big man, but after a month in that fucking dump, he had lost thirty pounds. He was weak. Frail. He didn't recognize me. He couldn't recognize his own son. He looked up at me and all he said was, *You got a cigarette, pal?* He whispered it to me like he was going to get in trouble. I gave him the cigarette and he walked right past me and tried to use it to open his cell door. Pushed the cigarette into the keyhole and turned it around and around. Even when it crumbled, he kept trying to unlock the door with it.

"He came home after a year, but was never the same. Never gained back the weight. Could never look me in the eye. He was still scared. Any loud noise would make him flinch. He wouldn't go out of the house or answer the phone. Those last two years he . . . I sometimes wish he had died before he did. It's a horrible thing to wish. But I do. I think about him now, and all I can see is a frightened old man trying to open a door with a cigarette. It's not fair. He was strong. He was good. He spent his whole life doing the right thing without ever expecting a pat on the back for it. He was my father, and that's how he should be remembered, not as a frightened old man. He shouldn't be judged on the last three years of his life when for sixty years he had been something else, something better. But that *is* how I remember him. It's not fair, but it's the way it is.

"A son should never have to remember his father that way."

He stared down at his shaking fingers.

"Dad . . ."

"I'm going to bed."

"It's only eight."

"I'm tired."

"But it's still so early."

"I'm tired," he repeated, but stayed in his chair, silently staring down into his lap.

"We're going to Israel, Dad," I said with as much authority as I could muster.

He looked at me for a moment and then turned away, returning his gaze to the blank TV.

"The deadline for registration was a month ago. We can't get food anymore and we can't leave the house without getting arrested."

"So we won't leave the house."

"They'll come for us."

"Let 'em." He sounded more defeated than angry.

"If they arrest us, Dad, they'll try and force us into taking the tag. If we don't take it, I think they'll kill us."

He looked up at me with empty eyes.

"Dad, if you take the tag, you go to Hell, if you don't take it, they'll kill you and you'll still go to Hell if you haven't . . . if you haven't accepted Christ."

"Have *you* accepted Christ?" he asked quietly.

"I . . ." The question surprised me.

No. I didn't know where that would lead me and, and I wanted to . . . I was waiting for . . . I needed . . .

"Look, what difference does it make? Mom and Sarah are already in Heaven. So is Scotty. You don't have to decide about the whole Jesus thing right now, just come to Israel and we'll have six years to figure that out. We'll all be together again, Dad, all of us."

He released control of his face and the excess flesh drooped down underneath his mouth, hanging off his chin.

"Dad, this is about forever."

"I thought it was about forever, too," he mumbled.

"What?"

"She was going to divorce me," he said quietly. His forehead became tense and the soft flesh accumulated around his eyes, burying them.

"What?"

"I never thought about leaving. Never. But your mother . . . I could see it in her eyes . . . she . . ." His eyes burrowed deeper into his flesh and his voice turned angry. "And then you come waltzing into the house telling me God took her away, acting like I ought be happy about that, like I ought dance around like some kind of fairy because God stole my wife. He already had my son, and now you say He's got my wife."

"But . . . but everything makes sense now, Dad. It's okay. We can finally do the right thing."

"I spent my life doing the right thing!" he roared. "Where did it get me? *Everything makes sense?* NOTHING MAKES SENSE!"

"But it will, Dad. The Bible's right, God's real, and we know what to do. We know what's going to happen and we don't have to be confused anymore. Everything, every single thing that's happening proves that the Bible's right."

The anger drained from his face and he smiled wistfully and nodded his head. "I know."

"You what?"

"I know." His lower lip began trembling. "You know, every day since I retired, I've thought about eating my gun. Every day. You left, your brother died . . ."

"Ma stayed."

"She hated me."

"She didn't hate you, Dad."

"DON'T YOU TELL ME! YOU LEFT! I STAYED AND I KNOW, SO DON'T YOU TRY TELLING ME, BECAUSE I WAS HERE!" He climbed out of his chair and stood in front of me, hunched over and gasping for air in between his words. "She didn't want me around anymore, didn't like having to see me all day, every day. This was my house, my *home*! She made me feel like I had no right to be here, like I was a nuisance. I spent my life supporting her, working my fingers to the bone. Not for me, for her. For you and your brother. And when I finally retire, when I can finally breathe again, you leave and Scotty leaves and she leaves. I was her husband. She was my wife!"

"Yeah but . . . but none of that matters anymore. I mean, it doesn't matter, because there's a . . ."

"A what? A Heaven? So what? I'll still be alone. I loved your mother. She was my wife, for Christ's sake, of course I loved her, I promised I would. I kept that promise, I never stopped loving her, I never stopped loving any of you. *You* stopped!" A tear squeezed out of his eye and ran down the wrinkles in his face. He wiped it away with his shoulder while holding onto his pajama bottoms, afraid to release them because they might fall off his frail body.

"But there's a Heaven, Dad. We can all be together there."

"Bullshit. Is God going to *make* them love me? I'll still be alone, only now, now I'll be alone forever. Don't you understand, it's worse now. Jesus Christ, I just wanted it to end, to stop. To rest, to go away and have it all stop. I just wanted to eat my fucking gun and make it all go away. And you took that away from me, Jim. Now, even death isn't the end. Now I have to be alone forever."

"It doesn't have to be that way, Dad."

"SHUT UP! SHUT UP!" He began panting for breath while tears tore down his face. "I stay and you all leave. Jesus Christ, I can't fucking breath, why can't I . . . why can't I catch my breath? I have to stay, I have to stay but no one stays with me. You all . . . Jesus Christ, even Molly. Even Molly left me. I can't . . . I can't do it anymore. I can't . . . I don't know what to do, I can't do it anymore, and now I can't even die. I'll always be . . . Jesus, why can't I breathe?"

His legs collapsed underneath him and he fell onto the floor sobbing. "What kind of man am I? What's wrong with me? I can't understand . . . How could Molly leave? How could she? I don't understand, I loved her so much.

How could she leave? Oh my God, am I really that bad? Am I? I try and I try and I try and everyone still leaves. Everyone's gone and you're going to go to Israel and I'm going to be alone again. Forever. I . . . Why would Molly leave me? Why her? I can't be *that* bad. I can't, Jesus, I can't breath. It has to stop. I can't . . ." He wrapped himself into a ball. "Make it stop. Please make it stop. I can't do it any more. Please."

"It's okay, Dad." I sat down beside him and lifted him into the air, cradling him in my lap. I was amazed at how light he was, how frail he had become. "It's okay. I promise I'm not going anywhere without you. You're not going to have to be alone ever again. I promise. I love you, Dad, and I swear to God it's going to be okay."

"Help me, Jim. Please. I need someone to stay."

I began crying through a smile. "I will. I'm going to save you, Dad."

The moment after I had uttered the words, there was a loud crash at our front door. It was followed by two more violent sounds and, after the third, our front door splintered apart and shattered onto the floor. Three kicks were all it took. For forty years, that door had served as a barrier, protecting and insulating us from the outside world. Three kicks were all it took to break through it. Four OWC soldiers, all holding handguns, stepped over the broken door and sauntered into the living room.

"William Lordan," the soldier in charge said, "both you and your son James have failed to comply with the deadline for registration. I've been authorized to place you both under arrest and to accompany you to a registration center."

My father stared up at the soldiers and I watched as his eyes flooded with sudden self-awareness, watched as he saw himself through the soldiers' eyes; weak, scared, and defeated.

Suddenly filled with energy, he leapt out of my lap and scurried across the room, grabbing his shotgun from the corner.

"Put the gun down, Mr. Lordan." The soldier's voice was calm and patronizing and he and the others pointed their weapons at my father in a lackluster, perfunctory fashion.

"Get the hell out of my house!"

"I told you, it's not your house anymore!"

"McBride? Is that you, you little weenie-wagger?"

"Stop calling me that!"

"Just put the gun down, Mr. Lordan."

"Get out of my fucking house!" He raised the barrel of his gun and pulled the trigger. An explosion erupted and chunks of plaster and wood fell down onto the floor in front of me.

This can't be happening. Not here. This is where I laid on the floor and played with my little green plastic army men. This is where I wrestled my brother, cramming his neck into a headlock and squeezing until he cried and promised not to read my comic books anymore. This was where I ate cereal and watched Hong Kong Fooey and Underdog every Saturday morning.

"Put the gun down," the soldier said in a more urgent voice.

They can't be here, in their dark blue uniforms, standing in front of the yellow striped wallpaper. Their heavy black boots can't be standing on top of the green carpet; their black guns can't be pointed at the old man who can't be my father.

"And stop calling me a weenie-wagger!"

Dad turned towards me. He smiled and winked.

"Weenie-wagger, weenie-wagger," he chanted before pumping another round into the gun's chamber.

The bullet split my father's face open, killing him instantly.

He's in Hell. In five billion years, when the sun dies and the earth is destroyed in its death-throes, my father will still be in Hell. And that five billion years will have amounted to little more than the first second of eternity. I will never see him again, never watch him yell at the TV again, never touch him again, never watch him wash a pan again, and never ever, be able to talk with him again. He is in Hell. Alone. Forever. And every moment that I'm alive and awake and capable of thought, I will know where my father is, I will know that he is in Hell and that he will be there, alone, forever.

When the billy clubs cracked down onto my skull, their touch felt as warm and as merciful as a lover's kiss.

Eleven

"Time to wake up, Mr. Lordan."

The voice was soft and pleasant, and it gently caressed me towards consciousness. My eyes felt moist, but when I tried to raise my hands and wipe away the tears, nothing happened. I focused my blurry eyesight and saw that I was strapped down into a heavy white chair. I tried moving my feet, but couldn't. The helplessness felt correct, and I allowed the tears to streak down my face without interference.

"Oh Jesus, Daddy. Oh my God," I sobbed through the salty tears painting my lips. I closed my eyes and continued to cry until a light cut through the darkness as a pair of delicate fingers gently touched my chin and raised my head. I opened my eyes and stared into the face of a young black woman.

"Time to wake up, Mr. Lordan." The woman smiled at me sadly.

I moved my eyes past her face and saw that I was in a small, empty room. The walls were painted white, as was the floor, the ceiling, and my chair. The lighting was harsh and intrusive, reminding me of a dentist's office. The woman slipped her fingers off my face and stepped back. She was wearing a white jacket that made her look like a doctor.

I returned her sad smile and began sobbing.

"I know this is a difficult time for you, Mr. Lordan, but it's important that we speak," she said quietly, while gently running her fingers through my hair.

I raised my head and saw that underneath her coat was a dark blue OWC uniform. The haze was slowly washed away in a wave of hatred.

"YOU FUCKING BASTARDS! YOU COCKSUCKING BASTARDS!"

She flinched and disappointment passed across her features as she turned away. She was silent for several moments, but then nodded and turned back to me with a fresh smile.

"My name is Louise Toth. Call me Lou." Her voice sounded genuinely friendly, her composure formal and relaxed.

"YOU KILLED MY FATHER, YOU FUCKING NIGGER!"

"Mr. Lordan, I'm here to help."

"YOU KILLED HIM!" Each word I shouted brought with it an accompanying jolt of pain. The pain felt appropriate and, if anything, not intense enough.

"I did *not* kill your father, Mr. Lordan," Lou said after taking a deep breath. "And my understanding is that the citizens who did shoot him were acting in self-defense."

"HE WAS AN OLD MAN!"

"He was an old man with a shotgun, a shotgun he had already discharged once. I read the report."

"HE WAS MY FATHER!" I strained my arms against the leather restraints. "I'M GOING TO KILL YOU, YOU FUCKING COCKSUCKER! I COULD HAVE SAVED HIM! YOU'RE FUCKING DEAD, ALL OF YOU! I SWEAR TO CHRIST I'M GOING TO KILL YOU!"

She sighed and covered her mouth with her hand. "This isn't going to get us anywhere, Mr. Lordan. My sincere condolences over your loss. I mean that. If you truly believe that the citizens who apprehended you acted inappropriately then you can certainly file a complaint. For our purposes, though, that's neither here nor there."

"Shooting my father's *inappropriate?*"

"Please, Mr. Lordan, I understand that you're upset, but I need you to calm down and listen to what I'm about to say." Her voice became slightly more rigid, though still remaining friendly. "James Henry Lordan, you have been arrested for failure to register as a citizen in the One World Community. You have been brought to this registration center so as to be officially offered citizenship. When you accept, you will be afforded all the rights and benefits of a free citizen of the Community. You will be allowed complete freedom of movement and offered satisfying work, which will be compatible with both your skills and temperament. You will have full access to food, shelter, education, and medical care. You will receive an identification implantation, which will . . ."

"Fuck you, nigger."

Lou stared at me silently for several minutes.

189

"All right, Mr. Lordan. You're obviously very upset and probably a little overwhelmed right now, so I'm going to cut this session short. Apparently, you've been living in Boston for some time, so I'm going to assume that you understand what's being offered. I'm returning you to your cell to allow you some time alone. But before I do that, I'm going to tell you something that you might *not* know. If you refuse citizenship, you will be officially categorized as a non-person, and your caseworker will be responsible for removing your harmful presence from society. If you refuse citizenship, you'll be escorted down into the basement and shot in the back of the head."

"Do it," I whispered.

"Excuse me?"

"Fuck you."

Lou rapped her knuckles against the door and stared at me. Her eyes were wide and sad.

I turned away.

Two guards entered the room, unstrapped me, cuffed my hands behind my back, and shuffled me out of the room. As I was led down a flight of stairs, I was unable to deny that Lou's sadness and sympathy seemed sincere.

The cell was dark and unlit, as was the hall. The only source of illumination was the light trickling down the stairs from the end of the hall. While my eyes adjusted to the darkness, an unseen voice sounding happy and haggard croaked out from the corner of the cell.

"A new roomy! Figures they'd send you in while I'm on the shitter. Hell of a way to get introduced, what with half a turd hanging outta my ass."

I saw the barest outlines of a bunk bed and stepped towards it.

"Bottom's mine," the voice said.

I climbed to the top.

The cell was cold and there were no sheets on the bed. I curled myself into a tight ball and stared at the wall. After a few minutes, the toilet flushed. He seemed to have difficulty traveling the few feet between the toilet and the bed, his feet dragging noisily over the floor. He cursed with each movement. The bed shook as he clumsily flopped onto the bottom bunk.

"So, what'cha in for?" he asked.

I said nothing.

He laughed an old man's laugh, full of phlegm and originating, not from his throat or voice box, but from the churning of internal organs.

"I'm just fuckin' whit'cha, boy. That's my joke. We're all in here for the same thing. By the by, my name's Stan."

"I don't give a shit," I said without turning away from the wall.

"Oooo! Got us a tough guy, huh?" Stan laughed his painful sounding laugh and I felt him rocking back and forth underneath me. "Yeah, I seen yer type before. Lots of anger, but not too much in the way of brains. I got yer number."

"Shut up, old man."

"Listen, Happy, if ya got any brains at all, you'll pay attention to what I got to say."

I stared at the wall.

"Ya got no idea what's commin' yer way. I can help ya through this, boy."

I pulled my knees up to my chest and squeezed.

"You listenin' to me, Happy?"

I squeezed as tight as I could and tried to disappear into the darkness.

"I'm talking to ya, boy."

"Jesus Christ!" I rolled off my bunk and landed on the floor with an impact that caused the pain in my head to flare. I crouched down and stared towards Stan. My eyes had grown accustomed to the dark, but Stan had pushed himself back against the wall, where the darkness was absolute. Only the barest outline of his figure was visible.

"Why can't you just leave me alone?"

"I want to help."

"Bullshit! What the fuck do you want from me?"

"You ain't got nothin' that I want, boy. I'm just telling ya that I can help."

"Yeah? Well, fuck you! All of a sudden, *everybody* wants to help. You want to help, that nigger bitch upstairs wants to help, and that faggot on the cross wants to help. Well where the fuck were you when I really needed help, huh? Where were *any* of you?"

He said nothing.

"Yeah, that's what I thought. Fuck you all."

The darkness surrounding Stan was nearly complete. I pushed through it, my eyes slicing through the black like razors, pushing into Stan's unseen eyes. All the hate and the anger and the rage, everything inside of me was pushed into Stan's eyes so he would know.

"Hey dumb-ass, do ya know you're trying to stare down my knee?"

"Fuck you," I mumbled, and climbed back onto my bunk.

Stan's crackling laughter shook my bed.

The harsh lights in the White Room blinded me as I was strapped down into the heavy chair. I heard clicking sounds and, as my eyes became accustomed to the light, and blurs became forms, I saw Lou sitting on a small white chair, typing into a laptop computer resting on a tiny white bench. After several minutes, she stopped typing and spun around to face me.

"Which do you prefer? Jim? Jimmy? James?"

"Mr. Lordan."

"Fair enough," she said, laughing and nodding her head. "Well then, Mr. Lordan, you've had several days to calm down and think about what I said. Now I . . ."

"What did you do with his body?"

"I'm sorry?"

"My father. What did you do with his body?"

"He was cremated."

"He was Catholic, you fucking cunt."

"Let's please try and stay focused here, all right? I am officially offering you citizenship in the OWC. Do you accept this offer, and all the responsibilities and privileges that accompany it?"

"No."

"Well," she said, nodding her head gravely, "I can't say I'm surprised, although I am disappointed. For the record, are you refusing citizenship due to religious beliefs?"

I stared blankly at her.

"Mr. Lordan?"

"Nigger."

"Well then," she said as she spun around in her chair and resumed typing, "I suppose that would be, *personal reasons of a non-religious basis*, then. Now . . ."

"Now you're going to shoot me in the face. Let's just cut the shit and get it over with. I'm sick of you and every other fucker on this planet. Just do it."

She stood up and wandered over to the opposite wall, leaning against it and staring at me. "Tell me, Mr. Lordan, did you even consider my offer? It's noon right now, you could be free and on the street by six. You'd have food and shelter, we'd see to it that you'd have fulfilling work. You could be a part of something decent. You'd have the opportunity to grow and evolve, the opportunity to become a better human being. You could be with us when we meet the Celestine Prophets as equals. Did you think about any of that?"

My father is in Hell.

"No. Are you going to shoot me or not?"

She sighed and rubbed the bridge of her nose with her finger tips. "No, I'm not going to shoot you. Not yet, anyway." She pushed herself off the wall and knocked on the door. The locks latched open and a large black man in an OWC uniform walked into the room, gently closing the door behind him. He stood next to my chair and stared down at me with neutral, disinterested eyes.

"Have you ever heard of Wilhelm Reich?" Lou asked me as she returned to her chair.

"Who the fuck is this? Why aren't you going to shoot me?"

"This gentleman's name is John Ridgeway. Wilhelm Reich was an Austrian psychiatrist who studied under Freud."

The blow was over before my brain had a chance to register what had happened. John's knuckles tore into my left eye, snapping my face and my neck to the right. My body jerked out of the chair and was snapped back down by the restraints.

"Eventually," Lou continued in a voice that betrayed no knowledge of the blow I had just received, "Reich broke with Freud and developed a radically different form of therapy. You're an educated man, Mr. Lordan, are you sure you've never heard of Reich?"

Underneath the skin, my blood pumped at a furious pace as the swelling began. "What the fuck is this?"

"Reich's ideas were such a radical departure from conventional psychiatry, that his writings were actually banned for a time in the United States and, in the late fifties, he was arrested and thrown into a federal prison, where he died. You see, Reich believed that our psychological problems were actually physical, that past psychological traumas were stored in our physicality. Those physiological blocks halted normal energy flow, and created a rigid, angry, ignorant, and potentially pathological character. Conventional forms of therapy didn't help any more than they would a patient suffering from cancer. What was needed to be healed was for the patient to experience physiological trauma, which jolted the blockages contained within the muscles, while simultaneously, re-experiencing the psychological trauma. All of which would force the patient to experience the deep sadness and hatred that lay undetected by the conscious mind. Only then, could the patient begin to change and grow. Only then would the patient be free to understand and move past the damage society had inflicted upon him.

"Reich understood the inseparable connection between mind and body. He understood that our society had traumatized us all, and that to exist within it, we needed to develop a shield, a mask, which, somewhere down the line, we forgot was a mask, and mistook for our true selves. Reich knew how to break that mask."

His fist dug into my cheek and I felt a surge of pain as my brain smashed back and forth against my skull. My skin pinched underneath John's knuckles and tore open.

"FUCK!"

My neck went slack and my head dangled. Lou grabbed my chin and raised my face. Blood dripped out from the gash on my forehead and drooled into my eye.

"I have to shoot you, Mr. Lordan. If I cannot convince you to change who you are, then *I* have to pull the trigger. We've trapped ourselves behind our shield, and it's stopped us from growing. For you to grow, I have to shatter that shield, because if I can't, than I have to shoot you. If I can't help you, then killing you is *my* responsibility, do you understand? I don't want to have to kill you, but I also cannot, will not, allow you to destroy the future of humanity."

"Wha . . . what are you talking about? I don't . . . Fuck you! Fuck you, you shot my father and *you're* going to judge me?"

"He was a malignant cancer and so are you. Why do you think the world is the way it is? Luck? Chance? A handful of leaders? The Devil? God? Who is responsible for the rape and the hate and the prejudice and the ignorance? *You* are, Mr. Lordan. God didn't make the world the way it is, people did. People like you. People like your father."

"Shut up! You don't talk about him! You never knew him!"

"No." She dropped my face and leaned back into her chair. "No, but I know you, don't I? And what are you but the inevitable result of who and what your father was."

"He was a good man!"

"*A good man?* Is that the best you can give me? Please. A surface description which means nothing. Words, Jimmy, those are just empty words. What does that mean, *he was good?* He didn't commit any crimes? He was kind to his family and friends? Every son thinks his father was a good man. That doesn't make it so. "

"He was . . . he was a human being."

"So was Ted Bundy. Your father was a virus who infected you with his hatred and his ignorance. Now *you're* the virus and, if left unchecked, you'll infect all of humanity."

"I don't have the slightest *fucking* idea what you're talking about."

"Oh, you're innocent! Is that it? Let me explain something to you, Mr. Lordan, men like Adolph Hitler, they don't lead society, they reflect it. People like you created him, put him in power, and then allowed him to act out your evil. And all the while, you sit back and deny any responsibility for his actions. All of our leaders, *all of them*, did *exactly* what we wanted them to do. The Holocaust wasn't what the *Nazis* wanted; it was what the *German people* wanted. People in America didn't go without food and medical care and housing because the *government* didn't care, they went without those necessities because the *American people* didn't care. Because *you* didn't care. It was all your fault."

"Shut up!"

"And the worst part is, you think you've got clean hands. You think you have the right to feel however it is you want, that you have the right to be ignorant and racist and hateful, as if you're not connected to the world. You were a teacher, Mr. Lordan, and you taught our children how to hate, because what else did you have to offer? You're as guilty as sin, Mr. Lordan, and we both know it."

"Who the fuck are you?" I asked through heavy, swollen lips. Blood seeped into my eye, half blinding me. "Who are you to lecture me about sin? You strap me into a chair and get this fucking nigger faggot to beat me. You shoot people in the head and *you're* better than me?" I laughed and allowed the blood to drool out of my mouth onto the white floor. "*I'm* the bad guy? Fuck you, you stupid cunt."

"Action has never been the final arbitrator of morality, Mr. Lordan. In Auschwitz, the Nazis erected gallows where starving inmates were hung for minor infractions such as stealing bread. When the Russians captured the camp at the end of the war, they used those same gallows to execute the Nazis. The action is the same, but should the judgment be?"

She stared at me and I turned away. The swelling in my forehead began to push down onto my eye. Everywhere I looked was white.

"Yes," Lou continued, "I have strapped you into this chair, and am having you physically beaten. But *why* am I doing this? Isn't that the question you have to answer if you're going to judge me? Why does a doctor cut, a mother spank, or a dentist drill?"

I heard the snap before I felt the punch. His fist dug into my open mouth, breaking off a tooth. The shock and the blow made me gasp for air and I sucked the tooth down into my throat. I gagged as the sharp bone dug into the soft flesh of my throat. I vomited. My shoulders hunched over while I gasped for breath and spat up blood and puke.

"FUCKING NIGGER!" I screamed, whipping my head towards John and hurling bits of blood and tooth and spit and puke onto his blue uniform. "Is this what they got you doing, boy? Is this how you're helping to build the perfect society? Yeah, they got you on the road to spiritual evolution. You're a fucking mule!"

"Is it possible for you to view yourself as anything other than a victim, Mr. Lordan?" Lou asked. "I understand that who you are is a direct result of the family that raised you and the society that surrounded you, but ultimately, don't you feel the need to take responsibility for who and what you are? Look at it this way, when a child is sexually abused, he is the victim, but if that child grows up and becomes a molester, is he still a victim? Forces beyond his control led him down that road, but at some point, doesn't he have to accept responsibility for what he's become? Don't you?"

"I was never abused and I never hurt anyone. I don't know what . . . You're insane."

"We were all abused and we all need to be healed."

"I'm going to kill you, you fucking bitch."

"You don't scare me, Mr. Lordan. *I'll kill you,*" she mocked, "*toss you in a ditch, take you out like yesterday's garbage.* You're a robot, a mindless slave to the dialogue you've read in books and seen in the movies. Your threats and insults are as flaccid and as shallow as you are. You're a scared little boy trying to fool the world. How many times do you have to use the word *fuck* before you realize that you aren't fooling anybody?"

"I don't . . . Why are you doing this to me?"

"Because no matter how false that mask might be, it still affects the world. You are a part of a community, and you either help that community grow, or you help to destroy it. You're an evil man, Mr. Lordan, and if I can't convince you to change, if I can't *help* you to change, then I'm going to have to shoot you. I don't want to do that. *That's* why I'm doing this. I want to save you, Mr. Lordan."

The knuckle plowed into my eye socket. I vomited until there was nothing left in my stomach. I floated in and out of consciousness and the world became blurry and unfocused. Shapes and objects became indistinguishable, bathed in black and purple and red. My eye-lid fluttered as water and blood flowed out from around its socket.

I wanted to cry harder. I wanted my mother to rub my back and tell me it was okay. I wanted my father to be standing behind me, saying nothing but assuring me with his strong presence, that this would all pass.

My father is in Hell.

"Do you know what this is, Mr. Lordan?" Lou whispered into my ear. "This is the beginning. This is only the beginning."

Twelve

My first concern upon regaining lucidity was not how badly I was injured or how much pain I was in, but the rag Stan was pressing against my face.

"Stan?" I asked, my voice heavy and slurred.

"What's that, Happy?" Everything was black, but the voice came from above, and I realized that Stan was cradling my head in his lap.

"Where did you get the water for the rag?" The words had to push themselves through puffy, torn lips, and sounded more like, *Ahhr id euh het heh whurhuh hor heh hruhu?* Stan seemed to understand what I was saying.

"Where d'ya think?"

"Just tell me that I don't have toilet water running down my face and into my mouth."

"Okay, ya don't have toilet water running down yer face and into yer mouth."

"Thanks." I attempted a smile, but my stiff face refused. "I do though, don't I?"

"Yep."

"Am I blind?" I asked.

"Nah, yer eyes are swollen shut, is all."

I ran my tongue around the inside of my mouth, painfully exploring the torn flesh and jagged broken teeth.

"How many teeth did they knock out?" I asked.

"Well," he said, after silently inspecting my open mouth, "I suppose that depends. How many teeth were ya missing before?"

"*How* . . .? None."

"Then they knocked out a shitload of `em."

I tried to lift my head, but a rush of pain stopped me.

"Simmer down, Happy. They worked ya over pretty good. Sit still and it won't be so bad."

"When are they . . .?" I swallowed hard. "When are they coming back?"

"Hard to say. They change it up so as to fuck wit'cha. Sometimes they won't come for weeks, sometimes they take ya three times in one day. What with the beating you just got, though, I'd guess they'll give ya at least a week to heal."

"How do you know so much about this place?"

"Been in this shithole for six months, boy."

"Six . . .!" I lifted my head and the pain flared. "AHHHH!"

"Stupid. Told ya to sit still. Don't listen to no one do ya, Happy?"

"The deadline was only a few weeks ago. Why have you been here so long?"

"How d'ya think the OWC stopped the rioting so quick? How d'ya think they kept the crime level so low? Ya think that was all community spirit? Anyone with a record got picked up in the first couple of weeks."

"I don't . . . If I don't accept the tag, they'll keep doing this for six months?"

"Nah. You, they'll shoot in three months. Maybe two."

"What's so . . . so special about you?"

"It ain't exactly a privilege." He laughed and, through the top of my head, which was pressed against his torso, I could feel his insides churning together like broken, rusted gears. I wondered how much pain his laughter cost him. "I'm what'cha call an anatomy."

"You mean *anomaly*?"

"Shut up, boy, I'm talking here. Ya see, technically, no one here's got the authority to classify anyone as a non-person. They gotta send away for authorization to some other department. Don't get me wrong, it ain't nothing but a circle-jerk, rubber-stamp department, but it's still gotta get done before they shoot ya. For some reason, they can't get the authority to shoot me. They keep sending my name out and the requests keep commin' back denied. Prob'ly just a computer fuck-up, but it don't matter, `cause without that authorization, they can't shoot me. Heh. Drives `em fuckin' nuts."

I remembered the White Room, the feel of John's knuckles and the cut of Lou's words.

"I don't know if I could take six months of this, Stan."

"*Six*? Boy, you ain't even gonna last the *two*."

"Fuck yoAAAHHH!"

"Big mouth don't help that pain much, does it?"

"I can take it. I can take anything those fuckers got to give."

"Mmm. I've had twenty-three cellmates since I been here. Ten were Christ-freaks. Them they just mess with for a week or two to make sure they're not faking it. Then they whack 'em. The other ten took the tag by the third session. Only three others held out for the bullet. You a Christ-freak?"

"Fuck God."

"Didn't think so."

"Fuck the rest of those faggots, too. I can take it. They can shoot me right in the fucking face, I don't care. I'll take the bullet before I take the tag. Shoot me right in the face."

"Actually, it's behind the ear."

"Right in the fucking face. If three lasted, I will too."

"That ain't good company you're lookin' to join. One of the three spent his last month trying to jerk-off after they sliced off his prick. The other one'd beat his head against the wall 'till he was knocked out, and then start all over again when he woke up. All day, *boom, boom, boom*, right into the fuckin' concrete. Bastards shot him just so they could grease him before he did it himself. The last one, he was gone long before they killed him. He just sat in the corner staring at nothin' while he picked the stitches on his stumps, where they had hacked off his feet."

"Bunch of faggots," I said without processing his words, "I can take it."

Stan sighed and I could feel him shaking his head.

"Yer anger's only gonna get you so far in here, boy. It's bullshit, and believe me, what those bastards got planned for ya, it's gonna tear away all of your bullshit. Whatever yer anger's hiding, shame, guilt, weakness, it don't matter what, 'cause they're gonna tear through and find it."

I pushed myself out of Stan's lap. White fire shot up and down my spine. I rose to my feet unsteadily, flailing my arms until I crashed into the bunk beds. I latched onto the top mattress and dug my fingers into it, fighting to maintain my balance and control my churning stomach.

"I don't care what they do to me, they can't take it away. It's all I've got left."

"Happy, if hate's all ya got, then you ain't got nothin', 'cause I swear to God, man, they're gonna rip it away and skull-fuck whatever they find underneath."

"They can't!" My broken teeth pulsed.

"They'll do it without breaking a sweat."

The pain trolled through my body like a shark, slow and thoughtless, confidant in its unchallenged superiority. My fingers tore into the mattress, ripping the fabric.

"Fuck you, Stan. You can't take it away, either. You all want a piece of me. Just fuck off. Fuck off and die. You can't have it. None of you can. It's mine. It's all that's left."

I smiled when the cell door was opened and two guards pulled me off my bunk and cuffed my hands behind my back. While the two weeks of rest had allowed me the time to physically heal, they had also begun nudging me towards a psychological breakdown. I refused to speak with Stan, spending most of my time trying to escape through sleep. It proved a wasted effort, as reality began bleeding into my dreams like a dark stain. Heaven and Hell, the White Room and my father's living room; they all existed as one single location, an indistinguishable fluid backdrop against which, any event seemed plausible. People merged in and out of one another as easily as the environment. Sarah, Scotty, Stan, Lou, Jesus, Dad, Morrison; they all phased in and out of one another, all offering promises and threats as vague and insubstantial as their physical reality.

If I accepted my father's hand, he'd suddenly transform into Lou, and I'd find myself surrounded by white, threatened with sharp, shiny objects, unable to retrieve my freely offered hand from her grasp. If I turned my back on a shadowy figure that looked like Morrison, I'd peek over my shoulder, only to discover that it had actually been Sarah, who would walk away from me looking sad and disappointed. I'd try and run to her, but find my feet already committed to walking in the opposite direction. I'd try and call to her, but my tongue would become thick and numb, rendering me mute and unable to reverse my rejection.

Waking from those dreams, I'd find myself back in my cell, in an environment every bit as nonsensical as my dreams. The Darkness in the cell surrounded me like a heavy mist. It wasn't a safe, anonymous darkness within which I could hide and take refuge; it was a living presence wrapping itself inside and around me. It was aware of my existence and knew my thoughts and fears. It smelled cold.

So, when the guards dragged me out of the cell and away from the Darkness, I smiled, believing with all my heart that after two weeks of being surrounded by black, the bright lights of the White Room would be a reassuring comfort, that they would allow me to reclaim my slowly eroding sanity. Of course, I was wrong.

I was stripped naked and strapped to a hospital gurney. My arms, legs, chest, neck, and head were all tightly secured to the table, leaving me utterly immovable. The guards left the room and I was alone.

I stared up into the white ceiling for what felt like an eternity. If the Darkness in my cell had been alive and intangible, the surrounding White was unbearably solid and lifeless. The Darkness was evil, but it was an evil that had been aware of my presence and acknowledged my existence. The White was utterly indifferent. It was unaware and inhuman. It extended outward to an infinity that strained my brain to be aware of, and then reversed itself, becoming solid blocks of pure symmetry, pushing towards me, threatening to crush and suffocate my existence. The White couldn't be spoken to, dealt with, or cajoled. It couldn't be bargained with, reasoned with, or begged. It crushed me into nothingness and stretched me into infinity, not with love or hate, but simply with its infinite, unbending presence. I couldn't turn away and it was useless to close my eyes, the White being so fully present that it destroyed the darkness of my own eyelids.

"You don't look very good, Mr. Lordan," Lou said.

I strained my eyes to see her, but remained silent, afraid of what I might say if I dared open my mouth, afraid of what might escape me. *I love you*, was not out of the question.

"I don't mean physically," she said while closing the door behind her. "Actually, your face has healed up rather nicely. I mean *you* don't look good." She placed her hand on my naked arm. Her delicate fingers felt cool and perfect.

If I accept the tag, I go to Hell. If I accept Christ, I go to Heaven and leave my father to burn in Hell alone. If I go to Hell with my father, I never see Sarah again. If I refuse the tag, they keep hurting me.

Lou stared down at me with compassion.

I dug my jagged, broken teeth into my tongue, fighting to stop the words and tears from escaping.

"This is all so unnecessary, Mr. Lordan," she said, tilting her head and smiling sadly. "Let's end this idiocy now. Accept citizenship in the OWC and you can leave. Why are you doing this to yourself? Do you really hate yourself this much?"

"You . . . you tell me that I'm all of these horrible things." My voice was quiet and uncertain. "You say that I'm hateful and ignorant. You say that I'm a . . . a virus. A disease. If all that's true, what difference will tagging me make? I'd only be doing it to escape the pain. Why would that make me any different? Any better?"

She removed her fingers from my arm and her shadow passed over me as she walked around the gurney and stood behind me. "That's a good question. The truth is, I *can't* be certain that you'll be any different. However, in my experience, a willingness to become a citizen of the OWC is a good litmus test of personality. People who refuse to join our community, even in the face of physical and emotional stress, display an uncommon reluctance to face and overcome their flaws. They refuse to see themselves as a part of something greater. They cling to a destructively self-centered concept of individuality.

"I'll admit that getting tagged is a cosmetic sign, but it's an important one. It shows a capacity to place one's self underneath something greater, a capacity to accept something larger than the self. In accepting citizenship, you become a part of a healthy family that can then help you to grow and evolve. It's a bit like alcoholic admitting that he has a problem and joining AA. It doesn't solve the problem, but it's the first, most important step in the healing process.

"Believe me, Mr. Lordan, I harbor no illusions. If you accept citizenship, you will doubtlessly walk out here thinking that you did so only to escape pain and suffering. But over time, you'll find that you discovered something inside of you that you never knew existed. The Community will help you nurture that part, help you to understand it and embrace it. Right now, you view yourself as the kind of man who would never accept the tag. When you accept it, you'll be forced to look at yourself in a new light. That's when the healing begins." She paused and allowed me a moment to respond. When I said nothing, she asked, "So, will you accept citizenship, Mr. Lordan? Will you allow me to help you?"

"No." I allowed the answer to flow out me instinctively. I was afraid to think, to decide. I nearly added a *thank you*. As it was, my refusal came out sounding both polite and uncertain.

"*No?* That's it? Where are your insults, Mr. Lordan?"

"What?"

"You never thought you were like that, did you? Be honest."

"Like what?"

"*Nigger, cunt, bitch, faggot.* I've read your file. Liberal Democrat, Liberal schooling. You sent money to the ACLU and Amnesty International. Tell me something, have you ever come anywhere close to acknowledging just how deeply you hate women, homosexuals, and minorities? Have you ever *really* looked at yourself?"

"I know I don't hurt people. I could never kill someone, or torture them. I'm not you."

"Is that how you justify it? *Everyone's worse than me, so I can't really be that bad?* You didn't call me a fascist or a sadist. No, *nigger* was the world that flowed so easily out of your mouth." She slid her face next to mine, gently placing her hand on my shoulder. "Come on," she purred, "be honest. It felt good, didn't it? After hiding those feelings for so long, it felt good to be able to lash out. You loved being given the justification to call someone a nigger to their face. You did, didn't you?"

Anger began seeping into my chest, slowly pushing aside the fear. "Yeah. Yeah, that was worth watching my father get shot in the face. I'm sick of your shit. Just shut up and shoot me. Either that or bring your spiritually evolved person-of-color back in here to kick the shit out of me again."

Lou removed her hand and took a step away from me. "There's a part of you that wishes he was beating you right now, isn't there? That way, you could avoid my questions and take refuge in the cover of martyrdom. Well, John won't be joining us today. He was an introduction, a way of knocking you out of your complacency and stripping you of any illusions of invulnerability. As I told you, he was simply a beginning. Today is when the real work begins."

She walked away from me and returned with a hospital tray. She pulled on rubber surgical gloves and lifted a scalpel off the tray. It was clean and sharp, just like it had been in my dreams. I wondered if I was dreaming at that very moment, but quickly dismissed the notion, realizing that even if it turned out to be true, it would be no consolation. My reality and my dreams had merged together so completely, that escape could no longer be found in either.

"Let's begin," she said.

With a look of serious concentration, she leaned over my torso and pushed the blade into the flesh covering my left rib cage. I bit down into my cheeks to try and stop myself from screaming. I averted the scream, but odd sounds escaped from my throat, and I squirmed on the table like a three year-old having a splinter removed. Lou slid the blade across me, my flesh yielding before it.

The cutting ended and I managed to take a quick gasp of air before the peeling began. I opened my eyes and saw Lou slip the blade under a corner of the slashed flesh. She lifted a tiny flap of skin, grasping it tightly between the tips of her fingers. Using her left hand to pull and her right hand to slice underneath, she peeled off the rectangular chunk of flesh.

"What are you doing?" I screamed.

Lou continued to peel.

It felt as though my flesh were being scorched by a blowtorch, a blowtorch that pulled fire from my chest rather than pushing fire onto it.

"STOP IT! JESUS CHRIST, LEAVE ME ALONE, YOU FUCKING NIGGER! STOP!"

The peeling took longer than the cutting and, once she had finished, she carefully placed my flesh on the hospital tray.

"You shot off your big guns too soon, Mr. Lordan. You should have started off by calling me a *watermelon* or a *spade*, that way you would have had the room to get meaner. You could have slowly worked up to *nigger*, thus conveying your growing hatred of me. Now, you just sound repetitive."

Blood bubbled out of the rectangular hole in my torso, spilling across my stomach. Lou reached around behind my head and I heard the slow whirl of machinery. She placed a tube in my hole, which began sucking up the red while she sponged away whatever remained. In the center of the hole were two white ribs, my ribs.

"That's what this is really about," I gasped. "You've got the power now, so it's payback time. *That's* your fucking lesson. Feel good to take back a pound of flesh from whitey?"

"So many justifications," she said with a smile. "This isn't you against me, Mr. Lordan, although I'm sure it would make you feel better if that were so. *We're all the same deep down*, right? All as hateful as you are. Well, this isn't about me; it's about you. You think I haven't had any black people strapped into that gurney? Any women? I'm not doing this because I hate you; I'm doing it because I love you."

"YOU HATE ME!"

"I . . . Okay. You need to believe that this is personal? Fine, here's how it's personal; I have a seven-year-old daughter. Lori. Lori has to live in this world. She has to be taught by people like you. She has to work for people like you. She even has to be friends with people like you. People whom, underneath their polite smiles, see her as nothing more than a nigger. She's a beautiful, loving human being, but because of people like you, she has to live in this world and be seen as a nigger. She's young, but over time, she'll begin to see herself that way too. I don't want her to have to grow up in that world."

"I'm not racist!"

"No? Then why is it so easy to call me a nigger? Why was it so easy to call John Ridgeway one?"

"He was beating me! You were hurting me!"

"So why not call us assholes? Sons of bitches? You obviously possess a wide spectrum of profanity, why call us niggers? I'll tell you why, because whether he was beating you or pumping your gas or running for President, John would never be anything but a nigger to you. My daughter would never be anything but a nigger."

"No."

"Yes. My daughter's *not* a nigger, Mr. Lordan. I don't want her to have to live in a world that makes her think she is. Believe it or not, I don't want *you* to have to live in that world, either. It can't be very pleasant living with all that hatred."

"You don't know a single thing about me, you fucking cunt!"

She pushed her face into mine and, for the first time, her voice sounded angry. "No," she hissed, "I know *everything* about you, Lordan. Everything. The problem is that *you* don't know anything about yourself." She leaned back and regained her composure. "And if you refuse to know the truth about yourself, if you refuse to understand the effect your hatred has on others, what motivation do you have in changing? You believe yourself to be harmless. You are not."

"I don't . . . Jesus Christ, why are you doing this to me? I'm not even a Christian!"

"Not a Christian?" She stopped dabbing away at the blood and looked at me with confusion. "What on earth does that have to do with anything?"

"Wha . . .? Everything! You're persecuting Christians for not getting the tag, but I'm not even one of them. I hate God!"

Lou regarded me in silence for several seconds.

"Mr. Lordan, *I'm* a Christian."

"What? I . . . No you're not. You can't be!"

"Why not?"

"You've got the tag! You're working for the fucking Antichrist."

"Oh my . . . !" Lou's eyes widened. "You mean to tell me that you honestly believe that Richard Morrison is the Antichrist? And that identification implantations are the Mark Of The Beast?" She placed her fingers over her mouth and gently giggled.

"He is!"

"Really? And tell me, who perchance isn't? Every crisis the world has ever faced has been called the Endtimes. How many men throughout history have been identified as the Antichrist? Did you know that Ronald Reagan's middle name has six letters in it? All three of his names have six letters. 666. Some people claimed that that meant that *he* was the Antichrist. Obviously I've heard these ridiculous accusations, but I have to admit, I'm shocked to hear that you believe them. Frankly, for all your obvious faults, you struck me as more intelligent than that."

"You shoot Christians, if I was one, you'd have already shot me."

"Possibly," she said, and nodded her head. "It's true that we don't spend as much time trying to help . . . well, *Christ-freaks* really *is* the most appropriate word for them. But that's not because of *our* agenda, it's because of *theirs*. They're so obsessed with the notion that Morrison is the Antichrist and identification implantations will damn them to Hell, that it's proven impossible to help them.

"It's sad, really. Such a twisting of what religion is intended to be. Being a Christian is supposed to be about growing, understanding, and loving. These Christ-freaks want nothing to do with any of that. With them, it's all about greed and fear. They're greedy for Heaven and fearful of Hell. It's all self-interest for them. They think accepting a tag means they'll go to Hell, so they refuse it. But there's no morality behind that choice, only a lust for Heaven. If they thought murdering a baby would get them into Heaven, rest assured, they'd do it. There's no love, no growth in these fundamentalist Christ-freaks, only greed."

"You're lying, you're just trying to fuck with me. You can't be a Christian."

"Of course I can. Obviously, after the Celestine Prophets, I needed to modify my beliefs somewhat, but that's what growth is all about. As a religion, Christianity has continually modified its doctrines. I believe in a man who lived in Jerusalem two thousand years ago. I believe he evolved to a level of spiritual awareness, which was unheard of at the time. Jesus was an extraordinary individual who accomplished what the Celestine Prophets told us we're all capable of accomplishing. He was crucified, but had evolved to the point where death no longer had any affect on him, and he rose from the dead to join the Celestine Prophets. The message of Jesus has been distorted throughout history. Read the Bible, Mr. Lordan, Jesus wasn't ordering us to kneel down, he was imploring us to rise up.

"The moniker, *Christ*, was tacked on to Jesus' name just as falsely as *Antichrist* has been attached to Morrison's. Both are true, but in a limited way. The Bible is a beautiful metaphor, which has been misinterpreted as a literal, historical document. Christ and Antichrist are not individuals; they are *us*, all of us. They are the dualistic qualities, which exist both collectively and individually in humanity. All religions speak of this duality, because they're universal metaphors telling of our innate capacity for good and evil. Christ and Antichrist live within humanity. The Endtimes are not a literal battle, but rather humanity's struggle to conquer the destroyer within while simultaneously learning to accept ourselves as our own redeemers."

"Everything that's happened . . ."

"Everything that's happened proves nothing more than our desperate need to avoid responsibility. We've read the Bible for two thousand years, and have subconsciously brought about the destruction that we mistakenly believed it foretold. We're destroying ourselves so that we can deny personal responsibility. Haven't you ever known anyone who would rather die than grow?"

"You're going to Hell!"

"No, I'm going to save you from yours. *You* are the Antichrist, Mr. Lordan. I'm going to help you become Christ." She snapped off her bloody gloves and pulled on a fresh pair. "And the first step is to show you who you really are, to help you understand how much pain you've caused."

"What are you . . . what are you going to do?" I sputtered.

"Do you know what racism is, Mr. Lordan?"

"Tell me what you're going to do."

"It's not an action or a thought or a word. It's a force. Words, actions and thoughts have kept that force alive, but racism is much larger than any of those things alone. It's a force that has been created through hundreds of years of slavery, segregation, ignorance, hatred, and ultimately, by acceptance. It's a force that exists above humanity, but couldn't exist without it."

"Black people," she said as she stared into my eyes, "have tried to create a similar force through an increasingly violent attitude. They tried to make white people afraid of them, and to some extent, they succeeded. Homosexuals attempted a similar strategy when groups like Act Up and Queer Nation exaggerated their homosexuality and then flaunted it, pushing it into the faces of heterosexuals. It made straight people uncomfortable, and there arose some power in that ability to offend, just as there existed some power in black people's ability to frighten."

"And that's okay, right? It's okay for blacks to be hateful and violent, because they're black."

"Of course not. One should be better than one's enemies. Besides, the strategy itself is fundamentally flawed. When black people played into racist stereotypes, acting like the *jungle savage*, they gained some power through intimidation. But while that tactic created a small reservoir of power, ultimately, it fed back into the larger force of hatred by reinforcing age-old stereotypes."

"I . . . Jesus Christ, woman, what does any of this have to do with me? Yeah, I called you a nigger, but my father was shot, and you were beating me. Words were all I had. I'm not a racist, I was just using the only weapons I had left. I'm not a racist."

"Jimmy . . ."

"Don't call me that!"

"I . . . All right. This is not about racism; it's about hatred. Racism is only one of the many ways you express the hatred inside of you. You can't evolve, you can't change until you admit to its existence. You have to understand the consequences of who you are."

"*I haven't done anything!*" I began sobbing and crying. "You're the ones who shot my father, you're the ones who beat me, you're the ones who are hurting me. I haven't done anything. Jesus Christ, will you stop? Please? Please stop. I just want it to stop."

"That's what I want, too," she said sympathetically, and snapped down her gloves.

"Jesus, whatever you're going to do, please don't. Please."

I began panting heavily.

She picked up the sponge and wiped the blood away one last time. When she looked into my eyes, any traces of sympathy had disappeared, replaced with a look of cold determination.

"Understand this, Mr. Lordan, every time you call someone a nigger or a cunt or a faggot, every time you look at someone and think those words, you are no longer simply acting as an individual. You are feeding into and drawing upon a force which has contaminated the soul of our species for thousands of years. You wrap your fingers around that accumulated power and wield it as if it were your own personal weapon."

"Don't do this."

"You know what it feels like to wield that force, the rush of power and control . . ."

"I'M INNOCENT!"

" . . .now you're going to understand what it feels like to be on the other side."

She leaned over my body and pushed her hand into the hole she had cut into my torso. Her fingers pushed underneath my lower rib, the back of her knuckles pressing up against my stomach and lung.

"STOP IT! STOP IT!" I pulled against the restraints, but couldn't manage even a millimeter of movement. My insides burned with an inescapable heat. "STOP!"

She pressed her fingers up against the small space between my ribs and began pushing herself between them. The tips of her fingers spread the ribs apart and it felt as though my entire body was being torn open.

"PLEASE!"

When she had edged herself far enough between my ribs, she slowly bent her fingers, wrapping them around my bone while looping her thumb around the other side. When she was finished, she held my bare rib snugly in the palm of her hand.

"GET OUT OF ME! GET OUT!"

My organs clenched into themselves in a vain attempt at allowing her hand more space. My heart pumped at a furious pace and I became terrified at the thought of it exploding. Next to my insides, her hand was cold and hard, like a brick stuffed into a drawer filled with helium balloons.

Lou turned towards me, speaking through tight lips. "*This* is what if feels like on the other side. You can feel me inside of you. You feel soft, don't you? A lie next to my truth, weak next to my strength, wrong next to my right. I own you."

I closed my eyes and her tiny hand with its delicate fingers felt larger than my entire body. I began convulsing, each shake stabbing into me like a thousand needles.

"OPEN YOUR EYES, BITCH!" she roared, leaning towards me with a look of hatred and disgust. "Good. Now quit shaking."

I tried to stop the shaking but couldn't.

"Nigger!" she snarled, and simultaneously clenched my rib.

I screamed.

She slapped me with her other hand.

"Shut up, cunt!" She lifted my rib, pulling it away from me.

I screamed.

She spewed words at me, lifting the rib with each howl.

"NIGGER!"

"FAGGOT!"

"BITCH!"

"CUNT!"

"MULE!"

Cold sweat pushed onto my flesh. My vocal cords became so strained that I feared they would snap. Each breath of air I managed to gasp felt like strips of barbed wire scrapping up and down my throat. I closed my eyes so tightly that it felt as though I had dragged my entire scalp down over my forehead.

"Yeah," she purred as she began slowly sliding her hand up and down my rib, "you like this, don't you, bitch? This is what you deserved all along, wasn't it?"

"Please . . ."

"Look at me when I'm talking to you, nigger!"

"Please . . ."

"You ain't gotta beg for it anymore, slut, I'm already giving it to you. Just tell me how much you love it. Tell me I'm right about you. Tell me you love it."

"Stop."

"TELL ME!" She pulled on the rib.

"I LOVE IT! I LOVE IT!"

Lou nodded her head. "I know you do." She gently slid her fingers from around the bone and pulled her hand out from my side.

It suddenly felt as though there were a million miles between my organs.

Lou stared into my eyes and I felt ashamed. I wanted to look away, but was afraid to. My eyes filled with water and my jaw trembled.

"I'm still there, aren't I, Mr. Lordan? You can still feel me inside of you. I'll tell you a secret: You always will. I own you, and you'll never be able to forget that. And now you know, now you know what you are. And now, now that you understand the humiliation you've caused . . ." Her voice trailed off as she reached onto the hospital tray and lifted up the flesh she had removed from me.

It was shrunken and discolored.

It wasn't mine anymore.

In her other hand, she held a thin needle with a long black thread gently trailing behind it.

"Please."

"Now that you understand the damage you've caused, Mr. Lordan, I'm going to impress upon you just how painful it is to try and heal those wounds."

"Please . . ."

"Shut the fuck up, nigger."

I slid down onto the floor and my hand fell into the toilet.

"How ya doin', Happy?"

"She raped me," I whispered.

"Two sessions and ya still ain't tagged. Not bad."

"She raped me."

I vomited all over myself.

"Jesus Christ, the toilet's right next to ya, all ya had . . ."

"SHE RAPED ME!"

Stan gently placed his hand on my shoulder.

"DON'T TOUCH ME!"

"Okay, okay." He backed away and sat down on the floor at the opposite end of the cell.

"Why doesn't she just shoot me?" I asked, while wrapping my arms around the toilet. "Why can't it just end? Oh Jesus, Daddy, I just want it to end."

I cried for what felt like hours while clinging onto the toilet.

I could still feel her hand on my rib.

By the time I let go of the toilet, the cell didn't seem so dark anymore, and I looked over at Stan, seeing him clearly for the first time. His feet had been cut off and there were dirty, ragged stitches cluttering his stumps. He only had one hand, and on that hand, only his pinkie and thumb remained. His facial features were lopsided; looking like a Mr. Potato Head that had been assembled by an angry three year-old. His left eye was missing and the skin around it had been removed, leaving the eye socket naked and exposed. His nose was nothing more than a mass of lumpy, mangled flesh spread across his face. The sides of his mouth had been sliced open and then stitched together, leaving Stan with a grotesque, perpetual smile. His right arm was bent at an angle which should have been impossible. His flesh was scorched and discolored. I was afraid to look between his legs.

"My God, Stan, how have you lasted this long?"

"Finally let yourself see, huh?" He laughed his painful laugh.

"I couldn't see before."

"More like *wouldn't*. Don't worry, though, I ain't offended. Don't suppose I was the most reassuring sight when you first got here."

He grinned a toothless grin and I ran my tongue around my own mangled mouth and felt afraid.

"I can't . . . I don't know if I can do it anymore, Stan. I don't think I'm strong enough."

"First thing you've said since gettin' here that ain't stupid."

"I can't . . . I think . . .I think I need God. I can't do it alone, Stan. I can't . . . Oh Jesus, I'm so scared. It won't ever end, will it? It won't ever end? I can't . . . I think I need God. I'm sorry."

"Don't apologize to me. Apologize to your father."

"What?"

"You heard me."

"But how . . .?"

"Ya talk in your sleep, boy."

"Goddamnit! What do I do? How . . .?" I clutched my hands around my head and squeezed. "I don't know what to do anymore."

"Find yer Inch."

"What?"

"Tell ya a story. Long time ago, when I was a kid, I ran away from home. Not because my father was a bad guy, just the opposite, he loved me. Loved me totally and unconditionally. I couldda told him I was gay, or a rapist, or a murderer, and it wouldn't have changed nothin'. He wanted a certain kind of life for me, wanted to help me. Wasn't a controlling thing, he just thought he knew what'd make me happy. Still, even if I'd have done things my own way, he'd have loved me, supported me. And that's exactly why I would've ended up doing things his way. He loved me, and if I'd have stayed, I wouldda handed my Inch over to him."

"But, what's your . . .?"

"Shut up, boy, I'm talking here. I left. Traveled around. Saw the world. I worked fishing boats in Alaska, spent four years eating outta garbage cans in Dublin, worked the pipelines in Texas, handed out flyers for sex shows in Amsterdam, and spent three and a half years in Chino for possession with intent. I've seen the world backwards and forwards, and the one constant in everything I've seen is this: Someone always wants to own yer Inch. Priests, wives, parents, politicians, hacks, convicts, bosses, kids; it don't matter where you are, there's always someone who wants yer Inch."

"I still don't understand what . . ."

"Ya wanna learn or ya just wanna hear yerself talk?"

"No, I want to hear what you're saying, but it's just . . ."

"Forget I gave ya an option. My mistake. Just shut yer yap and listen. The thing about yer Inch is, everyone wants it, but they can't buy it unless you're willing to sell it. There's always buyers. Some of their offers seem pretty sweet on the surface. Some suit'll offer ya a hundred K a year, only the Porsche rots in the garage while ya work yer eighty hour weeks and yer stomach eats a hole in itself and, before ya realize it, ya turn around and yer whole life's gone, pissed away in a blur. Or ya love someone, so ya give her your Inch and marry her. But now ya need her, and it ain't *yer* life anymore, it's *hers*. Some people sell their Inch for patriotism, so they can feel like they belong to something bigger than they are. Yeah, *join the Marines and become part of a brotherhood*, only, ya go where they tell ya and kill who they say, 'cause they own yer ass. Hell, ya even die when they tell ya to. Religion's prob'ly the biggest buyer. Ya sell your Inch for Paradise, but ya gotta believe what they tell ya to believe, no matter how stupid, otherwise, God'll take that Inch ya sold and send it right down into the Fire. And what've ya got to complain about? You sold it to Him.

"Me, I never sold my Inch to anyone for anything. And I never will. That Inch is the only thing that's ever really yours. It's the only thing that no one can steal."

"Are you talking about a soul?"

"Ya can call it that if you wanna," he said with a shrug. "A soul, dignity, self-respect, whatever floats yer boat. Trouble with calling it a soul is, once ya start thinking about it like that, it becomes real easy for some hump to convince ya that you *owe* it him. God, Jesus, America, Morrison, the Celestine Prophets, they all wanna lay claim, all say they got a right to it. Far as I'm concerned, it's just my Inch."

I stared at Stan with longing and confusion.

He shook his disfigured face and sighed. "Okay, ya wanna know what an Inch is? Tell ya another story. Back when I was doin' time in Chino, the Aryan Brotherhood wanted me to hook up with 'em. *Wall to wall niggers and spicks in here, we gotta watch each others back, blah, blah, blah.* Told me it was for my own good, but I knew. Just another bunch a bastards who wanted my Inch. Even wanted to brand a Nazi sign on me so everyone'd know whose property I was.

"I told 'em to go to hell. They didn't like that, so a few weeks later, four of 'em raped me in the back of the machine shop. Now, I ain't proud of that, but I ain't ashamed, neither, 'cause I wouldn't take it in the mouth. Wasn't a goddamn thing I could do when they held me down and took turns fuckin' my ass, but the only way they couldda gotten it inta my mouth was if I wouldda opened up for 'em. They knew it, too, and that's why they wanted me to open up. It was about owning my Inch, just like it always is. They knew if I'd have opened up, I wouldda been their punk forever. They cut me and they stomped me, but I wouldn't open up. Put me in the hospital for two months. Fuckin' hacks wanted me to rat out who did it, not 'cause they cared, but because they wanted to own me, too. Wanted me to be their fuckin' snitch. Didn't open my mouth up for them, neither.

"*That's* what an Inch is. It's that little piece underneath everything else, that piece that knows how fucked-up the rest of you is, the piece everything else is measured against. And *these* bastards?" He motioned over his shoulder, outside the cell. "They don't wanna tag yer body; they wanna tag yer Inch. They wanna brand ya like you was their freakin' cattle. That's what they're after. Ya ever wonder why they don't just hold you down and force the tag on you? It's 'cause they know it only means somethin' if ya let 'em do it. So they'll beat ya and mutilate ya and humiliate ya, but they won't tag ya unless ya say *yes.*

"You wanna keep saying *no,* then ya better find your Inch, boy. Find it and protect it. Ya can cry and scream and beg and curse. Ya can do any damn thing ya gotta do to get through it, but as long as you don't say *yes,* you win. Long as ya keep yer Inch for yerself, long as ya don't pussy out and give it to Morrison or God, you win. You win and they lose."

I looked down at my chest, at the painfully discolored rectangle of flesh. "I can't do it, Stan."

"Goddamn right ya can't." He smiled and the black stitches on his face wrinkled. "Not the way you been doing it, anyway. Ya got a lot of hate, boy, but you got no purpose behind that hate."

"I've got my reasons," I said angrily.

"No doubt. But those reasons are dead. Don't get me wrong, yer anger'll help, yer hate'll help. But only if they're protecting something good, something alive. Ya don't just talk in your sleep, boy, ya cry too."

"Fuck you."

"See? That's what yer hate's attached to, sadness and regret. That's not a good enough reason to keep fightin'. Yer hate ain't worth protectin'. Find yer Inch, 'cause then you'll have somethin' worth fighting for, somethin' worth protectin'. Just remember one thing; God can fuck ya in the ass as much as He wants to and there ain't a damn thing ya can do about it. But as long as ya don't turn around and suck Him off, ya still own yer Inch, and as long as ya own your Inch, you win. That'll get'cha through the beatings. That'll get'cha through Hell. Find yer Inch, Jimmy."

I was on the toilet when the earthquake struck. Heavy slabs of brick and concrete tore away from the walls, crashing all around me. The earthquake lasted for twenty minutes, and I stayed on the toilet, calmly waiting to die while God shook the building, twisting stone and steel as easily as water.

When it was over, it took me several minutes to realize that I hadn't been killed, that I was surrounded with rubble, none of which had even grazed me.

Stan was luckier. He was down on his knees, his ass jabbing up into the air, his footless stumps bent and wedged underneath him. His head had been crushed under a huge slab of concrete. The cell filled with a bright light pouring down from a jagged hole that had torn through all the floors in the building. I climbed up onto the concrete and stared up through the hole, at the pale blue sky.

The door to our cell had collapsed and I walked out into the hall and up the stairs. The hall was littered with glass, rubble and crushed bodies. A tiny noise came from the White Room and I followed it, pushing open the heavy door and stepping inside.

Lou was wedged underneath an immense slab of white concrete. Blood leaked from the corners of her mouth while she stared up at the ceiling with hopeless eyes.

"Help me," she whispered, in a voice so small that it couldn't have been the sound which had drawn me into the room. She hadn't noticed my presence, and pleaded in a voice that didn't expect to be answered, but didn't know what else to say. "Help me."

I walked across the mess and stood over her.

"Jimmy," she said, looking at me with gentle recognition. "Jimmy, please help me. I can't . . . I can't feel anything. I . . . My body . . . Something snapped. I heard it. Help me."

I continued to gaze down at her silently.

"Please, Jimmy. I have . . . I have a daughter. My daughter. She needs her Mommy. Lori needs her Mommy." A tear ran down her face, mixing with the blood smeared across her lips. "Move the rock, Jimmy. Please. Lori needs her Mommy, doesn't she, Jimmy?"

I left the room and walked into the hall, stripping a uniform off a dead guard and covering my nakedness.

I returned to the White Room.

"Please, Jimmy." Her breathing was shallow, her voice far away. "You . . . you kept saying you were better than me, that I didn't know you, that I was wrong. Prove it now, Jimmy. Show me that I was wrong about you. I . . .Oh sweet Jesus, I think I'm dying. I can't feel anything, I . . . Lori needs a Mommy. Don't let her Mommy die. Please. Please don't let that happen to her."

Her eyes opened wide while she pleaded. She had blue eyes. Beautiful blue eyes. I hadn't noticed that before.

"Please, Jimmy; show me that I was wrong."

Her eyes were the same color as the sky. They were an exact duplicate of the blue sky that had allowed me to see Stan's crushed body so clearly. The blue had shined into the cell because it had pushed through the ceiling and crushed Stan's head while he was on his knees. It had crushed him because he wouldn't give up his Inch. It had shot my father because he wouldn't give up his Inch.

"No. No, you were right, Louise."

She stared up at me with her blue eyes as I wrapped my hands around her throat and strangled the life out of her.

Thirteen

Her eyes were two black holes, a sucking, lifeless vacuum. I stared into that black and saw myself, lifeless and hollow. The blood on her face was dry and crusted. Her tears had stopped flowing. I was equally drained; my tears dried up, my blood congealed and solidified.

I continued staring into her eyes.

*I*srael, a voice whispered. *Leave this place now.*

I stepped over Lou's corpse and walked out of the crumbling building.

Boston was dead. For every building left standing, two had been reduced to rubble. The air smelled of soot and ash. Invisible particles of brick and concrete floated into my nostrils, causing me to sneeze. I stared blankly at the ruined city I had loved, the crumbled buildings, which had raised me.

"Good," I said.

Israel, the voice repeated. *To get there, you need to fly. Go to the airport.*

I began stumbling through the city, moving towards the airport.

Sounds of pain and desperation soiled the air. The individual screams merged together, creating a single sound, a single, perfect noise that said everything that needed to be said. It sounded like God's scream, like my scream. I stopped walking and allowed the Scream to wash over me. I straightened my spine and spread my arms towards the sky. Throwing my head back, I closed my eyes and dropped open my mouth.

Don't do this. Keep moving.

I calmly recognized the voice. It was my Inch.

It spoke softly, but clearly. It sat densely in the back of my stomach, welded onto the base of my spine. It was solid and real and it was mine.

Keep walking.

The Scream suddenly sounded tiny and ridiculous.

I began walking again.

When the day became night, the Scream became violent and angry because I was ignoring it.

I wasn't afraid.

My body had become intangible, swallowed up and made unnecessary by my Inch. My legs were tired and my back and head ached. Underneath the uniform, sticky blood seeped out from the hole Lou had raped.

It didn't matter.

My body had become a vehicle, an inconsequential machine carrying my Inch to where it had to be.

My Inch was safe, nothing else mattered.

*S*top.

I did, and noticed with indifference that I had arrived at Logan Airport. One of the parking garages had collapsed, but the main buildings still stood. The glass doors had shattered. I stepped through them, walking into Terminal E.

My Inch told me to look for a specific sign.

I did

When I located the sign, I was told to walk up the escalator and find a bathroom.

I did.

Go into a stall.

I did.

Pull your pants down and sit on a toilet.

I did.

Sleep.

I did.

I dozed in and out of sleep. When I was thirsty, my Inch told me to drink water from the toilet. When I became hungry, my Inch told me to ignore the hunger. When my legs became cramped, my Inch told me to stand up and pace around the inside of the stall. When the cramps left, my Inch told me to sit down. When I wondered how much time had passed, my Inch told me not to worry about it.

Someone entered the bathroom.

Hum quietly and casually and tap your feet.

I did.

Heavy black boots tromped across the white tiled floor. A fist pounded on the door to my stall.

"Open up," the voice said.

My Inch told me what to say, and I repeated its words and tone: "What the fuck! I been searching this airport for three hours, and I can't get three fucking minutes of privacy to take a dump?"

The soldier's shadow grew as he crouched down and peered under the stall. When he saw the color of my uniform wrapped around my black boots, he stood back up, mumbled an apology, and left.

The same thing happened four more times.

My Inch repeated its instructions.

When the bathroom became busy, and the people who were using it weren't wearing black boots, my Inch told me to stand up.

My head felt heavy and unbalanced. I began to sway.

Don't faint. Grab the walls. Steady yourself. Focus.

I did.

Good. Now pull up your pants and leave the stall.

I stepped up to the sink and failed to recognize the man staring at me from the mirror.

You look horrible. Splash water on your face. Get your hair wet and push it back. Straighten the uniform. You stink, wash yourself. Rinse your mouth out.

When my Inch was satisfied with my appearance, I followed its instructions and walked out of the bathroom, into the crowded airport. I found a monitor and slid my eyes down the words until my Inch found, *Boston to Tel Aviv.* My Inch told me where to go and, once there, told me to lean next to a bathroom door while it used my eyes to inspect the people passing by.

It locked my eyesight onto a man who possessed a passing resemblance to me and told me what to do.

I placed my hand on his shoulder.

"Yes?" the man asked.

"Where are you flying to, sir?"

"Why?" He sounded annoyed.

"Answer the question, sir," I said, hardening my voice as my Inch told me to.

"Israel."

"Let's see your passport and authorization papers."

"Why? Who are you?"

"Take a look at the uniform and guess. Your papers, now."

"No." The man stepped back. "Now look, my plane leaves in twenty minutes. I waited four months for authorization to go to Israel. I finally get it and the earthquake hits two days before I'm supposed to go. I had to wait another week and-a-half before you guys opened the airport. I come here and it takes me six hours to pass through all the checkpoints before I'm even allowed into the airport. *Six hours.*"

"Come with me, sir."

"What? No! You people have already gone over my paperwork fifty times!"

"Sir, this is strictly routine." I placed my hand on his elbow. "I promise that you won't miss your flight."

"You can't do this!"

"Lower your voice."

"You people have a treaty with Israel. I'm a Jew!"

"Sir . . ."

"No!" He broke free from my grip. "It's already taken me too long to get out of this madhouse. I followed your procedures, I didn't bring any luggage, I supplied you with all the birth certificates and papers, I even let you strip search me! I did it all, and I was told that all I had to do now was present my paperwork at the gate, and that's all I'm going to do."

I grabbed him by the back of the neck and pushed him into the bathroom. Two men were standing at the urinals and they turned and gawked at me.

"Get the fuck out of here!" I said.

They bolted out of the room.

"What the hell is this? I'm a Jew!"

I pushed him into a stall and smashed his face down onto the toilet bowl.

Do it again.

I did.

Do it again.

I did.

Do it again.

The soldiers at the gate flipped through the paperwork, smiled, and waved me through.

As I ran towards the boarding gate, I held on to the oversized pants I had stolen from the man whose passport I carried, stopping them from sliding off of my frail body.

I boarded the plane and was led to a seat. I sat down and stared straight ahead.

The plane took off and my Inch told me to stay awake until the food was served.

Two hours later, I finished eating my kosher meal.

Now you can sleep.

I passed out before it finished the sentence.

I dreamt of nothing.

"You've arrived."

I opened my eyes and stared at the Steward leaning over me.

"I'm sorry to wake you, sir, but you've got to get off the plane."

I stared at him silently and waited for my Inch to tell me what to do.

It remained silent.

I searched my body, but could find no trace of its presence, and allowed the steward to lead me off the plane.

I stood in line at Customs, waiting for my Inch to reappear.

Its silence was like a hole in the center of the universe.

At the head of the line, stood two soldiers, one Israeli, one OWC. Both men held machine guns.

I stared at the barrel of the gun and decided that, when I reached the front of the line, I'd drop down onto my knees and stuff the weapon into my mouth. I'd clamp my teeth around the metal and shake my head back and forth until it blew my face off.

"Papers," I heard.

The voice was far away and I continued to stare at the gun. I wondered what the steel would taste like.

"Papers!"

I wondered if I would smell the gunpowder, if the barrel would feel cold in my mouth, if it would feel hot when the trigger was pulled.

"Papers, right now." the Israeli soldier said, grabbing my shoulder and squeezing.

I turned towards him and stared at his angry face. I reached into my pocket, pulled out whatever was in there, and handed it to him.

He released his grip on me and I returned my eyes to his gun.

"Mr. Fedel."

I need to make sure not to push the barrel all the way to the back of my throat. I need to point it up, towards the top of my mouth.

"Mr. Fedel," the soldier repeated.

Reluctantly, I turned away from the gun.

"Long trip?" the soldier asked with a smile.

"What?"

"You look as if you've had a long trip. Welcome home." He shook my hand and returned Mr. Fedel's papers to me. "The Office of Assimilation is less than a kilometer away. You can catch the shuttle service right outside of these doors. Welcome home."

"What?"

He gently nudged me forward.

I took a few hesitant steps towards the exit.

The sunlight glared through the glass doors and I turned away from it, returning my eyes to the soldier's gun.

A man bumped into me and knocked me down.

After helping me up, he walked away.

I turned away from the gun and walked out of the airport.

I wandered south, into the desert.

"Israel," I said out loud. "This was the plan. Safety. Salvation." The words sounded pointless, my own voice pathetic compared to my vanished Inch.

I continued walking, but there was no passion beneath my steps, no purpose fueling my movements. With each step, I understood more and more how my father felt in his final years of life, no purpose in motion, but no other option.

I wanted to stop walking, to sit down and die, but realized, as my father had, that death was no longer a practical option, no longer an escape.

I don't want to go to Hell.

I can't go to Heaven.

I want to see Sarah.

My father's in Hell.

Stan was my friend.

God killed Stan.

My father is burning in Hell.

I continued stumbling forward.

The sun clawed into me, squeezed me dry like a sponge. If I could have, I'd have reached up and popped its fiery life out of the sky like a pimple. I would have dragged it down to earth and pissed out its inferno, trampling whatever was left underneath my feet.

I tripped and fell down into the sand.

The sun remained in the sky, its heat scourging me.

My father is on fire.

He is in Hell.

I can't go to Heaven.

I rose up out of the sand and continued walking.

Instead of walking forward, I began tracing my own steps, walking around and around in a huge circle. Mine were the only tracks and I wondered if I was the last living human. Sarah was dead, Mom was dead, Scotty was dead, Joe was dead, Molly was dead, Stan was dead, everyone was dead. There was no one left to wonder where I was or care if I was alive. Even Lou was dead. I had strangled the life out of the last person to know that I was alive. I had murdered the only person who still cared about me.

I dropped down onto the ground and tried to remember her living face. Instead, I remembered the feel of her windpipe as it collapsed underneath my grip.

I could have saved her. I could have moved the rock and saved her. I could have saved her and she would have come to Israel with me and we would have been happy together. Instead, I killed her.

I murdered a helpless woman.

I lifted my head up towards the sun.

It was my own personal spotlight. I was staring in a one-man show that nobody knew was playing.

God knows. God knows everything.

He knew I could have saved my father. He knew I had broken him and I could have saved him. He knew, and he allowed the soldiers to shoot him before he was saved. He knew, and He sent him to Hell.

The sand burned at my hands and knees. I searched the desert for shade and, when I found none, pushed my hands underneath the ground. No matter how far under I pushed, the sand was hot. It still burned.

I know I'm alone because if Sarah could have seen me, she would have helped. She would help. I know she would.

She's gone. Forever.

Everyone is.

Almost everyone.

I turned away from the sun and stared at the only person left. I stared across the sand at Jesus Christ.

It was a delusion created by a feeble mind. I knew that. He wasn't really standing in front of me.

He can't be.

I was losing my sanity and creating illusions. He wasn't really there.

He can't be. He can't.

He stood naked and covered in sweat. A twisted patch of wooden thorns pressed down onto His skull, causing thin streaks of blood to dribble down His cheeks. The bloody holes in His feet were covered with brown, crusted sand. He stared at me with quiet, sad eyes, and reached out to me. As He raised His arms, perfectly round droplets of blood fell from holes in His flesh, staining the desert floor.

"Do you love me?" I asked through cracked lips, my voice sounding like a dying gasp. "If you love me, then just help me."

Jesus remained motionless, his outstretched hands perfectly steady.

"No," I croaked. "No, don't make me come to you. I can't. Not after my father. If you love me, just help me. Friends don't . . . Family doesn't demand anything. There's no conditions in love. They just help. They just . . . Help me."

He remained motionless, His arms open.

"Yeah," I nodded, "yeah, that's what I thought. Stan was right about you. You want my Inch. If you love me, help me without it. Sarah never asked for it. That's why I gave it to her. Stan was right."

He said nothing.

"Where's my father?" I struggled back up onto my feet. "Where's my fucking father? He needed help. Another couple of days. A few hours, even. It's your plan; you could have given me another fucking hour! He was broke, ready to listen, Molly was . . . WHERE'S MY FUCKING FATHER?"

His face became sad.

"Fuck you. You get nothing from me. Nothing! Giving you nothing's all I got left. You took everything else. You and your Father. You sent *my* father to Hell, you fucking cocksucker. To Hell! Would you still love me if I sent *your* father to Hell? How much would you love me then?"

Jesus said nothing, but His eyes continued to meet mine.

"You had it easy, you fucking faggot. The blood and the thorns don't impress me. Who did you have to betray? You gave Judas the hard job, you fucking hypocrite. I don't need you; I'll make things right on my own." I turned my back to Him. "Get the hell outta here, you little bastard, you and me got nothing more to say."

I dropped down into the sand and heard something snap.

"Oh," I said quietly. "Oh shit."

A shadow passed over my eyes and a gentle hand touched my back. I raised my face out of the hot sand and saw a tall, thin man standing over me.

"Hello," he said. "My name is Bezalel Roth. Welcome to Paradise."

III
Revelations

Fourteen

"C'mon, wake up, fuck-nose. You can't sleep forever."

The words arrived from nowhere, uncoiling a thin beam of light down into the black. It was a darkness, the existence of which, I had not previously been aware, a darkness that did not surround me, but was *of* me. Was me. All traces of self had been dispersed by the black, so that I was no longer aware that I was different from the surrounding darkness. The coarse words and the light they had created brought me into awareness, separating me from the heavy, surrounding nothingness. The realization of self frightened me, and I felt a strong reluctance to reclaim my individuality. I tried to spread myself apart; to rejoin with the nothing, but the effort only ratified my independence. The words that I had heard continued to echo through me, each a single, perfect note. They tumbled over and around me, defining my contours and perimeter. Interacting with me and creating me.

I opened my eyes and found myself staring up at a white ceiling. There were cobwebs in the corner and they too were white. Even the shadows that stretched themselves behind the cobwebs and across the ceiling seemed to exist in a state of colorlessness. I tried to lift my arms and legs and found that I could not.

I smiled, confident in the fact that I had traveled around the entire world, from Boston to Israel and back again, only to end up exactly where I had begun, strapped down in the White Room.

I wondered if, perhaps, I had never left the White Room, if Israel, Bezalel, Jude, Mark, George, and all the rest had simply been a game, an elaborate psychological maze through which Lou had run my mind like an obedient mouse.

You killed me, Mr. Lordan, she would say as she entered the room. *I was helpless and begging to be saved and you murdered me in cold blood. You allowed that little boy on the boat to be raped and murdered in front of your very eyes. What's more, you acted as though his innocence, his faith in God were the cause of it. As if he were to blame. You set in motion the events that led to Mark Perry's death. And what about that man in the airport? The one you beat and stripped? Do you know what happened to him? Did you kill him? Put him in a coma? Did you care? Are you still going to tell me that you're a good man, Mr. Lordan? That I was wrong?*

I would shake my head, no.

We gave you what it was you wanted. We gave you Paradise. You were safe. You had people who loved you, who cared for you. And you hated it. You hated them. You spent two years in Paradise, and you walked away. You knew that you didn't belong there. You returned to our world, because you know that this is what you deserve. You know that this is who you are.

Do you see now, Mr. Lordan? Do you see that everything I said was correct? Do you finally understand who you truly are?

I would nod my head in agreement.

S taring up at the white ceiling made my neck cramp, so I released the muscles and allowed my head to roll onto its side. When it did, I saw an old man slumping deeply into a leather recliner.

I tried to say *Daddy*, but my throat wouldn't allow it.

Oh Jesus, I messed it up so bad.

It's my fault.

Not just mine, but mine, too.

But it's okay, Dad, I know what to do now.

I know how to make it right.

Everything's clear.

I don't have any more questions.

I know what I am.

I tried to focus my vision and, when I realized how blurry it was, blinked the heavy gunk out of my direct line of vision. Able to see a bit clearer, I saw that the man was not my father. The resemblance was there, but it was a superficial one. Both men were old and hunched with a mass of lines covering their faces, but that was where the resemblance ended.

My father's face had been a mass of wrinkles, but they were soft, sloping wrinkles that hid his face. The wrinkles on the face of the old man sitting across from me were hard. It was as though his face had endured a hundred paper cuts that left behind tiny, white scars. His eyes were small and receded, and I could see no color within them, only black shadow. He pursed his thin, red lips.

I blinked and my vision became blurry once again. I allowed the obstruction to remain centered and stared at the old man through the blurry filter, realizing that he *could* have been my father. I remembered seeing my father the first time after the Rapture, how shocked I was. He had looked vulnerable and sad, and not at all like the man I had grown up with or the man I had assumed he would have aged into. Sitting in the recliner across from me, staring through blurry eyes, I saw that man. He was hard and tight, possessing the face of a survivor who had seen the worst the world had to offer, and had become harder than that world. Not stronger, but more bitter. Bitter enough to weather a brutal world out of stubbornness and spite.

I stared at the man and realized that he was also the man that I had, on some level, assumed *I* would become.

The old man's head slowly turned towards me and he jolted in his chair, spilling the bottle of vodka he had been holding all over his shirt.

"Son of a slut!" he yelled, and stood up angrily while trying to wipe the liquid off his flannel shirt, succeeding only in grinding the booze deeper into the material. Attached to his belt was a large hunting knife. He continued pushing against his shirt, rubbing his hands down the flannel as though he expected the liquid to suddenly flow smoothly off him. He became more and more manic in his motions as he failed in his futile task, refusing to surrender to common sense.

"Look at what you did to me, you little fairy!" He walked over and slapped me across the face. It was a weak blow, and the feel of his dry, dead flesh scrapping across my cheek repulsed me.

The slap had turned my head and I gazed down at my body and saw that I wasn't strapped into a chair or a gurney. I was lying on a couch and my arms and legs were unencumbered. I tried raising my arms again, but they refused to do anything but shake. It was as though my arms were weighed down by heavy cinder blocks. My muscles had become as thin as mountain air.

I turned back towards the old man, who had resumed the impossible task of forcibly removing liquid from cloth.

"Who . . .?" I croaked, but was unable to say anything else. The word burned my throat. I tried to swallow down some saliva, but didn't seem to have any left, and the attempt caused my throat to clench and stab into itself.

"Shut up," the old man said, and glared at me through his dark eyes. He wiped away at his shirt for several more minutes, becoming more frantic until finally, he threw his hands up into the air and quit. "Shit me," he muttered, and walked away.

I looked around the room, but nothing I saw helped me make sense of where I was. Or rather, I saw more than enough to tell me where I was, but the conclusion made no sense. A bookcase filled with beat-up paperbacks whose spines were wrinkled white from use; a coffee table covered with empty bottles of vodka and ashtrays overflowing with half smoked cigarettes; a fake wooden entertainment center with a TV sitting in its center; a brown dead plant sitting on top of the entertainment center, along with several yellowing newspapers. Everything I saw told me I was lying on a couch in a normal apartment, but I couldn't accept that as true.

I pushed my eyes under the coffee table and into the corners of the room, searching for handcuffs or knives or leather boots or guns. I knew that as soon as I had accepted the normal environment as real, the walls would fall down, revealing themselves as nothing but false fronts for the White Room.

The old man returned wearing a new shirt and carrying a fresh bottle of vodka. He grabbed a chair and slid it next to me, staring into my eyes intently, searching for something.

After several minutes, he began laughing.

It was a dry, sharp laugh that sounded like his skin looked.

"Okay then," he said and leaned back into his chair while nodding his head. "Okay. I've been staring at your ugly face for longer than I'd care to remember, but I could never figure out what you were. Your eyes were closed and even when I pried 'em open, I couldn't figure you out. Couldn't see the truth within. Now I know."

I tried moving again, but could only accomplish a slight squirm as the muscles in my body fluttered like a beached sunfish.

"What the hell are you squirming at?" the old man asked, his voice dripping with contempt. "Your boyfriend ain't got his johnson up your butt, now." He lifted the bottle up to his lips and his sharp Adam's apple bobbed underneath his thin skin. "Look at you, the would-be savior. The redeemer. A gimp's what you are. A gimp and a fairy, lots of luck either of you got."

I inhaled a few painful gasps of air and managed a word: "Water."

"*Water?*" The request enraged him and his small black eyes became even smaller as he jerked himself out of his chair. "I'll give you some water, you big shitty!" He fumbled with his zipper and pulled out his penis.

I turned away as the stream of urine splattered up against my forehead and dribbled down into my eyes.

"You liked that, didn't you? Yeah, I bet you and the fairy do that stuff all the time, don't you?"

The chair creaked as he collapsed back into it without bothering to pull himself back into his pants. He chuckled for a few minutes and when he stopped, I could hear his heavy breathing.

I opened my eyes, which stung from his urine.

He looked into my stare and his black eyes narrowed. Leaning over, he pushed his face close to mine, his breath smelling of booze and uncooked meat.

"Let me tell you about my day, gimp. After your boyfriend got home, I caught a transport down to the docks. I'm too old to work there myself, but once or twice a month, I make it down. I like getting a look every once in a while and they let me have a taste of the fresh slabs."

His skin was not only wrinkled, but also seemed to be peeling off and flaking away.

"Buddy of mine tipped me off that today was going to be a good one, so I made sure I got down there early. They had just started unloading the boat when I got there. Usually, they'd just send the slabs upstate, but upstate's been backed up, so they hadda take care of things right there at the docks.

"It's hard work, too. Those boys work for a living. Used to be, they'd just put a bullet in the back of the head, nice and clean and simple. But ever since last year, when that Jew bastard stabbed him in the head, Morrison's had a hard-on to wipe out the Chinese and the Arabs. I watched it, too, right on the TV. It was like watching Oswald get shot. Historic. Morrison's giving a speech and that dirty Jew bastard walked right up to him and stabbed him in the head. I figured it was all over then and there, that my fun was finished. But three days later, Morrison gets on the TV and says he's been resurrected. Says he can't be killed, that he's the new Christ. He went around the bend; you can see it in his eyes. It's like he ain't even human anymore.

"And ever since then, he's been sending slabs over here like time's running out. He's been stockpiling weapons too, but he don't give the boys the bullets to take care of 'em. Don't seem right, giving those hard working boys enough bullets just to guard 'em, and then making 'em use machetes to finish 'em off. Upstate's got enough bullets, but when they gotta take care of things on the docks, all they got's machetes.

"Anyway, today, they get the slabs off the boat and separate 'em up. They take care of the young fellas first so they won't start any trouble. They take 'em into the warehouse, bring 'em one by one down into the basement, bend 'em over, and then WHACK!" He made a chopping motion with his hand. "After they do 'em, they take care of the old timers and the kids.

"Funny thing is, not one of the slabs ever does a thing. There must've been two hundred slabs on that boat and there were only forty guards. And the slabs know what's coming. Certainly they do. No one's that blind. But they don't run or try and escape their fate at all. No. They calmly follow the guards into the cellar, bending over the block of wood like meek lambs, and WHACK!"

His lips curled up in disgust and he spat on the floor.

"They ain't even human. Big shit, slabs of meat, that's all they are. I mean, take me. I'm an old man and I've lived a long, crappy life. Ain't much left to it, but I'll tell you this, if someone tried hacking my head off, they damn well are gonna have a fight on their hands. And y'know why? `cause I'm a human being."

He arched his sloping shoulders back and stuck his frail chest out. He nodded his head and then scratched his face.

"I ain't no slab of meat.

"I was talking to one of boys once and y'know what he says to me? He says to me, *Tony, if just one of those slabs, just one of' em put up a fight or tried to run, I swear to Christ, I think I'd let `em go. I'd bring it upstairs, give it some clothes, shake its hand, and let it go. You know why? `Cause it'd be a human being instead of a slab of meat, and I ain't gonna chop off the head of no human being. No, I'm gonna shake its hand and let it go.* That's what he tells me, and I believe him."

A thin line of piss touched my lips and burned the cracks.

"So anyway, like I was saying, they take care of all the men and the kids and whatnot. All told, it takes about twelve hours, and the boys're exhausted. The machetes they got are old and rusted. When they first got `em, they were nice and sharp, and they could take a head off in one clean whack. But that was four, five months ago. Now, they gotta put their back into it, and even then, it still takes five or six good whacks. And after that, they still gotta drag the bodies back onto the ship so they can be dumped in the ocean.

"So those boys are tired. But it don't take too long for `em to get their second wind, `cause now that all the garbage is taken care of, it's time for the treats. Nothing but the women left now. They're naked." His tongue pushed out from the corner of his mouth and dabbed his lips. "Can't hide nothing. No baggy sweater to hide a fat stomach or ass. No Miracle Bra to hike up their saggy, disgusting tities. The little slabs can't lie with their clothes no more.

"So the boys line `em up and we get to pick and choose. That's the main reason I go down there. I could go to Trump, but all the slabs over there are used. On the dock, you get `em fresh. The boys, they let me choose first. I'm sort of like a father figure and it's a sign of respect. I was feeling good today, so I took two of `em. Made one watch while I did the other. The whole time I'm sticking the one slab, I got my eye on the other, making sure she's watching and knows what she's got coming. And it knows, but it don't cry or look away or nothing. It just stares at me with meat's eyes."

He ran his hand through his white hair and a fleck of scalp attached to several strands of hair floated down through the air, twirling in a circle. "Now, don't mistake this for contrition or false justification. It's neither. I mean, who's left to make an act of contrition to? I'm not suggesting that those slabs want it or like it, although more do than you'd think. I'm just saying that it don't seem to matter much to 'em one way or the other. They're slabs and that's what it's like, like sticking your johnson into a slab of meat."

He stared at me for several minutes before turning away and staring out the window. He lost himself in thought and, for a moment, his eyes widened and I saw a flash of color amidst the black.

"Meat," he muttered, and then nodded his head and drank some more vodka. His eyes closed up again and the color disappeared behind the shadow.

"Wh . . . why?" I managed to ask.

"Why *what*? Why do I do it?"

I shook my head slowly.

"Why am I telling you this?"

I managed to turn the shake into a slight nod.

He pulled a cigarette and a lighter out of his pocket. The cigarette dangled uneasily in his mouth and he needed to use both hands to operate the lighter. He drew the flame slowly to the tip of the cigarette and leaned his face into it. Once it was lit, he sucked noisily on the filter, inhaling small breaths. He carefully pushed the cover over the flame and pulled the cigarette out of his mouth, awkwardly holding it with three fingers.

"You and the fairy ain't leaving any time soon. I know that, and I know there ain't a damn thing I can do about it. But when the fairy looks at me, I can see in his eyes that he thinks he's better'n me. He tries and hide it, even seems sort of ashamed of it, but I can still see the truth. I disgust him.

"And y'know, when I look into his eyes, I don't know if he's wrong. Perhaps he is something better than I. I can't tell. 'Course, I don't wanna be staring too long, cause he'll start thinking I'm looking for some butt-love. So with him, I'm not sure. But one way or the other, I don't like having some fairy looking down his nose at me, judging me in my own home." He took a short drag off his cigarette and exhaled before the smoke ever saw his lungs.

"I'm an old man. Too old for Morrison to put into his army and too old to work the docks. I could've gone to Europe. They say it's a paradise over there. I could've gone, but I didn't. I *choose* to stay here. Far as I'm concerned, *this* is paradise. I do whatever I want and there ain't no one left to judge me

"The fairy tries telling me that what I'm doing's wrong, he tells me with his eyes. I don't like that. So now you're awake and I figure you'll try and do the same thing. But I looked into your eyes, gimp, and you know what I saw? I saw the exact same thing I saw in the mirror before I caught a transport down to the docks this morning. I told you what I did because now you know who I am. I ain't ashamed of that. But you just remember, I know who *you* are, too.

"The fairy told me that you were in Israel, in the Christ-freak camp for a couple of years. He told me you came back over here, that you left that place to save some slab. He was real impressed by that, thought it made you some kind of a hero. I bet you think that, too."

He leaned back and crushed out his barely smoked cigarette.

"Well, you can sell that cat-shit to the fairy if he's buying, but not me. I looked into your eyes and I know why you really came back." He grabbed my wrist and held up my hand, pushing our tags next to each other. "You see that, gimp? *That's* why you're here. Same as me.

"This tag lets us do whatever the hell we want. Ain't no bishops or lawyers or judges or parents or anybody that can tell us differently. Ain't no God that can tell us what to do over here, either. This tag makes *us* god. You didn't come over here to save some stupid slab you haven't seen for twenty years, you came over here so that you could do whatever the hell you wanted to do. You came over here so you could be your own god.

"I know that. So don't you ever look at me like you're better'n me. I like doing whatever I want. I like not being told what's right and what's wrong. I like it here."

He dropped my hand.

It fell onto the couch like a dead dog.

"And so do you, Lordan. If you didn't, you never woulda come back."

"Jimmy?" George asked as he entered the room. "Oh my God, Jimmy, you're awake!" He ran over to the couch and hugged me. "Thank God!"

"Wa . . . water." I said.

"Yeah, yeah of course! You sound like you need some." He jumped up and ran into another room. When he returned, he held a glass of water and poured a few drops into my throat. "Don't drink too much," he said, and pulled the glass away from my dry, greedy lips.

He placed the glass on the table and stared silently at me. After a few moments, he leaned over and hugged me again. I could feel his tears against my face. "Thank God you're okay, Jimmy. Thank God."

"You fairies gonna hump now or later?"

George stood up. "How long's he been awake for?"

"What am I, his nurse?"

"You couldn't give him any water?" His voice sounded more disappointed than angry.

"Up your butt, Glass, I told you I ain't his nurse. Besides, you're the one who hoards away all our water. You think I'm gonna waste what little you leave behind on this gimp?"

"It would have been decent, is all."

"You don't like it? Leave."

"We're not going anywhere, Father."

"I told you to stop calling me that!"

George returned to me with the water and poured some more into my mouth. It was instantly absorbed into the walls of my throat, like a spilled canteen on the desert floor.

"Your . . . dad?" I asked.

George laughed loudly. "Did you hear that, Father?"

"Shit on both of you."

George continued laughing and squeezed my arm affectionately. "No Jimmy, he's not my Dad." He shifted his body so the old man and I could see each other. "James Lordan, allow me to introduce Father Anthony Zippco, my old parish priest."

"Shit on you two monkey-sucking fairies," Father Zippco muttered as he turned his back to us and left the room.

George dipped a cloth into the water and gently spread the cool rag across my face and throat.

"How . . ." I took a deep breath, " . . . long?"

The warm smile left George's face and he turned away from me. When he faced me once again, he had regained the smile, only it had become sad, and seemed to rest on his lips more naturally than the smile he had greeted me with. "A long time. Two years," he said quietly. "Two years."

Fifteen

My muscles had atrophied to an enormous extent over the two years. Recuperation was slow. It took two months to regain even partial strength. During the day, George would stretch my arms and legs and feed me. At night, he'd leave the apartment dressed in an OWC uniform, refusing to tell me where he was going or what he was doing. He refused to tell me much of anything those first few months. He said that he wanted to wait until I was back in shape, that he wanted me to focus on healing, but he seemed to be stalling more for his own sake than for mine. He didn't want to talk about certain things until he absolutely had to. For those first two months after waking up from my coma, all that George would tell me was that we were living in New York City, in a building that was owned by Father Anthony Zippco, George's old parish priest from Brooklyn.

When I entered my third month of lucidity, I could walk with minimal assistance and finally convinced George to talk about what had happened.

He sat down across from me, offering me a pack of cigarettes and laughing when I refused them.

"You got bit by that locust," he began, "and you went down. You split your head open on the car and then a whole swarm of those bastards ripped into you. They were swarming all over your body, climbing in and out of your mouth. I couldn't do anything."

"They didn't attack you?"

"No."

"Why not?"

"I don't know, Jimmy, they just didn't. Anyway, after about a minute, they cleared off you and moved on. You were a mess, covered in blood; unconscious, swollen, discolored, and muttering something about someone named *Sarah*. That was the last thing I heard you say for two years: *Sarah, your husband demands warmth, perform your wifely duties and warm me with your butt.* I heard sirens coming and I panicked. I threw you into the trunk and headed for New York. I knew we were going to be red-tagged and I figured we'd be better off hiding in New York, where I knew the area better. When we got here, I ditched the car, stripped the plates, and went into hiding with the rest of the Christians and non-persons."

"And me?" I asked.

George shrugged and smiled ruefully.

"You just never woke up, Jimmy. I'd find an abandoned area of the city and we'd hide out there for a month or two. I had a pretty good idea of how the OWC did their sweeps, so every time an area we were hiding in got too crowded, I'd move us somewhere else. During the day I'd sleep and take care of you. At night, I'd head out with the rest of the pack rats looking for food. We lived like that for six or seven months and then, just as winter was really setting in, I bumped into Father Zippco. He was coming back from Trump. I knew we'd never last through the winter, so I convinced him to take us in. We've been here for the last year and a half."

"I've been in a coma for two years?"

"Yeah."

"How did you know how to take care of me? I wouldn't know the first thing about it."

"I found a few abandoned bookstores when I first got to the city and got medical journals. I kept your muscles stretched out as well as I could. Any food I found I'd grind down into a pasty liquid, put it in your mouth, and then rub your throat until you swallowed it. It wasn't so hard."

"I . . . Well, why did Zippco help us? He obviously hates you."

"I blackmailed him," George said, his voice quiet. "He had convinced someone in the records department to delete the fact that he had been a priest. I told him that if he didn't hide us, I'd rat him out."

"That's great," I laughed. "But why would it matter that he was a priest? He's tagged."

"Yeah." George rubbed his face and looked past me, out the window. "Things have changed in the last two years, Jimmy. Morrison's . . . well, he's insane. Anyone who had the slightest connection to Christianity before the Rapture is arrested and executed. It doesn't matter if they've got the tag or not. I think he knows there's a tagger in Israel and he figures he'd better whack those people before they decide to go there.

"Take someone like Father Zippco. If he had a change of heart and got over to Israel, he could get the tag off. If Morrison whacks him now, while he's still tagged, he automatically goes to Hell."

"Zippco's got about as much chance of getting into Heaven as Morrison does," I scoffed. "Some people are beyond redemption."

George nodded his head and continued staring out the window, his face growing sadder.

He had changed so dramatically in the previous two years, that he was almost unrecognizable. He had shaved off his beard and his scruffy short hair had grown long, draping across his shoulders. His once flabby body had become thin and compact; skinny, but tight and muscular. The pudge that once surrounded his face had disappeared, his loose skin now taut and hard.

He had developed a tendency to shift his eyes away from me in the middle of a sentence, slowly turning his attention away and staring off into the distance. It wasn't a blank, absent-minded stare, but weighed down and heavy. He'd abandoned the blithe, arrogant demeanor he had carried himself with when I first met him and instead, carried himself with a sad confidence. His words were spoken with a quiet, measured stillness. His face was a blank wall which was occasionally cracked by moments of hesitation, through which his pain and regret could be seen.

"You took care of me for two years?"

"I kept thinking you were going to wake up. I never dreamed you were going to be in a coma for two years. Lots of people died from the locusts, some weren't any more affected by them then they would be by a mosquito bite. I didn't know what else to do."

"I . . . Thank you, George."

Waving his hands in the air, he dismissed my words.

"No. Thank you, George."

He looked down into his hands and twisted his fingers into each other. His forehead wrinkled into a frown and he shook his head.

"So, what now?"

"What?"

"What do we do now?"

"You keep getting better. You regain your strength."

"What about Jude?"

"She . . ." he moved his eyes away from me. "She's in New York."

"She's here? She's in the City? Where?"

"Not now, Jimmy." He shook his head. "Get better and then we'll talk."

"I . . ."

He stared at me solidly and I knew there was no way I was going to persuade him to say any more.

"George, what . . .?"

He turned away and stared out the window.

"George."

He continued to look towards something I couldn't see.

"Are you all right?"

He smiled thinly but said nothing.

Using a cane, I tried walking by myself. I moved hesitantly, my steps tiny and cautious. When I reached the bathroom door, I dropped the cane onto the tile floor and fell forward, catching myself on the sink. My arms shook as I dragged my bare feet behind. After steadying my arms and drawing up my legs, I took a deep breath and looked at myself in the mirror for the first time in two years.

When I saw the figure in the reflected glass, I gagged. My red hair, slightly touched with gray the last time I had seen myself, had transformed itself into an ugly mass of red and white splotches, neither color gaining dominance, each refusing to flow naturally into the other. My skin had become so thin and colorless that it appeared to be transparent. The weak flesh dug itself underneath my sharp cheekbones and stretched around my mouth so tightly that I was afraid a smile would cause it to rip and tear. My eyes seemed to have receded back into my skull and the green, purplish skin underneath them looked as if it were floating on black air.

My legs collapsed and I dropped down onto the floor. I grabbed the toilet, dragged myself over to it, and vomited.

I had expected to look different. The immense changes George had undergone had prepared me to see a similarly dramatic transformation in myself. I had not, however, expected that transformation to be so brutal. George's face may have reflected a deep sadness, but it also displayed a newfound strength of will and maturity, a stripping down of the non-essentials allowing what remained behind to appear pure and focused. George's new face and body quietly spoke of a reluctant warrior; mine croaked like a rotting corpse.

I began shaking. Leaning over the toilet, I grasped the seat with my hands and fought to control my trembling body. I panted heavily and felt myself on the verge of sobbing. Slapping my hands against the toilet, I forced myself to inhale deep, angry breaths. I swallowed the bile in my mouth and stared into the dirty toilet that possessed no water to wash away my puke.

Fuck 'em.

I struggled back up onto my feet and forced myself to stare into the mirror again. After several minutes, I curled my lips into a grin.

Fuck 'em all.

I snatched my cane off of the floor and left the bathroom. I moved quickly, no longer concerned with falling. Abandoning the cautious steps I had used to get to the bathroom, I swung the cane off the floor, throwing it in front of me. The tip slapped onto the floor and I fell forward, my arms trembling as I halted my weight with the cane and dragged my feet forward. I entered the kitchen loudly and collapsed down into a chair, dropping my arms onto the kitchen table where Father Zippco was sitting, twirling his jagged hunting knife between his fingers. The table shook and rattled. My cane made a sharp noise as it fell onto the floor.

"Hey there, Father."

Father Zippco turned his dark eyes away from his vodka and glared at me. His skin condition had continued to worsen. His flesh had stopped simply peeling off in tiny white flakes, and had begun to peel in large, thick strips. His face looked like an onion that had been blasted open by a bullet. Whole sections remained unmarred, while other areas, mostly around his left cheek and forehead, had peeled away layer by layer, leaving deep, ragged holes. Underneath the skin on his forehead, there remained only one thin layer separating his skull from the air. Loose meat hung from his ears and his nose.

When I had asked George what was wrong with Father Zippco, he shrugged and said, *The ozone layer's a mess and Father Zippco walks to Trump or some of the other rape camps at least a couple of times a week, so it could be the sun. Or it could be nuclear fallout. There's been rumors of a flesh-eating virus going around, so it could be that, too. These days, who knows?*

"How's it going, *Father?*" I asked with a grin.

"Get the hell away from me, gimp. I'm drinking here."

"When aren't you? In the four months I've been awake, I don't think I've ever seen you sober. What happened, *Father?* Get a little too used to drinking the Blood of Christ during Mass? That bottle of vodka remind you of the good old days, *Father?*"

His angry glare became an ugly grin. His gums were white, his teeth speckled with black. He dropped the hunting knife that the soldiers on the dock had given him as a sign of *respect*, and slipped a cigarette in between his red, flaking lips. He continued grinning, taking short, quick puffs off the filter and blowing out clouds of thick white smoke that had never floated any lower than the back of his mouth.

"That supposed to make me feel bad? Reminding me that I used to be a priest? Pressing my buttons ain't that easy, gimp. I know what you're thinking, that because I used to be a priest it's, what's the word? Symbolic."

"Ironic."

"Yeah." His ugly grin grew wider and uglier. "*Ironic*. You think me being what I am now considering what I was then is ironic. You're as dumb as everyone else, dick-wipe. You think if you toss a collar or a badge or a uniform on someone, it makes 'em different. You think it makes 'em special. Well it don't.

"I'm seventy-one years old. Joined the priesthood when I was seventeen. If I'd have wanted to get married when I was that age, or join the marines and go fight in the war; my parents and friends wouldda tried talking me out of it. Wouldda said I was too young, that I didn't know what I was getting myself into. They threw a damn *party* when they found out I wanted to become a priest.

"I spent my whole life sitting in a box listening to everyone else live life while mine passed by. I heard every possible sin in that confessional. Drugs, booze, men beating their wives and girlfriends and kids, and every sex act you could imagine. Incest, orgies, homos, lesbians, kids sleeping with kids, adultery, everything. Even heard a murder once. I'd tell 'em to say a few Our Father's and a few Hail Mary's, forgive 'em their sins, and then send 'em out into the world where they'd commit the exact same sins all over again. They were *living*. I just got to hear about it."

He brought the cigarette to his mouth and allowed it to dangle between his lips unsteadily. After a few seconds, he removed it without bothering to inhale any smoke.

"But that was okay, right? Because in the Heavens above, there was God. He saw that I was good and everyone else was bad. You think I didn't wanna go out and stick my johnson into some whore? Think I didn't wanna get drunk and high? Year after year, they came, confessing the sins *I* wanted to be committing. Sins I never indulged because the Lord our God was watching. Always watching. Always seeing.

"I was a good man, I followed the rules. And then, all of these people disappear and the Celestine Prophets tell me that everything I believed in was a lie. There is no God and there never was one. I crapped my life away on a lie."

His black eyes were full of hate and he angrily ran his hands over his forehead. Strips of flesh fell onto the table and he winced as his finger slid into the hole in his forehead, making brief contact with his naked skull. He drank from his bottle and then wiped his mouth with his sleeve, tearing a strip of skin from his lips. He cringed in pain as the flesh dangled down from the corner of his mouth, brushing against his chin.

"I wasted my damn life, afraid of getting punished by something that never existed. God doesn't punish, because there *is* no God. So don't think you can make me feel guilty by reminding me that I used to be a priest, 'cause all it does is remind me why I'm doing what I'm doing. That collar was a *slave* collar. I'm finally free."

"Who are you trying to convince, *Father*?"

"I'm not compelled to convince anyone of anything!" The flesh flapped and a bit of saliva slipped down it.

"Bullshit. You *reek* of guilt."

"Oh really? And who am I supposed to feel guilty towards? Who remains to decide what's wrong and what's right? Who remains to pass judgment upon me?"

"You were a priest, you know the Bible, you know this is God."

"If this were God, I wouldn't be here," he snarled. "I'd have been taken up to Heaven. I was a good man. No booze, no smoking, no swears. I was a sixty-five year old virgin! I followed the damn rules, so if this were God, I'd have been saved along with the rest."

"Bullshit. You're a sick piece of shit, Zippco, and you always were. It's just lucky for the rest of the world that that priest collar kept you under control for so long. You always *wanted* to do what you're doing now; you just never had the balls. In your heart, you've always been a pile of dogshit, and God knew it. When everyone disappeared, you just used it as an excuse to do what you always wanted. You didn't deserve to go to Heaven, you fucking rodent, and you know it. You're a baby throwing a tantrum because Mommy and Daddy went on vacation with the rest of the kids and didn't take you."

He turned away from me and I saw a quick flash of color in his eyes.

"Yeah," I continued, "but somewhere inside of you, you know the truth. You can try and look all mean and scary by waving that stupid knife around; you can smoke and drink and swear; you can even try and talk as if you've never had any education, which we both know is bullshit. None of it changes a thing. Deep down, you still know. I just hope I get to be there when you realize how full of shit you are. You've built up a slate of sins that can't ever be forgiven, you cocksucking corpse, and I hope I get to see the look on your face when you realize that you're going to burn in Hell forever."

His hands were trembling and the cigarette shook between his fingers.

244

"You going to smoke that, or just try and look all cool and evil with it?" I asked.

He jerked the cigarette up to his mouth, inhaling deeply and angrily. He held the smoke in his lungs for a moment before coughing it up and hacking.

I laughed and grabbed the box of cigarettes.

Tossing one into my mouth, I snapped open the lighter. The stale smoke burned my insides, roaming through me like a ball of fire. I pushed the deadly fumes out through my nose and grinned.

"**I** figured Park Avenue would've gotten a bigger taste of God's wrath," I said, looking up and down the street, surprised to see that it was relatively unscathed.

"Further down," George said.

"We going anyplace in particular?"

"Not really. I just wanted to talk to you without Father Zippco barging in on us. What do you make of him?"

"Zippco? He's a sick piece of shit."

"That's all?" George asked, disappointed in my answer.

"That's all." I lit a cigarette, the smoke hurting my lungs.

George said nothing and we walked several blocks in silence. At Fifty-Second street, the damage became much worse and we had to climb on top of the rubble. George navigated his way over the jagged mess smoothly and confidently, without paying the slightest attention to where he was stepping. He walked with a gentle confidence while I stumbled behind him, slipping despite the fact that I kept my eyes locked on the mess.

At Fifty-First street, we turned left and began moving towards Broadway. I halted and gasped at the enormity of the surrounding destruction. Huge chunks of jagged mortar spread out for as far as I could see. It was as if I had returned to the Israeli desert, but the miniscule grains of sand, while remaining infinite in number, had grown to the size of cars. I turned around in a circle and saw that the closest building that was still standing was half a mile away.

"Rockefeller Center," George said. "That's what you're staring at. Almost all the big buildings went down in the `quakes. Radio city Music Hall, NBC Studios, all of `em." He waved his hand over the rubble. "It was like dominos."

We continued moving, George gliding across the destruction as if it were smooth as water; me tripping and stumbling no matter how intently I measured my steps.

"We're going to get Jude tomorrow," George said.

I stopped walking.

"Well," I said after several minutes, "I guess you were right in that bar two or three years ago."

"Right about what?"

"Getting Jude'd be a milk run."

He didn't even try and smile. Instead, he winced as though I had just thrown sand into his eyes.

We moved down Fifth Avenue.

I stopped when I noticed we were surrounded by several stone crosses stabbing out from the rubble.

"What is this?" I asked, unnerved by the sight.

"The top of some old churches. They're still standing underneath all this mess."

"Jesus Christ, how far above the street are we?"

"Two or three stories. A lot of very big buildings fell."

We stopped speaking as two OWC soldiers a few hundred feet away stopped and looked at us. I tensed my still-weak muscles, preparing to run, but the soldiers simply shrugged and continued walking in the opposite direction.

"What the hell was that?" I asked.

"They don't do sweeps anymore. They already got most of the people, and the rest are dying from starvation or sickness. Besides, they're too busy with the work Morison's sending to worry about adding any more to their plate."

George continued to walk, eventually stopping in front of a tall, gold building standing upright amidst the destruction.

"What's this?" I asked.

George stared up at the building for a moment, but the sight of it seemed to hurt his eyes, and he shook his head without answering my question and looked away.

"George, what the hell's the matter with you?"

"I don't . . . What do you mean?"

"Look, I know I didn't know you very well before all of this, but you were different when you were in Boston. You were funny and confidant. You were . . ."

"Arrogant?"

"No. You were just different. I . . . Jesus Christ, George, why are you so fucking sad?"

"Why are you so fucking happy?" His words weren't angry, but simply a replay of mine, as if he could only ask the question by rolling it in *my* words. "You've lost two years of your life, Jimmy, and you don't seem affected by it at all. You're still the same. We've got about six months left before the End, and we still haven't gotten Jude and we're still not in Israel and you've still got that tag on your hand. How are you still the same?"

"I . . ." I shrugged and sighed. "George, do you have any idea how many times in the last few years I've woken up without the slightest fucking clue where I was and what was happening? My wife disappeared from our bed, I watched my father get shot in the face, I thought I was going to die in a nuclear attack, I spent a month getting tortured, a building I was in collapsed, killing everyone but me. I've wandered insane through the Israeli desert, spent two years surrounded by Christ-freaks in a camp protected by God, a month on a prison ship watching kids get raped. I've been beaten by an ex-student who worked in a death camp and got attacked by a swarm of locusts. *Locusts.*" I shook my head and laughed.

"You know, it just hits a point where you've got to laugh, or at the very least, not give a shit. I woke up from that coma and it felt like someone had scooped everything out of me. I can walk and I can talk and move and think, but I feel hollowed out. It's like I'm a balloon attached to a string. I don't know exactly where it's pulling me, but I don't really give a shit anymore. I've fought against that pull for six years. Fuck man, I've fought against it my whole life. I'm done fighting. I know what I am and I'm done fighting it."

George winced, and I watched him struggle to keep himself from crying. "Every time I close my eyes I see Mark Perry. I feel my finger pulling the trigger. I see his head explode. It was so easy to pull the trigger. I killed a man and it was easy." He stepped towards me and stumbled, throwing his arms on my shoulders to catch himself. "He was . . . he had blood on his face and he was helpless and he had blood all over his face and his eyes were open so wide and he was scared and I shot him. I saw him on the floor and I knew we'd get caught, so I killed him. It took me two seconds to decide. That was all. Two seconds was all that separated me from a murderer. Two seconds and I knew who I really was. I can still hear the gunshot. It's always there and it never leaves and I'm afraid it never will. I'm so afraid that I'll have to hear that gunshot and see Mark's face forever."

"You did what you had to, George. It's a fucked-up, evil world and sometimes you've got to do certain things to survive."

"Yes!" He squeezed my arms. "It *is* evil, and it's evil because of people like me, people who can shoot a man in the face just because he stands in the way of what he wants. He was tagged Jim, and I sent him to Hell because he was in my way. *We're* the reason the world's so evil. People like you and me and Father Zippco and all of us. We're all the same, Jimmy."

"Fuck that shit, George." I tried to pull myself out of his grip, but he was too strong and I was too weak. "You and me, we're nothing like Zippco."

"We're *exactly* like him! You look at Father Zippco and you see a piece of shit. I look at him and I see myself, a man who was always two seconds away from becoming what he really was. I see myself. I worked the docks in Boston, Jimmy. I helped send all those people to die. I'm a Nazi. Me! How am I different?"

"Zippco likes what he does. Likes what he is."

"Maybe he's just more honest with himself."

"Hey, you did what you had to, to save yourself. To save me."

"And that makes it okay? Who doesn't have an excuse for what they do? Who doesn't have a justification? I killed a man, murdered him when he was helpless. When I worked the docks, I wasn't sad. I didn't like it, but I also didn't go home and cry myself to sleep. No, I went home and slept in a dead man's bed. We're all the same, Jimmy. We deserve what's happening."

"SHUT UP!" I jerked myself away from him. "I'm sick of hearing that shit. I had a wife I loved, a home, a family, friends. I had a life! God took that away from me. There's no point to any of this shit."

"There is! I've learned who I am really am. It kills me to know, but God didn't create that, he didn't *make* me kill Mark, he didn't *make* me work on the docks. He created the situation that allowed me to see what I really am. Everything's happened so we can't lie to ourselves anymore. I know what I am now; I know what I've always been. I hate knowing that, but at least now the choice is clear. At least now I know what I'm choosing between. I can stay who I am and go to a Hell I deserve, or I can ask for help."

"So go. What the hell do you want from me? If you know what you've got to do, go and do it. Why did you even bother waiting for me? Waiting for Jude?"

"I couldn't go." He shook his head firmly. "I wanted to, but I couldn't. I don't deserve to be saved. I mean, I know that I can't really save myself, that I have to ask God to save me, but I couldn't even do that. I didn't deserve it. I . . . I stayed because if I helped you, if I helped Jude, if I did something good, I thought that maybe *then* I could ask for help. For forgiveness. I know that I still won't deserve it, but maybe I'll feel like I can at least ask for it."

"I . . . Okay, George." I felt the energy rush out of my body. "Look, man, what do you want from me? What do you want to hear?"

George stepped up to me, whispering like a starving man who's heard rumors of food. "Jude," he whispered. Tears swarmed down his cheeks and he stared at me desperately. "Tell me about Jude. Please, Jimmy. Tell me who she is. For three years, my entire life has revolved around her, and I don't even know who she is. Tell me who she is, Jimmy. Please, I . . . I need to know. I need a face."

I recoiled at the request. Jude had become a faceless goal, an abstract cipher, and something inside of me advised against allowing her a history, a story.

I raised my eyes to George, intending to refuse the request. But when I looked at him, looked at the only man other than Stan who had ever helped me without wanting something in return, I smiled.

"Jude. Jesus, where do I start with that?"

My smile grew as I remembered.

"There's different kinds of relationships," I said. "Occasionally, maybe once or twice in a lifetime, you find the kind that feels pre-destined. The kind of connection that you don't create or build or work at, because it already feels complete, as if it were simply waiting for you to stumble onto it. It's the kind of relationship that feels like it's always been a part of you. It makes you believe in fate or destiny. It can make you believe in God . . .

Sixteen

There's different kinds of relationships. Occasionally, maybe once or twice in a lifetime, you find the kind that feels pre-destined. The kind of connection that you don't create or build or work at, because it already feels complete, as if it were simply waiting for you to stumble onto it. It's the kind of relationship that feels like it's always been a part of you. It makes you believe in fate or destiny. It can make you believe in God. There's that. Then there's the kind of relationship you stumble into like a fucking moron because you see a great pair of tits. Jude . . . well, Jude was a full-figured woman.

She lived in my college dorm, but she never quite looked as though she belonged there. It was a freshman dorm and, while the rest of us were fumbling around the campus, trying to make friends without appearing too desperate, Jude sauntered in and out of the building with a bored look of confidence. Her dark black hair was clipped short and I never saw her carry a purse. She wore dark blazers over thin T-shirts and tromped loudly through the halls in heavy combat boots. She was constantly hanging out with at least two or three friends, usually men.

I gawked at her whenever she was in the hall and she caught me at it on more than one occasion. She never politely ignored my stares but instead, would lock her eyes onto mine, curling her lips into a knowing grin. I'd try holding my own, but would always be the first to look away, feeling embarrassed and ashamed. Her grin told the whole story; she was the woman, I was the boy, and we both damn well knew it.

When she knocked on my door at one o'clock in the morning, one month into my first semester, she greeted me with that same grin.

"You're *Jamie*, right?" Her eyes were glassy and her nose was red.

"Jim."

"Yeah, I've seen you around, Jimmy." Her grin widened and she lifted a bottle of scotch up to her lips. When she finished drinking from it, she wiped her mouth and stared at me silently.

I shifted uncomfortably from one foot to the other, my eyes darting back and forth, meeting her stare for a moment and then turning away. Jude's stare was unwaveringly solid, and she appeared perfectly content with both the silence and my discomfort.

"So," she finally said, "you're a freshman, huh?"

"Yeah. You're Judith, right?"

"Jude," she said. "*Judith* makes me sound like I'm a rich bitch. I'm not rich."

"So, um, what are you? A senior?" I lifted my hand and fiddled with my ear.

"I wish." She took another swig from her bottle. "Sophomore."

"Really? I figured you were older."

"I am." She pulled a cigarette out from her pocket and placed it at the center of her lower lip, rolling the filter across her flesh, and pushing it into the corner of her mouth. "Twenty-two, baby. I got a late start." She lit the cigarette.

"What happened?"

She blew smoke over my shoulder, into my room. "When I was eighteen, I took off to California with my boyfriend and spent my college savings."

"On what?"

"Drugs mostly." It was impossible to tell whether she was joking or not. She held up her cigarette. "Want one?"

I stared at the dark red lipstick smeared across the filter. "No, I um, I don't smoke."

She smiled, licked her lips, and returned the cigarette to the corner of her mouth.

"So your, um, your boyfriend, the guy you went to California with, is he . . . I mean, are you still with him?"

"Brian? Fuck no! We didn't last six months. Trouble was, we had spent all my money. My mother had co-signed a loan for me to go to BU and I blew that money, too. Had to spend the next two years waiting tables to pay her back before I could even think about going to college. I'm an RA and even with free room and board, UMass was all I could afford."

"Yeah? I was just too stupid to get in anywhere else."

She laughed and offered me a drink from her bottle. I shook my head and she put the bottle down on the ground and smiled. "You don't smoke, you don't drink, just what do you do, Jimmy?"

I attempted a suggestive smile.

Jude laughed at me.

"How old are you?" she asked.

"How old do I look?"

"Sixteen," she said after dragging her eyes over my body.

"*Sixteen*? Jesus, that doesn't do my ego any good. Eighteen."

"Something in your eyes," she shrugged. "Eighteen, huh?"

"Yeah. But wise beyond my years."

"That right?"

"Probably not."

"I didn't think so. Hmm. Eighteen. Young and corruptible."

"You think?"

"We'll see." She dropped her cigarette onto the floor and crushed it underneath her heavy black boot. "Nice meeting you, Jimmy." She bent over and grabbed her bottle before walking away.

"**H**ere," she said two days later as we did our laundry together, "I'll show you a trick." She removed the quarters I had placed in the machine, pulled a small nylon stocking out of her pocket, and stretched it over the coin slots. She pushed the money into the slots, over the nylon, and then jammed in the lever. The machine started with a kick and Jude quickly yanked the lever back, proudly displaying all five quarters, which were still resting on top of the nylon. She dropped the change into her pocket, lit a cigarette, and smiled.

"Sticking it to the Man," she said, and offered me a cigarette, which I refused.

She handed me the nylon and told me to try it in her machine. I mimicked what she had done, but the nylon jammed when I tried to pull out the lever. I tugged at the metal handle and, when it finally came loose, the nylon tore and only one of the five quarters remained.

"Well," she said, "you *semi*-stuck it to the Man."

A student walked in with his laundry and dropped his quarters into the machine.

"Sucker," Jude said, loudly enough for him to hear.

"Come on," she said, and grabbed my hand while she crushed her cigarette out on top of the white washing machine. "We'll wait in my room."

I closed her door behind me and, when I turned around, Jude grabbed the back of my head and kissed me. Step by step, I followed her lead in clothing removal. When she took off my shirt, I took off hers, when she removed my pants, I removed hers. Trying to show some initiative, I hesitantly slipped my fingertips under the elastic on her red underwear, but lost my nerve and quickly slid my hands onto her back.

Her lips tightened into a smile underneath my kiss and, in one deft stroke, she pushed me back onto the bed and yanked off my underwear. She dropped down on top of me and I ran my fingers across the back of her bra. She sat up smiling and unhooked it from the front, twirling it around on her fingertip before dropping it onto my face and jumping off the bed.

She slid her underwear down her legs and then stood still for a moment, staring down at me. The light was still on and she showed no inclination to turn it off. Her hips, legs and breasts were full, curvy and tough. She stood in front of me, naked and unashamed. Lying in front of her fully developed body, I suddenly felt ashamed of my nakedness, ashamed of my thin, slender frame.

I slid underneath the covers.

She hid a sweet smile underneath her fingers and turned off the light before climbing under the covers with me. Her body was softer than I would have expected.

She slid her tongue into my ear, around my jawbone, down my neck, onto my nipple, and then further down.

"Jesus Christ," I moaned, and after a minute, squirmed away from her and touched the back of her head.

"What's the matter?" she asked, raising her head and looking at me with confusion.

"Nothing," I said quickly. "Nothing. I just . . . Well, I'm about to . . . you know."

She shook her head.

"You know . . . come."

She laughed loudly before diving her head back down.

Half an hour later, she pulled me on top of her. I slid inside and, after several minutes, stopped moving.

"Oh shit," I panted. "We shouldn't . . . we shouldn't be . . . not without protection."

Jude nodded her head into my shoulder and wrapped her arms around me tightly. She made no motion to take me out of her and, as I began slipping out, I suddenly changed my mind.

Jude moaned and slid her hands down my back.

"Wait," I yelled after a few more minutes, and withdrew almost completely. "Wait, this is really . . . this is stupid. I mean, we shouldn't . . . Not . . . Oh Jesus, we really have to stop."

"Yeah, yeah you're right." She bit into my ear.

"Yeah. Yeah. Yeah. I mean, I want to, I want to so fucking bad, but I don't want to get you pregnant. I don't want to do that to you."

She licked my lips.

I dropped back down and pushed inside.

She dug her fingernails into my back and wrapped her legs around me.

After a few more minutes, I made a noise I couldn't control.

"Fuck," I said after rolling off of her. "I'm sorry, Jude. I was just so . . . That was really stupid. I'm sorry."

"Don't sweat it." She patted my stomach. "I'm on the Pill."

"You are?"

"Yeah." She leaned over the bed and pulled the cigarettes out of her abandoned pants.

"Well . . . well, why didn't you tell me?"

She shrugged while striking a match. "Kind of a test," she said. "Wanted to see if you'd care."

"I . . . Oh."

"Don't worry," she said, responding to my tone, "You passed."

"I did? But . . . I mean, we still . . . I didn't stop."

"Yeah, well, I've found it necessary to grade on a curve." She blew smoke towards the ceiling. "You didn't stop, but you tried to. You wanted to, and that's a hell of a lot better than anyone else has ever done. A-minus." She smiled and offered me her cigarette.

I took the cigarette from her fingers and, as I raised it, noticed the red stain her lips had left on the filter. I wrapped my lips around the stain and sucked.

W e holed ourselves up in Jude's tiny little dorm room, barricading ourselves as if the rest of the world was an invading army. Behind closed doors, we made ourselves a paradise. Jude traded her heavy black clothes for a pink robe. We talked quietly and spent most of our time under the covers, fucking and snuggling. She made me english muffins in her toaster, covering them with the perfect amount of butter and jelly. She never ate any, but with a proud, happy face, watched me devour them. She told me she loved me.

It was only when we ventured outside of the room that I felt uncomfortable in her presence. She slipped back into her black clothes and I always ended up feeling small. Jude seemed to know every person on campus, and friends of hers constantly greeted us. After being introduced as a friend, I'd be given a pleasant nod before being completely ignored. Jude's voice carried an edgy, slightly angry tone when she spoke to other people, and if the conversation went on longer than she was interested in, she'd simply turn and walk away. Before I knew what was happening, Jude would be clomping ten feet ahead of me in her heavy boots, leaving me behind to shrug an apology. Running to catch up with her, I felt like a little boy sprinting after his mother.

Occasionally, when Jude actually liked the person she was talking to, her conversation would last for more than a few minutes, usually ending with an invitation to get together with some people at a bar. Three times, Jude impulsively accepted before remembering my age and quickly withdrawing her acceptance.

"Jude," I said, after the second time it had happened, "if you want to go, it's okay with me. I don't want you not seeing your friends just because I'm not twenty-one."

"Do you want me to go without you? To leave you behind?"

"Honestly?"

"Yeah."

"No."

"Then fuck `em," she'd say.

Only once in those first few months did Jude accept an invitation. A friend of hers was the bass player in a band called Said And Done, and he invited Jude to come and watch him play at the Iron Horse. We sat through three bands while waiting for her friend to play; *Porn Star, Dyke Alert,* and *Fuck Death.* The music was loud and angry, all thrashing guitars and exploding drums, an orgy of noise that completely engulfed the singer's voice.

"How can you like this music?" I asked.

"What?" she asked.

"HOW CAN YOU LIKE THIS MUSIC?"

She frowned at me.

After the show, Jude's friend worked his way through the crowd and gave Jude a big hug before introducing himself to me. We shook hands and I felt the hard calluses on his fingertips. He was wearing a thin, sleeveless T-shirt, displaying his huge arms and a mass of black tattoos.

"How'd you like the show?" he asked me.

"I'm more of a Monkees fan. I kept hoping you were going to do a cover of *Daydream Believer.*"

He turned back to Jude.

I hovered around the two of them for an hour or so, feeling stupid and small.

Jude was quiet on the ride home, and seemed to be thinking about something that made her tense and uptight. It was only after we had returned to her room and closed the door behind us that she relaxed.

"You and me against the world, baby," she whispered into my ear after sex. "Fuck 'em all."

"I think I'm going to sleep in my own room tonight," I said, unwittingly introducing an apple into our paradise.

"What?" Jude's face and tone hardened.

"It's no big deal, I just haven't slept there for an entire semester. My roommate probably thinks I'm dead. Just for a change of pace."

"*A change of pace?*" What the fuck does that mean?"

"It . . . What's wrong?"

"Nothing," she scoffed. "Good. Sleep upstairs."

"I don't . . ."

"Are you still here?"

"Why are you acting like this is an insult?"

"Why *wouldn't* I? We've slept together every night for the past six months and now, for absolutely no reason, you tell me that you don't want to sleep with me anymore. What am I *supposed* to take that as? A complement? Just fuck off, Jimmy."

"Jude, I never said that I want to stop sleeping with you."

"Yeah Jimmy, you did. I'm sleeping here and you're not."

"I just thought . . ."

"Fuck off. If you don't want to go out anymore, just fucking say it, okay? Find some balls and say it to my face. Don't hand me this *change of pace* bullshit, just fucking say it."

"What? I don't want to break up! Jude . . ."

"Come on, be a man and say it to my face."

"I am saying it to your face; *I don't want to break up.*"

"Bullshit."

"Jude . . ."

"Get the fuck out of here. Do whatever you want, asshole."

"*Asshole?* Why are you acting like such a bitch?"

The blood drained from her face and she looked at me with pure hatred. Without taking her eyes off me, she reached behind her, grabbed a framed picture from her bureau, and threw it at me. The frame flew past my head and smashed into the wall behind me.

"GET OUT!" she screamed, and turned away from me.

"Jude . . ." I walked over to her and touched her shoulder.

"No." She jerked away from me.

"Hey," I said with a nervous laugh. "Come on, baby, I don't want this. I love you."

"Don't . . ."

I stepped up to her again and wrapped my arms around her.

She bristled at my contact.

"Jude, why are you doing this? I . . . Look, I'm sorry, okay?"

"It doesn't matter," she said, and nodded her head while stepping away from me. "I'm being stupid. Go on upstairs, Jimmy, it's okay."

"I don't want to go upstairs. Look, it was a dumb idea, let's just forget about it, okay?"

"No," she said calmly, and turned to face me. "You were right."

"Jude, I don't want to . . ."

"We'll sleep together tomorrow." She nodded her head and gave me a tight kiss. "I'll see you tomorrow," she said through a hard, false smile.

I never suggested sleeping alone again, but that didn't seem to matter. The damage had been done. Three or four times a week, she'd insist on having me sleep upstairs, in my own bed. Not because *she* wanted to sleep alone but because, she would say, it was obvious that *I* wanted to sleep alone. After spending an hour or two trying to convince her that that wasn't true, I'd become exhausted and relent. Jude would nod her head angrily, insisting that it was what I had wanted all along, only I didn't have the balls to admit it.

As the months passed, it took less and less to set Jude off, and once her anger was unleashed, it was impossible to stuff back down until it had expended itself. After the fights were over, I'd wade through the insults and accusations we had flung at each other, trying to trace the argument back to its origins, searching for the key to the anger, the colossal blunder that I must have committed to instigate such an explosion. I trusted that if I could just understand, I could fix it, that I could make it right. But when I'd finally pinpoint the exact moment the love turned into hate, the event was usually so small and insignificant, that I couldn't understand. I couldn't fix it.

She began going to bars and more arguments erupted when I suggested that perhaps we weren't spending enough time together.

"You act like I don't invite you, Jimmy, but I always do."

"I'm only nineteen, Jude, I can't get into a bar."

"They'd let you in if you came with me, I know the bouncer."

"Of course you do, you know everyone. Besides, they still wouldn't serve me. What am I supposed to do when you and your friends get loaded? Sit in the corner drinking a glass of milk?"

"Look, I'm not going to tell six people who want to go to a bar that we have to go to McDonalds instead because my boyfriend isn't old enough to drink. This isn't high school Jimmy; I'm not going to blow off my friends for you."

"When did I ever ask you to do that?"

"I don't know, maybe thirty seconds ago? You don't even like my friends."

"I like *you*."

"Doesn't seem like it."

And on and on and on.

"Hey, I saw Jude last night," my roommate said to me, one year after we had done our laundry together for the first time. "She was coming out of the Spoke with some black guy."

"*Jude* was? She was *with* the black, or . . .?"

"Oh." He shifted his eyes away. "No. I don't know. I mean, she was just talking to him."

"They were alone?"

"Ah, no. There were a couple of guys hanging around, so it probably wasn't just the two of them. I don't know."

It was not, I told myself as I stood in front of Jude's door, preparing to break up with her, that I had a problem with her hanging out with a black guy. It was that I had *no idea* that Jude had been hanging around with a black guy. If *I* had made friends with some black guy, *she* would have know about it. I would've *told* her. I was tired of feeling small and weak, sick of being the child to her adult. I took a deep breath and opened the door.

She was lying naked on her bed, quietly sobbing and squeezing Mr. Bun, a stuffed rabbit I had given her.

"Jude?"

At the sound of my voice, she closed her eyes and turned away.

The nigger raped her.

"Jude what happened?" I ran over to the bed and lifted her into my arms; discreetly trying to inspect her body for cuts or bruises.

"What happened?" I asked again, after failing to find any overt signs of assault.

She said nothing, but continued sobbing as I rocked her.

"It's okay, baby, it's okay. Just tell me what's wrong."

"My father . . ." She dug her face into my chest.

"I know."

"He died."

"I know, baby, you told me a long time ago."

"He hung himself."

259

I stopped rocking her. Jude had never told me how her father had died, only that it happened when she was young.

"I was ten." She dropped Mr. Bun onto the bed. "I got home from school and I went into the cellar and he was there. He was hanging from the pipes and there was a rope and his face was green and he was dead and his eyes were big and red and he had pooped himself and it was on the floor and he was my Daddy and he was dead."

"Aw, Jude. Jude, I'm sorry. I'm so sorry."

She pulled my shirt away from my chest, covering her face with it. "There wasn't even a note. He just left and he was gone."

"Jude, I . . ."

"You want to break up with me."

"What? No."

"I know you do. And you should. I'm such a fucking bitch and I know that you're going to leave and you should and I don't want you to. I love you and I don't want to be a bitch and I try to stop but I keep acting the same way and I don't know why or how to stop."

"Jude, it's okay."

"He didn't even leave a note. I never knew why he . . ."

"It's okay, baby."

"Don't leave me, Jimmy. I'm so afraid and I don't want to be alone and I don't want you to leave and I'm so bad and I don't want to be alone anymore. Don't leave me. Please. Please, Jimmy."

I cupped the back of her head in my hand and pulled her wet face up against my chest. Her naked white body suddenly looked young and vulnerable. All she was wearing was her red lipstick, which was smeared across her mouth. The dark color looked ridiculous on her, and I wiped it away with my shirt.

"I'm not going anywhere, baby," I said confidently, my voice sounding strong and right. "I love you and I promise; I'm not leaving. You'll never have to be alone if you don't want to be. I'll make it okay, Jude. I'll make things right. I promise."

"You'll never leave?" she asked in a small voice that mingled hope with fear. "You promise?"

"I swear to God."

"**A**re you sure you want to do this, Jude?"

"Yes. Don't you?"

"I just want to be sure it's the right thing."

"It is, Jimmy. It is. I know that things have been hard for the last year or two, but I think it's just . . . I kept thinking you were going to leave. Even after we moved in together. I just kept . . . ."

"My parents aren't even here."

"This isn't about them; it's about us. We've been together for more than four years, Jimmy. I wanted to do this after the first. I love you; I want us to be happy. Don't you?"

"Of course. No, this is good. I just wanted to make sure that you were good."

"Well it *was* my idea, Jimmy."

"Okay."

"But you're good with it? This is what *you* want to do?"

"Of course."

"You're sure?"

"I'm sure. I mean, hell, a Vegas wedding has a certain slimy charm to it, right? Listen Jude, are you sure you don't want me to go visit your friend with you?"

"Yeah, you go and gamble. I'll meet you back at the hotel."

"Okay."

"Just don't be too late, okay? Be back at the hotel by nine so we can get up early tomorrow. We have to be at the chapel by eight. Okay?"

"Yeah, that's fine," I said.

"Nine's good?"

"Nine's fine."

"Okay. Just make sure you're back at nine."

"Are you okay, Jude?"

"I'm fine."

"Are you sure you don't want me to come with you?"

"Yeah. Yeah, you go gamble."

"You're sure?"

"Yeah. Yeah, I'm sure. Go and have fun."

"Okay." I kissed her and turned to leave.

"Just . . .! Just come back!"

"What?"

"By nine, I mean. Just . . . I mean, just come back by nine."

She smiled nervously and walked away.

I played blackjack for three hours and met a dealer who decided that I was his best friend in the world until I ran out of money, at which point, his grimace told me that I had become his worst enemy and the drunk old man sitting next to me became his new best pal.

I wandered around the casino and became mesmerized watching the old ladies play the slots. They hunched over the devices, hanging onto them for support. When they pulled the levers down, they didn't use their arm muscles, but rather collapsed their whole bodies, allowing their dead weight to drag the lever down and then lift them back up. They sank quarter after quarter into the machines, but never seemed to discover any joy in the action, or even possess the slightest hope of winning. When they did occasionally win a small amount of money, they didn't smile or react with any pleasure, they simply scooped up the quarters, tossed them into the cup they held, and sank them back into the machine.

There were men in tuxedos walking through the casinos and showgirls dressed in ridiculously ornamented outfits which possessed as much material as the most conservative of dresses, but still somehow managed to display more than half of their flesh. There were hundreds of thousand of flashing lights, noises, and distractions, but that's all they were, distractions. Underneath it all, the heart of the casino was the old ladies with their polyester pants and plastic cups filled with rotating quarters. They worked the machines as if they were in a sweatshop and all the bullshit glamour in the world couldn't hide the depressing sight of their gray hearts pumping their jingling blood into the casino's veins.

I became hypnotized by the repetitive monotony of it all, and when I returned to the hotel, it was almost midnight. I whispered Jude's name into the darkness.

She shot out of the bed and leapt onto me, wrapping both her arms and legs around me.

"Where were you, Jimmy?"

262

"I'm sorry, baby, I lost track of the time."

She dropped off me as suddenly as she had latched on and walked back to bed sluggishly.

"Those casinos are so fucking depressing," I said, and lit a cigarette. "You know, I've got a theory about cities. Every major city in America represents some fundamental human facet. New York is our anger, LA our fantasy life, and Boston our intellect. You know what Vegas is? It's our asshole. Las Vegas is America's asshole, small, dirty, and the ultimate receptacle of all things unwanted. It's a corpse wearing too much fucking make-up, a dead city trying to hide its pale face behind too many gaudy lights and has-been performers. I can't wait to get married and get the fuck out of here. Jesus, let's get married and make something decent, huh? Something pure."

"Jimmmmmy," Jude said in a little girl's voice from the bed.

"You okay, Jude?"

"Mmmmm-hhmmmm."

"You sound weird."

"We're getting married tomorrow, aren't we?"

"That's right."

"After tomorrow I'm going to be your wife."

"Yeah. That's the way weddings usually work."

"I'm going to be your perfect little wife starting tomorrow."

"Yeah, huh?"

"Do you want me to be your dirty little whore tonight?"

"What?"

Jude turned over on her stomach and pulled her underwear down around her knees.

"Do you want to fuck me in the ass, Jimmy?" She crouched her knees underneath her and pushed her ass up into the air.

"What?"

"I know you do," she giggled. "We've never done that before, but I know that you want to. I look back sometimes, when you're fucking me from behind, and I see you looking at my ass. I see your eyes. You want to rape my ass, don't you, Jimmy?" She pressed her face into the pillow, her words becoming muffled. "I want to make you happy, Jimmy. I want to be your little whore tonight. I know you want to. Make it hurt, I can take it. I wanna be dirty."

"Jude . . ."

She reached across to the nightstand and pulled a mirror towards her. "I want you to get high with me and then I want you to stick your cock up my ass and rape me. Give me what I deserve."

I walked to the nightstand. There were two lines of heroin spread across the mirror. I put my hand on Jude's hip and pushed her onto her side.

"You son of a bitch, Jude."

"What are you mad about, snookums?"

"You said you were done with that shit. You promised me. You said if I took it with you that one time, that we'd be equal, that you wouldn't feel like I was looking down on you all the time. You promised that you were done with it."

"It makes me happy."

"I'm supposed to make you happy. *Me*! Not some brown shit you stick up your fucking nose!"

"Oh shut up, Jimmy. You're such a freak. Just fuck me in the ass. I know you want a clean little wife. I know you won't be able to fuck me in the ass after we're married. Last chance."

"How could you do this to me?"

"I didn't think you were coming back."

"Because I was two hours late? Is this shit why you had to see your friend from high school? Why you wanted to see her alone?"

"It was a wedding present."

"Fucking bitch."

"Get the stick out of your ass, Jimmy. Starting tomorrow everything'll be perfect. Now snort some shit and fuck me in the ass."

"Fuck you."

She reached out with her hand and grabbed the erection underneath my pants. "You don't *feel* mad, Jimmy."

I slapped her hand off of me.

"Fine, be that way." She leaned past me and snorted both lines of heroin. After a few seconds, she collapsed back onto the bed and spoke to me through a rubbery smile.

"Come to bed, Jimmy." Her underwear was still tangled around her knees.

264

My erection wouldn't go away.

"Come, come, come; come to bed with me," she sang.

I stood over her and began sweating.

I did want to fuck her in the ass.

I wanted to snort the heroin, rape her ass, and then maybe even smack her around.

I ran into the bathroom and scrubbed my face and hands in the sink. I stared up into the mirror and then back down at my erection that refused to go away.

I reached into my pocket and pulled out enough money for a cab ride to the airport and a one-way ticket back to Boston. The rest of the money, I left on top of the toilet.

"My white knight," Jude said quietly, as she drifted into sleep. "We're going to be married and I'm going to be your wife and everything's going to be good. Right, Jimmy?"

"Right." I walked over to the side of the bed, kissed her forehead, and pulled the covers over her.

"I love you, Jimmy."

"I love you too, Jude."

She smiled and looked as innocent as a child.

It wouldn't last.

I turned away from her and walked out the door.

Seventeen

"Jude's in a rape camp."

George was several feet ahead of me when he spoke the words. We were back on Fifth Street, on the same rubble we had crossed the day before, when I had told him about my relationship with Jude.

The words stabbed into me, cutting deeper than I would have expected. My weak legs buckled underneath me and I reached out to one of the protruding stone crosses, holding on to it tightly to stop myself from falling.

"She's *what?*"

"She . . . After everything went to hell for us in Boston, Jude managed to stay in hiding for another year-and-a-half. They caught her in a sweep about nine months ago. She was transferred around a bit and . . . well, you've heard Father Zippco talk about the place he goes. I . . . Jude's there. She's been there for the last six months."

"Oh Jesus. I . . . Oh fuck. Where?"

George pointed to the golden tower standing out amongst the rubble.

"Trump."

"What?" I pulled my hand away from the cross and quickly moved in front of George. "You mean to tell me that for the last six months, Jude's been in a rape camp less than two miles away from us and you just left her there?"

George flinched at my words and shook his head. "Jimmy, there was nothing I could do. I broke into an OWC barracks and hacked into their files to find out what had happened to her. Once I knew, I forced Father Zippco to introduce me to the right people, but I couldn't just go in and take her out. We have to . . .we have to buy her."

"We *what?*"

"Water, Jimmy. The droughts and the contamination have done so much damage that water's the only thing left that's worth anything. I needed to get enough water to buy Jude and bribe our way to Israel."

I pushed my finger into my temples and tried to focus on the details of what George was telling me, to push past the three words clinging to my brain: *Rape, Buy* and *Jude.* Telling George about Jude had been a mistake, an indulgent disaster. It had resurrected dead memories that should have stayed rotting in the ground. The memories had forced me into thinking of Jude, not as a goal or an excuse, but as the girl who made me english muffins in her pink robe.

Those memories hadn't bolstered my enthusiasm for finding Jude; they had done just the opposite. The memories had filled me with shame and guilt, they had submerged my brain into a thick fog I couldn't seem to push past. Everything was blurry and unclear, my head reeling with confusion.

"How . . .? Jesus. How much water?" I asked, not caring about the answer but trying to distract myself from the interior chaos.

"A lot. I rationed what Father Zippco was given, but couldn't save very much that way. He was only receiving enough rations for one, and there were three of us. I had to . . . to steal it. That's what I was doing all those nights when I went out. I'm a thief."

"You stole it to save Jude."

"Water's the only thing people need and I steal it."

"Look, anyone who's still over is no better than Father Zippco. They're fucking scumbags."

"*We're* still here."

"We have a good reason to still be here."

"You think Father Zippco doesn't think the same thing? That he doesn't have his own justifications?"

"Jesus Christ, Glass! Will you stop with the fucking self-recriminations? I am so fucking sick of watching you mope around as if you're the most evil person in the world. You did what you had to. We all did. You want to be a martyr, see yourself as a thief and a murderer? Fine, but why don't you try carrying it like a man and stop moaning like a fucking sissy. You made your choices. You are what you are, carry it like the rest of us and let's just get this fucking thing done with."

I walked ahead and George followed slowly behind me. The rubble tapered off at the end of Fifty-Fourth Street and we climbed down onto the cracked pavement. We moved past several OWC soldiers who took no notice of us. George was wearing his stained and torn OWC uniform and carried a gun. I was dressed in Father Zippco's baggy corduroys and flannel shirt.

"Is this safe?" I whispered to George.

He didn't answer me, but continued silently moving forward.

I stared up at the shiny, golden building, marveling at its opulence like a country hick who had just arrived in the Big City for the first time.

"How did this get through the earthquakes?" I asked, still marveling at the pristine, golden walls. "This looks like it would've been one of the first buildings to go down in a `quake."

"I wouldn't know," George answered in an abrupt, angry tone.

"Quit acting like a skirt, George."

I followed George up to the front of the building, to the revolving glass doors and the soldiers standing in front of them.

"Gimme yer hand, yeh?" one of the soldiers said in a bored Irish brogue.

"I'm here for Ron Hatch," George said, keeping his tagged hand in his pocket.

The soldier looked suspiciously at the two of us for a moment and then walked inside. Several minutes later, he returned with a burley, middle-aged man, who pushed past the Irish soldier and held his hand out to George.

"Hi, Ron." George limply grasped Ron's hand.

"Ronny," he said with a big smile. "I told you, call me Ronny." He looked over George's shoulder and motioned towards me. "This your pal?"

"Yeah. This is Jimmy."

"Good to meet'cha, chief."

He Chiefed me. I smiled without knowing why.

Ronny pushed past George and grasped my hand, his hairy, meaty forearms yanking my arm up and down.

"Did you check out the apartment I gave you the keys for?" George asked.

"Yeah."

"You count the water? It's all there, right?"

"Hey!" Ronny said with a hurt look on his face. "You're insulting me here. I trust you, chief. You tell me there's two hundred gallons there, I'm gonna believe it."

Ronny turned away and winked at me.

"Georgie's good people. I got a nose for it, y'know?"

Ronny patted his hands up against his chest like a drum. "All right then, boys and girls, let's take care of this." He clasped his hand onto my shoulder and pushed me up to the glass door, which was still blocked by the Irish soldier.

"Listen, Kelly," Ronny said, transferring his hand from my shoulder onto Kelly's, "me and these fellas here, we got a little business we need to take care of inside. No big deal, but it'd probably be easier all around if they didn't get scanned. No sense having a record of 'em being here if it ain't necessary, right? Unless that's a problem for you, of course. I don't wanna be stepping on your toes."

Kelly looked at George, then to me, then back to Ronny, all the while smiling smugly.

"Sure," Kelly said to Ronny. "I don't see the need to be clinging on to formalities. We're all friends here, right?"

"Exactly," Ronny said while nodding his head.

"O 'course, friends do right by their friends, yeh?"

"You gotta ask?" Ronny jolted back as if her had been struck. "Come on, Kelly, these here are good people. They're gonna do right by me, so of course I'm gonna do right by you. How's that ever gonna happen that Ronny ain't gonna do right by his friends?"

Kelly stepped aside and Ronny winked to us as we entered the building without being scanned.

"Fucking Micks," Ronny mumbled once we were through the doors. "Cocksucker wouldn't trust his own mother. Something wrong with a fella who can't trust his pals."

The sun pushed through the glass doors and reflected off the gold-plated walls. Soldiers casually strutted about, joking with each other and drinking from bottles of vodka

"You ain't never been here before, huh?" Ronny asked me.

"No."

"Well, I'll tell you, this here is the best goddamn Recreation Center in the whole freaking state. They ain't got these in Europe, y'know. It's funny, 'cause sometimes I hear the fellas bitching about the work, but I always tell 'em that they ain't got no Chinks or Arab's shooting at 'em over here and they ain't never gonna have nothing as sweet as Trump over in Europe. Don't get me wrong, they're good people, it's just that sometimes it gets on my nerves when folks don't appreciate what they got. Everyone's got their sob story, and everyone thinks their slice of shit-pie tastes worse than everyone else's, thinks it makes 'em something special 'cause not everything went right for 'em. I get sick of the moaning sometimes, is all. Still, they're good people."

He led us to the motionless escalators and we climbed up to the third floor. We walked to a gray set of doors and stopped in front of an old man standing in a puddle of vomit.

The old man's pants were dropped down around his ankles, soaking in the puke, and he held his flaccid penis in his hands. His red face trembled as he screamed down at the dead flesh, shaking it back and forth in his hands.

"You goddamn traitor! What's the matter with you? Do you understand what you're doing to me? Do you have any idea? Do you? Goddamn you! Goddamn you to hell!"

The old man ignored us as we squeezed past him. Once though the door, Ronny let out a loud laugh and squeezed my shoulder.

"That's Carl," he said. "Stupid mope comes in here at least twice a day. He goes into one of the rooms and, fifteen minutes later, comes out with his pants around his ankles, screaming at his prick. He never shows up unless he's stone drunk and then, after he fails, he leaves and comes back later even more drunk to give it another shot.

"Only thing that mope ever gives the slabs is a beating. You gotta feel sorry for a guy like that, am I right? I mean, he never shows up sober, so he can't get his pecker to stand at attention and obey orders. If he's gotta booze-up to get the courage to come here, that's fine, but after fifty times, you'd figure the guy'd catch on to the fact that it just ain't gonna work on the sauce, so either do without the sauce or don't show up, right?

"And, I mean, beating up the slabs and hollering at your joint's just misplacing the blame. You gotta feel sorry for a guy who don't have the guts to face up to himself and take the blame. What kind of life is that, going around in the same circle, always blaming the other guy? Or pecker as the case may be. I mean, how many times do you have to make the same mistake before you shoulder the responsibility?" Ronny laughed loudly and slapped George on the back. "Hey, you gotta laugh or you'll end up crying, right?"

We passed through a second set of doors, into a stairwell, and a blast of hot, sticky air pushed into our faces, its meaty, human stench sapping what little strength my legs possessed. George stepped up behind me and propped me up with his arm. I threw my arm over his shoulder and tried not to gag.

"You get used to the smell," Ronny laughed.

"Jesus, I hope not," I said.

"Oh yeah! Anybody'll get used to anything given enough time, Jimbo. Come on, we got a ways to go, we're headed to the seventh level!"

270

The stairwell was dark, the walls soft and wet. I closed my eyes, trusting George to navigate our ascension. Halfway up the first staircase, I noticed a quiet, muffled groan. The noise grew louder as we climbed, and was joined by a rhythmic thumping which sounded like dough being pounded into shape by an energetic chef.

"Jesus Christ, Garcia," Ronny yelled.

George stopped moving and released a long, sad sigh.

Reluctantly, I opened my eyes and saw a small, thin girl bent over the cold steel railing. She was naked, and standing behind her was a young boy who looked to be fourteen or fifteen years old. His pants were dropped around his ankles. He stopped moving and looked up at Ronny with an apologetic grimace. Ronny placed his hands on his hips and stuck out his chest with a theatrical display of disapproval, slowly shaking his head back and forth.

"What the hell is this shit, Garcia?"

The boy shrugged.

The girl was younger than the boy. Her fingers were wrapped around the banister, her knuckles pale white. She kept her eyes clamped shut and gasped for air.

"I don't know," the boy said in a sulky tone. "It's new meat. I'm just breaking it in."

"In a room, Garcia, not in the goddamn stairwell. Take it to a room."

"The rooms are boring," he whined.

"Yeah, well, they may be boring, but that's the way we do things around here. This is an official Recreation Center of the One World Community, not your personal playground. It's `cause of people like you that the stairwell's such a freaking mess."

"Okay, okay. I said I was sorry."

"Look," Ronny sighed, "all's I'm saying is there's a right way and a wrong way. So just finish up with the slab and next time, do it the right way, okay?"

"Okay."

"Okay. Don't worry about it, no harm no foul."

The girl opened her eyes for a moment and took a deep breath.

I dropped my arm off of George's shoulder and began following Ronny up the stairs. I held on to the railing and could feel the vibrations as Garcia began thrusting once again. I heard the same thumping noise I had heard before and realized that the noise was caused by the boy punching the girl's back every time he thrust his hips forward. Her backside was covered in red, purplish discolorations.

"There's only two," the boy growled as we walked away. "Slabs or saints. A saint wouldn't like this, a slab would. You're a slab, so if you make any noises, they better be the right ones. Make me know that you like it. Make the right fucking noises."

I released the vibrating banister and we continued up to the seventh level. Ronny moved ahead of us, bounding over the stairs like an excited child on Christmas morning. Behind me, George slowly and methodically plodded upwards.

"Sorry about that," Ronny said as he waited for us to catch-up to him. "Garcia's good people, but he's a little too enthusiastic sometimes, you know? I mean, he's got good intentions, but sometimes you gotta step back and ask yourself if what you're doing is the right thing. We live in a society, and sometimes you gotta think about someone other than yourself. One man's needs are not more important than another's no how important those needs feel, am I right? I mean, other people gotta use those stairs."

He shrugged and George caught up to us.

"Anyway, forget about Garcia, you gotta see this." He led us down a hallway and stopped in front of a door.

"Ron . . ." George said.

"*Ronny.*"

"Ronny, we're in a bit of a hurry, we should really . . ."

"No, no, no. You gotta see this. I didn't get a chance to show you the last time you were here, Georgie."

"I saw enough, Ronny."

"Ah come on, take a second and smell the roses. This'll only take a minute." He slapped his hand onto George's back and playfully pushed him towards the door while sliding open a peephole.

George stepped up to the slot and displayed no emotion on his face. His body remained absolutely still, except for his fingers, which were quivering.

"Ain't that something?" Ronny asked.

"Yeah," George answered in an empty voice. "Yeah, that's something." He stepped away from the peephole and smiled blandly.

When Ronny turned away, towards me, George's smile abruptly disappeared. He placed his hands over his face and inhaled deeply, turning away from us.

Ronny pushed me towards the door and I peered through the slot.

"This was my idea," Ronny said with pride. "Sometimes, the slabs we get in here think they're something special. You can see it in their eyes. The eyes don't lie, am I right?"

I stared into the room, wishing with all my soul that my eyes were lying.

"This shows 'em how special they are."

After a minute, Ronny shoved me aside and took my place at the slot.

I turned around and dropped back against the wall. My legs gave out underneath me and I slid down to the floor, desperately fishing for a cigarette in my pocket.

"That's Jack in there," Ronny said, his eyes glued to the peephole. "Purebred golden retriever. There ain't many purebreds left, but he is. He's a beauty, isn't he? Nothing more beautiful in the world than a good dog. Any man can't love a dog ain't a man in my book."

I tried placing the cigarette between my lips, but my mouth was numb and unable to grasp it. It dropped down onto the floor. I picked it up and it was wet.

"I send the new slabs in there if they got that look in their eye. I tell 'em what to do and that I'll be checking in on 'em from time to time to make sure they do it. I tell the slabs if they ain't doing what I told 'em to do when I check in, that I'll slit their throats. They do what they're told."

I pulled another cigarette out of the box and bit down into it with my teeth. The filter bent and sagged. I lit the cigarette with shaking hands.

"Yeah," Ronny growled, his voice abandoning its boyishness. The smile dropped from his face, which had suddenly become red and angry. "Show it, Jack. Show it who's boss. It loves it, doesn't it? It loves doing that to you. Show it. Show it. Yeah."

George rubbed his hands over his face and stumbled unsteadily over to the door.

"We have to go, Ron. Ronny."

"Yeah. Make it like it, Jack."

"Ronny," George repeated, and touched Ronny's shoulder.

Ronny jumped at the contact and spun around looking confused to see George. He shook his face and reclaimed his smile.

"Right. Right. That's something, though, ain't it? Didn't I tell you?"

George managed a tight smile and nodded his head.

I couldn't seem to inhale enough smoke to cover the meaty taste in my mouth.

"All right," Ronny said, and ruffled his hands through my hair. "Let's go get your slab."

Ronny led us down the hall and around the corner, to the end of the hall. He opened the peephole of another door and nodded his head. "It's there. You picked a good one, Georgie. It's older than we usually take, but it knew how to work its ass. I'm gonna miss that one. Jack will, too."

Ronny unlocked the door and began turning the handle.

George placed his hand over Ronny's, stopping him from opening the door.

"Can we get a few minutes alone with her? With it?"

"You fellas wanna get a taste right now, huh?" Ronny grinned and licked his lips. "Watching Jack and the slab got you worked up, didn't it, chief? Yeah, you fellas go on and have some fun; I'll be waiting around the corner when you're done."

George tried to mirror Ronny's grin. "Thanks. You're . . . you're good people, Ronny."

Ronny laughed and winked before leaving.

George grabbed the door handle.

I stopped him from turning it.

"Don't open the door, George."

"Why?"

"I don't . . . I don't think we should do this."

"*What?*"

"I . . . Look, I don't know, but there's this part of me, and it's telling me we shouldn't do this. That it's wrong. Maybe we should just . . . just . . ."

"Just *what?* Leave her here? Jimmy, you know what this place is. That's Jude on the other side of this door. *Your* Jude."

"I know!" I winced, hoping that Jude hadn't heard my voice. "I know," I repeated in a whisper. "But it doesn't . . . I've got this part of me, this inch telling me I shouldn't . . . I don't know. I can't think clearly, I can't . . . I don't know."

"*You don't know?* Get your fucking ass in there, Jimmy."

He turned the handle and shoved me into the room, closing the door behind us.

The small room smelled similar to the stairwell, but the odor was more concentrated in the room. It was so solid that I was sure if I pushed out my tongue, I could lick and taste it. I stumbled into the corner, clenching my stomach and staring at the floor.

George nudged me

"Talk to her," he said.

I kept my eyes locked onto the floor.

He shoved me again and I fell down, next to a dirty, soiled bucket. Next to the bucket was a pile of sex toys, most of which were stained red. I tried to control my heavy breathing and forced my eyes off the floor.

Jude was sitting on a torn mattress. The mattress was covered with orange and brown stains. She sat naked, her legs spread open. Around her neck was a thick, black dog collar. A chain was connected to the collar, shackling Jude to the wall. Her half-open, glazed eyes were caked with thick black eye shadow. Her lips were smeared with bright pink lipstick. Her emaciated body was covered with bruises and cuts and scabs.

Oh Jesus, what am I doing?

Jude stared up at the ceiling.

I can't do this.

"Which hole?" Jude asked in a lifeless voice.

I crawled across the sticky floor and grabbed the side of the mattress.

"Jude. It's me, Jude. It's Jimmy."

She dropped her head down and stared at me with dead eyes.

"I know who you are, Jimmy. Which hole?"

Eighteen

"Snuff it once you've had your fun," Ronny had said to George after ushering us past the guards and back out onto the street. Jude's thin wrist had looked like it might snap underneath Ronny's tight grip. He had refused to let her go, emphasizing the fact that the transaction would not be complete until he felt certain that George intended to honor the arrangement up to the very end. "Use it as long as you want, by when you're done, don't go soft and let it go. Snuff it."

Long after the three of us had returned to Father Zippco's apartment and showed Jude into the bedroom so she could sleep, the impersonal pronoun stuck in my head, feeling like an accusation.

I crushed out the cigarette I was smoking, realizing that, somewhere down the line, they had become too bitter for me to enjoy.

"You have to talk to her," George repeated for the tenth time.

My brain substituted George's *Her* with *It*.

"I can't, George."

"You have to."

"I . . ." I shook my head and threw a fresh cigarette into my mouth.

"Jimmy," George groaned, "I gotta take off in an hour to finalize the plans to get us to Israel. When I get back, the three of us have to leave right away. You have to talk to her, you have to explain what's happening and convince her to come with us."

"I can't." I sucked as hard as I could, trying to make the cigarette taste good.

"Why? Jesus, Jimmy, wasn't this what it was all about? Saving Jude? Doing something right for once? Doing something good? We've done that and now it's almost over. All that's left is talking to Jude. Go and do that so we can finish this thing."

"I can't! I can't . . . I can't fucking think." I stood up and walked into the corner of the room. My body felt tired and empty, my head heavy and cluttered. No matter how hard I tried, I couldn't focus my thoughts or organize the chaotic jumble of emotions wrestling through my brain. Only the word *It* stood out amongst the confusion.

"What's left to think about? Just get your ass in there and do what you came here to do."

"I can't." I pushed my fingers through my hair. "I can't, I can't, I can't. I . . . This is wrong, this is so fucking wrong!"

"*What's* wrong?"

"I . . . Jude's not an *It*. She's Jude."

"What does that *mean*, Jimmy? What the hell are you talking about?"

"It . . . I don't know." I stared at my cigarette and, not knowing what else to do, stuffed it into my mouth and inhaled. The stale smoke rushed into my stomach and gave me a cramp. "Fuck. Fuck! I don't want to go in there, George. I can't. I feel like I'm going to . . . I don't know what. It just feels wrong. *I* feel wrong. Jesus Christ, it feels like my fucking head's about to explode. It's all wrong. It's just, I think if I go in there I'm going to . . . to . . ."

The front door opened and Father Zippco walked into the room, looking haggard and pained. He winced as he quietly closed the door behind him.

"Oh God," he mumbled. "They didn't get any vodka down at the Distribution Office. I'm . . . I don't remember the last time I've been sober. I think I'm gonna be sick. I haven't been sober in three years, I . . . Oh my God, what've I . . . Oh my God. Do either of you have any vodka?"

"Shut your mouth Zippco," I growled.

"What?"

"I said shut up!"

"Look, I'm just asking if you've got any . . ."

I ran across the room, leapt over the couch, and slammed Father Zippco against the wall. "SHUT UP! SHUT YOUR FUCKING MOUTH!"

He looked up at me with frightened, sober eyes. Blue eyes.

His eyes were blue.

"I'm . . . I'm sorry, Jimmy."

"Fucking right you are, you sorry-ass son of a bitch."

"Leave him alone, Jimmy," George said as he place his hand on my shoulder. "Don't do this."

I dropped my hands off Father Zippco's shirt and felt the burst of strength drain out of my weak body.

Father Zippco's blue eyes dropped onto the floor and he looked as though he might cry. "I'm sorry," he whispered. "I need a drink. I need . . . What've I been . . .? I'm sorry. I'm sorry. I need a drink."

"Fucking faggot." I turned away from Father Zippco and saw Jude standing in the bedroom doorway.

"Anyone got a cigarette?" she asked.

Her eyes were freed from the heavy black make-up and she had pushed her hair back into a ponytail. Her left eye was puffy and discolored, but her jeans and T-shirt covered the rest of her cuts and bruises, and she looked exactly as I remembered her looking twenty years before. For a moment, it was as if those years had never happened, as if I were still eighteen years old, as if I were still clean.

"Jude . . . Hi."

She turned towards me and gave me the exact look I had always feared she was going to give me back before I had met her in college. I used to imagine sauntering up to her in the dorm, saying something witty, and introducing myself. Even in my head, I couldn't make her laugh or smile, my fears forcing her to turn to me with a look of simple indifference, a look that wondered why this ridiculous boy was wasting her time.

Standing in the doorway to Father Zippco's bedroom twenty-four years later, Jude gave me that look.

"How are you feeling, Ms. Gaunt?" George asked.

"I'd feel better if I had a cigarette."

"Ms. Gaunt," George said, his voice sounding strong and perfect, "I have to leave for a little bit, but it's very important that you speak with Jimmy. He'll explain what's happening, all right?"

Her expression remained stony as she turned towards me.

I tried to smile, but could only produce an awkward looking grimace of discomfort.

"A cigarette?" Jude asked.

Behind me, Father Zippco's breathing became labored.

"Jimmy, give her a cigarette," George said.

278

I stepped towards Jude.

"Oh sweet Jesus," Father Zippco gasped. "I know you."

I turned around to see Father Zippco staring at Jude as if she were an impossibility. He began taking small steps towards her, lifting up his arms and cradling one hand in the other, as though he were about to receive Holy Communion.

"I know you." His voice was filled with awe.

Jude regarded Father Zippco with the same cold indifference with which she had regarded me.

"You going to give me a cigarette or not?" she asked me.

"You were at Trump." Each step Father Zippco took was labored and pained.

"What?" I asked.

"Oh sweet Jesus, I know you. You're meat. You're naked and chained. You aren't . . . You weren't human. You were meat."

George flashed his eyes across the room, from Jude to Father Zippco to me.

"What the fuck is going on? Get away from her, Zippco!" I yelled.

"Who do I have to blow around here to get a cigarette?"

"My head's been so dirty for so long. It's all clear now. You're an angel of mercy sent by the Lord." Father Zippco unstrapped the knife from his belt and dropped it onto the floor.

"Jimmy!

I turned to Jude with a confused look.

"A cigarette?"

"What? Oh." I pulled the cigarette out of my mouth and handed it to Jude while returning my eyes to Father Zippco, who was continuing his slow pilgrimage.

"You're an angel. Christ sent you to me. You're an angel and I did so many dirty things to you. Oh Jesus, what have I done with my life? What have I done?" Tears streamed down his face.

"What the fuck are you talking about, Zippco?"

Jude slapped the lit cigarette out of my hand.

I turned towards her.

"How about one that you haven't already smoked down to the filter, Jimmy?"

I fumbled in my pocket and handed her the box of cigarettes.

Father Zippco dropped to his knees in front of Jude.

"Forgive me. I've been so bad. I made you do such horrible things. I'm so sorry."

"Jimmy . . ." George said from behind me in a worried voice.

"I knew. Sweet Jesus, I always knew. I didn't know I knew, but I knew. I wanted to be bad so much, I wanted to do dirty things for so long, and than He left me behind and I was alone and I was angry and scared. And I did such bad things. I was angry and I lied to myself so I could be bad."

"You son of a bitch."

"Forgive me, Jesus. I know I don't deserve it, but please forgive your evil son. I'm so sorry I was bad. Thank you. Thank you for still loving me and bringing this angel to me."

"You son of a bitch!"

"Jimmy . . ."

"Who's got a light?"

"Fucking cocksucker!"

"You sent me this angel so I could be saved. You still love me, Jesus." Father Zippco smiled broadly and hid his face underneath his hands, rubbing his palms up and down and causing chunks of dry, dead flesh to drop down onto the floor at Jude's feet. He raised his bloody face out from his hands and stared at Jude. "I see light streaming out from you. You're so beautiful. How could I not have seen it before? I see your light."

"Yeah, huh? I wish someone'd show me the light so I could smoke this fucking cigarette."

"You raped her!"

"Jimmy, don't . . ." George touched my shoulder lightly.

"Forgive me. I see your light."

I slapped George's hand away from me and pounced on Father Zippco, punching at his bloody face and his chest. My blows were useless, my muscles still weak from the coma. Whatever energy I possessed had been wasted when I pushed Father Zippco against the wall.

He continued smiling at Jude.

I punched harder but my arms were ineffective. I was too weak.

George grabbed me by my shirt and yanked me away.

"Get the fuck off me, Glass!"

"Calm down!"

"He raped her!" I lunged forward. "Don't you look at her!"

"Calm down!" George spun me around and pushed me up against the wall, easily containing my rage.

"Fuck you, Glass!"

"We have to talk."

"There's nothing to talk about. Get off me!"

"Maybe one of you big tough guys could talk about giving me a light."

"Ms. Gaunt," George said while holding me against the wall, "we need to discuss a few things. Would you mind stepping into the bedroom?"

She shrugged and did as George asked.

I struggled as he dragged me in behind her, spitting at Father Zippco as we passed.

He didn't notice the saliva landing on his face and mixing with the blood.

"Hail Mary, full of grace, the lord is with thee. Blessed art thou among women and blessed is the fruit of thy womb, Jesus. Holy Mary, mother of God, pray for us sinners, now and at the hour of . . ."

"Cocksucker!"

George tossed me into the bedroom and I stumbled down onto the floor.

Jude laughed.

"Okay," George said, "I have to leave, so we're going to do this quick. I think I can convince the guy I'm talking to tonight to take four of us instead of just three."

"What?"

"Ms. Gaunt," George said, ignoring me, "my only reservation is that, given the . . . history between you and Father Zippco, you might feel uncomfortable traveling to Israel with him."

"What? He's not coming with us! Fuck you, Glass!"

"If you object, he won't come with us," he said to Jude.

"Hey!" I yelled, waving my arms back and forth, "*I* object!"

"I don't even know who you people are," Jude said, turning around and staring out the window at the dark city. "Any of you."

"Jude . . ."

"So traveling with Father Zippco wouldn't be a problem? Not even with the history between the two of you, Ms. Gaunt?"

"You mean the rape," I said. "It's not a *history*, you fucking prick; it's a rape."

"Ms. Gaunt?"

"Do whatever the hell you want to do. I don't even recognize the guy."

"Good." George smiled happily.

"*Good? Good?* Is this a fucking joke? Zippco's *not* coming with us!"

"Jimmy, don't you see?" George asked, turning towards me with a look of ecstasy. "If Father Zippco can ask for forgiveness, if he can be redeemed after all that he's done, then so can we. If *he* can be forgiven, then surely *we* can."

"No!"

"This is God, Jimmy. God's showing us that we can all ask for forgiveness."

"Bullshit! Zippco spends four years raping people and jerking-off while women and children get their heads hacked off and then at the last minute, sobers up, gets a change of heart, and goes to Heaven? No! It doesn't work that way. He raped Jude. He's a fucking piece of dogshit and he stays here and burns in Hell, period."

"But Jimmy, if Father Zippco can be forgiven, then so . . ."

"No! Fuck you! Better we *don't* get forgiven than that piece of shit *does*. He doesn't get to go to Heaven while my father . . . No."

"Jude said she's okay with it."

"I don't give a flying fuck what Jude says, it's not about her."

George recoiled at my words. When he spoke again, his voice was cold and hard. "He comes, and that's that."

"George . . ."

"We can't ask for forgiveness if we're not willing to give it."

"It's not for *you* to forgive him, Glass."

"And it's not for *you* to damn him. He comes."

"But . . ."

"It's the right thing to do. End of discussion."

'I FORBID IT!"

"*You* . . .?" George looked at me with indignant amazement. "What the hell makes you think that you're in a position to forbid anything? *I* got you out of the camp, *I* dragged your sorry ass around for two years, *I* found Jude, *I* stole the water to get her out of Trump, and *I* arranged a way to get to Israel. What the hell have *you* done?"

I glanced at Jude out of the corner of my eye.

"I'll tell you what you did, Jimmy. You smashed a bottle upside Mark Perry's head and fucked us! If it wasn't for you, we couldda gotten Jude three years ago. She wouldn't have had to spend six months in a rape camp if it wasn't for you. I wouldn't have had to murder someone it if wasn't for you. That's what *you* did."

Each word he spoke stabbed into me. I turned to Jude, who refused to look at me, continuing to stare out the window.

"You don't get to forbid Father Zippco's shot at redemption." He stepped up into my face. "Who the fuck do you think you are, Lordan? What you say and what you think means nothing. What you want doesn't matter. As far as I'm concerned, you're just along for the ride, so keep your fucking mouth shut from now on."

He turned away from me.

I suddenly felt very clear, George's words acting like a splash of cold water that washed away all the fear and haze and hesitation. His words drowned any confusion from my head, leaving me empty and focused.

I turned around and walked out of the bedroom.

Father Zippco had climbed back up onto his knees and was saying the Lord's Prayer, his hands working an invisible Rosary.

" . . . *hallowed be thy name* . . ."

I walked past him, to the desk next to the door, and picked up the gun George had placed there.

" . . .*Thy will be done* . . ."

I walked in front of Father Zippco and raised the gun, pushing the barrel against the smiling, crying, decaying priest's forehead.

Behind me, George screamed something meaningless.

" . . .*forgive us our trespasses as we forgive those who* . . ."

"*I* don't forgive," I said quietly. The voice sounded familiar, and I suddenly realized that my Inch had never really disappeared, that it had merged so fully with me, that my voice and its own had become indistinguishable. I offered up a silent prayer of thanks to Stan, then pulled the trigger.

Father Zippco's dry head exploded. His body threw backwards, but he remained on his knees.

George dropped onto the floor and began sobbing.

"Oh my God, Jimmy. What have you done? Oh my God."

I dropped the gun onto the floor and lit a cigarette.

"*Now* try telling me that what I want doesn't matter, you fucking faggot."

Nineteen

I was the eye of George's storm, quietly and calmly sitting on the couch and smoking while he ranted and raged all around me, alternating between anger and sorrow, screams and tears. It had taken George all of five seconds to forgive Father Zippco for his multitude of sins, but he couldn't seem to find it in his heart to do the same for me.

I didn't care.

When George finally shut up and left to finalize the arrangements for our transportation, I arose from the couch gracefully, feeling strong and light. I crossed the room with a thoughtless clarity, casually stepping over Father Zippco's corpse and walking into the bedroom.

"Jude?" I asked with contrived hesitation.

The room was dark and I flicked on the lights.

Jude winced.

"Sorry." I returned the room to its darkness, closing the door behind me and walking over to the window. I stared up at the full moon, patiently waiting for Jude to speak.

"What are you doing here, Jimmy?" she finally asked.

I turned around.

The moon's reflected light pushed past the window, casting a pale white light over Jude's form.

"Would you believe that I'm here to save you?"

Jude laughed angrily and lit a cigarette.

"I didn't think so. It's true, though. I came here to save you and to redeem myself. Right now, George is trading hundreds of gallons of water so we can get to Israel. I lived there for a couple of years; it's a slice of Heaven. Everyone happy, plenty of food and water, nice people, and no rape or death or violence."

"Yeah, huh?"

"Yeah. It's like Woodstock, only without the sex, drugs and music."

"If it's so great, why'd you leave?"

"I told you, Woodstock without the sex and drugs and music. What kind of Woodstock is that?"

"Ha ha."

"I left for you. I came to save you."

"And I suppose that's why you shot that old guy, too? To avenge my honor?"

"Probably not," I said with a shrug. "I think maybe that one was for me. Maybe for you, too. Who knows? Who cares? So, you want to be saved?"

"Who the hell *are* you?"

'You know who I am, Jude."

"No. No, I don't. You're a fucking memory, Jimmy, a vague memory too stupid to stay that way. It strikes me that I've heard all of this shit before. *I'll protect you, I'll save you.* Grow up. It was kind of cute when you were nineteen, but at forty-two, it just plays as pathetic."

"There's no one else left, Jude." I picked at a hangnail and tore it down. "The whole world's dead or dying and you're all I've got left. I'm all you've got left."

"Jesus. You always were a drama queen, Jimmy." She blew her smoke towards me. "When are you going to get over yourself? The *white knight*, right? Twenty fucking years and you're still the exact same, still a self-centered kid who can't deal with his Catholic guilt. You never wanted to save me, Jimmy, you wanted to save yourself. Only, you never wanted to get dirty doing it, did you? Had to be the *white* knight. Well, there's nothing clean about me anymore, so why don't you just fuck off and take your act somewhere else?"

"No one's forcing you to be here, Jude. Leave if you want."

"What, you mean like you did in Las Vegas?"

"I'd say I'm sorry, but I don't think you'd believe me."

"Try me."

"I'm sorry."

"Fuck you. I don't care if you're sorry or not. You don't mean anything to me anymore. You're a footnote in my life. How often do you read the footnotes, Jimmy?"

"Was that rhetorical?"

"Piss off."

"I *am* sorry, Jude."

"I don't care."

"I'm sorry anyway." I sat down on the edge of the bed and softened my voice. "Leaving you was the biggest mistake of my life."

"I doubt it. And if it was, get over it."

"I tried. I tried so hard." I dropped my face down into my hands and tried to look sad. "I loved you so much, Jude, and I wanted it to work, but it was so hard. I didn't know how to do it. I was scared and stupid, but I tried. I really did."

"You failed."

"It never left me." I coaxed a crack into my voice and put on a faraway look. "I kept waiting for the feelings and the memories to leave, but they never did. I look at you now, lying here with the moonlight all over you and it's like we're back in our apartment, or the dorms. It's like it was all last week. I spent twenty years waiting for last week to get further away. It never did. A dream, a smell, a song; so many things stopped it from leaving.

"I remember," I laughed wistfully, "I remember the mornings, when I had to go to class and you were still sleeping. I'd look at you before closing the door behind me and the sunlight would be slipping through the corners of the shade, draping across your body. You never pulled the sheets up past your waist and you looked so fucking beautiful. Your skin was white and you were perfect."

"Let it go."

"Don't you think if I could I would? Do you think I wanted to drag those feelings around for twenty years? All the anger and all the fighting and all I remember, all I felt was the love. All I could remember was you laughing at me because I was afraid to come in your mouth."

She covered a smile with her fingers.

"I was in Israel. I was safe. And I hated it, because I wasn't with you. I couldn't stay there alone, knowing you were here."

"Jimmy . . ."

"I was a stupid fucking kid and what we had was the most important thing in the world, and now I'm a stupid forty-two year old man and it still is. I'm so sorry, Jude. I never should have left you."

Jude edged closer. "It was . . . It was a long time ago, Jimmy," she said quietly.

"I'm so sorry, Jude." I sobbed. "This is all my fault. Everything. I loved you so much and I let you down. I let everyone down. I'm so sorry for what happened to you. I'm so sorry for what I did, for what I let happen. I'm so fucking sorry. I know you hate me, but . . ."

"I don't hate you," she whispered, more to herself than to me.

"I fucked up so bad."

"It wasn't just you." Her fingers brushed across my shoulder. "It was . . . . It wasn't your fault, Jimmy. We were kids." She laughed. "We were just kids."

"I said that I'd take care of you. I promised."

"You tried. You were young."

"I fucked up! I lied to you. I said I'd . . . I'm sorry Jude, I'm so sorry."

"It wasn't your fault." Her hand pressed down onto my shoulder. I touched the skin on her wrist, hesitantly, almost as if I was afraid of her. She slid close to me and I pushed my face into her shoulder and began crying. She wrapped her hand around the back of my head and rocked me back and forth. I raised my face towards Jude and she looked down at me, her breath pressing against my lips.

The smile disappeared and her face became hard as she leaned in and kissed me. Her lips were tight and she plowed her tongue into my mouth, swirling it around as if she were searching for something. She pulled her hand away from my face and slid it down my chest, resting it on my groin.

"Jude . . ." I pulled away from her mouth.

"Jimmy," she whispered, and bit into my neck.

"Jude, don't . . ."

She tugged at my belt, skillfully yanking it open.

"Jude . . ."

The buckle flipped open and she unzipped my fly.

"Jude, don't." I grabbed her wrist.

"I want to suck your cock, Jimmy," she whispered in an excessively throaty voice before sliding her tongue into my ear.

I pulled her hand away.

"Please, Jimmy, please let me suck your cock. I want you to come in my mouth."

"No. Not like this, Jude."

"Please, Jimmy." She tried pulling her hand free. "Please, I *need* to suck your cock." She shifted her body and dropped her free hand onto my lap.

"No Jude, no!" I grabbed her shoulder and pushed her away from me.

"Well fuck you, then!" She pulled out of my grasp and slapped me across the face before standing up. "What do you want, you son of a bitch? What do you want?"

"I want to save you."

"FUCK YOU!" She slapped me again. "Where were you twenty years ago? Where were you when there was still something left to save?"

"I'm sorry."

"Those words don't change anything!"

"I know. But I'm still sorry. I love you."

"I HATE YOU!" She curled her open hand into a fist and punched me hard in the face.

I fell back onto the floor.

"I still love you," I said, and wiped the blood away from my split lip.

"You fucking asshole!" She ran towards me and began kicking my chest and face.

I wrapped my arms around her legs and she fell down on top of me, her arms swinging wildly. I grabbed her arms and held them at her side.

"Where were you, you fucking asshole? Where were you?"

"I'm here now.

"IT'S TOO LATE! THERE'S NOTHING LEFT!" She spit in my face. "There's nothing left!" She stopped fighting my hold and began sobbing. "There's nothing left, Jimmy. Where were you when they were doing that to me? Where were you when there was still something left?"

"I'm sorry."

"I hate you," she cried, and fell into my chest, wrapping her arms around me.

"It's okay, baby."

"No it's not." She rubbed her face back and forth across my chest. "It's not okay. They did things too me, they . . . they made me do things. They . . . Oh my God, Jimmy, they hurt me so much." She clawed at my chest as though she was trying to climb inside of me. "Why did they do those things? Why would they do that? I never . . . they did things, Jimmy. There's . . . there's nothing left. It's all gone. *I'm* all gone."

"Why didn't you take the tag, Jude?"

"It was all I had left," she said in a small voice. "It was the only thing I could still say no to."

"You kept your Inch, baby." I kissed the top of her head.

"What?"

"You beat 'em. You won."

"No. No they . . ."

"I don't care what they did, *you* won. You said *no* when it would have been easier to say *yes*, and you did it for yourself. You're stronger than they could ever be. You won."

"But I feel . . ."

"I know. I know how you feel, but you're wrong. They hurt you, but they didn't beat you. You'll get better, you'll heal. I'll help."

"I'm so dirty, Jimmy."

"Jude, you're the cleanest person on this whole miserable fucking planet." I carefully placed her underneath the blankets and smiled. "It doesn't matter what they did to your body; you never let them get anywhere near the place that really matters. You're good and beautiful and clean and perfect. They could never touch you. You didn't let them."

"I love you, Jimmy," she said, so quietly that I barely heard it.

"I love you, too, Jude." I pressed my hand against her cheek.

"Jimmy, will you . . . will you fuck me?"

"No. But I'll crawl under the covers with you and snuggle your butt. How about that? I'll wrap my arms around you and we'll close our eyes and pretend that we're back in your dorm room."

"You always . . .you always used to tell me that you liked snuggling with me more than you liked fucking."

"Yeah."

"I always thought you were lying."

"I wasn't."

"I know."

We woke up and smoked cigarettes while staring at the ceiling.

"Israel, huh?" Jude asked.

"Yeah."

"What's it like?"

"Nice people, no booze, no cigarettes, lots of praying. You'll hate it."

"But we'll be safe?"

"Yeah. Yeah, you will be."

"*We* will be." The end of Jude's cigarette glowed brightly.

"No. I'm not going."

"What?" She jerked upright.

"I'm not going."

"Yes you are."

"I can't."

"Of course you can. We're going together."

I climbed out of the bed and stared out the window at the crumbled city. "Jude, I don't know how much you know about what's been happening, but there's a reason behind this mess."

"What reason?"

"There's no time. George'll be back soon and then you'll have to go. I can't explain it now, but all the death and the suffering, there's a reason for it. When you get to Israel, you'll understand."

"What does any of this have to do with you not going? You have to go."

"No. The thing is, I know the reasons, and they're not good enough. I thought that if I could save you, if I could do something right, then I could stand in front of God and when He told me how bad I was, I could point to you and say, *There, what about that? I did that alone.* But I don't care anymore. Nothing I've done is anywhere near as bad as what He's done. My father, you, me, Stan, that kid on the boat, all of it, it's all wrong. It's not the way it should be and I can't . . . I don't belong there. I'm not going."

"Fine. But I'm staying, too."

"No, that's out of the question." I spun around. "Absolutely not."

"I'm staying with you, Jimmy."

"No. Jude, all of this, it was all about you. You have to go."

She laughed and jumped out of the bed. "Shut up, Jimmy." She placed her finger on my forehead and gently slid it down my nose and over my lips. "I'm a big girl and I can make my own decisions. I'm staying with you."

"You don't understand what's going on. Not really."

"And I don't care, either. I love you and I'm staying with you. If you don't want any part of Israel, I don't either."

"Jude . . ."

"Jimmy, do you really love me?"

"Yeah. Yeah, I do."

"And I love you. What else is there to talk about?"

"But you can't . . ."

"Jesus Christ, Jimmy, will you shut up? You always did talk too fucking much." She grabbed my wrist and pulled me under the covers. "It's all over, Jimmy. If you stay, I stay."

"I . . . Okay. If you're sure."

"I'm sure."

"Okay then. We're both staying. God help us."

Jude kissed me and undid my pants.

This time, I didn't stop her.

"Fuck God," she said with a grin. "Fuck 'em all. You and me against the world, baby."

I kissed her. Real gently, almost as if I were afraid of her. When I started touching her, I was tentative, soft. After an hour or so, things started becoming more intense, but I made sure that the focus stayed on her. I wouldn't let her do anything to me, it was all about her.

Pretty soon, I knew. I pushed her legs apart, only it wasn't really a push, or if it was, it was like pushing air. She pulled me on top of her and I slid inside. Just a little. She let out a throaty little gasp of consent and arched her back. I pushed myself all the way in and she inhaled like she was stuttering. I moved delicately. Lovingly, even. After a few minutes I pulled almost all the way out and looked down at her. She had her eyes closed and her chin turned up. The back of her head was pushed into the pillow and her lips were parted, opened up almost like she was trying to say something beautiful but couldn't quite come up with the right words. Corners of her mouth were curled into this faint smile. Right then, at that moment, she looked beautiful. Innocent.

Twenty

"**L**et's finish this," George said in a brusque voice when he returned. "Get Jude." He stared down at Father Zippco's corpse and seemed surprised that it was still there, that it hadn't been moved. He turned away and stared into the corner, refusing to look at me.

I leaned against the arm of the couch with my hands in my pockets, staring at George as though he were nothing more than an inconvenience, an unpleasant detail that had to be taken care of now that the larger task had been accomplished.

I lit a cigarette and blew smoke at him "We're not going."

"*Who's* not going *where?*" George slowly asked, and turned to face me.

"Who do you think, Glass? We're not going with you."

"Jimmy, what are you doing? I thought we were going to make things right."

"I *am* making things right."

George looked down at Father Zippco's body and then stared at me with cold, accusing eyes. "Where's Jude?"

"She's not going with you."

"Where is she? What did you do to her?"

"Piss off, Glass," I laughed. "Go to Israel with the rest of the Christ-freak faggots. You're used to going down on your knees; you'll fit in perfectly."

"Jimmy, if you did something to her . . ."

"What? You'll forgive me?"

"I'll kill you."

"Oh for Christ's sake, I'm right here," Jude said, emerging from the bedroom. She walked over to me and slipped her hand in mine. "I'm staying with Jimmy."

"We don't have time for this," George muttered, and rubbed his face. "The boat's waiting for us and the guy's edgy enough as it is. There's rumors flying all around that Morrison and the Arabs are mobilizing troops. Time's running out, so cut the shit and let's go!"

"Fuck you," Jude said. "I don't even know who the hell you are. I don't know you, I don't trust you, and I sure as hell don't owe you anything."

"But you know Jimmy, is that it?"

"Yeah, that's right."

"And you trust *him*?"

Jude hesitated for a moment and blinked her eyes at George's words.

"Look, we don't have the time! Gaunt, if you stay here with Jimmy, you could go to Hell, forever."

"*Hell?*" Jude laughed.

"You didn't even tell her?" George asked with a furiously astonished look.

"Fuck you, Glass," I said.

"You son of a bitch," George whispered, and stared at me with cold, clear, knowing eyes.

"What the hell are you two talking about?"

"Okay," George said to Jude," I don't have time to tell you everything, but right now, you're putting your life in Jimmy's hands. Do you really want to do that?"

"I . . ." She stared into George's face and then into mine. She began searching through my eyes and I turned away.

"Yes," she said, but it was a small word and a tiny voice, and it sounded more like a question than an answer.

"Jude, please," George said with a wince, "I'm not going to take away your choice, I'm not going to rob you of that, so the decision has to be yours. I know that you don't know me, but I've stayed in this country for three years so that I could help you, so that I could help myself by helping you. I have to leave now, and if you stay . . ."

"Hey, she already . . ."

"SHUT THE FUCK UP, LORDAN!" He turned back to Jude and dropped the hatred from his voice. "This is the fate of your soul that we're talking about. I know that sounds overblown and melodramatic, but it's also true. There's no time to explain right now, but if you come with me, I will. All I can tell you right now is that if you stay here, you're trusting your soul to Jimmy Lordan. Do you really trust him Jude? Do you?"

She turned and stared at me with pleading eyes I couldn't meet.

Her face turned to stone and tears ran out of her eyes.

"No," she whispered. "No I don't." She stepped away from me and walked behind George.

"Jude . . ." I struggled to find the words to seduce her with.

George stared at me with disgust.

"You fucking faggot, Glass. GIVE HER TO ME!" I stepped towards Jude.

George pulled his gun from his holster and pointed it at me.

"You son of a bitch, Jimmy. You self-centered, hateful, son of a bitch. You take one more step towards her and I swear to Christ that I'll kill you. I swear to Christ I will, and you know that those words mean something to me."

"What the hell are you doing, Glass?"

"What am *I* doing? I'm saving her. Remember?"

"I *already* saved her!"

"Well now I'm saving her from *you*, you fucking asshole. How can you do this to her, Jimmy? You have no right to drag her down to Hell along with you. Jesus Christ, how can you do that to her? How can you even *think* about using her to spit in God's eye?"

"I'm not . . ."

"Don't lie to me!"

"She doesn't even have the tag."

"And she doesn't believe in Hell or God. Who's gonna tell her what's happening? You? Are you going to help bring her to God?"

"It's her choice."

"She just got out of a rape camp, Jimmy. I can't believe you're going to use that to manipulate her like this."

"I'm not . . ."

"SHUT UP! I don't care what you think God's done to you and your father, you're not going to use this poor woman to try and even the score. It's not enough to turn your back on God yourself? You have to pull Jude down with you? He took one of yours, so now you're going to take one of His, is that it?"

"I . . ."

Jude stared at me with an unmoving face. Her stare was hard and cold, but she couldn't stop the tears from escaping her emotionless eyes.

"Jude, let's talk."

"We're leaving," George said.

Jude said nothing.

"GIVE HER TO ME!" I stepped forward and George fired a shot over my head.

"I'm not fucking around with you, Lordan. I *will* shoot you."

My whole body shook and I looked back and forth, from George to Jude and then back again.

"THEN DO IT! DO IT! Go ahead and shoot me, but you better not be a faggot about it. You better shoot me in the face, because if you puss-out and hit my leg or something, I'll still get to you. I don't care how weak I am, if you don't kill me with the first shot, I'll reach you and I'll choke your faggot ass to death. Piss away a shot on something that's not vital and my hands'll be around your throat before you can blink. It better be in the face, faggot."

"Is that all you've got left, Jimmy? Dying like your father? Is that the only thing left that'll make you feel clean?"

"FUCK YOU! I . . . FUCK!" I dropped my face down into my hands. "Yes."

"Jimmy, it . . . it doesn't have to be that way."

"I didn't make up the rules."

"Then try playing by them."

"Who's rules? Who do I fuck over, George? Sarah? God? Dad? Jude? Who's rules can I follow and still be a good son? Who's rules can I follow without selling out the people I love? Without selling out who I am? I . . ." I laughed. "Jesus had it easy. It's easy to tell everyone to abandon their families and serve God when your family *is* God."

"Jimmy . . ."

"No." I laughed quietly and shook my head. "No more talking. I'm sick of it. It doesn't change anything. It doesn't . . . it doesn't change *me*. You were right, George. There was a point to all this. I know who I am. Who I've always been. I can't hide from it anymore. The words are empty. They can't cover anything anymore. Can't hide the truth. That's all they were ever good for. Fuck it." I walked over to Father Zipcoo's body and gently leaned over him, picking up his knife before returning to George.

"Jimmy, don't do this."

"Fuck it. I . . . Oh Jesus. Jesus, I loved Sarah so much. I really did. Tell her that, okay, George? Tell her I really did love her. Tell her I tried, that I did the best I could. Tell her I'm . . . tell her I'm sorry."

"Jimmy, don't."

"Yeah. Here's how it's going to be, George," I fished out one last cigarette and lit it, "I'm coming after you. Right now. If I reach you, I'm going to stab you through the heart and you'll go to Hell and Jude'll be left alone. I swear, on my father's name, that if I reach you, I'll kill you."

"Jimmy . . ."

"And you know *that* means something to me."

"Jimmy . . ."

"I'm sorry I called you a faggot, George. I didn't mean it. Not really."

"Jimmy, don't make me . . ."

"I know it doesn't matter, Jude, but I'm sorry."

"It doesn't have to be this way. We can . . ."

"No. There's nothing left to say."

"Jimmy, is this really who you are? Does it really have to end like this?"

"Come on, George, you know how I feel about rhetorical questions."

I dropped the cigarette onto the floor and lunged.

The bullet split my face open. I died instantly. Just like my father.

Twenty-One

*A*bove me, I hear George weeping over my body.

And as I fall down into Hell and the lies slip away, I try and yell out to him. I try and tell him that he doesn't have to cry; to tell him that I'm not going anywhere I haven't already been for a very long time.

It's too late, though, to tell him anything, so I stop trying, and continue falling down into myself. Forever.

CPSIA information can be obtained
at www.ICGtesting.com
Printed in the USA
LVHW111406171022
730885LV00016B/388/J

9 780978 602444